FAITH AND THE DEAD END DEVILS

a sweetverse novel

KATHRYN MOON

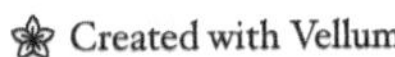 Created with Vellum

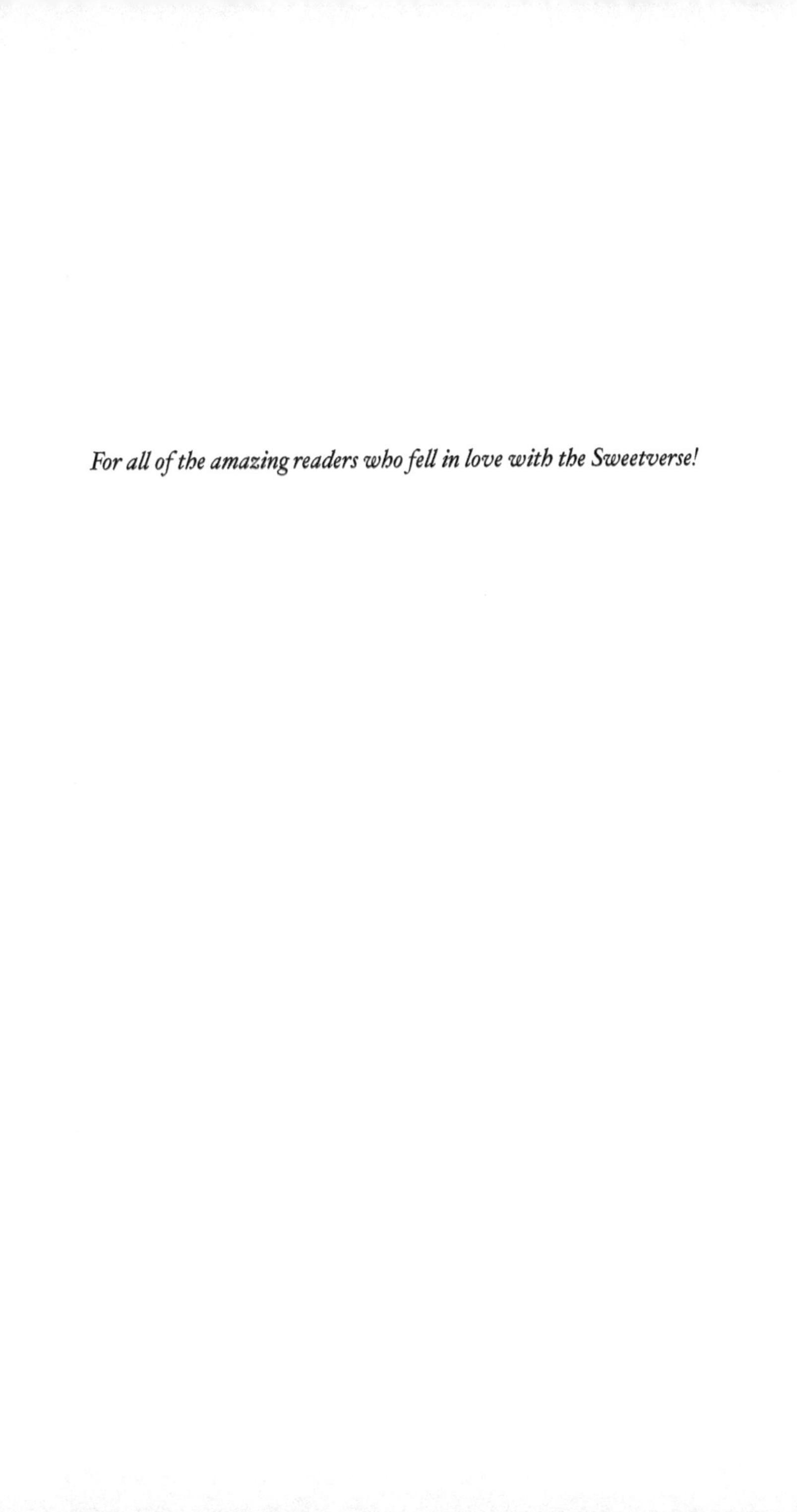

For all of the amazing readers who fell in love with the Sweetverse!

CONTENTS

KATHRYN MOON

Bear
1

My ears rang in a determined alarm as I dragged the lifeless driver out of the front seat, glaring at the gun still gripped in his fist.

A hand clapped on my shoulder and I clenched my jaw, the handle of my gun biting into my grip, finger safely pulled away from the trigger. Ghost released me as quickly as he'd grabbed me.

"Sorry," he said, although the word was swallowed by the siren running in my head and I had to study his mouth to catch what he was saying. "You good?"

"Not shot in the face, if that's what you're asking," I answered, glancing back down at the body at my feet. It was a near thing, the bullet cutting a few strands of hair short. Adrenaline was still whipping through me.

"King wants you at the back before we open it up," Ghost said.

"He's not a Western Wasted," I said, nodding my head toward the dead man.

The driver of the delivery van we'd intercepted was dressed conservatively, the kind of meek and mild-looking beta you'd expect to find going door to door with product surveys. But the van had been equipped with a goddamn booby trap, dropping spikes on the road that had torn up the tires of my bike and nearly my leg as I'd rolled free. And the beta had nearly managed to take me out first, trained well with the gun in his hand. I was trained too, ex-military, but in this moment I'd simply been lucky, and I didn't like relying on luck.

"Brothers are keeping an eye on the road but there's no sign of the Wasted," Ghost said.

My hearing was calming down after the too-close shot from the beta's gun. I bent and retrieved it from his still-warm fingers, then rummaged through his pockets, coming up with keys and a wallet full of cash, but no ID. Ghost pulled an open cellphone off the seat.

"Open to call, but no recent history," Ghost said, flipping up dark sunglasses and running tan, scarred fingers through his dark beard.

"Turn off location and then pull that apart. There's probably more security hidden in it," I added, glaring at the empty passenger seat.

Just one driver? For a full van's delivery?

We'd caught word that our MC rivals, the Western Wasted, were expecting a scheduled delivery via the Wasted VPs girl arriving bruised and bloodied on our doorstep. I warned King, president of our club, it could just as easily be a trap for us as a lead on what the Wasted were up to. They hadn't come right out and started shit yet, aside from a little light dealing of oxy in our territory, but all intel and signs pointed to a new MC looking to grow and eat up surrounding clubs. Interrupting a delivery that crossed our lines and taking whatever shit they were dealing would be, in King's opinion, a swift reminder of the laws of the one-percent.

Stay out of the way of the clubs who can crush you.

"You think it's a weak score?" Ghost asked.

I frowned and shook my head. "I don't know what I think."

"Bear."

I turned and marched toward the back of the van where King waited, glaring at the locked doors, alpha pheromones simmering with the same caution buzzing in my veins. At his side, Chance, a beta birthright member of our club, the Dead End Devils, had his back to the van and watched the progress of the other club members cleaning up the scene.

"We don't have much time," Chance said, pale eyes narrowed and tattooed knuckles clenched white at his sides.

King didn't blink. He stood with his arms crossed over his chest, staring at his own severe reflection in the smooth black of the van's paint job.

"Think there's a chance of explosives?" he asked me.

"You mean in the cargo, or it'll set off when we open the doors?" I asked in return, shrugging. "You hit the back hard, so it probably would've gone off already. Cargo is more likely arms or drugs."

King's gaze flicked to mine, icy, considering.

I respected our prez, but the man was a fortress of an alpha. I knew I looked the part of enforcer in size and appearance, but I had no doubt that of all the Dead End Devils, King would be the coldest and most brutal when it came down to it.

"I've got the key. There's no sign of any other device to open the doors. If we're walking into a trap, I don't think it's an explosive," I said.

King nodded, seemingly satisfied. "Open it."

Not volunteering his own ass, of course. But to their credit, neither he nor Chance stepped back as I took the keys I'd pulled from the van ignition and approached the door.

"We'll need the prospects to grab the product fast, pack it in the van," Chance said.

The key slid in, lock resistant as I turned it. King's question about explosives rang with the buzz of my injured ear drum, my hand steady even as my heart hammered in my chest.

But there was no beep, no quiet tick, no warning sound but a low, thin whine as I pulled the handle. The scent of burnt almonds clawed its way out of the crack. Momentum carried the heavy door open, even as my brain caught up with my instincts.

Slam it shut. Fuck! Fuck, fuck, fuck.

"Holy shit," Chance breathed, standing at my left. He peered into the open back of the truck, at the lattice of thin metal and the figure caught behind.

To the girl curled up in the cage.

King shifted, and Chance stepped out of his way without being asked, while I remained stupidly frozen in place. His breath hitched at the sight of the cowering creature, a mess of dark hair and long, pale legs in a stained black T-shirt. There was a glimpse of an eye so dilated, it was almost pure black peeking through the tangled strands. I couldn't hear her over my injury, but I knew by the way she was vibrating that she was warning us with a soft, wounded sound to *stay away*.

"How many?" King asked, voice flat.

"One," I said without opening the door any farther.

One ragged, angry, dangerous perfume. One omega in a cage.

The fucking delivery the Wasted were waiting on was an *omega*.

"The *fuck*," Ghost said, arriving at our small crowd. My shoulders went up to my ears, and I wanted to shove both King and Ghost out of the way. Chance too, for good measure, even if he was a beta. "Is that a fucking—"

"Ghost, get everyone out of sight," King said. "Take them round to the end of the tunnel. Bear...get her in the truck. Chance and I will load your bike in the back. Go directly back to your room. Wait for me."

"He's not taking her back to—" Chance started, voice cracking with anger.

And me? I was sick with relief. Yes, get the other brothers away from here. Get Ghost and King away from here. Find a way to get the omega out of the cage, get her somewhere safe, and—

"Do you suggest we leave a trafficked omega on the side of the road until the Wasted show up? If their plan is to sell her, they'll end up with pockets deep enough to buy us out of Dead End," King said.

My head whipped to stare at him, but his face was impassive, eyes meeting mine squarely and unapologetically. Heartless.

"And if she's meant for personal use, then...we're doing our good deed for the year," King added, mouth flat and humorless.

Ghost stared with a strange kind of horror into the cage for a moment before turning on his heel to follow orders.

"I'll...get the bike," Chance said, backing away.

King and I remained standing, staring at one another.

"Do you have something you'd like to say?" he asked.

My mouth opened, but my thoughts caught up first. He'd ordered the others away, for me to take the omega out of the cage and get her back to my rooms at the club. I knew why he'd chosen me. I was the only one of us with experience around omegas. My eyes flicked into the dark of the van, one eye staring back at me through thick brown hair. She hadn't said a word to us, hadn't uncurled from the floor.

King wasn't threatening to leave her behind for the Wasted to find, and he wasn't celebrating the sudden acquisition of an omega. He was making sure the other brothers hadn't seen her, didn't know there was an omega in a cage, who'd been about to be served up to a scumbag motorcycle crew. One new, but not so very different from our own.

Not that we'd ever ordered ourselves an illegally trafficked omega.

"No," I said, shaking my head. I glanced at the girl again. "It's going to take me a minute before I can get her out."

King didn't look at her again. "Quick as you can," he said. "Don't want the others getting curious."

I nodded, but I waited for him to join Chance before opening the door any farther. The omega winced and tucked her face to the floor at the sudden glare of sunlight.

"Hey...hey there..." I stalled out on what to call her as I studied her. Her spine was creating a line of ridges through the back of her T-shirt, and there were bruises all up and down her arms and an irritated ring around her swollen right ankle. I had to swallow my growl three times before I could speak again, my eyes latching onto a small tattoo on her uninjured left ankle.

"Hey Butterfly," I said, staring at the black and red dainty design of wings on her pale skin. I stepped slowly closer, perching on the open back of the van. It sank under my weight, and she trembled. "It's all right," I said, trying to make my natural gritty voice sound soothing. "I know I'm an alpha, Butterfly, but I'm not going to hurt you. Just wanna get you out of that cage."

She twisted, and I held my breath at the sight of her face. She was pretty, all delicate and feminine with big, dark eyes. Her stare wouldn't meet mine, and she kept squinting, like the light bothered her eyes. I tried not to think about what that meant for how long she'd been in a cage.

"I've got the keys," I said, lifting them in my fingers, jangling them. Her stare flicked and she flinched at the sound. "And then I'm gonna take you out of there. Give you a ride to somewhere you'll be safe."

She blinked and crawled forward, bumping her nose against a thin line of the wire, wrapping her fingers around the lattice. She breathed in deeply, whined a soft note, and then shuddered and took another deep breath.

She was deep in hindbrain, total survival instinct mode. A feral omega.

Fuck.

I'd had more than my fair share of experience with omegas, but never one this deep in their instincts. An omega in the frenzy of a heat was aggressive. An omega whose mate was in jeopardy was even more dangerous. An omega fighting for their life? I would have to move slowly and hope to god this little creature liked my scent. If my bike weren't destroyed, and she weren't a more important goal, I would've been riding toward the Wasted, ready to set them all on fire on her behalf.

Except they're not the ones who sold her.

I swallowed and reached toward the cage, putting my wrist to the wires. Her eyelashes fluttered over that near-black gaze as she scented me. She whined again, and I shuddered at the soft note of need. Not sexual. Just the imperative of an omega that needed an alpha's protection.

"I'm gonna unlock the cage now, Butterfly," I said, standing, pulling away only long enough to push the van doors open wider. She whimpered at my withdrawal, and the sound was a tangible yank on my chest. "You wanna tell me your name?"

She didn't make another sound, her fingers loosening from the cage as she scooted back. The shirt she wore was large, and it slid back on thin thighs, revealing a glimpse of underwear around her hips. Had she already been raped? I swallowed down the bile rising in my throat and scented the air carefully. Some thin wisps of betas, probably from handling her, and no hint of an alpha. Either she'd been cleaned thoroughly, or they'd kept her out of any alpha's reach.

"It's okay, Butterfly," I continued, as the lock protested each key from the ring I tried, metal jangling until I found the right one. "Just gonna get you out of there and take you somewhere safe, and then the rest will be all up to you."

Even if I had to defy King to make sure of it.

The poor little omega was shaking so hard at the back of the cage, she was making the walls rattle as I opened the narrow door. I pulled it open slowly, prepared for the girl to try and dive out and scramble past me, but she only stared. Stared and shook.

"Come on, Butterfly," I whispered, leaning back, offering her a clear view of the road behind me.

It wasn't much of a sight, to be honest. Our territory could be beautiful in its barrenness, but today was a gray day and it'd been a long time since we'd seen any rain. The world was dusty and baked from the heat of the sun.

I waited another minute until I heard King clear his throat too loudly to be anything but an impatient reminder to me that Ghost was trying to stall the others. And King was right—the last thing this omega needed was our whole crew to sniff her out.

"Come on, sweetheart. Let's get you out of that cage and cleaned up. Somewhere safe, I promise," I tried again.

I'd been holding my hand out for her, and I moved it slowly into the cage, just an offer. She stiffened, eyes on my hand, and my body translated the freeze of her muscles a moment too late. A warning.

She lunged forward with a snarl, and I barely managed to retreat before the pain of her teeth sinking into the heel of my hand reached my brain. I grunted, stiffened, and found that black gaze fixed to my own.

She'd bit me. Still had those dull little teeth buried in my flesh.

"Bear?" King called.

Her gums were red, pretty bow lips pulled back in a grimace, and there was no understanding or apology in that gaze. My chest ached for her all the same.

"We're good. Gimme one more minute," I answered, keeping my voice as low as I could for her sake.

Her jaw loosened, and for the first time I saw a little glimpse of soft brown around the dilated pupils. She dove forward again and I flinched, prepared for another attack, braced to take whatever violence she needed to lash out with. Her arms nearly strangled around my neck—nearly, but not quite. The cage was rattling as she crawled her way out, into my chest, face pressed under my jaw, hot breath rushing over my neck.

"That's it, Butterfly," I said, looking at the oval bite mark, the blood beading at the heel of my hand. I wrapped my arms slowly around her waist, absorbed her delicate trembles into my broad chest, and waited one last moment.

Her scent was still harsh, crispy and burnt, stress clinging to thick brown hair. Her fingernails dug into my leather cut, clenching down to press hard into the muscles of my back. Soft little notes of sighs and whimpers were muffled against my throat. She clung to me like she was trying to claw her way inside of me, use my body as a shield around hers.

I would've let her.

She held her breath as I turned and rose. The bite on my hand was throbbing, blood welling and slipping against the skin of her thigh where I held her to my chest.

Chance was at the back of the truck we'd brought and he stared at her with his usual suspicion, a furrow knotting on his forehead, but he didn't say a word.

"She good?" King asked, circling from the passenger side of the truck, ice blue gaze digging into the back of the girl's head.

"I've got her," I said, because no, she wasn't good. In fact, I didn't really want King to know exactly how rough this omega was. Didn't want him to know about the bite on my hand either. Not until I understood the repercussions too.

I managed to open the driver's door while holding onto the omega, and I slid her onto the bench seat first, untangling her from my chest for the brief moment it took to haul myself into the cab.

"See you at the club," I called over my shoulder.

"Keep her in your room till I make a decision," King

answered, watching the girl slide down onto the seat, press her head to the side of my thigh. She seemed to ignore his presence easily enough, but I was tense, waiting for King to reach in through the window. Would she bite him too?

He patted the outside of the passenger door. The girl flinched and whimpered, drawing a scowl to his lips. I turned the key in the ignition, then pulled away from the scene with a sense of one weight lifting from my chest while another landed in its place.

My ears rang in warning the whole drive back, an omen of change.

Thick, unfamiliar fingers catching in my hair, working out the tangles. Not the usual pair. The vibration of an engine, a new one, dense and heady.

An alpha's purr? A soft scent, safe. The smell of an imaginary home I'd built a hundred times in those moments before falling asleep.

Struggling, kicking, trying to bite through the strong arms as too many scents hit my nose. A low growl, gentle, warning. Stubbing my toe on a door frame and whining through the pain. Being surrounded by the home scent again.

A huff. Soft, humored, as I burrowed down into a pile of blankets.

My screech as I was dragged out again.

Warm, milky water, silky on my skin. Big hands in my hair. A broad, square face and blurry black eyes.

"Rinse twice, hmm, Butterfly?"

Another huff as I sputtered through the water pouring over my head.

Sniffing my own skin, rubbing my cheek on my shoulder, and finding the right scent. Me. Myself.

Faith.

Him too. The alpha. My alpha?

I ran my fingers over the soft collar that hung loose around my throat and drew it up to my nose. The scent lingering in the cotton was a bit sweet, a bit warm. The taste of his blood was still a sharp edge on my tongue.

I cleared my throat, opened my mouth to call for him, my hands searching the expanse of brown and white in front of me. *Where am I? Who are you?* But he'd said something a bit ago, and it had been quiet since. Had he left me?

Too much space to be a cage. Too bright. A dark shadow space to my right. I gathered my alpha's blankets and pillows and crawled slowly off the bed and into the shadows. *A nice small nest. Only I will fit here. Quiet.*

Smells like a home should.

A blue house with white shutters, bright lights on through the windows. A big tree in the front yard. A porch swing. Flower beds. A big dining room table, and a soft nest up in the...

No. Down in the basement. Safe, dark, cool.

The alpha made the floor shake as he returned, steps heavy but quiet. He froze, his breath caught audibly in that huge chest I'd clung to, and I knew he was looking at the place on the bed he'd left me in.

Would he be angry? Growl.

Then he exhaled, and I blinked at the sound of knees creaking.

"There you are, Butterfly."

I smiled. My alpha had found—

Not my alpha. He was scooting across rough carpet, his shadow appearing in the open brighter space of the closet doors. The closet where I was nesting. *Hiding.*

I frowned, hid my face in my hands, and tried to reclaim reality. My head was pounding, aching, as it had ever since—

The cement floor cracked against my skull, my shoulder throbbing at the sudden impact.

"Davis! What the fuck!"

"She fucking tried to—"

"She's merchandise! Her delivery date is coming up. What do you think her buyers are gonna say if we send her damaged? Not to mention the fucking boss!"

"Fine, fine."

But he'd dug his fingers in my hair to drag me back to the little room.

"Did you buy me?" I whispered to the massive blurry figure in front of me.

The alpha was huge and muscled, with dark hair and eyes and tattoos on his chest and arms smearing in my damaged vision. I'd been able to see clearly just a week ago. Something was wrong.

"No," the alpha said immediately. "Can't say we meant to find you either, though. Thought we were intercepting drugs or guns from a gang we don't want around our territory."

Which meant they were some kind of gang too, probably.

Adam's voice rang in my head.

"If anything ever goes sideways for us, I'm gonna find us the biggest, baddest, scariest alphas around and I'm going to make *them bond me." His grin was grim, determined. "That way we've got them on our team, fighting for us."*

"We both will," I'd said.

He stared at me a moment and that grin vanished, gaze solemn. "No. No, Faith, you're gonna have the fairy tale. The pretty house. The good pack. I'm just gonna take care of you in the meantime."

Apparently, it had never occurred to my older brother that we might end up separated. That I would have to figure out a way to take care of myself.

"You don't need to worry, Butterfly," the alpha said, and he shifted and rustled, leaning against the closet door that faced me, giving me space. "We're gonna get you to the Omega Center in—"

"No!"

Too loud. They'll hit now. Shrink, be small. Whine.

The alpha didn't strike. A big hand reached out, cupped my calf, warm and steady, and I sucked in a relieved breath, bringing a lungful of his safe scent along. He remained still as I found myself crawling toward him, a magnetic pull to that scent. Safe. Home. Soft.

Thick arms wrapped around me as I settled myself into the alpha's lap. He turned, shifting into the closet, and I sighed as the darkness swallowed up everything but the heat and bulk, the scent of the alpha.

"No?" he asked, and the question was gentle.

"No," I repeated.

We were quiet for a moment. My perfume was growing, and it almost took me by surprise. I'd grown so used to the smell of my own stress, and before that I'd been on suppressants for so long, I'd forgotten how sweet my perfume really was. It'd come in a couple years ago, late but not unexpected. My brother Adam and I had been on the run, and finding suppressants for us both had been a necessary challenge.

Does the alpha like my scent? I wondered. I'd been avoiding alphas for years. Knowing how I might affect one came with the risk of attracting their attention.

"You didn't like the smell of the club," the alpha said. "Too many scents?"

I nodded.

"We don't have anywhere else to put you, Butterfly. Omega Center—"

"No!" I snapped again, shuddering, still expecting punishment for arguing. But no hit came, and I swallowed up another soothing fill of this man's scent. "They'll find me there," I whispered.

"The Western Wasted?"

I blinked at the name. My *buyers*. But they didn't have me, and I shook my head.

A big hand rested on my left thigh, and there was a scratch against my skin. I picked the hand up and traced the scabs of dried blood left from my bite.

"The people who sold you?"

I dug my fingernails into his skin without thinking, and he flinched and grunted but didn't stop me. Just like he hadn't hurt me when I'd bitten him. Or thrown me off when I'd grabbed him. Or punished me when I'd fought him on the way in.

And he'd helped me bathe, but hadn't touched me or grabbed at me like the betas who'd guarded me.

This was a good alpha.

"Yes," I whispered, petting over the bite before releasing his hand and snuggling deeper into his chest.

"What's your name, Butterfly?"

I was tempted to tell him, but I shook my head. If he didn't know my name, he couldn't share it with the wrong person, and Omikron would be less likely to find me.

"Hmm, suppose we don't really do real names around the crew either. They call me Bear," he said.

I found my lips curling at that. Bear. Teddy bear? Or was he fearsome too? He was certainly huge.

"Bear," I said, breathing him in. Soft like fur.

"This isn't a good place for you, Butterfly. You smelled other alphas? They live here too. And some of them aren't much different than the ones who paid for your delivery," Bear warned, but he soothed the words by stroking my back.

And we were alone in this little nest. And the room only smelled of him.

"You can't leave this room. You can lock it yourself from the inside. And you can decide if you wanna open it to me. I'll give you the key," he said.

I wrapped my arms around his chest, protesting the idea of him leaving or not returning.

"I'll have to talk to King. He's in charge. I don't think you can stay here. I don't think you really want to. But we won't take you to the Omega Center."

I licked my lips. His taste was still on my tongue, and close to my mouth now. I wanted to bite him again.

Don't wanna leave. Safe here.

I whined, and Bear sighed, shifting and pressing me into a pillow. My arms tightened around him, and he didn't pull away. The floor was hard beneath us, coarse sheets tangled around my legs.

"Whatever happens, you're gonna be okay, Butterfly."

I chewed on the words, and Bear dragged the pillows I'd stolen from the other end of the closet over to where we were smashed in. He stuffed them around me until I was fully surrounded, extricating himself from my grip. I was drowsy and while I wanted him to stay, his scent was still surrounding me.

I was free of Omikron. I'd found an alpha to protect me.

My alpha. The thought rang in my head.

Adam had a plan. Find the biggest, scariest alpha around.

Bear wasn't scary, but he was huge and he belonged to some kind of gang. A pack?

Gunshots and screaming, the cage rattling around me, my shoulders crashing into metal as the van screeched to a stop. And then he had appeared in the ringing quiet minutes later. Bear.

Yes. Bear was dangerous. Dangerous for others, but safe for me.

I knew what Adam wanted for me. What I'd wanted for myself. Someday, after he and I had made sure other omegas were safe from Omikron, we would find our homes. Our packs. Pretty houses, nice nests, good alphas.

But I didn't know where Adam was, and I wasn't going to survive if I believed that I would magically find my way to some safe fantasy. Adam didn't trust alphas enough to seek their help before, and I wasn't going to take my chances with others when I had one right here who smelled like home and felt safe. What would a pretty house and a nice nest and good, normal alphas do to keep me safe from Omikron?

I needed Bear. I needed Bear's bite and bond.

Make him bite and bond me. Have him on my team, fighting for me.

I burrowed into the pillows, wrapped the sheet and blanket around me, and fumbled in the air in front of me, pushing the closet door shut to protect my nest. The dark was safe and simple, the only scents mine and Bear's.

Safe. Home. Alpha.

I kept to the back of club meetings.

As much as King liked to pretend that designation didn't affect the club, there were still only four of us betas who'd been sworn into the crew, and over a dozen alphas. I understood the precedent at the table, and I didn't need to humiliate myself by having an alpha boot me from his seat by will alone.

King sat at the head of the table, of course. There was an empty seat to his right for our enforcer, Bear, who was running late to church. At King's left, Ghost sank back into his chair, our road captain displaying the easy, confident, borderline lazy facade he liked to show off to the rest of the crew.

Across from King, balancing the table, was the VP Rider. My brother.

Before I'd sworn in to the Dead End Devils, Rider's seat had been where Bear's was now. King said he liked having Rider across from him, making their command over the club complete. But I suspected our prez really preferred keeping his eye on his closest ally and biggest rival. Rider and I were legacy in this club, our dad having been one of the founding members. And while old man Proof may not have ever found himself a seat of honor at the table, he'd had high ambitions for his son.

His alpha son.

So high, he'd got it into Rider's head that he was meant to be prez.

Somehow, both my brother and I ended up with chips on our shoulders.

"You're telling us there was no fucking cargo?" Skid asked, as the door to the room opened and Bear strode in like we weren't supposed to notice that he was a full twenty minutes late.

If Bear had become King's true right-hand, Skid was Rider's. If the skinny, sarcastic alpha was asking a dumb question at our church meeting, it was Rider who'd fed it to him.

"I'm telling you it's not cargo we can make use of," King said, raising his hands and feigning some of that casually calm air Ghost often wore. "There's no profit. No gain. Better rid of it. I promise you that."

Bear's chair screeched against the linoleum flooring, and King flashed him a glare but the bigger man kept his head ducked. I'd seen the damage Bear could do to not just one but a pile of men. If I hadn't, I would've assumed King had given him the position of enforcer just for show. But Bear could back up every inch of his enormous frame with physical power.

"Do we think it was a dummy van? That we lost the real score?" another alpha asked.

King and Rider held eyes across the table. King had filled Rider in on what happened, on what—or rather, who—we'd found.

"Could be," King said.

I watched my older brother's eyes narrow briefly. My position at the back of the room with the other betas gave me an advantage too, even in its veiled insult. Because it wasn't only Rider who'd found a position in this club. Mine just wasn't one I could flaunt. Spies rarely gain glory for their work.

King was a paranoid motherfucker, and my brother was restless. And I knew which of the two I would follow into battle. I'd sworn my vows to King; being under Rider's thumb too was an unfortunate side effect.

Sometimes, blood did run thinner than water. Or cheap beer around these parts.

"Cleanup went smoothly," Rider said, running fingers back

through thick sandy brown hair to where it was pulled into a tail at the back of his neck. "And it's not as though the Wasted would be surprised to find us breathing down their throats. Bit of unnecessary effort on our parts at the worst of it."

King dipped his head in acknowledgement. "And it's not as though we're about to stop keeping tabs on them. They're bold enough to run through our territory, we'll catch them again."

"And next time, maybe there'll be profit to it," Ghost chimed in, all sarcasm and cheer. King dutifully rolled his eyes as the rest of the table groaned or laughed or muttered their own frustration under their breath.

Skid glanced to Rider, who shrugged without returning the look. They weren't going to fight King further in the meeting. But Rider knew about the girl—knowledge that would be better used as pot-stirring bullshit in private. Only to the right club members. Not everyone would take issue with King's decision, either on the profit or pleasure side. Rider and Skid had their loud-mouth cronies, but in general, the club was made up of rough but decent men.

But I knew, and King knew, and sure as hell Rider knew, that there were a few of our brothers who wouldn't have minded a free chance at an omega.

I hoped for her sake Bear was late because he'd already gotten her well away from here.

"Girls have got dinner ready for you lot and put the good kegs on ice," King said, offering a dry smile to the stirring conversation. "Enjoy the night, brothers. Church is adjourned."

Chairs cried out their complaints as the alphas hurried out, wrestling at the door to be the first to get to a plate of food or a chilled mug of beer. Or, more likely, one of the club girls. King had called them all in for the night, eager to sate appetites and keep his men too busy and relaxed to ask questions.

The betas I stood with followed at a more sedate pace. We knew we'd end up last in line for every damned thing.

Skid left and King waved Rider and Ghost out, but Bear didn't bother getting up. I started to follow the rest of the room when Bear raised a couple fingers and met my eyes. Rider was already halfway out the door, and I figured it'd take him too long to notice I was missing. Ghost glanced back at me, paused, and then vanished too.

The three of us—the prez, the enforcer, and the spy—waited until the room was empty. I closed the door on the last beta to leave and listened there to make sure I didn't hear any sly comments.

"She's talking now," Bear said, breaking the silence.

I had no right being curious about a battered omega, but I found my way back to the table. I was as curious about why Bear wanted me present, as I was to hear news about the woman we'd found.

"But I can see her going in and out of hindbrain when she gets nervous," he continued, frowning at his own hands. "No name. And she says no to the Omega Center."

King scoffed. "Too fuckin' bad. What does she think her options are?"

Bear's lips tightened, hands fisting on his thighs, and I stared at the fingerless leather gloves he was wearing. Riding gloves in church? Strange.

"She says the people who sold her will find her at the Center."

I frowned at that. Wasn't the Omega Center designed to *protect* omegas? To make their heats and packs their decision? But King didn't look so surprised by the news, his initial scorn fading into thought.

"They'd register her, run her DNA in the database. Big enough trafficking organization might be capable of tracking her down, I think," Bear said, and his shoulders shrugged in an awkward movement. He was trying to sound casual, but it had to be as obvious to King as it was to me that he'd already come to some kind of decision about the omega and he did *not* want to argue on the topic. But he would.

"Bear," King said. A single, firm reminder.

Bear looked up, dark eyes hard and holding our prez's. They were the definition of two equal but opposite forces.

"Give me some time, I can get more information," Bear said.

King arched a pale eyebrow. "And in the meantime, we just...

fucking have an omega in the club? Around assholes like Skid and Numbnuts?"

"No. She stays in my room," Bear said firmly.

I cleared my throat and crossed my arms over my chest. "You're talking about one alpha or another. And King and I both saw the way she glued herself to you," I said.

"I can handle myself," Bear said, and I was surprised by how confident he was. He looked to King. "I know how to manage omegas, and I know how to manage myself. You know this."

King dipped his head, and I scowled at being left out of some vital piece of information in the conversation. "Doesn't change the situation. Still an omega in a club full of horny fucking alphas, half of whom wouldn't know impulse control if it bit them in the ass. She may not smell great now—"

Bear's expression twisted, and it gave him away. The omega's perfume was already clearing up. "I'll get her suppressants," Bear said. "I know how to work the system."

My eyebrows bounced at that. Had Bear been bonded at one point, or...?

"You have a job to do around here," King said, just an edge of a bark in his voice.

"I know," Bear answered, his eyes flicking to me. "And I intend to do it. I'll need time away from her anyway."

"Wait—" I said, already sensing the direction this was headed.

"If Chance will keep an eye on her when I'm busy—"

"What?" I laughed.

King's head turned back and forth, glancing between us. "You trust Chance?" he asked Bear.

Bear shrugged, and my head spun. "*You* do," he said to King, a slight challenge in his tone. "So you tell me. Can that omega trust Chance?"

King's jaw clenched, and we stared at one another through a brief stretch of silence before I realized he was waiting on my answer.

"Yes," I said slowly, frowning, sensing the walls of the trap go up around me. "But—"

I was the beta. As if that made me less of a predator, a danger, than an alpha.

"It'll be up to her," Bear continued, ignoring me. "But if Chance's loyalty is to you, I know he won't sell her out from under us. And he can't bite her."

My teeth ground in protest. I could bite her. It just wouldn't mean anything. Fuck this.

"Maybe I'd just rather not be a fucking omega's babysitter," I said, but the words sound weak and petulant to my own ears.

"If we can't take her to the Center, what are we supposed to do?" King asked.

Frustration blazed through my veins. I was being talked over, ignored. My dull fingernails bit into my own palms, and Bear shot me a wary glance, like he knew my anger was about to boil over, and beta or not, that warranted caution.

"Find her a pack that can keep her hidden," Bear said. "Get her a new identity. Quickly. We don't want to know what she's mixed up in. But we caught her before she was in the Wasted's care, which means we crossed the traffickers, not another MC. And if they do have a network that has influence with the Omega Center, then..."

King sucked in a deep breath and let out a low growl, rolling his head on his neck and grimacing at the tired cracks.

"You're not making a persuasive argument to me about why we should keep her longer than we have to," King muttered.

Bear and I glanced at one another. Maybe I was a safe bet to watch the omega, because in a single moment of wondering if our prez would send a young woman back into the hands of the traffickers who had caged and sold her, I knew how *wrong* that sat with me.

"I've got a few contacts I can consider," King said slowly, tracing a pattern of wood grain on the long table as he thought. "We may need to think about sending the crew out on a pleasure cruise if this is going to take more than a few days. Scared feral or not, an omega *is* going to get noticed around here. I'll talk to Ghost."

"And Rider," I said quickly. "Better to get him out, away from temptation."

Bear rumbled with a growl that suited his road name. "I need to get back to her, get her some food. Chance, I'm gonna make a run for stuff she'll want tomorrow."

I nodded. Arguing was pointless and truth be told, the more I thought about it, the more I preferred the idea of being the little omega's guard than anyone else in the crew. The other betas had loyalties to alphas I didn't trust, and I couldn't imagine any of the alphas but King and Bear resisting the urge to knot an omega. Not if they were offered the invitation, at least.

"I'm only conceding under the terms that she *does* leave, Bear," King said.

Bear nodded, but he didn't meet the prez's eyes.

"We're not a pack. We're not taking an omega. It's only going to fuck up the crew," King added.

Bear nodded again, but when he looked up there was no sheepish apology on his hard face. "It's her staying here for the time, or me taking some leave while I figure out where to place her."

"We need you here," King said, frowning, reluctant acceptance of the corner Bear had gently backed him into.

I headed for the door as the pair of them rose from their seats.

She was staying. The huddled bruised creature from the van. The omega. I stepped out of the meeting room into the hall that bridged between the club bunk house and the bar. The clubhouse was an old motel King had bought and closed for the crew's use when the old club house I'd grown up in burnt down. It was a little run-down, pretty filthy, but still a far cry better than the death trap of my childhood.

The party hadn't waited for our prez. Music was already blaring from amps, a round of pool was brewing a minor argument between two prospects, and one of the club girls was serving shots topless, letting the guys suck salt from her tits.

I told myself not to, but my eyes had already started their search, the destination too familiar by now.

Ghost was in a corner booth with Rider and Skid. Lilah was on his lap, facing him, pressed so close to his crotch I couldn't tell if they were already fucking or not. They'd get there soon.

Lilah was Ghost's flavor of the week, but I could tell by the way his green gaze was drifting through the room her time was running out.

And I knew where he'd wander when his interest for her ran dry. The interlude between one woman and the next. Ghost's dirty little secret.

I hoped it took Bear and King a nice long time to find that omega a decent pack. I hoped Ghost rode out with the club and I got a break from watching him laugh half-heartedly at my brother's filthy jokes and fuck every pretty girl his aimless gaze landed on.

I hoped he didn't find his way back to my bed before they left.

But if he did, I knew exactly what I would do to him.

When that lazy gaze drifted in my direction, I turned away, heading toward my own room. I was up on the second floor, nearly across from Bear's corner room, and I passed my own door to stand in front of his, pausing to listen.

Bear's mellow, almost bland scent was there on the door-frame, where his shoulders brushed, and there was no hint of the burning perfume I'd caught from the omega. I waited for a shuffle of steps, or a whine of warning, but it was silent within.

I walked back to my own door. Bear would be back soon to keep an eye on her and I'd hear anyone coming down the hall in the meantime. Babysitting duty could start tomorrow.

I woke, breathing deeply, sighing with relief at the homey, safe fragrance surrounding me. There was a growling sound—no, just deep, heavy snores from outside of my nest, and I listened with my eyes closed to the sleeping alpha.

Bear.

Safe, my brain reminded me as I started to tense. I shifted, sitting up, and realized how sticky my skin was. Sweaty. I was twisted up in blankets and sheets, surrounded by pillows. Was the alpha sleeping on a nearly bare mattress? The room was dark, and my obscured vision left me practically blind, just a few smudges of shadows as a map.

But darkness in Omikron's compound meant I was alone, left in peace, and it'd gone from being frightening to comforting. I wasn't alone now, but Bear was asleep, snoring like his namesake. My head was clearer in this moment than it had been in weeks or even longer.

There were voices nearby, a feminine cry of pleasure rising up from the floor below, a dull and distant thump of music far off, a few shouts and laughs.

No crying, no whines, and no whimpers. No other omegas in distress.

I was safe now. Bear was safe. I needed Bear.

I played the mantra in my head for a few minutes, listening to him snore and the enthusiastic woman crying out downstairs. My skin was warm, even as I peeled out of the blankets, and the repetitive sounds from below had an embarrassing effect on my body, warming me from the inside out.

A woman on her knees, crying out as an alpha pumped into her from behind. The red light of the camera watching from the top left corner of my little room, the volume rising higher as I tried to hide my gaze.

Safe. I am with Bear, and I am safe. I am safe here.

I came back to the present and tried to let the heat simmering through me feel welcome. This was not Omikron trying to force arousal, manufacture my heat. This was just the sound of a woman having a good time downstairs and the smell of an alpha who was keeping me safe.

I reached out and found the closet door, wincing at the squeak, pausing as it tapped against something on the floor.

A trap?

Bear was still snoring as I reached out between the crack, fumbling over the rough carpet until my touch crinkled against a thin bag. The alpha's throat cleared as I touched the plastic.

Food!

"Hey, Butterfly. Left you some—" Bear let out that soft rasp of a laugh as I broke free of the closet and descended blindly on the food.

A sealed bag of chips. A heavy aluminum can. There was a sandwich too, unwrapped, and I lifted it from the styrofoam plate but couldn't convince myself to bring it to my mouth.

Sometimes the meals I'd been fed made me sick. Sometimes they made my skin feverish and my insides twist, laced with drugs trying to induce a heat.

I helped myself to the chips, and Bear made the mattress squeak as he rolled over. Outside of my nest, light from somewhere outside made the foggy shapes of the room a little clearer. Bear's arm moved above his chest. He was on his back now. I opened the can and sipped slowly, surprised to find it was lemonade, rather than beer or soda.

"You sleep okay?" he asked.

I nodded, and he hummed. He could see me fine.

Downstairs, the woman's moans were growing longer, more languid and satisfied. My perfume was blooming, sweet and sticky. A surprising burst of heat in my core released an unexpected wetness. *Slick.*

My eyes widened, but Bear made no sound. He'd dressed me in a huge shirt and a pair of men's briefs that barely hung onto my slim hips—his own clothing, not another woman's. I was going to make his underwear smell like my arousal, and his shirt would mix our scents together.

"You don't have a pillow," I whispered, drinking more of the lemonade, running my tongue over my teeth. I would ask him if I could have a toothbrush tomorrow.

"Don't worry about it. I'll get you more for your nest tomorrow. Clothes, bath stuff. Everything you need," he said, his voice thick with sleep.

Safe. A good alpha. I needed him. His protection, and...

And I needed a way to relieve the throb between my legs. I put the empty chip bag aside and pushed the can out of the way, crawling slowly toward the bed, finding it with my hands in the dark.

"Whatcha need, Butterfly?" Bear whispered, words slow and slurring softly as I climbed up. He would fall back to sleep if I let him.

I could crawl into my nest, touch myself. But that would be like it was in my cell, trying to hide my sounds, my tiny movements from the cameras, from whoever was watching, from the humiliating reality of being trapped and horny and observed.

His chest was bare as I braced my hands there, his skin so, so warm. He stiffened as I swung one leg over his hips.

"Butterfly—"

"I need this," I whispered, sitting down on his lap.

Should I have undressed? He was wearing sweatpants, and I landed directly on the waistband, the knotted tie against my clit. The pressure was like a finger and I let out a pleased whimper, rocking on top of him without thinking twice.

Bear's hands wrapped around my wrists, gentle but lifting up, trying to move me. I wasn't sure I had the courage to fight him, but I was already lost to the tiny point of relief that one bit of friction had provided. I sighed and moved, scooting down a little farther to the pressure of his hips, rubbing myself there. My eyes fell shut, and I was in the middle of a rhythm, steady and slow, grinding, when I realized my hands were still on his hot chest, his fingers wrapped around my wrists.

"I need this, alpha," I said again. "Please."

Bear wasn't breathing, but his heart was thumping fast and hard under my right hand, and there was a nudging and swelling against my ass.

One large hand slid up my arm, skipping the loose shirt sleeves, to cup the side of my neck. I leaned into his touch, his hand surprisingly cool on my throat, and marveled at the delicious pressure and gentle fire in my core. I moaned freely, matching the woman downstairs, and Bear's thumb stroked over my pulse.

"Shit," Bear muttered, and my pace stuttered for a moment. "You're burning up, Butterfly."

"Mhm." I nodded and gasped. I tugged on the hand he was still holding, twisting in his grasp and struggling for a moment to push his hand under my shirt, up to my breast.

"When was your last heat?"

He sounded so calm. I was sure that was his cock growing thick and stiff behind me, but he didn't move otherwise, didn't take anything for himself, didn't push me away.

"I-I—Ohhh!" I managed to wrap his huge hand around my breast, and finally Bear grunted, fingers flexing briefly.

I realized that whoever was downstairs had finished, fallen quiet, and it made me shy of my own voice. I pressed my lips together and swallowed my whine as my shameless humping grew frantic.

"It's all right, Butterfly," Bear murmured. "Take what you need."

I left his hand on my breast, returning my own to his chest to steady me in my desperate rocking. His thumb brushed over my nipple, and I shuddered at the way the touch rushed through me, down into my core.

"Again," I gasped.

This time he took my nipple between two fingers, rolling it gently, not pinching but playing. My mouth fell open, but I refused to cry out. Bear's hand on my throat moved to my jaw, and then two thick fingers slid between my lips. My eyes widened, but I sucked on his fingers gratefully.

Suddenly, the chest beneath me vibrated, a low and heady sound rising up. Tears stung my eyes, and I squeezed them shut as Bear started to purr.

Safe. Home. Alpha.

It was a sound I knew to my bones without ever having heard before. It made my muscles unwind, making room for pleasure to flood in, to swallow me from head to toe. My orgasms on the run had been hasty, urgent releases, taken in shameful moments in the shower, or awkwardly with friends in the dark. This was slow and thorough, while tears rolled out of my eyes and over my cheeks as I shuddered and soaked the borrowed underwear.

Bear pulled his fingers free of my mouth and I gasped for air, still coming. His hand grasped my hip, continuing the rock and slide of my body, pulling me up so I was on his bare stomach. My eyes flashed open as I realized what he was doing, rubbing my release through the thin knit underwear directly into his skin, and it made me shake with another wave of toe-curling pleasure. I sagged forward, trapping his hand on my breast, wiping my tears off on his shoulder, and Bear kept me moving, kept the heat simmering in my cunt.

"You can...you can knot me," I mumbled into his skin.

I was starting to gain control of my own muscles again, moving myself on his stomach, aware of the slick and easy path I'd created there.

Bear pulled both hands away and then slid them under the shirt, up my back, petting me as I rocked.

Knot me. Bite me. Keep me safe.

But he didn't pull my shirt off over my head or push the fabric out of the way to plunge that now hard cock inside of me.

"Keep going, Butterfly," he murmured, ignoring my offer. "As long as you want. Just take what you need."

I gritted my teeth at the new pound of desire pulsing through me, rougher and more demanding than the one before. I whined, and Bear rolled us onto our sides, creating a gap between my hips and his stomach.

"No—" I whined, but it was short-lived as he pulled a hand from my back and pressed it through the fabric.

"Inside or outside?" he asked, the question almost empty of personal interest.

"In-inside," I stuttered.

He rubbed over my clit, and I realized why he was hesitating.

I reached down, pushing at the slit in the briefs, shoving Bear's hand past the wet fabric to touch me directly. His fingers were calloused and rough, but I was slippery and I arched with a cry as he studied me.

Did he not want this, not want me? If he didn't, if I couldn't make him want me, what would I do?

"Alpha," I whispered, reaching for his cock, finding it through the thick cotton of the sweatpants.

Bear's purr rumbled as I studied his length and rode his fingers.

"Alpha, I want you."

Bear shuddered, bucked into my hand, leaned forward until I was on my back, two fingers pushing into me, thumb circling my clit.

"You can have anything you want, Butterfly," he rasped, his cool brow pressing to my fevered one. His hair was curly, I realized, as it slipped across my cheeks.

I hiccuped as he fucked me with those thick fingers, braced my feet on the bed and rocked into the touch.

"But not my knot tonight," he added. I whined, and he nuzzled his nose against my cheek. "Too soon."

I had a plan. I needed Bear. I needed his bite and bond. Needed him to keep me. Keep me safe.

And yet for some reason, those words brought the same comfort and relief as his purr. I moaned and my cunt sucked on his fingers, and a pair of thick lips grazed over my open mouth as I came. My hand tightened on Bear's cock, and he purred and rubbed himself into the muffled touch, but no more.

"That's right, omega," Bear purred. "Coming so pretty for me."

I gasped at the words and the way they made the heat of release flash all over, right up into my cheeks.

"You want another?" he asked, purring through the words, drawing a shiver up my back and another aftershock to make me whine with a brush of his thumb.

I nodded, and Bear brushed another kiss over my nose. He had a nice mouth. I shifted, stretched, and studied it with my own—not quite a real kiss as we nuzzled our noses together. He was scenting me, like an alpha should to his omega. He was taking care of me. Keeping me safe. Satisfying me.

Not hurting me, refusing to rush.

I licked my lips and caught a taste of him too. He had a very nice mouth.

I released his cock, and he didn't make a single sound of protest.

I'd never had time to explore an alpha before, never been near one that I knew wouldn't bite me or knot me without my permission.

I am safe, I reminded myself.

Bear rubbed his cheek to mine and then against my neck. I arched my throat, and he only grazed a kiss over my pulse, no hint of teeth. I needed his bite. But maybe I could take just a little time first?

No knot tonight.

Maybe tomorrow night.

And maybe tonight...

"I want you to lick me," I whispered, my eyes wide at the words.

Bear purred louder, nuzzled against my collarbone, huffed a laugh. His fingers pulled out of me and I whined, until those slick fingers hooked into the waistband of the briefs, pulling it easily down my hips aside from the wet cling of it on my cunt.

The room was dark and full of my perfume and his scent. I could just make out the enormous shadow of Bear's head and shoulders as he scooted down the bed. His hands found mine and placed one in his hair and the other on the back of his neck. My thighs spread to make room for him, and the air was too cold on my wet pussy until Bear puffed a breath over the spot.

"Take what you need," he purred, patting my hands where he'd placed them, then cupping my thighs and spreading them a little wider.

I arched my hips forward and found that mouth on my sex, groaning as his full lips spread me open, tongue flicking at my opening.

Take what you need. Take him.

I dug my fingers into his hair and did exactly that.

I stood at the foot of the bed, staring into the closet, frowning. I could still taste sugar and almonds and coconut and something floral on my lips, and somehow "Butterfly" had managed to slip back out of the bed and into her makeshift nest after having her way with me.

My lips twitched.

Shyly, sweetly, bashfully having her way with me. Sweet little omega.

It was difficult to remember the number of problems she posed when I was still coated in her scent, so I moved slowly toward the attached bathroom, cranking on the shower. I'd leave the door open to be sure I didn't miss anything, but I needed to wash off and clear my head.

And also jerk off.

Resisting her skittish offer of getting my knot in was more challenging than I'd expected. If she'd been a little more relaxed, begged instead of that careful 'you can,' I probably would've had her pinned on my cock in five seconds flat. Most alphas wouldn't have needed much more encouragement than the half-hearted request.

But I'd worked as a service alpha to omegas in their heat for five years before finding my way to Dead End, and I knew when an omega was really ready for a knot.

Butterfly was going into heat. She was feverish, throwing off perfume, slick running eagerly. And only a heat could send an omega out of a cage and onto an alpha's cock. Her still being half feral probably didn't help. She was operating on instinct and her instinct demanded to be bred.

I grimaced as I stepped into the spray of water. I'd never reversed my vasectomy, but I would get tested today to make sure I was clean and safe for her. She'd need toys for her to use so she had an option that wasn't me. Packaged food because she wouldn't touch the sandwich I'd left her—a smart but inconvenient defense mechanism. And everything else an omega might want.

Chance would have to keep an eye on her and maybe even help me sneak all this shit up to my room. Bubble bath and twinkle lights weren't my usual fare, and if someone saw me carrying in bags of goodies, there'd be questions.

I licked my lips, groaned at the flavor I found there, and reached down to my own cock. It jumped eagerly into my hand, knot swelling fast and hard, aware of how I'd denied us both the night before.

But fuck, it'd been worth it just to watch her have her own pleasure, selfish and sweet. She was underfed, but she had a nice curve to her waist and soft handfuls of breasts. I'd get her back in fighting shape. Get all the vitamins and protein bars I could find.

And I'd make her come as often as she asked. Watch the color smudge over her cheeks, her eyes drifting wildly as if she were searching for some explanation to the sensations I drew out of her, her tongue flicking out over her lips as she fought for breath, pretty nipples sharpening to points.

I grunted and used both hands, one for my knot and one to stroke myself. Her hands were smaller than mine; she would need both of them to stroke me too. I'd worked with dozens of omegas, servicing them through their heats. I could pace myself through Butterfly's too if it came to it, although it created issues with the plan I'd just presented to King. We either needed to introduce the omega to a pack she liked in the next couple days before the heat really set in, or there'd be no turning back until it was over.

And it worried me how much I liked that prospect.

Been too long since I knotted, I tried to tell myself. *Been too long since I fucked anyone period, actually.*

I groaned as I caught another whiff of the omega's sweet and slick perfume, beautifully sexual, and then my eyes widened as I realized why. She was standing in the doorway of the bathroom, dark eyes fixed to my hands on my cock.

My chest rumbled with a purr automatically—that hungry look on her face seemed to communicate directly to my cock, making it jump in my hand—but I cleared my throat as she stepped forward.

"No." The word was gravel, the direct opposite of what my body wanted, but it made her pause and frown. "Gotta wash you off, Butterfly. Or the others will know."

"That's not washing," she said, and I laughed.

I expected her to stay, to keep watching, but her eyes narrowed and her brow furrowed, like she was trying to get a better look and frustrated with the result. Maybe staring at dick wasn't her thing? Fair enough. I savored the sight of her in my T-shirt as she turned away. She was bare under that shirt.

I groaned, closed my eyes, and tried to recall the dark shadows of her on my bed from the night before, fueling my fantasy to the finish.

———

CHANCE OPENED his door after the fourth knock. His eyes were red, and his gelled-back hair was half mussed from sleep, pieces still held together with product. Chance had a dirtbag look to him that seemed to invoke automatic distrust in civvies, and sexual attraction in young women. Tattooed up to his ears, pierced, and constantly scowling. Handsome too. He could pull more trade than half the alphas in the club when he wanted, although he rarely bothered.

I couldn't catch much of his scent under the aftershave and

occasional whiff of cigarettes, but it was the usual whisper of a beta.

"I need one of your shirts," I said.

He blinked, reaching a hand up and scrubbing it over the stubble that was starting to stab through the intricate design on his throat. "It won't fit."

I glanced down the length of the hall and lowered my voice. "To test your scent on her."

Chance grunted and turned, leaving the door hanging open. His room was...surprisingly clean, actually. He was meticulous about his looks. Maybe he was about cleanliness too. He dug into his closet and pulled out a rumpled black T-shirt, tossing it to me.

"What are you gonna do if she hates it?" he asked.

"Make you leave your door open and keep an eye out," I said, shrugging.

He scowled. "Like that won't look fuckin' weird?"

"Less suspicious than if she's throwing a fit," I said, leaving him standing there and heading back to my room.

Jerking off hadn't really relieved any of the pressure from the day before, and I wasn't in the mood for Chance's perpetual dark cloud of a personality. I'd seen a few moments of obvious trust towards him on King's part, but mostly what I observed from Chance was a general sense of being pissed off at the world for denying him an alpha's designation. Futile anger.

I slipped back into my room and found Butterfly in her nest again, curled up and watching me from the shadows. "I need to go out and get you supplies. I have a...friend I'd like to let keep an eye on you. If you're comfortable."

I held out the T-shirt. Under normal circumstances, introducing an omega to a beta would be a non-issue. Betas were inoffensive—biologically speaking, at least—and there was no ceremony for an introduction. But until I was sure Butterfly was totally out of her hindbrain and feeling secure, I needed to tread carefully and operate on the rules of instinct.

Scent knew best.

She reached out and accepted the garment, running it through her hands first before drawing it slowly to her face. Her nose wrinkled immediately, and my heart stuttered, but she didn't throw the T-shirt back at me.

"Beta," she said, frowning, gaze going distant.

I lowered into a crouch, watching every minute shift of her expression. "Better than an alpha," I said.

She scoffed and shivered. "Not really."

He can't bite you or knot you, I thought, but didn't bother saying. A beta could hurt an omega; she was right. And she'd obviously seen plenty of trouble without it coming to a bite.

I opened my mouth, ready to reject the idea, tell Chance to do his best work as a guard dog from outside, when she stuffed her face into the fabric and breathed deeply. Her eyes closed, brow furrowing, and I watched her in silence. She drew away slowly, blinking.

"It's a nice scent," she murmured. I bristled, unnecessarily jealous, and she added, "Kind of spicy. He won't touch me?"

"Absolutely not. He'll get you food if you ask. Drinks. Make sure no one bothers you." She took another deep whiff of the shirt, and I wrestled with the absurd urge to tear it out of her hands and replace it with one of mine. "You can even close the doors to the closet if you want. Don't have to talk to him. Get some rest," I suggested.

She hummed, and I clenched my hands as she looked up at me, tucking the shirt into the tangle of the sheets around her. Was that a conscious choice or not? Adding his scent to her nest seemed like a good sign.

"How long will you be gone?" she asked.

I tallied the tasks in my head. She'd need toys. Suppressants, although I wasn't sure if they'd take since her fever had already started. Good food and indulging treats. Clothes. More bedding. And pretty shit. All the little trinkets and decadent decorations the omegas I'd worked with seemed to have on hand for themselves during their heats.

"Most of the day," I admitted reluctantly.

She started to whine but swallowed the sound before I had to say anything. "Okay."

I held still, absorbing her acceptance. I should've waited until the last possible second to shower. I wanted to stuff myself into the nest, rub my scent all over her, make her come again for agreeing. But I needed to walk out of here without an omega's perfume clinging to me, and anyway, it was already late in the morning.

"Good girl," I said, purring for her as I stood, backing away before her blooming scent could catch at my legs. "I'm gonna let him in as I leave," I said.

She nodded, reaching out and missing the edge of the door as she reached for it, catching it on the second try. I paused at the sight and watched as it slid shut on a creaky track.

Shop and come back. Ask her more questions tonight. Suck on her clit till she thrashes and loses her breath again.

Chance came to his door as I opened mine, and I nodded. His hair was back in place, eyes clearer, and I blinked at the sight of him holding a book as he crossed the hallway.

"She says no touching," I whispered, although the hall was empty again and most of our club brothers wouldn't be up until one of the girls started cooking lunch.

Chance shrugged. "Figured that was a given."

Which was a comforting remark, I decided. Still, I fought the uncomfortable clench of my stomach as he stepped into my room and shut the door behind him. I stood in the hall, waiting and listening for a whine or a whimper. There was nothing. Chance didn't even say a word.

I rolled my shoulders and headed for the stairs. Shop quickly. Get back soon. She'd managed this long without me. Surely I could handle a few hours of separation.

The beta outside of my nest was quiet. He made the bed creak when he first entered, and there were twin thumps against the floor, shoes dropping, but then it was silent. Just the whisper of...paper? Pages turning.

I peered out of a crack in the closet door, but it was difficult to make anything out when everything was blurry. He was just a black shadow on a white bed.

My fingers played in the soft cotton of his T-shirt where I'd stuffed it at my hip. I tried to sleep, but I was too aware of his presence outside the closet doors. He wasn't like Bear. His scent wasn't *home*. But it was safe. Not chemical or sour or bitter, like the betas who'd been on rotation. Pleasant, even.

We existed in quiet together for a long time. Was he watching the closet the way I was watching the thin stripe of light coming from outside? Or was he able to ignore me?

I was just starting to feel my own hunger when a sudden series of booms sounded. I stiffened and gasped, trying and failing to swallow a whine.

Someone was knocking on the door.

"Bear!" a low voice bellowed from the hall.

The bed didn't creak this time, but I caught the flicker of

shadow as the beta moved. I cowered in my sheets as the knocking pounded again, and the beta's figure blocked the light through my door. There was a soft rustle, and then the door of my nest pushed in slightly, pressure from the outside.

"Shhh," the beta whispered. "It's all right. They'll leave."

"Bear! Wake the fuck up!"

I buried my whimper into a pillow.

"It's all right," the man outside my nest repeated. He was closer now, and that clean and soapy spice scent filtered into my space. "I can't answer. They'll leave."

More knocking. A muffled, distant call. And then a soft, "Damn, where the fuck he goin' this early?"

"He's leaving," the beta whispered.

And sure enough, a soft thud of footsteps shook the floor and softened in retreat.

The beta sighed with me, and the quiet from just a minute ago returned. But he didn't move back to the bed.

"You okay?" he asked, after a moment.

His voice was nice too. Simple and clean, like his scent. I nudged at the closet door, and the pressure released, light flooding in and making me wince. The glare passed and the beta shifted, sitting fully on the floor. He had lighter hair than Bear, but there was something strange going on with his... Oh, those were tattoos, blurring his skin into a mottled gray.

I nodded.

"Hungry?"

I licked my lips and nodded again.

"Bear told me you'd want sealed food, but not what kinds. What sounds good?"

My lips twisted. What I *wanted* was about fifty different things at once. Tacos. A sheet cake to myself. Ice cream in a waffle cone. Pizza bagels. But imagining any of it on a plate in front of me...

"I don't know," I said instead.

The beta moved restlessly. I wondered how he'd managed to stay so quiet and still on the bed, because now that he was up close, I could watch the way his hands were constantly traveling, rubbing over his arm, scuffing at his jaw, the back of his neck.

"Guess I'll just grab whatever I can find," he said, moving to rise.

My hand snapped out, slapping around his wrist, and he stilled. Bear was gone, not back for hours. And this beta, whoever he was, was my protection. If he left the room. If someone else came knocking...

"I'm not that hungry," I lied.

He snorted but settled and made no move to take my hand off him. His wrist was thick, and I was tempted to explore more of him, just to get a better sense of who was in front of me. He shifted again, pulling out a glossy rectangle.

Ah, a phone.

"I could reach out to King. He doesn't want the others to know you're here. He'd make sure no one saw him in the hall too. He could bring us food?"

"Would Bear trust him?" I asked.

It took me a moment of squinting to realize the tremble of his head was a nod.

"Okay."

"He's also the prez of the club, so sending him on an errand is a bit of a ballsy move on my part, but circumstances being what they are..." The beta trailed off with a soft laugh.

"What's your name?"

"What's yours?" he parried quickly.

Faith Robins. My brother is Adam Robins. I need to find him. I need him to find me.

I said nothing. My body trusted Bear, but that didn't mean he couldn't use my name or my brother's name at the wrong time, to the wrong person, and send Omikron in my direction again.

"Chance," the beta said.

"Bear calls me Butterfly."

A sharp laugh cracked out of the beta's throat, and he stifled it quickly. "Jesus. I'm...not going to do that." The blur of his hand reached for my face before I could pull away. "How about I just call you 'omega'?" he said with a slightly comical growl.

I tensed at the word and shook my head.

"Fair enough," he murmured, not releasing me.

He wasn't supposed to touch me. Then again, my hand was

still holding his wrist, warm and muscular in my grip. And Chance was gentle, holding my jaw between his thumb and fore-finger, the others resting against my throat, little tingles of heat. My cheeks warmed, and I realized he was studying me.

"Birdy," he said. My eyes widened, and he continued, "Little bird in her cage."

"Not much better than Butterfly," I said, frowning.

He laughed again and it was a warmer sound. His phone chimed and he pulled away at last. I forced my hand to let go of him too, although I missed his warm skin immediately, a human anchor in the fog of my vision.

Chance's laugh continued as he read whatever message was sent. "King is gonna regret not bringing the club in on this. Grabbing lunch is prospect shit."

"Prospect?"

"Prospect members of our crew. Motorcycle crew," Chance explained.

I recalled the roar of engines before the chaos. Motorcycles.

"Bear, Chance, King... You all have funny names."

"They're road names, Birdy. You join a motorcycle crew, you give up your civilian life and you take a new name. Bear's kind of obvious—man is stacked. King's been lordly all his life as far as any of us can tell, but it also happens to be his last name."

"And Chance?"

He shifted again, moving away from the nest to lean his back against the bed frame. He stretched long legs out in front of him, and I reached out, studying the black denim fabric with my fingers.

"Chance is my real name, actually. My dad belonged to this crew. Gave me and my brother our road names as soon as we were born. It suits, I guess. Not lucky, not unlucky. Just sitting on that knife's edge, waiting to see which way I topple."

I sank back into my pillows, found his T-shirt under my hand, and tangled my fingers in the soft fabric in lieu of grabbing onto the beta. "I think I was born unlucky. I..." I pressed my lips together briefly, debating how much to say, before I found some of the words spilling out anyway. "I lost my parents straight away. And...obviously, it didn't get a lot better later."

"You're an omega," Chance pointed out.

"That's not lucky. Most omegas are packed up before they've even finished fully mentally developing," I said. It was Adam's speech, not mine. I'd been the optimistic one. I'd believed in the fairy tale for a *someday* we never reached in all our running. "And going into the system as an omega is...living as a product alphas are just waiting to buy."

Chance was quiet, and I ducked my head. A lot of betas resented omegas. Maybe he did too. Maybe I sounded like a privileged girl whining about her pedestal to him—a pedestal I'd sat on while being auctioned off.

But he moved again, shuffling close. And in spite of that supposed no touching rule, he reached into the nest, finding my hand and gripping it in his.

"Good point," he said simply, and I relaxed. "Can't exactly argue your shit luck after yesterday."

"Yesterday was an improvement," I murmured.

His hand squeezed mine. "We'll keep working on that, okay, birdy?"

If Chance's name had left him hanging in the moment between good luck and bad luck, in the opportunity for things to go right or wrong, mine had been the constant belief that all the horrible might one day suddenly be replaced with something nice.

Nice had come in little moments. Brief pauses with Adam as we suffered through. Nice had been sleeping for eight hours. Having a spare room to stay in instead of a couch. Money to eat real meals or, even better, groceries and a kitchen to cook them in.

At the moment, nice was an alpha whose touch set me on fire and who seemed to want nothing else but to keep me hidden and safe. Nice was a beta who smelled good and who held my hand and agreed that in spite of winning the supposed designation lottery at birth, I'd been dealt a shit hand in life.

I didn't know how to find Adam. I could barely see, let alone get my way onto the server we used to contact him. I'd just been stolen from the men who'd paid to own my body.

I wanted to keep nice. I had nice in my grip right now and

absolutely no intention of letting it go. I would dig my teeth into nice like an alpha and claim it for myself.

————

"This was not the agreement."

"I know."

The words rumbled in my ear from the chest my head rested on. Chance was tense, and my arms tightened around him.

"Don't get up," Bear said. "I'm relieved, actually."

Chance didn't really relax, but he didn't move either.

My head had started to throb again after an irate sounding alpha had dropped off a huge tray of bizarrely chosen food—more cans of lemonade, string cheese, a sleeve of crackers, an unopened bag of pepperoni, a can of olives, a box of cookies, and a jar of peanut butter—and I'd had a strange but satisfying feast to myself, with Chance watching from his spot on the bed.

He'd read aloud from his book with a bit of coaxing from me, and had eventually let me draw him into my nest when I couldn't stop tossing and turning. I'd fallen asleep at last with him curled around my back.

And now Bear was back, staring at us from the bed.

"Hey, Butterfly."

"Hey," I croaked.

There was an obscure bulk of bags on the floor around Bear's feet, and he'd turned some lamps on, their bright orbs of light making the space confusing with too many shadows.

"King's got work for me tomorrow. We're going forward with sending the crew out. Can you stay with her?" Bear asked.

Chance's hand stroked the length of my back through Bear's shirt, just once, and his chest shifted as he nodded.

"Thanks," Bear said. He breathed deeply, then let out a heavy sigh. I wiggled in the cramped nest, sitting up and squinting at him. "Butterfly, when was your last heat?"

My cheeks flushed at the question. He'd asked the night before too, and I'd avoided answering. There was a firm edge to his tone now that told me I wouldn't be able to skirt the subject a second time.

"I've...never had one before."

"Shit," Chance said, scooting back, sitting up against the wall of the closet. "How old are you?"

"Twenty-two," I said, wanting to smile at the tangible relief from both men. "Ad—the omega I was traveling with and I thought it didn't come in for me because we never really had time to rest? We were...running."

"The omega you were traveling with," Bear repeated.

"Please don't ask," I whispered, and I found Chance drawing me back into his chest.

"She doesn't have to trust us right away. We don't need to know everything," Chance said.

Bear cleared his throat, and I thought I heard a bit of that huffing laughter. "Agreed. Okay. Chance, does she feel feverish?"

"Um." Chance passed a hand over my forehead and then my throat. "Not right now, but she was a little heater while she was sleeping."

Oh no. I thought. And also, *This will help*.

"Butterfly, I think...I think probably the delay, the...trauma and then relief of yesterday, and...to be honest, my scent—"

"I'm going into my first heat," I finished for him.

There was a pause, and Chance clapped a hand over his mouth.

"Yes," Bear said.

Last night, I'd helped myself to climbing onto an alpha. I'd been itchy and hot, and I'd *needed* to feel him, touch him.

I'd been pulled out of a *cage*, rescued from being sold, *and I'd climbed onto an alpha and humped him just to make myself come*.

"Okay. That makes sense," I said, my voice small.

"I got suppressants for you today—"

"No," I said sharply.

But Bear continued, "And some...things you can use to take care of your heat. I can move out of this room temporarily—"

"No."

"We can find a different way to make sure no one knows you're here for a couple days, and then everyone who can't know about you will be gone with plenty of time for you to—"

"No! Stop!" I cried out.

Chance released me, and I scrambled out of the nest, up on shaky legs, tripping over bags and into Bear's lap. I grabbed onto his shoulders with tight hands, wrestling myself into his chest.

"Stop it. No pills. No pills, please." My cheeks were flushed with shame for the weak sounds my throat was making.

The pills made me sick. They made me hot and itchy. Cameras watching.

"Shh...it's okay, Butterfly, I've got you. But you need options, okay?"

Paper rustled behind me, and Chance whistled. "What—Is this what I think it is?"

"It's a knot."

"No pills," I begged, my throat tightening, stomach starting to heave.

Bear purred, and the sound was forced, but it still did the trick. "It's important that you know that you don't *have* to have an alpha for your heat. Or anybody. That's all, Butterfly. This conversation is going to get...delicate, do you want Chance to go?"

"Like you're doing such a great job by yourself," Chance muttered.

"No," I said.

Bear sighed and nodded, his chin bumping my shoulder, arms circling me. He pulled me from his chest, and I fought for a moment, letting out a sob of protest, before relenting.

"We'll come back to the heat. Next thing is..." He reached up, and I flinched as his hand came close to my eyes. "What's going on here?"

I stilled. His thumb ran just under my eyebrow. "What—what do you mean?"

Bear was quiet.

"Nothing," I lied.

"Your head's not bothering you?"

I chewed on my lip.

"Butterfly, tell me what this says." He twisted around me, reached down and pulled up a box, passing it into my hands.

I looked down, but I already knew the answer to his question. I couldn't read the words. And the box was non-descript, white with pale lettering that was even harder to make out, especially with lamps on and confusing shadows and my eyes filling up with tears that made it all worse.

"I—They hurt me. I hit my head on the floor. The next day, everything was fuzzy," I whispered.

Chance sucked in a breath and Bear sighed, as if they'd passed the air between them.

"Has it gotten worse or better?" Bear asked.

"Worse for a few days. Then stayed the same."

"And headaches?"

I nodded slowly. Bear took the small box from my hands. "This is a fancy CBD bath bomb. Scent enhancing, just right for omegas. Got a bunch of that kind of stuff for you. And lots of blankets and pillows for your nest. A whole pantry of snacks. Truffles. Everything I could find that you would know hadn't been tampered with."

Another sob broke free, this one in earnest. I fell forward into Bear's chest, and he bundled me up in his arms, rubbing my back, his purr vibrating through his chest into mine.

"It's gonna be all right, Butterfly. We'll figure it out, okay? We're gonna have to talk about some ibuprofen for your head. I'll do whatever I can so you feel comfortable, okay?"

His comfort just made me sob harder. He knew exactly how vulnerable I was now, right down to not being able to see clearly. Knew I was afraid of food, of pills. Soon, he'd know that the idea of being left alone with arousal terrified me too, made me feel like I was being watched, studied.

"I can take all this to the laundromat," Chance said, quiet under my crying. "Wash the store smells off so she can have it clean and how she likes."

"Start a bath on your way out," Bear said. "Grab that bag, the purple one."

I moaned into Bear's shirt, shaking with my crying, so fucking *relieved* to be taken care of that it physically hurt inside of me.

Relieved to finally have my heat, to have that dreaded threat arrive not on the road with my brother while we were in danger, but *here*. With an alpha and beta that didn't frighten me. That were safe and nice.

"Jesus, you thought of fucking everything," Chance murmured.

I sobbed because I was actually excited. To be spoiled. To have a nice bath with expensive omega products. To know what else Bear had found me. What food and clothes. To eat truffles from a box all in one sitting so I would know they were safe and *mine*.

Bear shifted me on his lap, cradled me, and tucked my wet face back into his warm throat. He rocked me and I wept with the sweetness of it.

"It's okay now. I've got you, Butterfly. It's okay."

I scowled at the number in my phone. Would calling Preston Bowers create a favor I would have to pay later, or one he'd owe me? Did he have the right connections to hide an omega? Powerful enough, but safe for the girl too?

He was the omega's best option in my catalog, but he didn't feel like a sure thing, and I'd already debated the risk for the better part of an afternoon.

After prepping a lunch tray for a hindbrain omega who wouldn't let go of her guard dog. Chance was acting like a knot-whipped alpha and he didn't even have the right designation.

She needed to go.

I set my phone face down on my desk as a soft knock hit my office door.

"It's Bear." My crew knew to announce themselves and not waste my time.

"Come in," I called.

Bear had arrived to the club on the back of a cruiser Harley nine years ago. He'd been huge, silent, and it hadn't taken longer than an hour for one of my guys to take offense with him—either at Bear's size or the sudden interest of all the club girls. I'd watched from the corner as the stranger had laid one after another, brothers and prospects alike, flat on their back. When the Devils had given up trying to beat his ass, he'd sat right back on the stool and continued his beer.

I'd recruited him to the crew on the spot, knew I'd wanted him as my enforcer the second old Beggar was ready to retire.

Bear was still huge, still generally silent, still able to knock any challenger down to the floor. He'd been loyal to me for his entire tenure of six years, never asked a question that wasn't worth considering. I needed him, now more than ever.

"She's alone?" I asked as he shut the door behind him.

He shook his head. "In the bath, Chance is with her."

Bear made it halfway across the room before I smelled it, that same heady scent that had gusted over me when Chance opened the door to Bear's apartment earlier. Omega perfume. Sweet enough to make my mouth water, needy enough to make my blood rush to my cock.

"Fuck. She's all over you," I said, sitting up in my chair even as I wanted to push back, escape the influence of the perfume.

"I'm careful. Avoiding the others. Didn't have time to wash her off again," Bear said with a shrug. He stopped short of the chair in front of my desk, dark eyes meeting mine, and a warning bell rang in my ears. "Her heat's coming in."

My jaw clenched at the announcement.

"I can see her through it, but it'd be better if the others weren't around. There's not gonna be any chance of hiding her during..." Bear drifted off.

During the fuck fest of the omega's heat. No hiding her perfume as Bear knotted her for a week straight. Probably no hiding the sounds either.

What's it like? my hindbrain wanted to shout.

"Better to get her settled elsewhere, don't you think?" I asked.

Bear tried to hide his reaction. He did a decent job, actually. His hands twitched, but he didn't clench them into fists like I suspected he wanted to, and he forced his eyes away from mine, clearing the growl out of his throat before speaking.

"Maybe. Might not go smoothly at this stage," he said with a shrug.

"And the suppressants? Will they help?"

"Not enough," he answered quickly, and his hands stuffed into his jean pockets.

He's hiding something.

Bear had told me what he'd done for a living after the army. Fucking omegas seemed like an alpha's dream job. Amazing pay, getting your knot squeezed regularly, soft beds and twinkle lights and whatever other shit the little princesses supposedly needed to see them through. And he'd walked away from it, landed in Dead End, of all places, and seemed content to stay.

I'd seen that as a good sign. He'd seemed to understand what our brotherhood was about, a bond stronger than the forces of our designation. I didn't care who my men fucked, whether or not they shared pussy with one another, but we were a crew, not a pack. The Devils came first.

Certainly not after a fucking omega.

"You're getting attached," I said.

Bear's stare whipped back to me, eyes narrowing. He held his tongue for a moment. I generally respected this alpha's ability to think first before running his mouth. Now I wished I could rip whatever thoughts were running through his head right off his tongue.

"I don't care about the drugs. I don't care about the guns. I do the work you give me," Bear said, pulling a hand free of his pocket and bracing it on the back of the chair in front of him. "But if you want me to *not* give a shit about a young woman who's been kept in fuck knows what kind of conditions, auctioned and sold, hurt, frightened, then I am not working for a leader I can respect."

The alpha in me wanted to bark, to lunge over my desk and snarl into Bear's face, remind him that in spite of his size, I was in charge. But that was designation. I swallowed it down.

"You're worried her being here will test this brotherhood in a way you haven't been forced to before now," Bear continued. "You're probably right. But if you believe in the words you lead with, you'll believe in our crew and our bond."

Fucker was right, of course.

"She's a person first," Bear said.

I pressed my lips flat and held my hand up before he continued preaching. "You're right. I hear you. Omegas don't bite."

Bear let out a sharp and startled laugh, and his hand dove back into his pocket. "Right. Exactly. And I know how to keep my teeth in my mouth. So calm down, old man."

I grunted and scowled, and Bear backed away from my desk. Had he already knotted her? I debated the idea of going out on the road with the others, uncertain if I really wanted to be stuck in the club during an omega's heat.

Bear was right. I did trust him not to lose control. *I* was the untested one.

"Keep me updated," I said, reaching for my phone.

Bear nodded. "Of course. I'll do as much scent canceling as I can. It'll be easier when the others head out."

I wasn't so sure about that, but I nodded and he let himself out of my office as I turned my phone face up, swiping past the lock screen.

The best solution was to get the girl out of our lives, and fast. I weighed the risks and made the call.

My eyelids twitched as the floor beneath me trembled with his approach. I could smell him coming. Warm, safe, comforting.

"How did you know about my eyes?" I asked as Bear shut the door to the bathroom behind him.

I hadn't been fully aware of the tub the day before when Bear had cleaned me up, but it was impressively deep. Decadent. Not a normal motel tub. Chance said Bear had gutted and redressed the bathroom a few years back. Made sense. He was a big man.

"You fumble when you reach for things sometimes, and it didn't strike me right away, but...the way you looked at my cock while I was showering," he said.

My lips twitched. "Can't blame a girl for trying. Hands-on study will be required."

Bear sat on the edge of the soaking tub and I shifted, resting my head against his thigh and sighing as his fingers brushed the back of my neck.

"We gotta do something about it, Butterfly. Doctors—"
"No."

Bear sighed, and his hand cupped my throat. "And if there's

more going wrong than just vision and headaches? That's a big enough deal already."

I shuddered and tried to hold onto the present, reaching wet hands up to Bear's wrists to use him as my anchor. My fingers brushed over his palm, and I found the rough welt and scabs from my bite, a soft thrill rushing through me. Bear purred, and my breath hitched, gentle warmth and worry in my chest cutting through some of the old memories trying to creep in.

"Can I start by agreeing to...to take the ibuprofen?" I asked.

"Yep." There was a quickness to the response that belied its casual tone, but he didn't say anything else.

I trusted Bear. I trusted this alpha. I'd already offered myself to him on a silver platter. He would give me what he said. I could trust one little pill.

Relief for my head would be nice.

I didn't realize I was shaking until Bear was stroking my back, his hands sliding into the water. "It's okay. You tell me when you're ready. It's okay."

"W-will you get in the bath with m-me?" I asked. I was shivering in hot water, panic settling in like a layer of snow in my veins.

Bear shifted, and I fought the urge to claw and grab at him. "Gimme a sec. Sending Chance out for the night."

It was on my tongue to protest that too. I trusted Bear. Chance was nice. I had so little security, I wanted to latch on to every new piece. Cling to them and build them up around me, pieces of my nest. I held my tongue, listened to the murmured exchange of the men.

"I'll be back tomorrow, birdy," Chance called, and then the door shut again and fabric rustled.

"You're shaking," Bear said.

"T-trying not t-to," I said.

"Don't fight it. Let your body shake it out. Take a deep breath."

Chance had lit a bunch of candles for my bath and then left me to pick and choose which products I wanted to add to the water. It was silky now, the surface still thick with bubbles, and I tried to take Bear's advice, to breathe and accept the shudders rushing through my muscles. It helped a little.

The candles made the room confusing for me, but I understood the enormous soft brown shadow moving next to the large tub. Bear tied his long black curls back, and I squinted again at the dark blur between his legs, black hair and red-brown cock.

He laughed, and I realized some of the shaking had subsided. "That look on your face could make a grown man wither if he didn't know better. Scoot forward."

I had to drain some of the water out before Bear could sit down in the bath with me. We finally settled with his legs stretched around me, chest and cock at my back, arms wrapped over my chest. Calm rushed over my head, down into my chest, and all the way to my toes. I grasped the hand I'd bitten, tracing the mark with my fingertip.

"I'm sorry," I whispered.

"No, you're not," Bear answered.

I blinked. There was a whisper of humor running through me, another thread of worry, and I suddenly wondered if the feelings were...*mine*.

"What do you mean?"

Bear's hand turned, tangling our fingers together, my smaller palm nestling easily into his. "You're not sorry, and you don't need to be."

I swallowed, pressed the heel of my hand into his, rubbed our skin together and studied the sharp edges of the bite. He was right about me not being sorry, but I wasn't sure about the rest.

———

MY EYES WIDENED, cup at my lips and small, sweet pill on my tongue. My throat convulsed, and Bear held my hand steady, coaching me.

"Breathe, Butterfly."

No one ever fed me pills. It even tastes like ibuprofen. Just drink the water.

"You don't have to take the pill," he said. I frowned, swallowing a gag, and Bear cleared his throat. "I mean, I want you to, but—"

I sucked in a deep breath, opened my mouth wide, and choked down the water, spluttering and praying that it took the pill down with it. Bear wiped my cheeks and pulled the cup away as I coughed and swallowed.

"Good girl," he said, cupping the back of my neck and drawing me in to kiss my forehead.

I was bundled up in my nest, shivering again, and Bear packed the new blankets he'd bought around me. He'd purchased a bunch of foam and a yoga mat, building me a small mattress that would fit into the closet, and I eyed the space. It smelled too new, but I had Bear's blankets and pillows and Chance's shirt with me to help.

Bear's bed was dressed with fresh blankets and pillows, nothing plush or soft like he'd gotten for me.

"I need y-you," I whispered.

Bear sniffed, and I realized he was scenting for arousal.

"I n-need the distraction. You feel good." And I felt sick, but that had been the case even before I'd taken the pill. My body was playing tricks on me.

Bear grunted and shifted, twisting on my makeshift bed. He lowered me down into the pillows, his arms wrapped around me. The nest was dense now, like lying in a cloud, but Bear was heavy around me and hard with muscle. I liked the contrast.

For several minutes Bear did nothing else, just slowly relaxed on top of me, giving me his weight. The closet was too narrow to wrap both of my legs around his hips, but with a shift and a squeeze I managed to hook one around his back. The fabric of his sweatpants, the hard angles of his hips, pushed into me, and I sighed at the perfect distraction I'd been hoping for.

Bear's purr started, vibrating against my breasts, loosening my muscles just enough to understand my own pliable shape in his arms. The way my back curved up, hips pinned down, the arch of my neck to press my face to his throat.

"Better," Bear observed, and I nodded. His nose nuzzled my ear and I shivered. My perfume bloomed, and I realized it'd gone acrid earlier, sweetening now in earnest.

I whined as he hunched, pulling his chest away from mine, but the sound was softened as his lips brushed over my forehead again, down my nose with feather-light touches, his breath rushing over my skin. So gentle. The tightness in my head eased, but I knew it couldn't be the medication yet. It was this alpha.

By the time he reached my lips, he'd touched every other spot on my face and I was arching up, little begging notes in my throat. The press of his mouth to mine was as soft as the kisses and brushes, just our lips learning the way we fit together. Bear's purr thickened and his hands slid down from my shoulders, pushing my breasts into his chest, his hips carving forward into mine.

He was the definition of an alpha, the fantasy of a man I'd been picturing since I was a teenager.

Sudden possessive urgency bolted through me, my fingers digging into his back, mouth parting to claim his, to bite and lick, to pull him into me. His purr darkened and rattled, and I twisted until I felt the weight and ridge of his cock against my sex. He'd dressed me in a pair of silky, thin pajamas, and it was as if I could feel every thread of fabric that separated us, the faultless muffled outline of him.

Bear answered the kiss, tongue stroking against mine, plunging in the same rhythm of my arching hips. His hands slid down to my ass, and I gasped and surrendered as he ground me into him, purr rushing down my throat, right into my cunt. I whined as he pulled his mouth away, wet lips dragging against my cheek to tongue my ear. He was tugging me down and I moaned as a thick bulb of flesh fit between my thighs—his knot. He was pushing me against his knot, stimulating us both on the swollen base of his cock.

"Fuck me," I gasped. "Knot me."

Bite me, I thought, recalling my plan, although the words tangled on my tongue as one of Bear's hands slipped out beneath me to shove the door of the closet back and out of the way. My leg fell off the bed, and then he was there, rutting between my thighs, more fully plastered to my body. My nose pressed to the base of his throat, hands pawing at his bare back, down to the waistband of his sweatpants, pushing them aside to grab handfuls of his ass.

The muscles in my grip flexed, and we groaned together. I pushed and whined and writhed beneath him, Bear hissing as I yanked at his clothing, my own shirt riding up, until a wet kiss of precum soaked through my thin shorts.

"Bear, please!" I muffled the words against his neck. "I need you. I need your knot, alpha. I need...I need—"

Bear's pants were down, his hands were inside of my shorts, squeezing my ass, sliding between my cheeks, down farther until he found my dripping cunt.

"I need your bite!"

He froze, but only for a moment, and then snarled, dragging me back up to his chest. My head bumped against the interior of the closet, and I gasped as a hot tongue stroked up the length of my throat, once, twice, a third time.

I shuddered, my eyes wide, heart pounding. I'd been at the edge of an orgasm, and it only seemed to tangle tighter with Bear's mouth on my throat. I needed this. I needed him. He would keep me safe. He would protect me. He—

Bear's lips and teeth wrapped around my throat, tongue circling the oval of pressure, preparing me. I trembled, victory and—and—

Terror.

We stilled at the same time. My body was tight, preparing for the bite. I needed him.

I *did*.

Bear's tongue swirled again, and I shuddered with pleasure. His back trembled.

And then the pressure on my throat eased. Surprise and worry twined around me, but instead of making me more anxious, they seemed to calm me down. They weren't my emotions.

They were Bear's. I winced as he pulled away briefly, sighed as he kissed my throat.

Curiosity. Still worry.

The hand I bit found one of mine on his ass, pulled it away and tangled our fingers together, palms brushing and the scabs of my bite mark scratching me. I whined and squirmed, wanting to hide my face back into his chest, crawl away from the truth, what I'd already suspected and he certainly now knew.

"I'm gonna keep you safe, no matter what," Bear whispered, sitting up briefly, twisting to his side and wrapping us together. His cock was still hard and a little slick, pressing to my closed thighs. "As long as you need me, Butterfly."

I swallowed hard but Bear kissed me, a little nip on my bottom lip. Thick calm was replacing the curiosity, an intentional drug, but one I was grateful for.

"I didn't—There's a—"

Bear rubbed our palms together again, pulled our hands between our chests, his knuckles over my drumming heart. "There's something like a bond," he said.

"I didn't know it would happen," I rushed out.

"I didn't think you did."

My breath gusted out of me, body going limp, and Bear adjusted us again, sorting out my clothes first, and then his.

"But you are trying to get a bond bite so you have an alpha to protect you," Bear said.

He sounded calm, but whatever I'd created by biting his palm offered me a glimpse of hurt, disappointment.

"You. So I have *you*," I whispered.

"That's not how it's going to happen for you, Butterfly. I'm going to make sure of it, okay?"

I'd rushed it. Bear was a good alpha, which meant that he wasn't going to bite at the first chance. I hid my scowl against his chest, and he wrapped his arms around me. He needed to *want* me as his omega, not just have the opportunity to get his knot squeezed. I'd messed it up.

"It's going to be okay," he said, kissing the top of my head, soothing my back with slow strokes of his hands.

The edge of the orgasm I'd missed out on now made me feel raw and temperamental. I wanted to ask Bear to leave the nest. I wanted to bite him again, because whatever this was—too quiet to be a real bond, but just enough to make us aware of one another—it was something, better than nothing.

I wanted to bite Bear because I needed him. I wanted him. Did he trust me less now that he knew what I was after?

He found my chin and lifted it, passed those slow soft brushes of his lips over my face again, and the anger softened. My headache faded into the background, and this time, I thought it probably *was* the ibuprofen.

"Sleep, Butterfly," Bear murmured.

T he crew was drunk, girls were half-naked, and the floor was slick with beer as I stepped out of the ladies' room. Lilah was inside, cleaning herself up, satisfied and confident she'd done the same for me. I'd gotten off, but there was no real relief in it now—not for the past couple of days, actually. I scanned the room, looking for the answer. Booze? I'd had my fill, and I didn't want a hangover the next morning as I prepped bikes for the ride.

Lilah was expecting to ride out with me on the cruise. She hadn't said so, but I saw that look of victory in her eyes as it was announced. Now would be as good a time as any to live up to my road name. To slip out of the little tangle of her grip on my cock, leave her attentions for someone else to enjoy.

She'd have her feelings hurt for a bit, but like any of the other club girls could reassure her, this was just who I was.

The backdoor to the bar opened and a haze of cigarette and weed smoke floated in, a tempting flavor on the air. But I didn't want to dull the night.

I searched the faces of the room, a wry smile curving on my lips.

Who was I fooling? I knew what I wanted to finish off the night.

Who I wanted.

I turned and headed for the motel stairs, jogging up out of sight, just as the bathroom door squeaked.

The upstairs hall was empty, quiet. King was still in his office, and the only other club members I'd seen missing from the bar were Bear and Chance. Bear would be guarding the little omega we'd accidentally acquired. And Chance...

I slowed as I approached his door. There was a whiff of sweetness at this end of the hall, along with a dull and slightly chemical cover of scent-canceling products. Most of the brothers wouldn't take the time to notice, but I figured it was good we were heading out soon.

I knocked on the door to my right and was surprised by the almost instantaneous movement I heard from inside. Usually, Chance made me wait.

"What's up, is sh—?"

I blinked as his door opened, paused at the open and almost excited expression on his face, watched it fall and shutter into nothing as he stared at me. The change created a similar gravity in my chest, not so different from the heavy feeling that always hit me when I looked at him.

Chance was awful and perfect all at once. Beautiful and dismissive and disgusted. The air around him simmered with contempt, a more potent cloud than the fog of smoke I'd witnessed in the bar. A more potent drug to me too.

"Damn, never seen that look on your face before," I said, not joking but forcing a grin for the effect.

He was my weakness, as much as I tried to hide it, but I knew there was something mutual, some power I held too, small as it was. I was an outlet, and I *needed* the electric charge that existed between us.

His eyes flicked over my shoulder to Bear's door, and I stared blankly back at him as he stepped out of my way, his door open to me.

He didn't ask what I wanted like he'd done early on. Now we both knew.

What's up, is sh—Is she...? He'd been expecting Bear at the door? Expecting news about the omega?

"Where were you today?" I asked, sliding into the room.

"Since when do you look for me during the day?" Chance asked, the latch clicking shut with a soft bang.

Since a year ago, at least, I thought. *Maybe longer than that.*

"You're not on watch duty too, are you?" I asked, my eyes narrowing. Bear had been out, I'd seen him leave...and King certainly wasn't asking me or Rider to watch the girl, so...

Chance blinked back at me, eyes cold. Had I imagined that openness that had been there in the first second?

I opened my mouth to goad him, but he cut me off. "You seriously came here with your dick still wet?"

My teeth clacked shut, and a thrill rushed through me.

"Lilah—"

Chance stepped forward, and my eyes dropped to the floor. His feet were bare; his hair was wet, loose. I wanted to dig my fingers into the strands, knowing he'd never let me. "I don't give a fuck about Lilah. And don't give me any bullshit like it has shit to do with her when you just busted and you still haven't had enough," Chance spat out.

I cleared my throat, heat rising up from my chest. I was taller than the beta in front of me, a little thicker in muscle too. It wouldn't matter when my knees went weak at that tone and my cock twitched with interest.

Chance's hand snapped out, grabbing at the hair at the back of my head, yanking on it and making me stare down my nose at him. I panted through my nose, but I knew what expression I wore. Fuck, it was reflected back at me on the mirror behind Chase's shoulder. Need. Shame. Hunger.

"The girls are great. You're just a filthy slut," Chance snarled.

Breath rushed out of my parted lips. Relief and arousal.

Chance tugged on my hair, and I fell to my knees, practiced and eager. I dove forward, sucking in lungfuls of him, my face in the soft crotch of his cheap sport shorts. Sharp and fresh beta tickled the back of my throat. I needed more.

He pulled my face away from him and I sighed. He was towering above me now, glaring down with those ice chip eyes, tattoos like a pattern over his chest for me to trace with my tongue. Beautiful and angry. I questioned, not for the first time, whether this was really a game. Did he actually hate me? It made me queasy as much as it made me hard.

"Lilah deserves better," Chance muttered, brow furrowing.

"She can go find it," I said, swallowing hard, wondering if I could get away with nuzzling back into his hips. "I'm done with—"

Chance scoffed. "Fucking course you are. Just when she started to look fucking excited. You are such trash, Ghost."

He meant it. He was right. Lilah deserved better. I was trash. Trash to women. To Chance too.

He knew as much, but he still opened the door.

Except this time, he didn't open it for you.

"Well?" Chance asked, eyebrow arching. "We both know why you came here."

I nodded and reached out, groping him through the thin fabric, pulling eagerly at his length.

"With your mouth," Chance ordered, using the fistful of my hair to tug me forward, my moan muffled as I pulled his shorts down and wrapped my mouth around his half-hard length.

This was mine. Chance was mine, in a weird and backward way. My real relief. The only person who knew me well enough, who had the sense to understand any of us well enough, to know what an actual dirtbag I was and to hate me for it. To want me in spite of it too.

I groaned, a purr in my chest, and sucked him deep, that clean flavor striking my tongue in earnest now.

Chance sighed as he grew hard on my tongue, his hand in my hair gentling, stroking down the side of my face. "The one fuckin' thing you're good for."

I sucked in agreement and relished the sight of him above me, chest heaving in desire at last, eyes glaring down.

———

I'D BARELY FINISHED COMING, my T-shirt wrapped around my cock, my face buried in Chance's mattress, when he pulled roughly out of my ass. I howled and my cock spurted again, the pain an uncomfortable but not unwelcome surprise.

I waited for his weight on the bed as I sagged, for his warm skin against my back. It never came. I rolled over, just in time to watch him step into the bathroom, water rushing in the shower a moment later.

I hissed as I pulled my shirt away from my wrung-out cock. My ass was still throbbing, the bruise of Chance's grip at the back of my neck still ached, and I was still high from coming a second time in a less than hour, forced out of me by the pound of his fucking.

And he was washing me off.

I stood, tried to find the dignity I didn't usually bother with —not in his company—and walked on weak legs to the open door of the bathroom. He hadn't taken off his shorts until he'd reached the tub. His head was down, water running over his back, hands braced against the wall.

"Didn't realize till just now, but I think I prefer you reaming my ass with a perfunctory cuddle after," I said, heading to join him under the water.

He looked up, pushing out from under the water, and I stopped. He wore the same warning stare now that he'd sported when I'd walked into his room.

There'd been some kind of ease between us when we were done lately. Comfortable touching. And Chance always looked... not happy, but...tired and unguarded.

Faint praise, I thought.

He looked tired now. And angry. And disgusted. But maybe not with me.

"I think I'm done with this," he said, the words echoing off cheap tile.

I stiffened. "What?"

He turned in profile, thrust his face into the water and scrubbed it with his hands, pushing back his hair as he stepped out again.

"I'm done. With the visits and the fucking."

"With me," I said.

Chance stared at me, and for probably the first time, I had

the urge to...to not come crawling to him in need of being stepped on, but to try and be a fucking alpha. To be a bolster for him. He looked so fucking exhausted. But even in our limited frame of a relationship, I knew he would never want me playing that role.

Chance nodded slowly. "Yeah. With you. This."

I opened my mouth to ask why and then shut it again. Why wouldn't he be?

You're such trash.

I'd just taken for granted that he was fine with that. Wanted me.

A million familiar questions ran through my head. *You're telling me this now? After? Why do you get to decide for both of us? You can't just cut me off.*

It was a taste of my own medicine, and it went down bitter as acid as I swallowed.

"I think I would've rather you just...not opened the door the next time I knocked," I said, forcing out a laugh.

"That's you, not me," Chance said, glancing at me, turning off the water. "I'm asking you not to knock."

I narrowed my eyes, watching with a familiar sick hunger as he toweled off his body. A body I craved, had memorized the sight of, and yet had barely been allowed to explore.

"I'm trying to figure out how she factors into this," I said.

It was the wrong thing to say. Chance's stare returned to ice, and naked as he was, smaller and beta as he was, every muscle in him screamed *threat* as he stepped forward.

"She fucking doesn't. I'm sick of this, and I'm done. Now *leave*, Ghost."

And the truth of it was, threat or not, Chance didn't cow me. Not when I didn't want him to. I was in too much shock to move as he stepped forward, face growing red with anger when I didn't flinch. He wasn't powerless, but we weren't on even footing either. I could bark and I would win. We could fight and I would probably win, although neither one of us would be in good shape after.

And Chance would never fucking forgive me.

I dropped my shirt on the floor, left him fuming up at me in the bathroom to go grab my pants from where he'd torn them off me before throwing me onto the bed. Strengths I'd wanted from him, and could've prevented. Maybe. Did I choose to be power-less with Chance, or had he stolen all of it from me long ago?

I licked my lips as I headed for the door, his cold eyes watching me from the bathroom, his taste still on my tongue.

I'm asking you not to knock.

Because maybe he *would* open.

I clenched my jaw and didn't bother checking the hall as I strode out of Chance's room, feeling reckless, almost wanting to be caught with the secret I'd been hiding for so long.

I'm asking you not to knock. I wasn't making any fucking promises.

Bear's unspoken reprieve in the night only lasted a few hours before I woke, sweaty and grinding on his thigh. He'd let me finish myself off without comment before dutifully sinking his fingers into me, kissing me through my moans and whimpers.

I'd lasted the rest of the night, but when I woke, it was Chance with me, not Bear.

Chance paused in his reading, taking a deep breath and then clearing his throat.

"I'm sorry," I whispered, aware of the cloud of perfume I was creating.

"It's fine," he said, automatically.

I shuddered and twisted in my nest. He was sitting on Bear's bed, and the mattress springs creaked as he shifted.

"Have you...have you tried any of the things Bear got you yesterday?" Chance asked, the words careful. "You don't have to answer. I just... If you want me to leave you alone for a bit, I can keep an eye on the hall."

"No!"

"Okay."

Chance cleared his throat again, lifting his book up. Just as he started to read out loud, a cramp rushed through me, curling me up into a ball and bolting dull pain in my core. I whined, and Chance's feet thumped to the floor as he hurried to my side.

"Birdy...you need me to call Bear?" Chance asked.

I didn't think it was a coincidence that Bear had left early this morning, or that as sweet as he'd been in the night, he'd also been slightly dispassionate, giving more than taking. He knew I was trying to trap him now.

"I'm calling—"

"No," I gasped out, reaching and catching Chance's hand. "No, I don't...want to bother him."

Chance scoffed. "I don't think he'd consider it a bother."

"Would you...can you curl up with me?"

There was a slight pause, and then the nest bed was dipping as Chance climbed in, wrapping himself around me. He couldn't purr and he didn't have that weighty presence like Bear's, but he was warm against my back and held me tight to his chest. The ache in my bones remained, but the panic ebbed.

I took a deep breath, and with his fresh scent came something else. The spice that was familiar to him, but something syrupy too.

"You smell like an alpha," I said without thinking.

He stiffened against my back. "I—Sorry. I thought I... Want me to wash off?"

"It's not much. I didn't notice till just now," I said. I twisted and buried my face into his throat. "I don't mind it. You're mostly yourself."

Chance grunted. I wanted to ask why he smelled like a spicy, syrupy alpha. The scent made my mouth water, like I needed to drink it down. But he was still tense, and I'd been clumsy yesterday with Bear. I needed to do better.

"He's leaving with the others tomorrow, so..."

I blinked at that admission, at the way it made Chance tighten further. "Are you upset you have to stay because of me?"

"Relieved," he said immediately.

I wanted to know more.

"Just let people talk, they'll usually tell you everything you need to know. If they don't, offer them something vulnerable first. People like the

exchange," Adam had said, coaching me through little cons as we traveled from one state to the next.

I waited, and when Chance didn't continue, I chewed over what to offer. Vulnerable. I had plenty of vulnerable places. If I offered one to someone else, would it leave me open to be hurt further, or would it lessen the burden?

"In the...place where they kept me," I started, and Chance shifted, moving back to look at my face, probably. "They wanted me to go into heat. They would pump synthetic pheromones in the room, and run...porn on a projector. They gave me toys too."

"That's sick," Chance whispered, arms tightening around me.

I nodded, ran my nose up his throat and heard the catch of his breath. I just needed to smell him, catch that whiff of alpha mixed with his scent, let it chase the sterile memories away.

"I don't want to be alone in here when I'm like this. It makes me feel like they're still watching."

"It's just us, birdy," Chance said, petting my back. "Just you and me here."

I considered finding a way to touch Chance, mostly to have him touch me back, relieve some of the ache in my core. The cramping had subsided for the moment, and I was still embarrassed about being caught out by Bear.

Chance couldn't bite me. He couldn't claim me and bond me. But this moment was comforting and hushed, and there was something selfishly beautiful in that. I didn't have to manipulate him into keeping me; I only had to let him hold me.

———

"She's been like this since the afternoon."

I burrowed deeper under my pillows, where my alpha's scent was still thick and heady. He was in the room, standing tall and dark outside of the nest, but I could sense him, the soft frustration and worry. I whined into the bedding.

"Did she take anything? Eat?"

My beta answered in a low tone. I'd gagged down another pill when my head had started to throb and the sunlight in the room made my eyes water. I'd eaten a box of wrapped chocolates and fumbled my way through a little snack pack.

Resignation simmered at my edges. I was disappointing my alpha.

"She needs a better nest," Chance said.

Chance. Chance and Bear. Not *mine*.

"I've got plans, just needed the club to clear out. Tomorrow."

"And there's something else..." Chance trailed off.

Vulnerable. I'd given him a secret, and now...

I listened, whining in my nest as Chance explained what I'd confessed about Omikron's treatment.

Anger. I sat up with a snarl and reached out, slapping for the closet doors and slamming them shut as Bear called for me.

———

LEGS TRAPPED, wrists clasped. Heat radiating into my back. Safe, home. *Need*.

I squirmed, and the alpha purred, the sound stuttering as I rubbed my ass against the hard length behind me.

"Not like this, Butterfly," the alpha purred.

Bear.

My breath hitched and I settled.

"Come on back to me, sweetheart," Bear murmured, nuzzling the back of my head. "You're safe here."

I was hot, sweating through my thin pajamas, my skin sticking to his where he'd crossed our arms over my chest. I was constrained, but gently so, and I winced against a foggy understanding that I'd pawed and tried to bite at him before he'd settled us like this.

"Sorry," I mumbled.

"It's okay," he said, and this time, there was no anger or resignation or frustration. Just calm. Just...something tender and possessive, a binding sensation that I sighed into, relaxing in Bear's hold. He didn't free me, and I didn't want him to.

"Knot?" I'd meant to say it like an order, but it came out as a question.

Bear purred for a few minutes, keeping me calm. "Not like this. I need to know you're with me, Butterfly."

Adam would've been bitten and bonded by now, I thought, and the reminder of my brother, missing him and not knowing where he was, the little hint of anger at being torn out of reach and left on my own, brought me back to myself. My breath hiccuped, and Bear gave up my wrists, arms circling my chest like thick and comforting bands.

"This is stress, not heat," Bear said in my ear, misinterpreting my sudden tears. "It's gonna be okay. This will pass."

He let me cry, and while I wanted to twist in his hold and distract myself with the press of his lips, making him settle his weight on top of me, I let his purr do its work, falling back into the weight of sleep, or something like it.

"ABSOLUTELY NOT."

"He's here now, and he drove two hours. I can't reschedule."

I woke, vibrating in the nest, a fire of anger licking at my skin, and I was snarling before I even realized it wasn't my anger. It didn't matter. My alpha's rage would be my own.

"You should've fucking *warned* me," Bear rumbled, a feedback loop running between us.

The other voice at the door was familiar yet not, hard and sharp. "You're too attached. I didn't trust you not to try and talk yourself out of what has to be done. She *can't* stay."

"I—I know that. But fuck, King, she's..."

"She's got the chance to be safe. With a *pack*. That was the idea, right?"

A pack. I needed a pack. I needed Bear.

I blinked and climbed out of the closet nest, tiptoeing over rough carpet, my body protesting. I had the urge to sink into a crouch or onto my knees, to hunch my shoulders up around my ears and raise my arms in front of me.

Bear had started another soft growl, but he cut himself off abruptly as I rounded the corner. Over his shoulder another alpha stood, and based on the prickle running over my skin, he was staring back at me. Bear turned to face me, revealing more of *him*, King. The prez. He was shorter than Bear but still taller than me. He smelled rough, masculine, and it made my belly cramp and my breath catch.

He jerked at my stare. "She's receptive, at least. The others are gone. Preston is waiting."

Bear growled and caught the sound again, holding out an arm for me. "Let her change first."

"Five minutes. No more."

Bear shut the door on the other alpha before he'd stepped away, one hand remaining on the surface of the door.

"What's going on?" I asked.

Bear let out a heavy sigh, and I tipped my head as bit by bit, what I was feeling from him seemed to bury itself, hide away.

"Come here, Butterfly," he said, reaching his other hand out in my direction.

I crossed to him with a sinking stomach.

Butterfly had been silent ever since I explained the situation: that there was another alpha here to meet her, to potentially take her away, keep her safe, offer her a home and a pack to protect her. I'd tried to hold myself back from sharing my own emotions, but it meant I couldn't get a read on hers either.

She'd dressed in silence, face blank, and when we'd reached Chance's door, drawing him out, she'd taken his hand rather than mine. I was trying not to examine how much that bothered me, and the fact that it meant King might be right about my being too attached.

Fucking King.

I'd heard the crew ride out at dawn, and I'd actually sighed with relief. I could let my guard down a little bit with Butterfly, bring her out of the room if she wanted.

Listen to her beg and whine and gasp with pleasure without worrying about who might hear and question the sounds. Let her perfume flood my room until it embedded itself in the walls.

I tightened my fists. Too attached? Who, me?

There's a bond. Or something like it—a little softer and quieter and easier to push aside, from what I knew about bonds. A definite thread tied between Butterfly and me. What would happen if...when...if Preston Bowers walked out of the club with her at his side?

A growl rose in my throat as we reached the bar, and I buried the sound. I needed to be calm, or Butterfly would pick up on it. Because as much as I thought King was an absolute bastard for springing this on me, and her, he was right. She needed a pack to protect her. One with money, connections, a real fucking nest.

But I knew for a fact she'd be taking everything I'd gotten for her into that nest and those alphas would be stuck smelling me for days. Good.

Preston Bowers was, as far as I understood, the grease behind the wheels that turned the state. He wasn't a politician and he wasn't a businessman, or at least not outright; but he had hands in both of those worlds. And he wasn't so squeaky clean as to not be tangled up somehow with our crew. King probably paid him off to keep our asses out of minor offenses. I wasn't sure how I felt about him being chosen for Butterfly, but it wasn't like King would know very many alphas who *weren't* dirty in some way.

Bowers stood in the middle of the room, looking like he both owned and hated the bar. I hoped to god the former wasn't true. He was dressed in some kind of preppy-casual costume that I was sure had cost a small fortune. He didn't look at us right away, surveying the stains on the ceiling before slowly turning in our direction. He was handsome, clean-cut, and in decent shape.

King stood behind him, holding my gaze, a warning in his stare. *Don't interfere.*

"This is her?" Preston asked, as if I were likely to parade out some *other* omega we had on hand.

She was dressed in a pair of soft leggings, cheap foam flip flops, and a loose hoodie layered over my T-shirt. She had her own, but she'd pulled mine from the nest with a defiant jut of her chin and I...

I hadn't had the fucking sense to stop her. I'd *wanted* her in it.

Her hair was brushed, but it was already starting to go wild around her head, and altogether she looked small and fragile and wary. And so fucking beautiful it took everything in me to force myself to step back, to give room for Preston to move in.

King didn't know Butterfly couldn't see very well; he didn't know she had headaches. He hadn't given me time to tell him that she'd slid back into her hindbrain yesterday, stress and the heat muddling her into a state of biological emergency. I should've forced the knowledge onto him and Preston, maybe it would've changed things...

Maybe that was what I was afraid of.

Preston stepped forward, surveying her like a fucking car or a piece of furniture he was considering for his house.

"You are in rough shape, aren't you, little omega?" he said in a purr.

Chance tried to release her hand but she was clinging to him, and she let out a soft snarl of warning to Preston, who paused briefly. I kept my smile under control as he glanced at me, tried to bury the pride in my chest.

"She's stressed, it's understandable. Maybe we should talk first, about what I know of her state so far," I started.

But the man scoffed and stepped forward again, just out of reach. "Omega," he said, and the hairs on my arms stood on end at the command in his voice. "You need to behave—"

I glared at King, my entire body stiffening at the bark in this asshole's voice. King's eyes were narrowed on Preston's back, his scruffy jaw clenched, and I missed the moment my girl had enough.

There was a snap in my chest that drew out my growl, tuned in chorus with Butterfly's, and I twisted around again just in time to watch her swing a clawed hand in his direction.

"Fuck," I bit out, lunging forward as Preston caught her wrist.

That didn't stop my little butterfly. For a jealous moment, I wondered if she would bite him too, but I watched with a panicked pride as she headbutted him in the sternum. She clawed and scratched and shoved at him, Chance reaching for her with wide eyes.

"Little bitch—" Preston snarled, his hand tightening to white knuckles as my own did the same at my sides, ready to lunge at the other alpha.

"Enough!"

King's bark was stronger by far, cutting through Preston's hiss and stilling Butterfly, even pausing my own steps. Chance wrapped his arms around her waist, pulling her away, and Preston stomped forward before I caught him by the shoulder.

"She's feral," he growled.

"Of course she is," I snapped. "She's frightened. Traumatized. I tried to explain," I said, glaring back at King briefly. "Chance, get her back to the nest."

"She smells like you," Preston pointed out, narrowing his eyes and glancing between me and Butterfly.

My girl was shuddering and whining and warning us all with her soft snarl, and all I really wanted to do was shove this fucker out of my way and scoop her up. I watched to make sure she let Chance guide her back to the hall, and then I stepped between Preston and the view of them.

"We don't know how long she was kept locked up. We don't know what they put her through. We don't even know her fucking name yet," I said, glaring down at the bastard of an alpha that had tried to bark an omega into submission. "She needs *care*."

Preston puffed up, and there was power to this man, but I didn't like the flavor of it. He smelled like cigars and exhaust, luxury, and I was sure that suited him. *It didn't suit her*.

"You didn't give me time to get her under control," Preston said.

My hands clenched, and I opened my mouth to explain what fucking control meant, when King interrupted us.

"Bowers, my man is right. We rushed this."

"She's at the edge of her heat," Preston said, glancing back at King with an obvious gleam of interest in his eyes.

He would still take her if we let him. He wanted her heat. He and his pack would try and stifle her into accepting them.

I would kill this asshole—and King, if I had to—before I let that happen.

King crossed his arms over his chest, gave me one quelling glare, and looked back to the man he'd invited into our club, invited to Butterfly. "We'll handle it."

I swallowed hard and stepped back. King's words were final. I had plenty to fucking say, but I'd wait until we got Preston Bowers back to his fancy fucking city life before I said my piece to King.

Preston scoffed, and I stiffened as he glanced down the hall, before turning back to King. "You wasted my time."

"I did." King nodded, and his jaw ground before he added, "I owe you."

"You can send her our way when you work some of that crazy out of her," Preston said, brushing his hands over his clothes. There was a tear in the cuff of his polo shirt, somewhere Butterfly had caught her claws.

"We'll see," King said before I could tell the man to fuck right off to hell.

Preston rolled his eyes, and I paced to the bar, helping myself to a beer and keeping my back to the pair until I heard the door to outside open. I turned at last, watching Preston march to his sports car as the door swung shut. King approached the bar out of the corner of my eye.

"You fucked up," I said, unable to keep my mouth shut at last.

"You did not keep me—"

"You didn't fucking tell me you arranged this. That you'd even found someone. I could've told you she'd regressed. I could've given her warning instead of making her feel like I—the person she was attempting to trust—was springing a complete stranger on her to just fucking *haul her off!*"

King sat at the bar, staring impassively back at me.

"Not to him," I growled.

His eyes blinked, and his shoulders sagged slightly. "No. No, not to fucking him. You're right. That was..."

"He barked at her." I stared hard at King.

He turned his face away, a little color of shame in his cheeks.

"Tell me you don't fucking—"

"Of course I don't fucking approve of barking at an omega," King hissed at me, eyes flashing before he leaned forward into the bar. "Get me a fucking beer if you're going to ream my ass out."

Considering it permission for all the speaking my mind I planned to do, I went ahead and got the man a beer.

"I just wanted her out of here," King muttered. "She's...got those little claws in you, Bear."

I wanted to deny it, but I needed King to cooperate with me from now on. And to get that, I was going to need to be honest. "I want to see her through her heat. I want to know she's safe. *Personally*."

"You want to *keep* her safe," King said, punctuating the words with a swig of his beer.

I stalled with my own gulp, glaring back at King while I wrestled with the truth. "Yeah. I do. Hell, I want to keep her, period. But that doesn't mean I think I *should* or that I've fucking decided to. It's just that I know I can be what she needs right now. And I'm not going to let you pawn her off to the first available alpha just because you're fucking terrified of her."

"I'm not—"

"You're terrified that you're fucking powerless to resist her. That she could whine and you'd have your knot in her before you could blink. But guess what? You think like that, it's what'll fucking happen," I growled. "King, she's tiny and she's terrified. She wants to be protected. If you can't do that without losing control, then I don't want her here."

King scowled. "I'm not going to fucking knot her. I just..." He trailed off and blinked, and I knew that he didn't have the faintest idea of what it would be like to be alone with Butterfly.

"You ever been around an omega?" I asked.

King blinked and shrugged. "Not really."

"It takes some getting used to. Breathe through your mouth if you like their scent. Tasting is intense, but it doesn't go straight to the brain like a good deep whiff. Purr if they're stressed, but stop if they're getting aroused. At least if that's not your goal. Cuffing your hand around their wrist or the back of their neck will settle them down. Doesn't have to be hard," I said watching him. "Better if it isn't, in her case."

He was absorbing the information, eyes trailing over to the hall that would lead to where Chance and Butterfly had disappeared.

"And if you'd *asked* me, I would've said that we should've met Preston outside. It smells like fucking alpha dick and beta pussy in here. Her body would've been on high alert."

"Bowers was an asshole. I should've told him to back off the second he called her 'little omega'," King muttered, drinking again.

I relaxed slightly, glad our instinct on the other man had hit in the same place.

"The longer she's around, the more the others will notice," King said slowly, not looking back at me. "Guys like Skid and Nutso get interested. And—quit fucking growling, asshole—and I wouldn't stand for them around her anymore than you would, okay? She can't stay because if she does, she won't be safe. And fighting the rest of the crew to try to set those boundaries? It would break the already fucking thin ice the club is on at the moment."

My eyes narrowed. "You think a coup is coming?"

"I think Rider would love the excuse to start one," King said, blinking. "Was only a matter of time. I stalled by giving him the VP seat."

Is the crew worth keeping together in that state? I wondered. But this crew was King's life.

The weight lowered onto my shoulders now too. If King lost me because of Butterfly, a head seat he knew was loyal to him, he was left with Ghost as road captain, Rider as VP, and Nutso as money. Nutso and Rider had grown up in the club together; they and Skid were closer than Rider was with his own brother, Chance. And Ghost had slid easily into their circle, although I wouldn't write him off King's card yet either. Still, it wasn't even, and it didn't bode well for my prez.

And yeah, if I dangled Butterfly in front of the others' noses, that might be what would happen. Not that I had any intention of giving them a chance to even *think* about so much as touching her.

The damp label of the beer bottle brushed against the bite on my hand. It was healing, the teeth marks a little red pattern on my skin. When I brushed my thumb over the marks, a tremor ran through my chest, Butterfly's stress. I wanted—no, *needed* —to get back to her.

It might already be too late, I thought, staring at King. Maybe the bite wasn't a full bond, but it wasn't a lack of one either. Maybe my omega had claimed her alpha and it wasn't a matter of deciding if I could hold onto her—it was a matter of figuring out how. Preferably without completely screwing King over.

But she would come first, I thought. My omega would have to come before the club. I didn't know if King would ever accept that.

"How long will the heat last?" King asked, voice grim.

"Week or so, once it really hits," I said, thinking about her temper and her arousal lately. "I don't think we're quite there yet. She needs a better nest. Hell, I need a better nest than my tiny fucking closet."

King's expression was sour. "So you get a week-long fuck-fest, and I gotta hold the gates and my dick too?"

"I won't hold your dick for you," I said, flashing a grin. "But I can tap in Chance for breaks if you need something. Something *important*," I said.

King blinked at that. "Chance. O-okay."

Was he surprised I'd let a beta help an omega out with her heat? He didn't know shit about shit when it came to this.

I drank down the last of the beer and wiped my mouth on my sleeve. "About Bowers."

"I'm not inviting him back," King said quickly.

"Good," I growled and then shook my head and caught his eyes. "It's not that. He knows about her now. You can't take that back."

King scrubbed a hand through his short beard, smoothing thumb and forefinger over his mustache. "I know."

"It could mean trouble."

King nodded and repeated, "I know."

"Pay up that favor to him. Soon," I said, arching an eyebrow.

King arched one right back. He knew. He knew he'd fucked up. Time would tell how much. In the meantime...

I cleared my throat and tossed my empty bottle in the trash. "I need to see how she's doing."

"Right." King was quiet for a moment, watching me as I grabbed one of the bottles of fruity hard cider he kept on hand for some of the girls. "Bear..."

I turned my head. He was sitting at the bar, glaring meanly at the bottle in his hands, lined brow furrowed.

"Nothing," he grunted after waiting in silence a moment. He shook his head and pushed off from the bar, carrying the bottle on his way to his office.

I could call him back, but I had somewhere more important, better, to be.

The door opened and shut, the thin walls of the motel room apartment trembling. I trembled with them, pressing my face to the deep wall of my nest. Chance's hand was clutched in mine and he sat on my bed, facing the room, legs stretched out ahead of him.

"What the fuck was King thinking?" Chance whispered.

I heard Bear's knees creak as he crouched down, his warm scent wrapping around me, making my shudders loose and heavy.

"We talked. He's... Fuck, Butterfly, come here," Bear called, voice breaking slightly.

I shook but didn't move.

Bear was supposed to be safe. He was supposed to keep *me* safe. Instead he'd let another alpha look at me, touch me. He would've let me go.

"Can you give us a minute?" Bear asked.

I tightened my fingers around Chance's, and he squeezed back, remaining quiet for a moment. "I'm not leaving until she says it's okay."

I gasped and tugged on Chance's hand, pulling his side into my back. Bear grunted, cleared his throat. I ignored him.

"Right. Okay." He sighed, and I swallowed the whine in my

throat as a weary longing tugged in my chest. "Actually, okay, yeah. Stay here. I'll be back."

Bear moved, and I stiffened, turning my head just enough to watch his legs walk away from the nest. Chance wrapped his free arm around me.

"You can call him back," the beta whispered in my ear.

I shook my head, but I whined as Bear disappeared out of the room again.

"King surprised us, birdy. Bear didn't know that man was coming. He wouldn't have let him take you," Chance said, and then added in a low, dark tone, "*I* wouldn't have."

I blinked at that. Chance was a beta, but he'd been every bit as much careful with me as Bear had. Gentle. Kind. And he'd helped me push the alpha away, took me back to the nest where it was safe.

I turned in the tiny amount of space and grabbed onto Chance's shoulders before he could pull away. His features were a little clearer today than before, and I wondered if I was getting better. My fingers traced up the patterns on his throat to his jaw, and his muscles flexed under my touch as he swallowed.

"You mean that?" I whispered.

Chance sighed and his face blurred as he leaned in, resting his forehead against mine. "Of course I do. I don't even think King would've—"

I tipped my chin up, nuzzling my nose to his cheek, and his words died as my mouth grazed against his. His lips were already parted, and they fit easily against mine. Chance was frozen as I took his upper lip in a careful studying tug. His breath rushed over my lips, minty from toothpaste.

"Birdy," he whispered as I pulled away, but I silenced him again, taking a turn on his bottom lip, flicking it with my tongue.

I was granted a choked sound, almost a groan, and Chance's hands moved slowly around my waist, a tentative embrace. His mouth pressed back, sliding against mine, head tipping to catch a new angle that left us open to one another. He tasted sharp and clean like cucumber, and his chest brushed against mine with deep breaths as we kissed.

My fingertips traveled up, studying the line of his cheek-bones, the curve of his temple, up into the soft and loose strands of his hair. Chance moaned into the kiss as I touched him, his hands tightening on my back, drawing me closer in tiny increments. He was tense against me, and I soothed my hands down to his shoulders as our tongues licked gently against one another, parting again to nibble and nuzzle at each other's lips.

Chance panted and groaned, his arms circling my waist and twisting us in the tiny nest, pulling me on top of him. His scent didn't drive me into a frenzy of need like Bear's, but there was a slow trickle of warmth running through me the longer we kissed, a comforting kind of arousal with no immediate need of a destination.

His kisses traveled to my jaw as I caught my breath, whispering presses on my skin and deep breaths rubbing my breasts to his chest.

He can't bite me, bond me, I tried to remind myself.

Chance paused at the corner of my jaw by my ear, breathing me in, a slightly wet kiss searing hotly to the spot.

He pulled away, and our mouths returned to one another like patient magnets, licking, teasing, studying.

No, this beta couldn't bond me, couldn't mark me. And maybe he couldn't keep me safe from another alpha. But he could kiss so sweetly, it made my toes curl. He made me feel safe and calm again.

His hands slid up under my T-shirt, pleasant scorch marks against my lower back, and he pulled away, stroking his nose against mine.

"How'm I doing?" he asked in a low slur, voice rasping with a drowsy desire.

"Hmm?"

He licked his lips and his tongue skimmed against my skin too. "Been a long time since I've kissed anybody. Like this. Just 'cause it feels good to," he murmured.

I blinked, his nearness all smears of peach and gold and brown. Was that true? Was that why his heart was racing under my palm?

"Don't stop," I said, pulling just far enough away to catch an unfocused glimpse of his eyes.

He made a soft, low sound in the back of his throat and then turned us slowly, kissing my lips, my cheeks, my nose, above my eyelids. When my back was against the mattress again and his weight held me there, our legs tangled, his mouth returning to mine.

These were decadent kisses, tender and aimless. I caught my breath with him and sank into the easy drowning of the touches.

———

I woke as Bear returned to the room, but I was too soft and cozy after the seemingly endless make out with Chance. For the first time in what seemed like forever, I was relaxed. I'd been on an endless high alert while held by Omikron, and even before that with Adam, things had rarely felt *safe*.

With my face to the closet wall and Chance wrapped around my back, my body unwound from slow strokes of his hands and deep and patient kisses, I rested.

I rested through the snap of the door closing, the clatter and thumps from outside of the closet. I even frowned and ignored the closet doors being opened, reassured but annoyed by Bear's familiar scent.

I did not rest through the sound of a fucking drill.

Neither did Chance, the pair of us bolting upright.

"What the fuck?" Chance spat out.

I glared up at the sudden bright light from the outside of the room, from the massive shadow of Bear in front of me.

"You need a proper nest, Butterfly," Bear announced, voice gruff and abrupt. "One I fit in. *We* fit in," he corrected.

We? But the answer was immediate, as Chance wrapped an arm over my shoulder. I blushed as I imagined being surrounded by the pair of them, and then grew even warmer at the immediate heat blooming between my thighs and the obvious sudden appearance of damp arousal in my sex.

"That's... Did you just drag in a fuck-ton of lumber?" Chance asked.

"King helped. Think we can probably milk him for a little guilt for a while," Bear said. He crouched down again, and this time, he didn't ask Chance to move or leave us—just reached over the beta and wrapped a warm hand around my ankle. "I'm sorry, Butterfly. I should've told King to fuck off this morning. I should've ripped that worthless alpha's dick off as soon as he opened his mouth to speak to you."

I bristled and growled at the reminder of the stranger alpha, but Chance pulled me into his side, dragging a kiss up the side of my face, and it didn't matter that he was a beta. It calmed me.

"You're staying here for your heat," Bear said.

I tensed and blinked at him. "But not... Where am I supposed to go after?" I asked, struggling to control my omega whine.

Bear's fingers stroked around my ankle, sliding under the cuff of the leggings to find my skin. "I can't promise you that you'll be safe with me, Butterfly. And I won't keep you, I won't let *any* alpha walk away with you, unless I know you're going to be safe and happy from here on out, okay? You're with me until we find you that. Or until you say otherwise."

I tugged at the hem of the shirt I wore, twisting it around my fingers until it bit into my flesh, studying him, considering the words.

Chance cleared his throat. "You need help putting this together, or can I walk her out? Let her get some fresh air, finally."

I perked up at that. "Outside?" I whispered. "Will...will anyone see?"

"It's just us and King here now. Yeah, go on," Bear said. "Get some food and show her around a little."

I licked my lips, hesitating as Chance rose from the nest.

"I'm gonna take care of you, if that's what you want," Bear said softly to me, still holding onto me.

I considered his words, considered my still-prickling anger at being led out to another alpha earlier, the subtle rejection of him deciding I would be passed along after my heat.

"What if...what if what I want is suppressants? And a..." I swallowed. *A car.* A car I couldn't fucking drive. Not with my injury and my headaches and my blurry vision. "A different plan than another alpha. I don't want that man."

"He's never coming back here, Butterfly. He'll never touch you again," Bear said with a growl.

I relaxed slightly.

"And you can have suppressants. I can get you some. And we can plan," he said.

And what if what I want is you? I wanted to ask. But Chance was standing, watching us, and Bear had already kind of refused me that, hadn't he? *I can't promise that you'll be safe with me.* No, not quite a refusal.

I sighed and reached up, Chance's hand clasping mine immediately and pulling me to stand in the nest.

Bear leaned back to let me step out, his face turned up to gaze at me. "I'm sorry, Butterfly."

"I know," I said. But I didn't feel safe this morning, and I hadn't quite forgiven Bear for that yet.

Chance led me to the door, bending and helping me into my flip flops. Bear rustled behind us, the sudden whirr and roar of a drill making me wince.

I didn't recall arriving here very well, and I'd been too stressed this morning at the idea of being tossed to some new alpha to really notice my surroundings, but Chance was patient with me as I followed his lead down the hall, the sound of construction echoing after us. I paused, unsettled that my nest was being tampered with, but Chance's thumb stroked the back of my hand and curiosity won out.

"Our club's an old motel. Died out ages ago when the freeway redirected everybody well away from Dead End," Chance explained.

"Dead End?"

He huffed. "Yeah. Shitty fucking name for a town, and it fits too well. There's not much left around here, but King probably owns most of what's still standing."

"Bear listens to King," I said, peering in an open doorway but only finding shadows.

"He's prez of the club."

"Like the head of a pack," I said.

Chance paused in his step and huffed a laugh. "Yeah, but don't let him hear you say that. King fuckin' hates the idea of pack."

I frowned and leaned into Chance's side as he wrapped an arm around my waist to guide me down the stairs. "What do you mean? Pack is... He's an alpha."

Chance grunted. "Yeah. And so are most of the guys in the club, although it's big for a pack. I dunno if it's 'cause he liked club life or grew up in a fucked-up pack dynamic, but he's adamant it stays out of the club."

Chance's voice lowered as we walked down the stairs. He pointed into a darkness ahead of us, where a thin strip of light stretched across a gray floor. "That's the club, the bar. King's office is open. We'll go out this way," he said, steering me to the left, to a pair of glass double doors.

If King refused to accept pack dynamics, was that why Bear resisted the idea of bonding me? Or was that just because...of me?

"Does that mean all the alphas are feral?" I whispered, slowing my steps as we neared the door.

It was golden and pink through the doors, evening already, and he pushed one open, letting in a sudden rush of dry heat and air that smelled faintly of asphalt. I paused on the threshold as Chance walked ahead of me, blinking at the outside world.

We were in a desert, bristly thin weeds growing up through baked earth, and what looked like an abandoned storefront across the road. I stepped through the door slowly, stumbling slightly over the ledge, down off the broken sidewalk to the craggy parking lot. We were under the awning of the motel, and I turned back to study the chipped orange paint of the building and then around at the barren sketched blurs of the world around me.

Adam and I had been in the desert when I was grabbed too, and I was uncertain how far Omikron had moved me, or even how long I'd been missing at this point. Sudden tears rose in my eyes, and Chance hurried around me, closing the door and stepping in front of me, his hands cupping my face.

"I haven't—I can't remember being outside in..." Since the

night Adam and I snuck around the back of an industrial shipping port where we thought omegas were being trafficked, since
I'd been grabbed from behind and quickly put under with a shot
to the neck. "So long," I whispered.

"Shit," Chance whispered. "Come on, there's a bench outside
the laundromat. And a better view."

I followed his lead away from the motel, across a pitted and
cracked parking lot, over some scorched dry weeds and grass, to
a small and seemingly abandoned strip of stores.

No, not abandoned. There were a couple cars at the far end,
and a muffled tone of music.

Chance sat us down facing the road, and the empty expanse
of the desert ahead of us, all color and shadow washed in vibrant
tones by the sinking sun, distant mountains blue on the horizon.

"I dunno if King really knows how a pack works, or how to
avoid one. There's some guys who are definitely feral in the crew,
yeah. Some loners, or just assholes, maybe. And King keeps
himself separate. But a guy like Bear? Who's just kind of loyal
and orderly anyway? He might as well be in a pack, as far as I can
tell."

Chance was rambling a bit, filling me in and distracting my
head from some of the panic setting in. I was sucking in deep
lungfuls of air, even as it dried out my throat, my fingers wrapped
around the splintering bench I was seated on, listening to the
grit of the sidewalk scrape against the bottoms of my flip flops.

"Birdy, you okay? You need to go back in?"

I shook my head quickly, blinking again and swiping away the
wetness. "No. No, keep talking."

Chance's arm stretched out behind me, a grounding touch
against my shoulders. "'Kay, um... We call each other brothers.
King says we're closer than a pack, better. But to be honest, I
think that's what he'd like to see. It's the same food chain as
anywhere else. Alphas on top. And the few betas who can
stomach sticking around trailing at the bottom."

His voice was rough, bitter, and I slid one of my hands onto
his thigh, gripping the muscle and making his words stall briefly.

"At first, I stayed because it was all I'd ever known. I grew up
in this crew. Been running around some of these guys since I was

in diapers. And then...King took the prez seat right before I was ready to prospect. He's a lot cleaner than the last prez, wants the club to thrive, not just party to our deaths. Suits some of us better than others. He means what he says, even if not everyone gives a shit. Means it when he says designation doesn't factor into the club. It does, but I appreciate he's fooling himself into thinking otherwise."

I grew used to the air moving over my skin as he talked, turning with the shift of the barely-there breeze. Grew used to the sounds of a dog barking in the distance, the far off motor of an engine. Chance paused as the single lit shop at the end of the row opened with a bell clanging on the door, and two men exited. I stiffened, but his fingers stroked back and forth over my shoulder and if the men noticed us they did nothing, heading directly into their car.

"Just a convenience store. Pretty much the only thing open when the guys are out on a ride," Chance said to me. "Cigarettes, beer, and burgers."

"Burgers?" I asked, my mouth watering.

"Want one?"

The saliva turned to ash, and my heart sank as I shook my head. I did want one, desperately, but I also knew I wouldn't stomach the bite.

"You okay?" Chance asked, cupping my shoulder.

I nodded, blinking at the ball of glaring golden light soaking into the horizon. "Can we stay till the sun sets?" I asked.

Chance scooted closer to me and I sighed, settling into him. "Long as you want, Birdy."

O ur steps were slow and dragging as Chance and I moved through the empty hall of the motel, shoulders brushing, hands linked.

It'd grown chilly and dark before I'd finally stirred from the bench, and Chance had taken me past the open office door that smelled strongly of leather and olive oil, to raid the kitchen for my supper. He'd stood to the side, watching me make myself a mess of a sandwich, and had wiped the few tears from my cheeks as I'd eaten food I'd prepared for myself.

My room—Bear's room—was silent as we approached, and I couldn't tell if the turning of my stomach was nerves left from eating, or excitement for my new nest, or apprehension at seeing Bear again.

"About what Bear said earlier," Chance said, interrupting our quiet, pausing halfway down the hall. "About your nest and... fitting in it."

He cleared his throat, moving nervously in front of me, and I found a slight smile curling up the corners of my lips.

"I've never had a heat before, and I've...I've never been with an alpha before," I whispered, for once relieved that I couldn't see clearly, that I could blush and avoid his gaze and the world wasn't focused enough for me to make out his expression. "I'm not..."

"I don't have to be there," Chance said, his voice flat, misreading my stumbling words.

"I want you there," I answered, my face flaming with warmth. "I want you with me. But maybe not...all at once? Right away. Umm..."

Chance leaned in, and I froze until his hands cupped my cheeks. His mouth landed against mine, as soft and thorough as earlier, and I sagged into his chest, relieved at the interruption.

"You say when, birdy," Chance rasped, soaking up my hum of agreement with another press of his lips.

A door opened at the end of the hall, but Chance ignored the sound, sipping on my mouth as I clutched at him, both of us aware of the eyes that watched. He pulled away, nipping at the corner of my jaw, and then turned me to face the doorway where Bear waited.

"Got a surprise for you," Bear called.

For the first time in hours, I reached for that little thread of him in my chest and found him. He was bright, kind of spiky, but it was excitement, not irritation, and it made my steps lighter as we approached.

"Is it a surprise if you woke us up with a drill and told us what you were doing?" Chance muttered.

"It is, yeah," Bear said, although I didn't think Chance had meant for him to hear the question.

He stepped back as we reached him, and the room was dark, but there was a soft orangey glow ahead that revealed the curves of his thick arms and narrow hips. And with his excitement mingling and my own tossed and turned emotions from the day, I gave up resisting and reached for him. His skin was warm and familiar under my hand, and he bent over me, kissing the top of my head, running a hand through my hair. The room smelled like lumber and a little metallic, and I wrinkled my nose, moving slowly forward.

A new, huge structure protruded from the closet, into the center of the room, with squared sides and a peaked roof. The bed was gone, and Bear's minimal furniture had been pushed to the far wall. Chance released my hand and I reached out, touching the new, strange wall to my left.

"Shit," Chance muttered. "You weren't kidding."

"It's just plywood and soundproof foam for now," Bear said as I squished my fingers into the dense foam.

For now, I thought.

I found the edge—which was carefully padded by what I was pretty sure was a foam pool noodle—and stepped around to the front, my lips parted on a gasp. The source of the dim glow was revealed, little opaque golden bulbs shimmering through a curtain of thin fabric. The peak of the nest's roof went up to the top of the closet, but even so, Bear would have to duck or crouch to get inside. I wouldn't, though.

I pushed the fabric aside, blinking at the glimmer of the lights strung up and down the peaks in a zigzag and around the sides of the nest. It gave the small space an all-over light that made it easier for me to make everything out. Bear had moved his bed frame out and pushed the boxspring and mattress into the nest, a perfect fit to either wall he'd added. Even with the mattress, the space was overflowing with pillows and blankets.

"There's a thicker curtain we can pull down over the opening," Bear said as I stood, still staring inside.

This was a nest. It was bigger than the tiny closet, that had felt secure and private, but still small enough for me. Especially once Bear or Chance joined me in it. A nest made for me.

My chest burned and my hands were clammy as I knelt, ducking under the curtain and sliding my knee onto the mattress. The walls inside of the nest were also padded, but these were wrapped in a golden yellow fabric. The bed was denser than I remembered Bear's being.

He'd taken apart his bed and moved it into the nest he'd built for me, dismantled his closet—although there hadn't been a whole lot in there. Still.

He did all this, and he wanted me to leave?

Or maybe he didn't want me to. Maybe King would make him, or maybe he believed it would be better for me.

What could be better than this?

I dove into the pillows at the head of the bed, wiping new

tears away on the soft fabrics before either Chance or Bear could see them, rooting around in the blankets, grinning as I found my scent and Bear's and even hints of Chance's. The mattress was pushed into the closet, with little wooden tables stuffed into the corners on either side.

I twisted and rolled in the blankets, tangling myself with a relieved sigh, rearranging the pillows around me. Chance laughed softly, and I realized they were watching me fuss and nest.

"You like it?" Bear asked, surprisingly hopeful, uncertain.

I pushed my feelings in his direction as I nodded and blinked up at the lights.

"They dim," Bear said, and then just a moment later, their bright glow softened and I sighed again.

I stretched in the bed, and a little happy whimper rose up from my throat. My legs rubbed together, and I realized I was still fully dressed, which suddenly seemed unacceptable. I wanted to be squirming around in my new nest with...

I blinked and sat up on my elbows, staring at the men watching me from the end of the bed. My cheeks warmed. Chance was slimmer than Bear, but I knew the weight of them both, and at the moment...

Chance cleared his throat, reaching in and squeezing my foot briefly. "I'm gonna let you get settled for the night," he said. I whined, and he laughed. "I'll be back in the morning. Give you time to adjust in here."

I swallowed and blinked. With the comfort of the nest around me, I did see his point. Part of me wanted to tell Bear to leave and ask Chance to stay. I knew that if I did, they would listen. Another part of me wanted the *alpha*, which seemed wildly unfair to Chance.

The last and most reasonable part decided I probably needed to talk to Bear. To thank him for the nest and maybe forgive him for earlier. Or at least make him promise to never do anything like that again.

I sat up completely, crawling to the end of the bed, and Chance met me in a firm and unapologetic kiss, even with Bear just to the right of him. His tongue stroked in against mine, and the two men's scents mingled and clashed around me, comfort and arousal fizzling in my veins.

I sighed as he pulled away, my fingers tangled in the thin cotton of his T-shirt until it pulled and I released him, sagging back into the dense cushion of the mattress. Chance left with a few parting words to Bear, their voices muffled as I burrowed into a pile of pillows, nose wrinkling at the remaining sterile fragrance. I moved the pillow, and my hand landed against a broad chest. Bear chuckled and covered my hand with his. Outside of the nest, the apartment door clicked shut.

"Never seen Chance looking so...comfortable. Happy, I think," Bear said.

I twisted and pushed pillows away, blinking up at Bear's shadowed head. Whatever he'd put down on his old mattress made it so I could barely feel him moving around me, and my hands searched for his skin until I grabbed onto his wrists.

"Really?" I asked.

Bear nodded, dark curls swinging down over his shoulder. "He usually looks like someone just shoved dog shit under his nose. Around you, he looks relaxed. Someone could mistake him for friendly."

"He's nice," I said, frowning. I fought an irrational urge to kick or hit Bear in Chance's defense, and it distracted me from the slow progress of the man settling down at my side.

"He's an asshole." Bear grunted as I knocked him in his stomach, the muscles flexing under my hand. "No, I mean—not to you, which, *good*, he fuckin' shouldn't be. But he pretty openly hates most of the rest of us. But I like the way he looks at you, Butterfly."

I chewed on my lip, curious fingers studying the planes of Bear's stomach. He was relaxing, that muscle softening, and I wanted to press into the cushion and strength of him like I burrowed into the nest. His hand squeezed as I started to pull away, and he shuffled closer, pushing pillows and blankets aside to wrap an arm around me.

"I'm sorry," he said softly, and I stiffened. "I fucked up this morning."

"Did you want me to leave with that alpha?" I asked. I

wanted to pull away from Bear, to slide into a corner of the closet again and snarl at him until he left me alone. Or I wanted to want that. In reality, the soft perfection of this nest left me boneless and comfortable and craving Bear's closeness.

"No! Or—" Bear cleared his throat and settled on his back.

I twisted, and since I couldn't make out the fine details of his expression on my own, I reached a hand out, strangely pleased by the tangle of his furrowed brow under my fingers.

"I *do* want you to find a safe place, a good pack," Bear said, and then he rushed on before I drew away. "But even if Bowers had been that, had been fucking decent and gentle and sweet to you, it woulda killed me to watch you walk out of here."

I sighed, leaning forward and dropping my chin on Bear's chest, his arms circling me to stroke my back. I licked my lips, and Bear's chest vibrated with a purr.

"How's your head?" he asked, voice gritty.

"A little achy earlier. Took a pill while I was with Chance," I said.

He hummed, crunching forward and pressing a kiss to my forehead. "Good girl."

The words caused an immediate clench in my core, and I trembled through a sudden burst of need, Bear's purr picking up.

"What if I want you to be my alpha?" I whispered.

I couldn't see clearly, and I suddenly reconsidered the idea of letting Bear find me a doctor, if only so I could watch his face and *know* what he looked like when the question burst out of me.

His purr didn't stop, and his hands on my back clenched. He dragged me up onto his chest, and my legs spread eagerly over his hips, fitting us together.

"Is that what you want, Butterfly?" Bear growled. "Tell me."

I pressed my hands to his chest, squinted down at him, and fought my own bruised eyesight to try and force him into focus. It didn't work, but it made him rumble with laughter under me, the added vibration thrilling my core where I was pressed to his hips.

"Yes," I said firmly, frowning and glaring down at this perfect man. "I want you. I want Chance."

"Because you're scared?" Bear asked, but one of his hands slid up to clasp the back of my neck in a possessive hold.

I opened my mouth, but I didn't like the answer in my head.

"We stole you from the men who bought you," Bear said. "They're gonna give us trouble for it. And I think we can handle them, but it might get ugly. And Butterfly, you haven't told us what else is coming. I can't say for certain that King will risk the club, and I can't say for certain that Chance and I alone can handle the trouble, although I do promise I will try my fucking hardest."

My heart sank in my chest. He was right. I was fighting to survive, clinging to Bear and Chance, trying to drag them into my tornado as if it might calm the winds, when in reality, it might just leave them in as much shit as I was.

I whimpered and Bear rolled us, settling me into the mattress, brushing my long dark hair off of my face.

"What I will promise is that as long as I am the best alpha to take care of you, that is what I will do," Bear whispered, cupping my jaw in his huge hand, tipping it up to feather a kiss over my lips. "And I am absolutely the best alpha for your heat, Butterfly. That I *do* know."

My breath hitched, and his thumb swiped over my bottom lip. *Sometimes you have to be vulnerable first.* Adam's words echoed in my head.

I blinked up at Bear, his purr still thrumming through my bones, his hand on my back holding me tight to his chest and hips.

"Faith," I whispered. He was quiet above me. "My name is Faith."

It was a small kernel of truth—useless, really. Bear was right that I needed to tell him about Omikron, and I *knew* I was being selfish and cowardly by not saying anything. Omikron could be on their way, for all I knew, and the thought gave me shivers.

But I settled as Bear offered me more of his weight, head bowing to nuzzle against my cheek, marking me with his soothing scent, a false sense of security washing over me.

"Faith," he whispered, kissing my jaw. "Hmm...Courtney."

I blinked and he drew away, staring down at me. "Courtney?" I asked, lips twitching.

He laughed. "Yeah. Why, you think everybody just sticks with Bear around here?"

I grinned and Bear growled, ducking down and nipping my jaw again, drawing out a giggle and a shudder of pleasure. "I like it," I said.

"Mmm, I like Faith," Bear purred. His tongue flashed out, and I gasped at the searing flick on my throat. "Like the way she tastes. How she feels under me."

I whined, spreading myself beneath him, arching into his huge frame on top of mine. I'd had a couple of rushed experiences with sex, both with betas, trying to hide my activities from Adam in the next room. They'd mainly been brief, and while one of the betas had gotten me off, the anxiety of hiding, worrying, had made the orgasm a little dissatisfying. Every instance of being touched by Bear, his weight on top of me, his fingers and mouth on my sex, was more powerful than either of those connections.

"Like these little sounds she makes too," Bear purred in my ear, and I blushed but couldn't restrain the next soft whimper in my throat as he rocked on top of me.

"Bear!" I hiccuped and then tried again, pleading, "Courtney!"

He laughed and paused, arms cradling my neck and hips. "Kinda funny hearing that, actually. Sounds pretty from you, though. Again?"

He surged back and forth and I called his name, drawing a groan from his throat and a twitch of hardness against my thinly-covered sex. "Your voice gets me hard, Butterfly," Bear growled. "Don't care what you call me."

I licked my lips, squirming under him until he raised himself up enough for me to pull my T-shirt off over my head. Bear's purr thrummed as I bared myself, and I stretched on the bed, arching my back a bit to present my breasts to him.

"A-alpha," I murmured.

Bear groaned, his hips landing squarely against mine, cock thick and hard, pressing perfectly against my clit. "Goddamn,

Butterfly." He lifted himself again and I whined, trying to chase the pressure. His hand pressed to my stomach, pushing me down, and even that force was arousing in the moment. "You still upset about this morning?"

I blinked and shook, trying to think through the throb of my cunt and the tight ache of my nipples. But the mention of the morning made me tense, and I nearly rolled away before thinking through my reaction.

"A little. I forgive you, but it scared me," I admitted, trying to clear my head.

Bear hummed in agreement. "You feverish? Hot?"

Suddenly, I understood what he was asking. Was I horny because of my oncoming heat? Was I still angry with him for this morning, but also in need of release? It mattered to him what I was asking for and why. I was hot, but it was cooling quickly. The uncomfortable itch and clawing sensation that came with Omikron's drugs was missing. There was an ache inside of me, but it was just a familiar sexual craving. My heat might be coming, but my body was content in this moment to find its own natural needs.

I sat up, my face close enough to Bear's to make out some of the bristle of shadow on his face, the thick line of lashes on his eyes.

"This is just how you make me feel," I said, rubbing my cheek against Bear's. "I need you. I want... I want this between us before the heat hits."

"This?" Bear rasped, but he was leaning in, driving me to my back again.

I licked my lips, and his purr rattled against my throat as he pressed a kiss to my pulse. My previous experiences had been urgent crashes, just desperate moments that needed an outlet. I hadn't needed to spell out what I wanted, because I hadn't had a chance to really speak.

My mouth dried up at the thought of spelling it out now.

"Do you want my mouth on these needy tits, Faith?" Bear growled, my name on his tongue as erotic as the offer.

I sighed and arched my back in offering, his breath rushing

over my chest. But he didn't move closer until I whispered, "Yes."

I moaned as Bear licked a circle around my nipple and then moved to press a kiss between my breasts. But he ignored them further, hunching his back. His hands scooped my hips up and I stared, eyes wide and lips parted on a pant, at the foggy image of his face between my thighs.

"You want my fingers in this greedy cunt?" he asked.

God, yes, because his fingers were huge and perfect and they curled so wonderfully inside of me. But that wasn't all I wanted.

"Your cock," I breathed.

Bear stilled. "My cock?" he rumbled. "My cock where, Butterfly?"

I growled back and Bear huffed a laugh, starting to lower my hips. I spat the words out, that rough animal living in my chest clawing out her demands on my tongue. "I want your cock in my greedy cunt."

Bear was quiet and still for a moment, and I caught a rough breath, staring back at him as well as I could.

"I want your knot, alpha," I said, my voice surprisingly clear, just the slightest tremor at the end. And when he still didn't move, didn't speak, I found myself continuing, "I want you to fuck me with your cock until I come, and then I want you to stuff me with your knot."

Bear's hands tightened around my hips, and he let out a gusting breath that might've been laced with the words, "Jesus fucking christ," before suddenly he was on top of me, pushing me into the mattress, his mouth fused to mine in a brutal and starving kiss.

His fingers hooked into the hips of my leggings without him tearing away from the kiss, and I clasped my hands around his broad face, whining into his mouth as his tongue stroked against mine. He pulled my underwear down with the leggings, and I felt the stick of arousal clinging to my sex before I was bare. I drew my legs up to my chest, helping Bear wrestle me out of the clothing.

He snarled and purred into the kiss, lips ravenous and tongue thrusting as I struggled to catch my breath. When my legs were free, I wrapped them around his hips, shamelessly rubbing myself on his hard cock through his sweatpants, gasping and yanking my lips away to cry out at the friction of cotton knit on my tender, slick flesh.

"Gonna make this nest so rich with your perfume, it soaks into the walls, Butterfly," Bear hissed, scratching his teeth over my jaw, sucking a hickey on my throat. I nearly came at the draw of pressure, a meaningless mark so similar to the one I craved from him.

"Bear, please!" I reached around his back, clawed up his shirt to find his flesh.

He ducked and I nearly screamed until I realized he was shedding the layer, shoving the fabric into the depths of my nest and then pressing himself down on top of me, skin to skin.

I caught my breath and blinked at him, my lips already aching from his kiss, cunt tingling with the promise of release.

"You're so beautiful," he said, the words gentle, all the animal urgency from a moment ago sapped away. His thumbs stroked my cheekbones. "Seeing you like this, all pink with need...makes me so fucking hard, omega."

I hadn't expected that simple word, my designation, to cause a flood of sensation in my core, a sudden urgency to be touched, *consumed*. I whined, trying to climb into Bear, and he purred, moving his mouth farther away to my brief disappointment.

Until his fingers were tugging gently at my nipples, tongue and lips dragging over my chest, sucking one breast and then the other, back and forth as I thrashed and squirmed beneath him.

My legs around his hips pushed at the fabric of his sweatpants, wiggling them down inch by inch, until the sticky damp head of his cock was suddenly kissing my clit. I keened and froze as Bear pulled roughly on my nipple, one hand abandoning my breast to push himself the rest of the way free.

His cock slapped against my slippery sex, and we both let out quick bright shouts at the contact, Bear's voice muffled against my chest. He bucked immediately, his length stroking my hypersensitive skin, and I trembled as I clung to him.

"Gotta kick these off," Bear muttered, pulling away from me, hissing as I scratched his back in protest. "Need to be touching you, Butterfly."

I reached for his cock, wrapping my fist around him, grinning in victory at how slick I'd already gotten him. I'd been embarrassed of my own arousal once, but I couldn't recall that shame now, seeing the shine of my need on his length.

"Fuck. Fuck, I—" Bear growled, pushing my hand away and quickly yanking his pants off and out of the end of the nest.

I blinked at the cool dark of the room beyond the nest, and then Bear was drawing the curtains down, shuttering us inside. I stroked my foot against his hip, surprised by how even that little detail eased thin threads of tension in my body until all that was left was desire. The need to have this alpha—who had sheltered me and seen my weaknesses and needs, who had built me a nest—as close as physically possible.

"Bear," I murmured.

He returned to me, perfect weight and broad frame, one hand holding the back of my neck as he dove down for a plunging, stroking kiss. His other hand reached between my legs, fingers sliding inside of me, curving immediately.

My hands on his arms and chest found him trembling. It was as if it were him struggling against the sudden physical imperative of a heat, the need to fuck, to be claimed. I gasped as his thumb stroked my clit, and he pulled his mouth from mine, guiding it down my throat, over my collarbones, back to my breasts as he fucked me roughly with his fingers.

"Need you ready, soaked, nice and stretched for me," Bear growled before fastening his lips to my breast.

"I am ready—please, Bear!" I cried out, spreading my thighs farther apart, working myself on his fingers.

But he only moved to torture the other nipple, biting at it playfully, swirling his tongue in a hot, wet circle around the puckered flesh. His fingers on the back of my neck stroked and massaged, a confusing soothing motion that contrasted with the urgency of his fingers in my clutching cunt.

It didn't take long. Bear had already learned my little triggers, to start in a wide circle around my clit and then work his focus to the underside until I couldn't control the shaking in my legs.

He knew how to find the softest place inside of me, where his knot would fit later, and mimic the same swirling motion there.

His purr thrummed through my breasts, down into my core, and my fingers clutched and tangled in his long curls. The obscene sounds of his sucking lips and plunging fingers made my face flush with a thrilled embarrassment, until the noise was rushing and pounding with my pulse.

I came with a cry of his real name, and Bear's head lifted, body tense against mine, his growl echoing with the high notes of my voice as my pussy clutched and coated his fingers in my release. I was catching my breath, shaking through the soft tremors, as he shifted, a blunt nudge joining his gentling fingers inside of me.

I blinked and stared up at his hovering face, soothing my hands down to his bristled jaw. He was getting himself ready, stroking himself with my glossy release, belly rumbling against mine with the purring melody that hadn't faltered since we'd kissed.

"I need you," I said.

"You do," Bear rasped.

And there was no hesitation, just a slight pressure, in and out, sinking a little deeper with every second. I moaned as he worked his way inside of me, gentle but persistent. He was thick, and while two fingers might've felt like a good stretch in preparation, at least three would've really been needed.

"Oh fuck," I gasped, chest heaving. There was a soft burn, but he was stroking against it, transforming the sting into a pulse and a heat that soaked into my very bones.

"Don't close your eyes, Butterfly," Bear hissed, before I'd even realized they were falling shut. "I need to see this look on your face. I need to watch how good I make you feel."

I whined, bracing my heels into the too-soft mattress, trying to raise my hips to thrust myself onto his length, almost wishing for more pain to distract from the heady pleasure.

"I'm gonna earn this," he whispered.

I reached up to my aching breasts, just trying to find a contrast to the slow stretch, the blooming pulse of pleasure in my cunt with every driving thrust from Bear's hips, but he groaned as I gripped myself, and I could've sworn I felt him swell inside of me.

My fucking eyes. I wanted to see his face too, although the way his hands shook on my hips as he drew me just a little farther onto his length was rewarding.

"Fuck me, alpha," I panted, licking my lips, noting the clutch of his fingers in my ass. "Knot me, Courtney."

He groaned, and I memorized the power that flooded me at the sound, the floating sensation.

"You gotta come for me first, Butterfly," Bear snarled, and his hand shifted, brushing over my clit, but his next thrust was rougher. "You gotta make me so slick and wet I slide right in, baby."

I whined, reaching back and clawing into the pillows, trying to find the leverage to shove him inside of me.

He leaned down, catching my mouth with his, our tongues tangling immediately, and drove in so deep that his knot pressed to my opening. I gasped, and Bear sucked on my bottom lip, moaning in protest as he pulled out nearly to the tip again.

"Come, Faith," he growled, and this time it was more of a demand, born of his own desperate need to be filling me up.

His thumb was on my clit, clumsy and desperate, and his thrusts were rough, missing the rhythm that he'd touched me with, occasionally pressing hard as if he could barely resist seating his knot in me.

I didn't know what was better—the full stretch and pound of Bear's cock, or the thrill of making him wild and needy, feeling the threads of his control unravel with every plunge inside of me, the claw of his fingers in my ass as he forced himself to pull out again.

He'd lost his finesse from minutes ago, and he let out the most beautiful groans. I squeezed, baring down on his length, crying out at the strike of him inside of me, forcing my orgasm closer.

"Come. Come on my cock, omega. Come for your alpha."

Mine, the starving creature in my chest snarled, and I came with a bright cry, squeezing at Bear's shoulder, pressing my breasts to him, arching my throat. He gasped against my neck, sucked a kiss that was insufficient to what I craved, and then his arms were tight around me, pulling me closer, closer, pressure like fire at my sex, making me howl.

Bear was huge, and his knot pushing into me gave me a brief moment of terror, like I was splitting myself in half, but I was still shuddering through waves of release and the pain was confused in the process.

And then there was only dense, pounding pleasure as he locked inside of me. My breath rushed out of my chest, and my legs and arms twined tight around the massive alpha as he sank in. Bear moaned and the sound was in my throat, echoing in my head, in my toes, drumming through my core. He rocked, and I whined as a new rushing beat of release struck me.

It was too much and I wanted it to continue forever. There was no room for thought, and that was a sudden relief. I pressed my face to Bear's skin, let his scent flood my lungs, and gave myself over to instinct and ecstasy.

I was going to lose my goddamn mind. It had been years since I'd serviced an omega, since I'd knotted anyone, but that was no explanation for the feral edge of my hindbrain taking over. That was all my Butterfly, Faith.

I reared up, pressing my palms into the mattress, and watched her wild face twist in agonized relief as my knot dug into her cunt, burying her in a new tide of sensation.

She was exquisite. Sweet and snarling, tender and demanding. And she had my knot in a vicious chokehold that made me fight to not cross my eyes and come at the first clench of her muscles around me.

Fuck, I was *dying* inside of her.

My teeth ached and I could *smell* her pulse, the air clogged with her thickly sweet perfume, almonds and coconut and a dense garden bursting with every beat of her heart. She was inside of my lungs, in my bloodstream, probably soaked into the roots of my hair.

I held my body still, testing my own faint restraint, and watched her settle and breathe.

"More," she moaned, reaching for me.

Lightning was licking down my spine into my balls, and there was no *reason* to resist coming. As long as Faith was squeezing and whining and sucking on my knot with that perfect cunt of hers, I would stay hard, drive us both mad with pleasure. Except I didn't trust myself not to sink my teeth in her.

She wanted me. She wanted *me*, my bite, wanted our souls fused together.

And King was right—I was already attached. I'd *never* wanted an omega this way before. Never wanted to possess and protect any of my clients, to bite them and leave them limp and helpless on my cock until they couldn't do more than come for me.

"More, alpha," Faith snarled, dragging me closer.

I took her lips with mine, aware of how swollen I'd already left her pretty little mouth, that pout dangerously full as it was. I worked my knot inside of her, stroked my tongue around hers, buried my growls and purrs in her throat, and fought the siren's call of her next orgasm as she whined and milked my knot.

How long could I last?

I needed a mouth guard.

I needed to take her from behind next, push her face-down into the pillows and make her present like a good little omega.

I groaned and tore from her mouth, the tension snapping in me as release clawed its way free of my cock, flooding between us.

Faith gasped and I forced my eyes open, her face slack and dreamy as I coated and filled her with snapping thrusts of my hips. Still, the craving didn't slack. She was thrumming and clenching around me, keeping my knot swollen and hard.

She whined, twisted, and arched, and I ducked down, feasting on those pretty, full breasts she offered.

I would give her everything. I'd destroy us both. I'd tear the nest down around us until we were shredded pillows and sweaty, boneless bodies.

"More," my pretty Butterfly whispered, softer now, tangling me in her long legs and arms like I'd caught myself in a lovely spider's web.

"Yes," I snarled, biting at her mouth, fucking her on my hard knot.

More and more, until our bodies couldn't take another second.

———

I WOKE to the soft tap of fingertips crawling over my chest. One breath—one snag of the taste of the air—and a purr was bursting from my chest.

The nest smelled obscene—fully coated in our scents and the tang of sex. My cock was *sore,* and for some insane reason that made me grin.

A moment later, I had the sense to wonder if that meant Faith was sore too, which was a less pleasing prospect, and I fought the heavy glue of exhaustion that was sealing my eyes shut.

"Butterfly, you okay?" I asked, stretching a limp arm down to wrap around the small woman attached to my hip.

She'd ridden me like a queen in the night, gasping and whining out nonsense begging words, coming on my knot repeatedly before collapsing like a limp doll on my chest. With a mix of amusement and shame, I recalled that she'd been riding because I was too weak and wrung out to keep fucking her on her back.

"I'm fucking amazing," she murmured, a sweet little sing-song note in her voice. "Was that my heat?"

A laugh burst out of me, and I hissed. Christ, even my abs were sore. "Shit, Butterfly. That was just the start." In fact, I wasn't even positive that last night wasn't just us. Alpha and omega, our base urges together.

But no, this wasn't just designation. I'd been with plenty of omegas, and none of their scents tangled up in my brain like Faith's. None of them looked so perfect spread on my knot, so sweet and pink and inviting beneath me. I was trained in caring for omegas, for their physical and emotional needs, but it'd never been as natural and as *necessary* to me before.

Faith's cheeks were flushed, and there were red smears on her throat from my beard, bruises from my claiming kisses. She smiled and squirmed, eyes wide and breath catching.

"Sore?" I asked, rolling into her, kissing those marks with a gentler goal.

The nest was still cozy and dark, barely lit by the bulbs around us, but there was a strip of sunlight cutting through the dark curtains past our feet.

"Just...aware," Faith murmured.

She'd given me her name, a soft promise of a word that suited her and made my chest ache. I licked a bruise and resisted the urge to wrap my arms around her like a vise. Someone had hurt this woman, treated her like careless cargo. I wanted to tear the world to pieces until I found them and destroyed them, but what was more important was simply holding her here, keeping her out of their reach.

My fingers dug into Faith's hips and she hummed, curving into my chest before hiccuping again and stiffening.

"I'm so sticky," she whispered, and I lifted my head to find her cheeks pink and lips twitching.

I grinned and she reached up, tracing the line of my mouth with her fingertips. I nipped one, and she jumped.

"Bath or shower?"

"Mm, shower. You're...a little clearer today, but also kind of..." She frowned and squinted, blinking for a moment as I waited. "Double."

My cheer faded slightly. I'd gotten a concussion in high school during a football game and had double vision for a few days. But I didn't know how long Faith had been dealing with this and what it would take to help her recover.

She squeaked as I scooped her up off the bed, kicking open the curtains at the end of the nest. She hid her face in my neck as I carried her out, the room bright with midday light. I made a list in my head. Faith needed to shower, needed to eat. Needed to see a fuckin' doctor. I wasn't sure I would win that last battle, but I had to try.

I'd set her down in the tub and just gotten the water going when a knock sounded on the apartment.

"Might be Chance. You good, Butterfly?"

Her eyes were shut and she had her hand braced on the ledge

for balance, but she was smiling and sighing, face ducked under the water.

"Good," she said, stretching that marked-up throat and making my mouth water.

The knocking hit again and I scowled, now certain our visitor was, in fact, not Chance. I ducked out of the bathroom, shutting the door behind me, and went to hunt for a pair of pants.

"Gimme a minute," I called to the door.

I only bothered with a fresh pair of sweatpants, fully intending on jumping into the shower as soon as I was done with whatever this was about. And if I opened the door a little too aggressively, allowing the mixed scent of Faith and me to gust over King, it was only a minor payback for the interruption.

King's jaw dropped, eyes going black with dilated pupils, and a brief, stuttering purr rose from his throat. He stumbled back, aborting the sound with a rough swallow, and narrowed his eyes at me.

"Fuck," he snapped.

"What do you need?"

King's fists were clenched at his side, eyes scanning around me into the room as if he were searching for her. "It started already?"

"Close to. Not quite," I said, fighting my smirk as his eyes widened at that announcement.

Yeah, I thought. *This is just the appetizer.*

"I...got a call from Chappy," King bit out.

My hand tensed around the door handle. Chappy was the prez of the Western Wasted.

"They know?" I asked, glancing at the bathroom door. King's eyes followed mine.

"Didn't say so clearly, but they wanted a meet here. I assumed it was to sniff her out. I refused, demanded neutral territory or their own, since they called the meet. But fuck, I can't take *you*. You reek of her."

I arched an eyebrow at King. *Reek* implied that the way this room smelled right now, the way I smelled, wasn't making his mouth water and his dick hard. Which, given the way he was swallowing and hunching, I was sure it was. King was a commanding presence in every way, and I was enjoying this sudden uneven playing field he found himself on.

"I *can* shower," I said, trying not to laugh. Although it was true, there probably wasn't a single thread in this room that didn't smell just a little bit like Faith now. "You wanna deal with this when it's just us? Someone has to stay here."

King's scowl deepened and his lips parted. I recalled the advice I'd given him the day before about breathing through his mouth. And boy was he breathing, chest heaving as he tasted Faith's pleasure.

"Can't stall for two weeks. I don't want them to think I'm nervous," King muttered.

The bathroom door opened abruptly, a cloud of sweet steam cutting between us as Faith appeared. She was dripping wet but wrapped in a towel, leaning against the doorframe, and the bright smile on her lips faded as she found King and not Chance in the doorway. But she didn't shrink.

"Oh. I..." She turned her head, blinking at me.

"I'll join you in a second, Butterfly."

"There's not...not another alpha?" she asked, frowning.

"No," King snapped out before I had to reassure her. "No more alphas till—" He cut himself off, looking at me in a rare panic. "I'm...sorry about that. Bear, come find me when you're...done."

And then King turned on his heel and all but raced down the hall, boots stomping a tempo of panic.

Faith blinked and I swung the door shut, a slow grin growing.

"He's afraid of you," I whispered, waggling my eyebrows and crowding her back into the bathroom.

"Afraid?" she asked, breathless.

"Never been around a needy little omega before," I teased her as her eyes widened. "Probably thinks you're gonna take a bite out of him like you did me."

She gasped as I scooped her up, whipping off her towel and hauling her over my shoulder. I kicked my sweatpants to the floor, hand groping at Faith's ass.

"You told him?" she asked, voice high and nervous.

"I didn't, actually," I admitted. I probably should have, not that King was any less suspicious of my interest in her without knowing about the bite.

I carried her under the water with me, purring at the slide of her damp skin as I dragged her down my body. Her cheeks were flushed, lips still swollen from the night before, and she wiggled her hips as my cock stroked between her thighs.

I wanted to spend another day between those thighs, knot her right here and now, and watch the bliss take her into that hungry insanity she'd found last night. But King wasn't known for his patience, and Faith's heat would demand plenty of hours and sweat and desperation from us both when it hit in earnest.

I stepped back, bending to kiss her forehead, and focused on my list for the day.

"Hold onto me while I wash you," I said, and Faith hummed her agreement. "I got an idea I wanna run by you."

She beamed up at me, gaze unfocused and smile bright.

I knew this woman wanted protection, wanted to cling to the first person who'd made her feel safe in who knew how long. And maybe, with enough time, she would find her footing in the world again and the feeling would fade. Maybe she'd be ready to find a full pack, rich and safe and gentle.

But I wasn't sure I would be ready to let her go. I'd never considered myself a selfish person, but the more time I spent with Faith, the more the urge grew.

To bite her, keep her, claim her.

And if I was going to be selfish in that way, then I needed to be right for her in every other way. That would take some help.

Faith

15

I fidgeted on the couch cushion, squished between Bear and Chance. My eyes were closed, head tilted down, and I was taking shallow breaths, trying to only catch the familiar flavors of the men at my side, rather than the oppressively masculine alpha pheromone coating the room. My eyes flicked up and opened briefly at the thought of him, King. There were two of him, white-blond hair and gray beard twisted in a scowl. He was glowering at the three of us from the other side of his desk, and I shivered at the slice of those cold eyes.

This was *his* territory, and we were the invaders. In spite of what Bear had said earlier, I wasn't convinced this man felt anything but contempt for me. But I'd noticed yesterday that the rest of this "clubhouse" stank of too many scents, fresh and stale, beta and alpha. Here in this room, it was only the rough leather and smooth olive of King.

Chance's arm draped over my back, delivering a solid and comforting squeeze of his hand on my shoulder. I closed my eyes again and rubbed my cheek against Chance's shoulder, marking him with my scent. His breath hitched and then his arm tightened, face nuzzling into the top of my head. Through the curtain of my hair, I thought I felt the burn of King staring at us with hostile curiosity.

"You can change your mind," Bear said to me in a low voice.

King made a garbled sound of protest, but it died quickly as Chance and Bear glared back.

I had to swallow down the immediate answer of *Yes! Take me back to the nest.*

"No, I... It was bad enough when everything was fuzzy," I said slowly. "I don't want someone else...touching me, but I'm getting scared about what happened."

The double vision made me queasy. At least when my vision was fuzzy, I'd been able to keep my eyes open, but now I had them squeezed shut, when all I really wanted to do was finally get a good look at the handsome faces around me.

Bear purred to soothe me, bending down and kissing the crown of my head, and I glanced at King. His two faces were staring at me, eyes narrowed, brow furrowed. Was that suspicion or worry on his face? And who was it directed at?

Strong fingers found my hand at my side, tangling our grip together, and I looked down at Chance's hand knotted with mine, surprised at how simple touch made the world feel solid around me.

King's phone chimed from his desk. "Molly's here. I'll get her."

I stiffened as the alpha rose from behind his desk, crossing the room.

"Molly's a former Catholic sister turned trauma nurse," Chance said to me, which Bear had already mentioned. "She's on our books mainly 'cause..." Chance cleared his throat and spoke over my head. "You think she's back with him?"

Bear scoffed. "Think he'd be this uptight? No, they've been done for years." Bear's fingers brushed through my hair, soothing trembles that made my muscles tight. "She's a beta. Very quiet, almost no scent. She's not going to touch you 'less you say it's okay."

I nodded, but ragged memories clouded my vision of the room, figures in white suits forcing needles into my arms, into my neck, strapping me down when I fought. Footsteps thudded in the hall, approaching King's office, and my blood was ice in my veins.

I'm with Bear. Omikron hasn't found me. I want to be better, I chanted mentally.

King's steps were unmistakable, heavy alpha stomps into the room, the huff of breath as he threw himself back into his seat, the chair squeaking in protest. And strangely, the gust of his scent as he passed cleared my head a little, made Chance's grip on my hand solid again. The next set of steps moved slowly and softly into the room, letting their feet scuff on the floor, making a large arch around the couch. I shuddered and stared at those innocuous white sneakers, the illusion of four shoes like some kind of monster at the corner of my vision

"Hello, honey," the woman, Molly, said gently, taking a seat in a rolling chair.

Just look, and you'll know it's safe, I told myself.

The woman in the chair had thick, dark hair threaded with silver, and warm golden skin crinkling at the corners of her eyes. She was attractive, older, and my chest panged at the look on her face as she stared back at me in double. I hadn't seen an expression like that since my second foster home and the older woman who'd cared for Adam and me with real gentleness, actual compassion. This woman had all the kindness and sympathy King seemed to lack, and she waited patiently while I shook through my nerves, a soft whine clinging in my throat.

"The boys say you hit your head a while back. Do you remember how long ago that was?" Molly asked, her eyes drinking in every detail of me as I struggled to hold her gaze. Chance's grip squeezed mine with the rhythm of my breaths, and Bear's hand landed on my thigh, anchoring me.

"I think...a week before...before they found me," I whispered out, trying not to let my head drag me back to those moments.

"Were you unconscious?"

I nodded.

"Same amount of vision loss the whole time?"

"It started off just a little blurred and...I couldn't track time well, but I think it took a couple days before everything was just foggy colors," I said.

"And it's improving again?"

The questions were gentle and also clinical, and I found it easier to breathe the longer we spoke.

"Better since Bear convinced me to take ibuprofen for the headaches."

"And is your vision still foggy or clearer?"

"Almost clear."

"That's good. And the ibuprofen helps with the headaches?" Molly asked, leaning forward.

I nodded again, finally lifting my chin, frowning through the confusing picture of two identical women blinking back at me.

"A severe concussion can cause swelling that presses on ocular nerves," Molly said softly, glancing briefly at Bear and Chance before returning her focus to me. "The improvement from intense obscuring to this point is promising. Seeing results from an MRI would help, but almost two weeks out from the incident...the worst would've happened by now, if it was going to. As long as your headaches keep lessening, you should be okay, but I'd really like to double-check everything at the hospital."

My heart hammered and my head shook, the whole room topsy-turvy in double as I shook. "I can't...I can't go to a hospital."

"Butterfly," Bear started.

The whine in my throat was annoying and frantic, and I fought through it to speak. "No. You don't... As soon as I put my name down, anything, security footage—" My words cut off, eyes wide and frantic before squeezing shut with a huff of frustration.

"The double vision is worse than blurring," Molly said to me, ignoring my fit of panic to speak to me calmly.

The doctors or whatever they were who worked for Omikron had spoken around me, consulting with handlers and each other, never me. Molly was not like them. Bear trusted her. I caught my breath, closed my eyes, and settled before nodding in agreement.

"I might be able to get you some lenses that disrupt that. How was your vision before the injury?" Molly asked.

"Fine. Normal, I think," I said, shrugging my shoulders, as if I were capable of being casual in this state.

"I'll see what I can do," Molly said with a nod. She licked her lips, glancing at the men to either side of me and then over her shoulder at King, who was pale and silent. "If it's all right with you, honey, I'd like to speak to you alone."

"No," I whispered immediately, even as King rose from his seat. "Not alone."

Bear's hand patted my thigh. "How about Chance stays with you? That way, Molly doesn't have to deal with us alphas?"

I frowned and swallowed, but leaned into Chance's side. "Okay." I would've preferred to have them both, but Chance would keep me safe.

Bear kissed my head and followed King out of the room.

Molly was silent for a moment, and I risked a glance at her, finding her staring back at me so long, I wanted to press her into speaking.

"Are there others?" Molly murmured at last.

The soft, hopeless cries in the night. Scratches against the wall. Unfamiliar perfumes that made me anxious and uncomfortable.

"Yes."

"And my hospital, it's not—"

I licked my lips and interrupted her, aware of how extreme my worries sounded, the idea that some monstrous limb might reach into a hospital to find me. "I don't know. I don't know for certain but they—It's—I'm not crazy!"

"Hey," Chance soothed, stroking my shoulder, squeezing my hand. "No one thinks that, birdy."

"No, you're not, honey. Chance is right—that's not what I'm thinking. Just wasn't sure if I needed to be worried about my patients," Molly said, scooting forward, testing a careful hand on my knee, smiling at me when I didn't flinch. "I've got some medication for you. Just to keep your blood pressure down. King mentioned your heat is coming in. I also have suppressants, which I'll leave if you decide you want them."

I remained silent, and Molly glanced at Chance warily.

"I also...want to make sure you're comfortable being here," Molly said to me, in a low voice. "If you need an alternate—"

"No!" I gasped, realizing she was offering to take me away, away from Bear.

"She's not taking you anywhere," Chance said. "Not unless

you *wanted* to leave. She's only asking 'cause she's worried about you locked up here with alphas."

"Exactly," Molly said with a nod. "I trust King, but you have options. I would *find* you options."

"I want to be here. With Bear and Chance," I said.

Molly paused, but nodded. "Okay. There is evidence that an omega heals up much better with a trusted alpha on hand. Purring alone is great for an omega's blood pressure."

"Bear can barely stop around her," Chance said, and Molly's lips twitched.

"Good," Molly murmured. "Now, back to the heat. Are you covered for birth control?"

I stiffened and blinked. "I...I don't know. I was on birth control before, but I don't know...how long. And they gave me shots, but I don't know what for."

Molly frowned at that. "I would need a blood sample to tell, but I don't want to create unnecessary risk. And I don't want to double you up. "

"Bear told me he had a vasectomy," I whispered, blushing at the memory of the discussion. But I was glad it hadn't needed to come up the night before.

"I'll use condoms, unless there's something else I should do," Chance said.

Molly stared at us briefly, then glanced at the door. Was she wondering about King?

"I can get you a shot too, if you want one," she said to Chance.

With the focus off of me for the moment, I cuddled into Chance's side as they discussed the offer and he requested to be tested.

"I've been careful, but I don't want to assume...former partners have," Chance said.

"I can handle that for you easily. That should cover us for now. Please don't hesitate to have the guys contact me if you have any worries. I'll work with you, I promise. Nothing you're uncomfortable with," Molly urged.

I nodded and softened into Chance's side, marking him with another press of my cheek. "Thank you."

Molly sighed and rose up from her chair. "I'm gonna have a quick word with them before I head out."

Chance waited until she'd walked out to twist and kiss my forehead. "You did good."

I hummed in his arms, following eagerly as he pulled me onto his lap. It was our first moment alone since the night before, and I wanted to fall back onto King's couch and drag Chance over me, let all three of the men's scents mingle into a reassuring combination as I begged for another of Chance's gentle kisses.

"I feel like such a coward," I admitted under my breath.

"You're the absolute opposite, birdy," Chance said, tipping my chin up.

I smiled, eyes shut, and the last line of tension on my forehead was brushed away by his mouth. "My name's Faith," I whispered. "I told Bear last night too."

Chance paused, his lips grazing over mine. "Brave Faith," he murmured.

The door opened again, and I ignored the heavy footsteps as I arched into those soft lips, Chance's kiss like gentle breezes, now accompanied with hungry wet flicks of his tongue. I dug my fingers into his shoulder, wanting to drag him on top of me, chase that hunger until his feather touches were deep and feeding my own cravings, but I also enjoyed this careful embrace.

"We'd better clear out before King gets back," Bear said from above.

Chance paused and I pulled away from the kiss, blinking. "Can we go outside?"

"'Course we can. I got another surprise for you yesterday," Bear said. I arched an eyebrow, and he grinned at me. "Trust me. You'll like this one too."

B ear and I sat on the painted metal picnic table in the shade of the clubhouse, watching Faith float in the cheap kiddie pool Bear had purchased. I fought the grin that wanted to claim my features as I recalled her giving me her name, her little unconscious whimpers as I kissed her. She trusted me. She *wanted* me. As if I were an alpha, like Bear.

Faith arched in the water, showing off the deliciously small black bikini Bear had gotten her, and I figured this surprise was as much for us as it was for Faith. I was the lucky asshole chosen to coat her in sunscreen, my greedy hands finding her sensitive, ticklish places, and the spots that made her perfume bloom. I cataloged the information for later.

"Big difference in a few days," Bear murmured, smiling softly and swigging back his beer.

I hummed my agreement, trying to see the bundle of terror and bones we'd found in the back of that cargo van. Watching her fight that fear, conquer it as she'd spoken to Molly, had filled me with a pride that didn't feel rightly mine. I was claiming it anyway. This girl was mine, as long as she kept reaching for me.

Bear had also bought Faith a floaty tray, and today she'd let me help her pick out her food and arrange it to her liking. It was such a small gesture, but the trust behind it was heady.

"She's eating better," I said.

"Doesn't choke on her pills either," Bear said, obvious pride puffing his chest.

"Walking a little bowlegged after—"

Bear barked out a laugh and Faith flapped an arm, glancing in our direction before softening back into the water.

"She needs a pack," Bear said, lowering his voice.

The gulp of beer I'd just taken went down as hard as rocks in my throat as I swallowed. "Sure," I said, voice flat.

"Pack she trusts. Likes," Bear said.

Duh, I thought, but there was an almost teasing note in the words that made me look at the alpha. My usual scowl was on my face, and for once it didn't feel so natural.

Bear arched an eyebrow and I scoffed, not even sure I wanted to voice what I thought he might've been saying. "I'm a beta," I said, spitting the words and their bitter flavor out.

Bear shrugged. "She doesn't care. Why should I?"

I sucked in a breath and held it, turning back to stare at the young woman floating in the pool. She *didn't* care. She'd talked to Molly about me being involved in her heat. Kissed me and clung to me with such sweetness, it made me dizzy.

"One alpha and one beta don't make a pack," I said, because the offer was ludicrous and so fucking out of reach, it made me angry he'd dangled it in front of my nose in the first place.

"True. Not one big enough to keep her safe, at least," Bear allowed.

Which ought to be the end of it, so why didn't it sound like Bear was done?

"King would sooner take your patch away before he let you turn the club into a pack," I said.

"You think I want some of these fuckers going anywhere near her?" Bear asked.

Why did this bastard sound so fucking casual about this?

"Not many of us I trust that well," he continued.

"King." The name fell out of my lips, and I glanced at Bear again. He was still quiet. Totally out of his mind, but with a calm confidence. Insanity would do that to you, I guessed. I shook my head and continued. "You trust *King*. You wanna call his fucking bluff on *pack*?"

Bear shrugged. "She likes his scent."

It was my turn to laugh, but the sound was ragged and too harsh. Faith looked over again, but her eyes must've been bothering her, 'cause she shut them almost immediately. That sobered me. She *did* need us.

But *King?*

"I think you need a backup plan," I muttered. King's focus was on the club, on holding it together and keeping his crown in place. Bear didn't even know half the shit-talking going on under the surface of the club.

I respected King. I sure as shit didn't want to be in a club led by my older brother, have him constantly rubbing my nose into my designation. But did my determination to keep King crowned make me less interested in the idea of being part of Faith's pack?

"You're probably right. Her heat is my focus for now. That and just...this," he said, nodding his beer in her direction.

This. This girl floating in a kiddie pool, soaking up sunlight she hadn't seen in weeks at least, relaxing for the first time in as long, if not longer.

"We don't know her. We don't know what we're up against," I said.

Bear nodded. "I know. And the Wasted are sniffing."

Fuck.

My hand clenched around my beer. The Wasted wanted her, or the product that they'd paid for.

It should've made me even more reluctant to get involved in this half-baked scheme of Bear's. Here was trouble in a pretty package that, by all rights of designation, should never have even been offered to me.

"You're insane," I said under my breath.

"Mhm. And?" Bear asked. Knowing, smirking bastard.

"And I'm insane too." And filled with a possessive demand to keep Faith safe and happy and *mine*.

No way in fucking hell was I letting the Wasted touch my birdy.

Bear clapped a hand on my shoulder, and I let out a heavy sigh.

"We need to get King on board," I said.

"Probably. I think it'll happen." Bear stretched his long legs out in front of him, crossing them at the ankle, leaning back into the table.

Apparently, getting their knot strangled all night made burly, surly alphas into cheerful puppies. How nice for them.

The backdoor from the bar clanged open, a gunshot of sound in the dull quiet of Dead End. Faith sat up, water splashing against her cheek. Bear and I twisted to see King standing in the doorway, glaring at the low afternoon sun heading toward the horizon. A moment later, his eyes were on the omega, and she squinted back at him, adorably disturbed.

"Meet's tomorrow night," King said, gaze finally drifting to Bear, who grunted in answer.

My eyes bounced between King and Faith, Bear's mission buzzing through my head. Her eyes dropped back to the water, hand swishing patterns through the surface, and King stared. I couldn't tell if it was hate or hunger twisting his expression. Probably both.

His throat cleared twice, but Faith's attention was long gone, or at least she was pretending so.

I remained riveted to the pair, the charged silence of the yard, until King finally managed to spit out words.

"You need anything, princess?"

I turned away to hide my surprise, but Bear was openly smug, grinning down at his hands.

Faith's head shook, eyes flicking toward the door. "Thank you."

It shut without another word.

"This might work," I muttered to Bear.

"It will."

I actually hoped so. And that fucking scared the shit out of me.

"SHE'S WORN OUT, should be good to sleep through the meet. Heat's probably good to start properly tomorrow, so she's gonna be snoozing her way up to it. But if she does wake up—"

"Bear."

"—it won't take much to settle her down again. Get her off a couple times, then be real sweet—"

"Jesus, Bear!"

"It'll need to be penetrative. Eating her out will just rile her up," he continued.

I had the sudden urge to stuff my fist into the larger man's mouth. "Are you seriously prescribing a sexual routine to a grown woman right now?" I snarled out, speaking over Bear's explanation of how to massage Faith's sensitive opening.

He blinked at me, trailing off, and I was as aware of the tense silence falling between us as I had been of every minute detail he'd already offered. I'd barely had the time to do more than kiss her so far, and she and Bear had holed up together again for the rest of yesterday. Being told how to satisfy her was as humiliating as it was arousing.

"I am, yeah," Bear said, eyes narrowing. "Because this is her first heat. And it's about *her*, not us. And yeah, I'm being clinical now, because it helps me focus and resist the urge to dive right back into her nest and knot her into complete oblivion like I would really fucking like to."

I swallowed hard but refused to drop my stare.

Bear let out a slow breath. "There are condoms on the right table. If you fuck her, use them. She will need pressure just inside, like she's being knotted, or she'll get antsy and emotional. Okay?"

"Okay," I said, hands fisted in my pockets.

Bear rolled his shoulders and glanced away at last. "Sorry. I know I've been hogging her and you two haven't had much time to—"

I didn't want to listen to Bear's half-hearted apology or the reminder of what I *hadn't* yet with Faith. "You're the alpha," I said, cutting him off with a shrug.

Bear snorted. "That's not it. I won't lie and pretend I've been altruistic about this, man. I've been keeping her to myself 'cause I'm a greedy bastard."

I blinked, my gaze finally falling to our shoes.

"Service alphas are great, but a lot of omegas hire betas for their heats too. All that matters is that she likes you, she wants you, and you'll be good to her. The rest is just getting creative."

I wanted to growl at Bear, but it would've been ridiculous on several levels. The man was practically twice my size, never mind our designations. So instead I settled on a nod.

"Either way, you should hang around tonight," Bear said.

My brow furrowed. "Around?"

"In the nest. Even when I get back. She wants you too," he said, a bit stiffly.

His offer clicked in my mind. I didn't have an issue fucking around with a guy in the mix, but Bear and I weren't interested in one another, and I wasn't sure if he'd be spending the whole time trying to make sure I didn't touch him.

"You good with that?" I asked, frowning.

He snorted. "Two to four partners on board is pretty standard in an omega heat," he said. "Are *you* good with it?"

As long as I didn't end up feeling like a useless third wheel as the beta, I'd be fine. I shrugged and nodded, just as King's boots stomped up the stairs to catch us in the hall.

"You ready?" he asked Bear.

Bear arched an eyebrow at me.

"We'll be good. She'll sleep, and if she doesn't, I'll make sure to stimulate like a knot," I said, taking Bear's somewhat humiliating instructions seriously for the moment.

His shoulders relaxed and he dropped one enormous hand on my shoulder for a moment, removing it before I could bristle.

"Keep an eye out," King called to me, scowl in place. "They know the rest of the brothers are on the road. I don't trust them not to pull bullshit."

I wasn't sure how I was supposed to nurse a horny omega and guard the whole damn clubhouse on my own, but I nodded. "Home base is covered. Good luck."

"You too," Bear said, the corner of his smirk just barely visible as he passed me.

King tossed him a can of scent canceling spray. "You smell like candied pussy. You'll have the Wasted humping your leg."

I choked on my laugh and crossed the hall toward Bear's door as the two alphas griped at one another on their way down the stairs. Bear's room was quiet, coated wall-to-wall in Faith's rich and syrupy perfume. The nest looked bizarre from the outside, an enormous structure taking up the majority of the space, but Bear had left the curtain slightly parted, and I caught a glimpse of the languid omega sleeping inside. I wanted to melt into that mattress and curl up with her, but King's warning lingered.

The Wasted might try and take an opportunity to push their luck with us. Those nasty little fuckers were hungry for the territory King had built up. Dead End might be the ass end of the desert, but King had formed impressive connections with all the surrounding cities, working toward growing the club's reach and bringing in more traffic to our nearly ghost town.

The Devils had been a bit of a parasite on the town when I was a kid, dealing drugs too frequently and close to home, letting other gangs creep over our borders. King had reorganized the businesses, cleaned up what was left of the neighborhood, and beaten back the circling wolves. We weren't good men, but he strove for a sustainable balance between criminal and functional, and I respected that.

Faith hummed in the nest, blankets rustling, but she settled just as quickly. I took the spare chair in the corner and turned it to face the window, where I'd be able to see the road. I'd circle the club in a half hour or so, come back to her, keep her and the clubhouse safe while everyone else was away.

Not all of the Devils thought I was enough to be their brother. I wasn't enough to be more than a midnight secret to Ghost. But I would prove that I was enough for this omega, to be a man in her pack.

I woke in the nest, already entirely aware that Bear had left, if only because if he'd been with me, we would've been wrapped around one another like we had been for the past couple days. I sat up, reaching for the dial that turned up the lights in the nest, squinting around me.

Bear had said when he left that Chance would join me, but I was alone on the bed.

"Cha—"

The door to the bedroom opened, and I stiffened at the quick and soft approach of light footsteps. I froze, curling in on myself as the curtain at the foot of the nest flipped up, but I recognized the pattern of tattoos on Chance's skin before I made a sound.

"Shh, Birdy. We got company."

I curled up on the mattress, blinking back at the beta. He was shockingly, breathtakingly handsome, clearer than ever, with beautifully sharp features I wanted to trace with my tongue. "Company?" I mouthed.

"Couple of guys. They're outside. I'm gonna deal with them. Do you wanna stay here, or can I find you a hiding spot where I can keep an eye on you?"

The idea of leaving my nest made me want to scratch and claw and shove Chance away from me, drawing up that instinctual beast that circled restlessly in my chest. But worse than that was the idea that Omikron might have found me.

"Suits?" I managed to ask.

Chance blinked those pale eyes, wavering in and out of focus in front of me. "Huh? No, no. These are some of the Wasted crew. They assume they can sniff around 'cause Bear and King are out and the rest of the Devils are on the ride. I'll set 'em straight."

Not Omikron. These were the men who'd bought me. I released a rough breath, oddly relieved. I reached out, and Chance's arm was tense under my hand, practically vibrating with the urge to chase off whoever was here on his territory. *The Devils*, he'd said. I wasn't sure about the other men, the ones out on the road, but I was growing partial to the two I'd spent time with.

And the jury is still out on King, I thought. His alpha scent made me ache, and I'd shivered in the desert sun's direct glare when he'd called me princess the day before, but I wasn't sure if I trusted him—although I'd caught some of what Chance and Bear had discussed, and was mulling it over in the back of my mind.

A pack. I shoved the question aside and forced myself to focus on the present.

Did I trust Chance to keep me safe?

Yes, the feral creature in me growled. I didn't want to hide in my nest without any idea of what was happening. "I want to come with you," I said.

His hand grasped my elbow, and I crawled out of the nest with his gentle tugging. I started toward his chest, and he stepped back.

"Believe me, Birdy, I wanna bundle you up in my arms and carry you down to hiding, but I don't want these guys to smell you on me. Can you walk?"

I nodded. Bear had fed me the medications Molly had prescribed at some hazy point this morning before he'd left, but my vision was still a crisscrossed double layer, and everything spun a bit around me as I stood. Still, I would do whatever Chance said.

"Good girl," he whispered. "Come with me."

He took my hand and guided it to his back, allowing me to steady myself as he led the way out of Bear's room. I held my breath as we walked down the hall. The scents in the clubhouse were growing stale, but it still left me raw and irritated to be surrounded by so many unfamiliar and abrasive smells. Chance paused at the top of the stairs, picking up a shiny can, and I caught my breath as he started to spray us both.

It was chemical and sterile, and I tugged myself away, gagging, before I realized what it was. Scent-canceling.

"Sorry," Chance whispered, catching me again. "Gotta be safe."

I closed my mouth and squeezed my eyes shut, nodding, ignoring that clawing sensation in my chest again and the immediate urge to rub myself all over Chance, to mark him up as mine again.

"When we get to the bottom of the stairs, you duck behind the motel desk into the office. There's a two-way mirror in the room so you can watch. Under the carpet, there's a trapdoor. If anyone makes it past me to the front doors, you go down the trapdoor and you lock it behind you, 'kay?"

No! I wanted to scream. Adam and I had done everything together, every step of the way. Then again, that hadn't stopped an Omikron thug from grabbing me from behind, dragging me away with a fist over my mouth before I could scream for my brother. I didn't blame Adam for my choices to fight at his side, but I was tired, I couldn't see straight, and I didn't want to end up captured by anyone who had anything to do with Omikron.

"Okay," I whispered.

Chance yanked me closer, kissing me squarely on the forehead. He paused at the edge of the stairs, leaning to look around the corner, his hand wrapped around my wrist where I was still braced against his back.

"Okay, go now, birdy!"

I scurried out around his side, dashing for the motel desk, fumbling my hand to keep track of the space, ignoring the churn of anxiety and nausea in my stomach. Chance paced out with determined steps as I ducked out of sight and through the partially opened door.

"Close it," he hissed, and I did so as gently as I could.

The old clerk's office was musty and smelled like a mix of alpha pheromones. There was a couch pressed to the wall beneath the two-way mirror, and I withheld my whine as I realized that most of the scents came from that spot. People had been fucking on it, probably for many years. It stank of old scents and made my roiling stomach even worse.

I squinted through the mirror, kneeling gingerly on the cushions. Chance's broad shoulders stood squarely in front of the main doors, his arms hanging at his side. I focused on my view rather than the scents, rubbing a thumb absently over my shoulder and wiping away the frost of scent-canceling spray Chance had used on me.

Suddenly, a shadow passed in front of the door and Chance leapt into action, banging the door open. The other man was taller and thinner than Chance, lanky and missing the corded muscle of my beta. He was equally tattooed but stood in shadow, too far for me to make out clearly.

Their voices were dull and muffled, but with Chance standing in the open doorway, I caught most of the words.

"What the fuck do you think you're doing here?" Chance asked.

The other biker laughed. He wore a leather vest like the ones I'd seen on Bear and Chance, but his was painted with white bones like a ribcage. "Just came round to grab your prez."

"You know full well he's meeting yours at Hank's."

Chance filled the open space, solid and straight, but the other man wove back and forth so much, I almost felt seasick at the sight of him. Another figure, in the same kind of painted leather cut, appeared from the opposite direction, strolling lazily closer, the two of them crowding around Chance. The new figure was big. Not quite as much as Bear, but much larger than Chance, and he seemed even more unsteady on his feet than the first.

"Hank's, huh? Funny. Must've been some wires crossed," the first Wasted said.

The second Wasted's voice was lower and hard to catch, words drifting in and out. "... smell fuckin' sweet..."

"Rook's right, you do smell awfully sweet," the first creep said, leaning forward enough for me to see the broad and uneven grin on his face, teeth stained and marred and chipped.

Chance replied, quiet and flat, and the pair roared with laughter, the larger one—Rook—stumbling back and nearly falling on his back as he tripped off the sidewalk.

The Wasted was a perfect name for these assholes, and bile crawled up my throat at the thought of either of them touching me, grabbing me out of Chance's reach.

"Now that we've cleared that up, why don't you fucking losers get off Devil's territory before I help myself to the right of kicking your worthless asses?" Chance snarled, clearer now.

"Never met a fucking beta who smelled so sweet," the skinny man said, still grinning. "You got a sweet little beta pussy in there with you? Wanna share?"

"No, friend, I just make sure your mom coats herself in knock-off omega perfume before I fuck her six ways to Sunday," Chance answered. His voice lowered again, face leaning into the other man's, words snarled too softly to catch.

Rook broke out into even rowdier laughter, bent completely over and howling into the gravel, but the skinny one sneered back at Chance.

"Fuck off," Chance said, straightening. "I won't say it again."

Rook straightened, snorting, and reached out an arm, swatting at the other guy. "Hear that, Skinny? Your boyfriend won't give you another warning."

Skinny grinned, and all three men seemed to grow still. I held my breath, clutching at the back of the filthy couch, wanting to yank Chance back to me, and also...craving something much darker. I wanted to see those men ripped apart. I secretly wished I was powerful enough to do it myself, to tear them down for threatening what was mine.

Skinny's voice was quiet as he spoke, and I understood his

words more by watching that foul mouth than hearing him clearly. "Just can't help myself. Gotta chase that scent."

He stepped forward, an arm reaching past Chance's shoulder to grab the edge of the doorway. Suddenly, the animal rage in me gave to panicked terror. I'd forgotten to find the trapdoor, and if the man pushed past Chance, he could reach me before I'd made my way under the floor.

Except before I could finish that thought, Skinny was on the ground. I gasped, but there was no way any of them could hear me over their sudden shouting. Rook reached for Chance, but my beta's elbow was back, knocking roughly into his nose before he could do more than grab those beautifully broad shoulders. I watched, mouth open as Chance dragged Skinny away from the door, tossing him into the broken parking lot, and then spun, swinging a determined fist into Rook's face.

He swung again. And again. My fingernails dug into the back of the couch, the ragged leather scuffing under my grip as I watched Chance beat at the larger man, the sight doubled in my messy vision. Two fists for every strike, one crack of impact. It didn't matter. One or two, Chance was fierce and feral and terrifying. He kicked Rook in the gut and then spun again, going after Skinny before he had a moment to get up.

Rook rolled to his belly, and I wanted to scream a warning to Chance as the larger Wasted man rose to his knees, but my beta moved like a whip crack. Chance snapped around, the toe of his boot flicking up into the underside of his enemy's chin. Rook let out a bellow, and I squinted through the blur of movement as Chance reached for his own foot.

Skinny was up, Rook was on his ass, and suddenly the whole scene went still. Sunlight reflected in duet off the sharp edges of two knives, extended from Chance's hands in either direction. Blood dripped from his knuckles, and I didn't know if it was Chance's or the other mens', but it made me feel wild and urgent, fighting against my own tense muscles to keep from running out of hiding to grab at my beta.

Soft words were spoken, and Rook only managed to get on one knee before Chance had the blade biting against his throat.

He was fierce, dangerous.

Mine, the creature in me howled.

Skinny raised his hands, wavering side to side as he backed away slowly, stumbling in the uneven parking lot.

"Gonna fuckin' regret this," Skinny said as Chance shifted just enough to let his buddy rise. Little flecks of red hit the cracked pavement as the bigger man spat to the ground.

"Bullshit," Chance called back. "You're gonna go back and explain to Chappy that you got your asses handed to you by just one Devil. And if he sends any more of you fuckers around here, it'll be the same story, except you won't be going back with a warning. This is our fuckin' territory. It's staying that way."

"Sure thing, sweetheart. We'll see," Skinny hollered, but he was out of view to me now, Rook edging warily around Chance.

An engine roared to life, and low in my belly a monster gnawed with hunger as I stared at Chance's back.

I didn't care about territory. I didn't care about Devils or Wasted. Chance had protected me, as promised. Viscerally, effectively...*brutally*. A base, instinctive, ancient part of me approved of the blood on his hands on a shocking and sexual level. I pressed forward into the cushions of the couch, ignoring the old, faded scents of other alphas and betas, grinding my hips there as I watched Chance standing still in the parking lot. A second engine joined the first, their snarls now seeming pathetic. They were the sound of surrender, not victory. Chance had scared them away.

And now I needed Chance, needed those fists to loosen and touch me, that cool mouth to press over mine.

My breath was uneven, my breasts aching as I humped weakly at the cushion. The gesture only relieved the craving for movement, lacking pressure and focus.

My eyes fell shut as I listened to the growling retreat of the other men, my memory clarifying the blur of Chance's movements, the strength of his arms, the sharp strike of his fists, even the cracking sound of impact.

I opened my eyes again just as Chance turned. His focus was on me, or so it seemed, as if he could see through the mirrored reflection behind the desk directly to where I knelt, panting and aching. He glanced once more at the road and then pulled the door open, stepping inside and locking it behind him. He almost seemed like the man I recognized, quiet and patient. But there was a grim quality to his expression now, and his shoulders were tighter. He paused again at the door, not moving closer to me, and my own impatience won out.

I hurried off the couch, ignoring my weak legs, and opened the door to the office just as he rounded the desk.

We both froze, and I fought the discomfort of my vision to stare back at him. I caught a whiff of an overly musky alpha scent lingering around him. He'd fought an alpha. My hand slapped against the desk counter, and my knees shook.

"Did you watch?" he asked, voice soft, face turned slightly to the side.

I nodded and swallowed. "Are they gone?" My voice was ragged.

"Yeah. I'm sorry, bir—"

I cut Chance off, throwing my body into his, clawing at his shoulders as I tried to climb into his chest, my back arched and chin raised. My mouth slanted over his with a muffled echo of surprise rising from him and a low moan from me.

Chance had always been so sweet to me, so gentle, and I wanted to return the favor to him, but I was starving for his touch, biting at his lips. A strange, primal part of me wanted him to be as rough with me as he had been with the Wasted.

For a moment, he gave no response, only parting his lips to let me thrust my tongue inside, searching for his fresh and slightly soapy flavor. Then, as fast as he'd spun and kicked the larger man, Chance's arms were around my hips and my back was slammed into the mirror. It shuddered behind me as I groaned in approval. I spread my legs and then jumped, Chance's hands catching my ass eagerly, squeezing hard, as I wrapped my thighs around his hips.

His tongue curled around mine, both of us crying out as I started to grind again, this time to a much improved result. Chance's jeans were rough against the soft fabric of my leggings, his stirring cock a more direct pressure against my needy sex.

One hand tightened on my ass to the point of a beautiful aching bite, and his other slid up my back to fist my hair in his grip. Chance's mouth pulled from mine, our breath loud in the quiet hollow space. If the Wasted came back now, they would see us together. They'd see me wrapped around the beta, moaning like the desperate omega I was. I stared at the doorway as Chance dragged his lips and tongue and teeth to my ear.

He leaned in hard, stealing my breath and forcing a whine from my lips as he dug his hips between my thighs. "Did watching me fight those assholes make you wet, birdy? I can feel your slick soaking into my fucking jeans."

"Yes!" I gasped, rubbing and hiccuping as Chance bit on the lobe of my ear.

"Because it made you scared?"

I blinked and then shook my head, and Chance pulled away. This close, I could make him out so well. The lines of his cheekbones as they carved down to the muscle of his jaw. The perfect aquiline arrow of his nose. The eyebrow sharpening as it arched.

I licked my lips and his gaze flicked to my tongue, green eyes going darker. "Because it made me feel safe," I whispered.

Chance blinked, and then I was breathless again, his tongue deep in my mouth, rough and hungry, every inch of his chest pressed to mine. His body surged, bucking and pinning me in place. His hand in my hair tightened and twisted, pulling on the roots. I moaned as I sucked on his tongue, the mark of pain in my hair enhancing the edges of the pounding in my cunt. Chance's grip on my ass squeezed in time with his rocking motions.

My hands tore at his T-shirt until it was wedged far enough up his back that I could scratch at his skin, the muscles flexing under my grip in that same hard and determined rhythm. There was only one conclusion, and Chance grunted and pulled away from his forceful demand of a kiss as my nails dug in. I came with a shout, the sound almost mournful, the birth and death of pleasure in one moment. I leaned in and rubbed my breasts into his chest, eyes shut, trying to extend the wave rushing through me.

Chance's movements slowed, although they were just as deep, only stopping as I squirmed. He stepped back a fraction, and I braced one foot on the ground before reaching between us and grappling at his waistband.

"Fuck me," I gasped. Once was not enough. That feigned game of sex was not enough. I needed his skin. His teeth—

My head cleared as Chance laughed, grabbing at my hands and drawing them up his chest. Chance couldn't bite me. He wasn't an alpha.

In spite of that, the idea still sounded wonderful.

Chance released my hands and wrapped his arms around my hips again, lifting me up into his side.

"Not here, birdy. Be a good girl and clean me up, and then I'll make you come until you can't see straight."

I snorted at that. "That's hardly an ambitious marker. How about until I can't walk straight?"

"Deal," Chance growled, spinning us out from behind the counter and heading for the stairs.

I was coming to understand why Bear was walking around on clouds while simultaneously looking like someone had wrung him out like a dirty dishcloth.

I'd taken Faith into the shower with me, and she'd been a slippery little sexual monster the whole time, barely letting me wash the blood off my fists—the Wasted chumps'; I was only a little swollen and bruised—before she had her hands on my cock and was rubbing that hot pussy against my hip.

Now, with her dripping wet and clamping around three fingers, swollen lips open on a moan, I understood.

This shit was heady.

"More," Faith whined, not even done fluttering and already fucking my fingers with pretty little jerks of her hips.

Her dark hair was plastered over slender shoulders and an arching chest, inky arrows down to her waist, deep and rusty pink nipples peeking through the strands. I'd traced the tan lines of the bikini she'd been wearing, lapped at the pale skin I'd missed seeing before, and sucked a bruise onto the inside of her thigh after going down her.

Heady and constant. I was starting to prune and the shower was getting chilly.

"Fuck me, Chance, please," she panted, reaching to me with trembling hands.

She needed a knot, but she never begged for one. Just my name. My cock. My fingers.

"Please," she whined once more, stumbling forward.

I caught her in my arms, pulling my fingers free of her soaked pussy, hiding my grin as she sobbed out her objection. I'd seen her wild and anxious and frightened, but I hadn't realized that same desperation would be applied in urgent, explicit demands for fucking. I'd imagined my little birdy as shy and skittish. But she grew claws and sharp teeth to express her hunger, liked when I pinned her in place or bit around her nipple.

She was perfect.

Faith clung to me as I cranked the water off and then bundled her up in my arms. She would feel better in the nest. Also, that was where the condoms were.

It made me feel safe.

I'd made an omega feel safe, not by restraining myself, not being gentle. I'd been strong, fucking angry, and powerful. She'd seen all that, and it had made her wet. For *me*.

Faith's lips latched onto the corner of my jaw as I lifted her out of the tub. She liked that spot, kept nibbling on it and whimpering as I worked her up.

"Fuck me," she whispered, as if I could somehow forget that a beautiful woman was begging me to be fucked.

Not likely.

"Nest first, birdy," I said, but I only did a cursory sweep over our skin with the towels before tossing them on the counter and carrying her into the bedroom.

She shivered and snuggled closer, and I glanced at the dark fuchsia hue of the sky outside the window. How much longer did I have with Faith?

She wants me, I reminded myself. If Bear came back, he could wait his turn.

Faith hurried ahead of me into the nest, diving in as I opened the curtains, and I paused on the threshold, staring in as she settled.

She spread out on her back, legs stretched to either side and knees bent, a shameless offering. Her pussy looked as deep and pretty and pink as the sky behind me, open and shining with arousal, gaping with need.

"What do you need, birdy?" I asked, just to hear her say it again.

"You," she moaned, rocking her hips up into the empty air. No hesitation, no shyness.

Shameless desire, all for me. I fell to my knees, a little dizzy at the declaration and her thick perfume in the nest. The curtains hit my back as I drew them down. The light was golden in this enclosed cozy space, little droplets of water catching the bulbs' glow like stars on her skin.

That cunt flexed in eager welcome as I reached out, brushing a hand up and down the inside of Faith's thigh, and she wiggled her way closer like she could just help herself onto my cock.

"Condom and lube, birdy," I chided, tapping two fingers over her clit and making her gasp.

"I don't *need* lube," she huffed, but she was stretching an arm back to where Bear had said I would find it, breasts pointing high in the air in invitation.

I leaned forward, ducking my head and wrapping my lips around one of those sweet offerings, sucking on the budded tip. She was probably right. Even after showering I could easily slide two fingers back in, which I did eagerly.

She dropped the supplies within reach, and then her hands were stroking through my wet hair, holding my mouth to her breasts. I nudged my ring finger at her opening and wiggled in with a soft resistance that just made my omega moan and rock into the touch.

"Yes, yes, *more*, please."

I grinned, nibbling my way over to her other nipple, and teased her with the press of my pinky finger.

Faith's grip in my hair tightened, her back arched, and her slippery sex sucked the digit in.

"Oh god, Chance, yes!"

My eyes widened, and I pulled away from her breast with a little trail of saliva catching in the air before breaking.

Faith was working herself onto my hand eagerly. I stroked

inside of her, and she moaned as I found that spongy, soft opening ring Bear had explained to me. She fucking took four fingers like a queen.

Like an omega, I reminded myself eagerly.

I cleared my throat to try and hide the ragged need in my voice. "Bet you'd like all five fingers in you," I said, and Faith's eyes widened, staring up at the ceiling. A moment later, she grew even hotter and slicker, and it slid out to pool in my palm.

I glanced at the lube and realized she was definitely right. At least where it concerned her cunt. A filthy, hot, depraved idea occurred to me. One Bear might disapprove of later. But my birdy?

"You want that, birdy? Want my hand filling you up?"

Her mouth was hanging open, chest heaving, and her eyes fell shut as she nodded.

"Look at me, Faith," I snapped, and her eyes flared wide again, chin tucking to her chest. I arched an eyebrow, letting my fingers sink deeper, stroking around her lips and clit with my thumb, petting her thigh with my free hand. "Do you want me to stuff you with my hand?"

Her tongue wet her lips and her eyes were practically black, but she rocked on my hand and more glossy desire slipped out. "Yes," she said softly.

Jesus. Holy angels. This fucking woman.

"You want my fist, birdy? You want my fist working you like it's a knot? Making you scream?" I tried to sound calm, but the tremble in my words was obvious.

"Fuck yes," Faith said, thighs shaking.

I stroked her with my thumb and she shuddered and fell limp again, but her heels spread farther apart in offering.

It seemed easy at first, and Faith moaned in gratitude with every subtle adjustment.

I shifted, hovering over her to be sure that slack and dazed expression on her face didn't switch to pain. The first knuckle of my thumb went in smoothly, like her body had just been waiting for the full set. Faith was breathing like she was running a marathon, her cheeks flushed and lips swollen, looking like an absolute wet dream. I could feel the resistance of her opening, the cramp of my hand where she crushed already bruised knuckles, but she just kept leaning in, swallowing me up. It wasn't until we got to the second knuckle that her brow furrowed.

I glanced down and groaned at the sight of her stretched on my hand, red and wet and so tight, I could feel her pulse.

"Don't stop," she whimpered.

I twisted my hand, let the ridge of my fingers stimulate her hypersensitive flesh, and Faith thrashed and released a high-pitched keening sound. I didn't want to hurt her. I'd seen Ghost's knot plenty of times, and it seemed roughly fist-sized, maybe a little less. Bear's was probably bigger. But was that different for omegas?

"Chance," Faith moaned, rocking and bracing her heels against the bed, eyes rolled back.

Not pain. *Need.*

I nudged as she ground down, and then with a sudden pressure around my hand that stole my breath, I was in, and Faith...

Faith was losing her mind. She howled and immediately began to pulse and gush around me. I curled my fingers slowly and the change made her wild, shaking and panting and whining and coming on my fist like I was giving her the world's best orgasm with a cherry on top.

"Yes, yes, yes, oh fuck, don't stop—" she pleaded. I shifted, sank in a little farther, rolled my wrist, and a sudden splash of fluid hit my lap as Faith screamed and squeezed my hand like a throbbing vise.

I couldn't breathe. My cock was painfully stiff, sticky head nuzzling between Faith's asscheeks. I reached down with my free hand, stroking my length in an attempt at relieving the pressure there, but it only made the ache worse. I needed to be inside of her.

Faith moaned and squirmed on my fist, hands clutching the pillows behind her as she trapped herself in an endless cycle of release with hitches of her hips.

"You want more, birdy?" I asked, hopeful and doubtful at the same time.

"Yes, yes, yes, more!"

I abandoned my desperate cock, teasing my fingers around

Faith's stuffed opening and then down to her ass. "You wanna be filled here too?" I asked, biting my own lip as she gasped and stilled, my fingertip pressed to her hole.

If she said no, I would get her off until she couldn't stand anymore, finish on her belly, and rub my scent into her until even Bear would notice the mark.

"More," she whispered, wiggling again, crying out in pleasure, gripping on my fist and slicking me up.

My breath hitched at her answer, and I had to twist and strain to reach the lube.

Sometimes I was cruel to Ghost, fucking him without enough prep. He liked it that way—he didn't come to me because I was sweet to him. But I wasn't going to mess up with Faith. She needed to be stretched and ready. The orgasms were making her crazy and horny, but it wasn't about to make her ass prepared to take a cock for what I figured was probably the first time.

With a clumsy, one-handed fumble, I coated my fingers in lube and bent down, kissing Faith's stomach and breasts, distracting her as I reached for her puckered hole.

She grabbed onto my head eagerly, trying to pull me up to her mouth, but I laughed and worked my way down to her belly button instead, licking into the little dip and tasting her sweetness. She tensed as I pressed a finger to her hole, and I wedged my index finger in to the knuckle and paused, letting her test the sensation. Remembering the way she responded to filthy questions, I teased her.

"You gonna open here for me too, birdy? Let your man stuff your greedy holes?"

Faith whined, and I hissed as she tightened further. I shifted my knees a little more, let my breath cascade over her clit.

"You wanna know what it feels like to be stuffed with my fist and cock? You gotta let me in."

"Lick," Faith whispered, and my heart leapt into my throat.

I blinked up at her, black eyes watching my lips hover over her sex, her swollen clit practically pulsing before my eyes.

I pointed my tongue out, stretched it towards her clit, barely pressing, and Faith growled and ground down on my fist. My finger sank into her ass, and her mouth opened in shock.

I lapped at her once in reward, and she collapsed, going soft, letting me in a little deeper.

"It's good, isn't it? Your needy pussy likes to be filled. And your ass..." I tested a second finger at her hole and she flexed, granting me tight entrance. "Oh yes. Your ass is a little slut too."

Faith gasped, and I only wondered if I'd pushed her too far for a moment before she was fucking herself between my fist and fingers with fresh urgency.

"You're gonna have to help me put the condom on, birdy," I said, grinning as I twisted my hands, scissoring my fingers in her ass to stretch a little more. She hissed and wrinkled her nose for a moment, but just as quickly pushed herself deeper on my fingers.

This was probably not what Bear had in mind for getting creative...or maybe not. Maybe he'd tried all sorts of shit working as a service alpha. I hunched, licking and sucking on Faith's clit —couldn't knot an omega and eat her out at the same time as an alpha, so I had that going for me—as I added a third finger, and she came, one hand flying up into my hair.

She was ready.

I rose up to my knees, gently pulling my fingers from her ass, grabbing the condom packet and ripping it open with my teeth.

Faith was limp, but she blinked at me and reached down to help. She was clumsy, maybe a little inexperienced, but I guided the condom on and passed her the lube, my head falling back with a groan as she stroked me with far too gentle hands. One day, I would teach her how to jerk me off, to swallow my cock. I wondered if she'd let me hold her face and fuck that mouth. I'd be sweeter to her than Ghost, but I had a feeling she'd like to be used a little dirty. We'd take it slow to start until I knew for sure.

Not that double-stuffing her with my fist and cock could rightly be considered slow.

I rocked into her hands, testing my resolve to not just finish like this a little too closely, and waited to catch her eye.

"You good, birdy? You want this?"

Her eyes were black with desire, chest and cheeks flushed, lips wet, but I wanted to hear her voice too.

"I want everything from you, Chance," she said, and I thought my heart might've died in my chest for a second. But it beat twice as hard a moment later, and I leaned in, catching her lips in a slow, deep kiss, stroking her tongue with mine, rubbing my knuckles inside of her and fighting my grin as her cunt clasped me.

My hand was starting to cramp, but I wasn't fucking giving up this moment until I had to.

I pulled away as Faith gasped for breath, settling back on my heels and pulling her over my lap with my hand on her hip.

"Spread those cheeks for me, birdy."

Faith's eyes widened, face red, but her trembling hands reached for her own ass, gripping hard and spreading like such a good girl. A perfect, sweet slut. She hiccuped and gasped as my fist shifted inside of her while she moved. The new angle distracted her long enough for me to position myself at her ass, pressing in slowly.

She'd contracted a little as I'd gotten the condom on, and I watched her face shift. The tension folding her brow at the initial pinch and burn, the rapid rise and fall of her chest as I breached the resistance, sinking in. I squirted more lube onto my length to be safe, and then started to pump.

Fuck. Fuck, I could feel the pressure of my fist. And Faith's expression was going slack and helpless, her breath short, eyes searching the empty space above us.

"Tell me, birdy," I called to her, drawing her back to me. "Tell me how it feels."

"So full," Faith whimpered.

I fucked in deeper, ignoring the way her squeezing my cock mirrored the clench of my heart, the sharp spike of pleasure in the base of my spine.

"Too much?" I asked, but I already knew her answer.

"Nooo," she moaned, rolling her hips into me. "So good. I—I —Oh god, Chance, I'm going to come again."

She was; her cunt sucking on my fist, ass tightening and trying to refuse me deeper entrance. But I was addicted to the feel of her, and I slid in easier with every thrust, well-prepped for her, forcing her to take more of me.

"Play with your breasts, make them pretty and pink for me, and I'll suck on them as you come on my fist," I snarled.

Faith obeyed immediately, and I gaped at the sight of her, ecstatically mindless, all sensation and need. She pinched and pulled at her nipples, grabbed the flesh of her breasts as she shuddered through one release and into another until she was too deep in the storm to focus on the process. I bent over her, wrapped an arm around her back to arch her for the taking, and bit down on one breast roughly before soothing it with my tongue.

I sank as deep as I could in her ass from this position and used my fist to stroke myself as I fucked her, sucked on her tits, drove us both into a frenzy of grunts and cries. My balls were slick with Faith's pleasure, and her ass was so tight around my cock it was like I was being strangled from there to my throat.

"Oh, Chance, oh—I—I—"

Faith howled, legs knotting around my waist and body tensing as a head-to-toe shudder claimed her. It claimed me too. I drove as deep as I could as she dragged me down with brutal flexes of muscle around my cock, buried my groans into her breasts as I bucked weakly to my finish, lightning behind my eyes and sweet almond and coconut on my tongue.

Our breaths were ragged as we stilled. My thighs burned and my fist pounded with the need to be freed and my dick felt... tenderized, actually. I grinned into Faith's skin, and her fingers stroked through my hair.

"Wow," she whispered.

I laughed, sitting up just enough to look at her. She looked slack and soft and sleepy, eyes blinking slowly. She'd bitten her own lip and it was swollen and red, but I couldn't reach it like this.

"Mmm," she hummed, shivering with an aftershock. I bit back my groan. I needed to escape, but I hated the idea of moving, separating from her, so I braced through the gentle clamps and shudders and caught my breath, nibbling on a nipple until she started up again.

Too much.

I pulled free slowly, cock first, hand gently flexing and stretching, carefully dragging out. Faith came again with a whimper as my knuckles tugged out, but we both sighed as she settled quickly. My hand was red and a little swollen...and wet as hell. I brought my fingers to my mouth and licked, groaning at her flavor. She had coated me and she tasted like fucking candy, and I found myself suddenly starving.

Faith watched with a hazy interest as I cleaned the hand that had been in her, and I blushed as I realized I probably looked like a little kid who had stuffed his whole fist in cake batter. But she didn't laugh. She stretched and sighed, a lazy smile spreading over her lips. Her sex was red and swollen, nipples bitten, new marks from my kisses decorating her skin.

"That was fucking incredible," Faith breathed out, casual and honest.

My dick almost got hard again at the praise.

Her arms flopped back over her head, total surrender and ease. Because of me. Because I'd fucked her so good, even as a beta when she was an omega approaching her heat.

I glanced down at myself and realized I was kind of a mess and I needed to get rid of the condom and clean up. But all I really wanted to do was spread myself out over Faith and kiss her until she fell asleep...or wanted to fuck again. I wasn't really sure which sounded better.

"You just gonna stare or will you cuddle me?" she mumbled.

I laughed and rose up to my knees, groaning at the stiffness. "Clean up and then cuddle you. Maybe stare too."

She hummed, frowning slightly and glancing at the curtains behind me.

I dove in, pressing my mouth to hers for a quick, rough kiss. "Super fast. I'll be right back." She sighed and nodded and I scooted away, moving quickly to the bathroom.

I was in the middle of washing up when I heard the bedroom door open. I'd left the bathroom door partially open, and I kicked it farther to find Bear paused at the entrance. He was sniffing the air curiously and I froze, glancing down at the floor to where my clothes had been abandoned.

Bear grinned, and he didn't look like he gave two fucks that I was buck ass naked in his bathroom.

"I take it you guys had a good night," he said in low greeting.

I huffed out a laugh, overly aware of my still slightly sore hand that had just been wrist-deep in the omega only a few feet away from us.

"It ended on a high note," I admitted, deciding to leave the details out. "But we had a visit from a couple Wasted early on. They never saw Faith, but they might've caught a whiff of her on me. I chased 'em off."

Bear's hands clenched at the news and he pulled his phone out, typing quickly—probably a text to King to let him know. "She's okay, though?"

"See for yourself," I suggested with a shrug. When he looked away I swallowed hard, a sudden spark of nerves buzzing through me. I couldn't decide if I'd feel better with clothes on, but I'd promised Faith a cuddle and I wasn't letting Bear get in the way of that, no matter what.

I followed him out, the room now dark aside from a little glow from a flickering street lamp outside. He parted the curtain of the nest and his response was immediate—a soft smile and a low, warm laugh.

I glanced in and found Faith sprawled like a starfish, lips parted and sleepy breaths puffing out.

"Wore her out, huh?"

It was impossible to keep my chest from puffing with pride as I answered, "Got creative."

Bear's phone chimed, and he frowned at the screen briefly. "Hmm...King wants the details. Come curl up with our girl, and we can brief him in text," Bear said.

And without another look, he kicked off his shoes and started to undress.

Our girl.

I ducked into the nest, lifting one of Faith's legs to slide into her side, drawing her into my chest to make room for Bear...or just to be greedy.

"Smells like a satisfied omega in here," Bear said. "Did you use the vibrating knot toy?"

I blinked at that, a smile sneaking onto my face as Faith rolled to face me and buried her nose in my throat. "No, but I will next time," I said.

Bear only stripped down to his briefs, but there was enough light to tell that his knot would almost definitely be as big or bigger than my hand. Man was terrifyingly hung.

"I used my fist as a knot," I blurted out.

Bear blinked and then flipped and flopped back onto the mattress. "She fucking loved it, didn't she?"

I sat up and nodded. Faith's lips were curling up at the corners, and I had a feeling she was listening to us.

"I, uhh...fucked her ass too."

Bear's eyes widened. "At the same time?"

I nodded.

His mouth opened and closed a few times. "Well," he said finally, brow slightly furrowed but the rest of his face relaxed. "I'm a little jealous now. Think she could take both of us at once?"

I would die, I thought, but it would be worth it. I glanced down at Faith. Her lips were parted and her breathing was growing a little heavy against my throat. I grinned and stroked her hip.

"I think she'd take us both and beg us for more," I said, leaning down and kissing her ear, letting my tongue slip in briefly. She shivered but continued to pretend to sleep, so I figured she was still satisfied with my efforts.

"Greedy little omega," Bear purred fondly.

"Our girl," I whispered, kissing her ear again, nibbling on the lobe. I settled finally and reached across Faith, and Bear passed me the phone, open to King's texts.

I could tell Bear about how hot Faith had gotten watching me fight the Wasted, but I was strangely possessive of that fact. I'd share her with him in all sorts of ways if we were going to be pack, but I wanted to keep that one kernel for myself for now.

Faith's lips pursed against my throat, a secret kiss, and I smiled as I typed out a message.

One appeared from King as I was typing. *Send Chance down to tell me himself.*

I frowned at the summons and then remembered Bear's plan to rope King into accepting Faith. I opened the camera and turned it to face me, glancing at Bear and arching an eyebrow. Faith and I were on the screen. She was still pink-cheeked with pleasure, marked with kisses and playful bites, and her breasts were hidden against my chest and under her arm, but there was a soft curve of one on the side. Bear grinned and nodded at me. I snapped the picture and then sent it to King, adding, *Can't, sorry. Here's what happened.* to the start of my original text.

A response bubble popped up, blinking at us for a few minutes, but no answer came and it eventually disappeared.

I wasn't sure if that was progress or not, but I figured King could come and find me if he had a problem with it. But he never did, and the three of us fell asleep in the nest, tangling closer together until Faith was sandwiched between me and Bear, wearing a dopey smile even in sleep.

I probably wore one too.

I thought the heat had started the first time Bear had knotted me. Or the night Chance had basically fisted my brains right out of my pussy and then taught me that anal was terrifying and fantastic and necessary.

I'd been wrong both times.

I'd managed to wake the next morning, shower, eat a meal, and feel halfway normal as I floated in the kiddie pool, watching a storm roll past Dead End from the west, clouds rolling across the sky for two hours without ever bringing any rain.

Chance and Bear took turns hanging out with me, but King was demanding their attention and he wouldn't come near me.

I'd heard Bear's plan and caught Chance sending the photo of us to King. They wanted him to form a pack for me. They hadn't said so to me directly yet, but they were right that King was the challenge, not me.

I would accept the surly, silent alpha. I needed a pack. And his scent made me wet.

What they failed to realize, on some level, was that I was their best weapon. They were trying to coax King's interest without alerting me to the plan.

But as my skin grew hot and tight and the sun came out from

behind the threatening clouds, clarity came in the form of hind-brain instinct and a sudden rush of arousal bolting into my core like molten candy.

I stood from the pool just as Chance glared up at the sky from where he'd been throwing knives into a round target.

"Ready to head inside?" Chance asked.

I nodded and shivered as a surprisingly cool breeze circled the backyard. Slick fluid kissed my inner thighs.

"Bear is in King's office?" I guessed, stepping out of the water.

"Think so. He'll be done soon, though. We can head upstairs or get you a snack."

I walked toward the door, picking up the large towel left for me, but not wrapping myself in it. My skin was too hot, and I didn't want to bury my scent in cotton.

I could take Chance to the kitchen, coax him into fucking me there...

Instinct rebelled immediately. It was close to King's office, but too full of scents and too open. No, I had a plan.

"Can I go grab Bear?" I asked, chewing on my bottom lip as I walked backwards toward the door, Chance following me.

"From King's office?" Chance asked, brows raising. He glanced over me head to toe, and his smile twitched with humor. "Actually, yeah. I'll meet you guys upstairs?"

I nodded, and Chance smiled warmly at me as I bumped into the doorway. He leaned in, opening it for me, rubbing his cheek to mine.

"Take my towel?" I rasped as cold air-conditioning rushed over my skin, pebbling my nipples.

"You got it, birdy," Chance said. I wasn't sure if he realized who exactly I was intending to bait, but he winked at me and seemed to understand the general idea. Maybe he just thought I would be as tempting to King as I meant to be to Bear.

We parted, heading in opposite directions.

King's office door was open and I slowed as I approached, letting his scent and some of Bear's drift in my direction. My skin flushed further, breasts growing heavy and sore, pussy throbbing as I breathed them in, let my perfume bloom. The voices inside paused, and I stepped through, keeping my gaze down to avoid King's.

"Fa—Butterfly, you okay?" Bear asked.

He was seated in front of King's desk, and I hurried there, aware of the sharp points of my nipples now visible through my bikini top, my arousal pooling more than the swimsuit could really contain, my perfume heavy around me.

I ignored King's shadow behind his desk, pretended my entire focus was Bear, and reached his side. Without hesitating, I climbed over the arm of the chair and into Bear's lap, straddling him.

Bear stiffened in surprise, and I moaned as I pressed myself down. "Heat's starting," I gasped out.

It was true. The effect of pressure on my clit was immediate, and the resulting blaze inside of me was like a house fire where all the windows had been thrown open. Even though I'd come with a goal, I forgot about King's presence at my back—his perfect view of my bare skin and barely concealed ass—as I started to rock and grind on Bear. I hid my face in the familiar shoulder and panted out a breath, helping myself to the friction that instinct craved. Bear purred for me and I shuddered.

I would come like this, in front of King, if Bear weren't quick to remove me from the room. Would he let it happen, just to tempt his friend? His hands grasped my thighs, and he pushed me down for one second. Behind me a soft rumble sounded, and I wasn't sure if it was a growl or a purr.

"I need to go," Bear said, hauling me up in his arms, holding me in place even as I squirmed into him. "Only call for emergencies."

"Got it," King's strangled voice answered.

Bear backed us up for a moment, then turned on his heel, and I looked at the other alpha for the first time. His knuckles were white, gripping the arms of his chair, eyes immediately fastened to mine, dark and angry and...yes, hungry. I worked myself against Bear's growing erection and wet my lips, gasping as I stared back at King. Bear wrapped an arm around my hips and pressed me to him even harder, offering relief and more fuel to my needy sounds. Then we slipped into the hall and out of sight, leaving King behind to his resentment.

Bear hurried toward the stairs and stopped before we crossed in front of the main doors, twisting and pinning me to the cold, flat wall.

He dug his hips into mine, growling into my ear. "You are a wicked girl, aren't you? I should deny you my knot for that game," Bear teased.

"Why?" I answered in a breathless whisper, leaning back to gaze up at him as he continued his slow grind. "Aren't we on the same team? Fuck me here."

Bear's laugh was low and dangerous. "So he can hear you? Smell you? Think about what it would be like to drop you onto his own knot?"

I whined and nodded. I'd liked the look in King's eyes, liked the idea of him watching me sink onto Bear's cock right in front of him, not touching or speaking, needing me and denying us both.

Bear swallowed hard at my nod, glanced down the hall like he was considering my offer, and then back over his shoulder, scowling.

"Too dangerous. Dunno if the Wasted are coming back." That sobered me a little, but then Bear's eyes lit up as he added, "But I can do this."

He shifted and I gasped as he pushed my swimsuit crotch aside, thrusting two fingers inside of me without preamble. I cried out in approval, squirming on the digits, and he pressed his thumb to my clit, letting me find my own release on his hand like he was just another toy for my use. I could see the corner of the double doors on my left, could turn my head to the right and stare at the beam of light over the carpet from King's office.

I grew louder for the hell of it, letting the reluctant alpha hear me whine and whimper and moan on Bear's fingers. A shadow stood in the doorway, stretching across the dingy hall carpet. He was listening—listening and not closing the door on us. Just wanting. Would he step into the hall to watch?

Bear pushed his thumb in a slow, hard circle, callous digging in, and I came with an honest, soft cry of release, shuddering and collapsing against his chest.

"More," I hissed as Bear pulled his fingers free.

"More," he agreed. "But in the nest. Not out here."

King's shadow retreated as Bear carried me up the stairs to my nest.

———

"COME ON, baby, be a good girl for me, won't you," the alpha purred.

I whined and stretched my neck, squirming on the dense point of pleasure and pressure in my core, gasping and managing one word. "Bite!"

Gentle hands pet at my back and shoulders, a mouth grazed up and down my spine, and a second pair of lips sucked on the throat I offered.

I sobbed as I shuddered through a wave, the gesture of a soft mark on my throat a relief while also being a cruel taunt. It wasn't enough, but it made the fog of the heat clear a little from my brain.

"You need to eat, birdy," Chance murmured, wrapping an arm around my waist, bringing his other hand up to my lips, tracing cool fruit over my swollen mouth. Juice dripped down my chin, and Bear's mouth sought it out with his tongue. Mango.

I bit and the flood of fresh, spicy juice made me hum with pleasure. Chance fed me the whole slice and laughed as I caught his fingers with my teeth, sucking him clean too. I settled on Bear's lap as they took turns feeding me fruit from their hands, letting me lick them clean. Bear's knot eased in my core, and I couldn't decide if I was heartbroken or relieved as he pulled free, laying me back in the bed.

How long had it been so far? I didn't know. The fog had set in heavily when Bear and I had reached the nest. I wasn't sore, but I was keenly aware of how well I'd already been fucked, and how much more I still wanted.

Chance's kisses replaced Bear's touch, his mouth brushing

back and forth over my chest as my alpha sagged at my side, watching us through tired and happy eyes.

I reached for Chance's face, tipped it up to mine. He had dark circles under his eyes too, and a small teeth-mark bruise on his throat. I suddenly remembered Bear's fingers tangling in my hair, his voice ordering me to release Chance, and I blushed as I traced a finger around the mark.

Chance just grinned at me. "Chompy little omega. Trying to claim your beta?"

A possessive hunger surged through me and I moaned, drawing Chance to my chest, taking his lips with mine. He tasted like mango too, and we challenged one another in the kiss, tongues tangling. Chance settled between my hips, plunged his cock into me with one stroke, and I gasped as he picked up the rhythm Bear had abandoned.

"This what you need, birdy?" Chance asked, voice ragged as he fucked me in steady, slow thrusts.

"Yes!" I cried, spreading my legs to take him deeper. Bear grabbed one thigh, holding me open and teasing the sensitive skin on the inside.

"Slutty little pussy needs one cock after another filling her up," Chance said.

"Hey, be nice," Bear growled.

"Don't be nice!" I said, clutching Chance's back, grinning back at him as his eyes brightened and Bear laughed. "Keep going."

Chance's smile was a beautiful contrast to his words, all warm and affectionate.

"No, birdy doesn't need nice. Birdy needs to be stuffed, needs to be filled up with cum until it gushes out of her," Chance said, breathless as he grew rougher and faster.

"Pressure," Bear said, and Chance rolled his eyes.

"She doesn't need a knot right now," Chance answered Bear. "Do you, birdy? You want a knot, or you want me to fuck you hard, make you splash all over me, make you scream?"

"Yes, that! That's what I want," I gasped, rocking up into his thrusts, the perverse sounds of our bodies colliding spurring me on.

"And then later, when you start scratching my back and whining and you think you can't come anymore, we'll show Bear how well you take my fist." Chance picked up my hips, changing the angle of his thrusts, rubbing my inner walls.

I howled and arched as I came, and Bear and Chance both laughed. Then the fog of need rose up again, and it was only pressure and glorious agony once more.

———

"How did you get into being a service alpha?" I asked.

Chance was snoring softly at my back, and Bear looked like he was about to drop asleep himself, fighting the urge to keep me company. I was restless, aware of the desire hovering at the edges, waiting for its next moment to strike.

"I only did one rotation in the army, but it was enough to get me through my alpha growing pains, teach me the discipline I'd need," Bear said. "There's a couple pipelines for alphas who leave the military. Most common is security, of course, but servicing is actually a close second. I probably would've gone for the former if a buddy hadn't already lined me up an interview with the Heat-Ease agency."

"Were you excited?" I asked.

Bear snorted. "I was. Didn't realize what I was getting myself into."

I wagged my eyebrows as he glanced at me, and he sighed and continued.

"I passed the interview fine. But the training was...a little humiliating. They can't just let an alpha get his knot in an omega for the first time on a job. We had to practice," he said.

I blinked at that, staring back at Bear's dark eyes as he arched an eyebrow.

"On silicone," he said.

"With people watching?" I asked, tensing, thinking of the camera in the corner of my little cell.

"In the room," Bear said, huffing out a laugh and shrugging. He squeezed me into his side, twisting to press a purring kiss on my forehead. "But I get it. Even on my first job, with three of the pros with me, I kept it together, but the reality was over-whelming. I went a little wild. Nothing the omega wouldn't enjoy, but I'm glad I was prepared, had partners."

I hummed in thought. "How old were you?"

"Twenty-two. Way too young to want a pack, way too horny to fuck up and lose a job that good."

I tiptoed my fingers across his broad chest. "Did you have regulars?"

"A few, towards the end."

"Was there ever an omega you...wanted to bond?"

Bear purred, started to roll and push me to my back. "No," he said, voice low and heavy. "We always wore the muzzle, it was mandatory. But even without it, there wasn't anyone I would've bitten."

My breath was frozen in my chest as Bear shifted us, not bothering to guard me from his weight, from the dark pressure of his gaze on mine.

"Why did you leave?" I asked.

"I stopped feeling...human, I think. I felt like a tool. It's not about the alpha during an omega's heat, at least not in the agency. Sometimes, even just at home alone, I forgot how to be myself, serve myself."

My brow furrowed and I reached up, cupping Bear's face above mine. He was a little hazy, but something had been happening during the heat. I wasn't sure if it was just Molly's guess being correct—that I would heal with the right medica-tions and time—or that this good alpha above me and all his purring was doing the trick. Either way, I was grateful to be able to study him now in all his richness and strength.

"I quit and left town, searched for a way to be selfish again," Bear said.

"And ended up tripping over an omega who can barely func-tion, who doesn't know how to manage her first heat," I said, a little bitter worry slipping out in the words. Would Bear resent how much I needed him?

If he did, it didn't show in his broad smile, in the glitter of his gaze as he settled his hips into mine and ducked his head to whisper in my ear.

"Butterfly, if you think I'm not being selfish by stealing this time with you, you haven't been paying attention."

I gasped as the head of Bear's cock dipped inside of me. His hands stroked down my sides softly before taking a sudden bruising grip of my ass, pulling me onto his length.

"If you think I'm not taking *very* personal enjoyment from fucking you..." He paused, groaning and thrusting into me a few times, my whines immediate and embarrassing. "That I'm not kissing you 'cause I love the taste of you," he added, mouth claiming mine as we moaned and moved together.

My legs wrapped around his hips, the space he filled so familiar to my muscles now that my inner thighs understood the ache of his hips as a fact. His hand slid back up to my back, arms circling and tightening around me.

"Even holding you is selfish for me, Butterfly. I wanna be good to you, I do. Wanna do right by you. But there's nothing about the way you feel right now, the way that you're looking at me, that I'm not enjoying selfishly."

"Bear," I gasped, riding him as he gazed down at me. "Bear, I want you. I want you to be—"

His head dove down, lips colliding and caressing mine in a hushing, possessive kiss.

"I know, Butterfly. I know. Just a few more pieces to put together first," he whispered against me. "And this," he said, stroking in and out of me. "This first."

I caught his face in my hands, pulled him back down for another, bit and sucked at his lips as he fucked me gently, thoroughly, until neither of us could stand it and our bodies grew urgent and demanding again.

———

I woke to the sound of growling, stiffening between the broad male frames that surrounded me. But then the hollow gnawing of my stomach clawed through me and another growl echoed.

Oof. I was starving.

The frenzy of the heat had renewed after a few quiet hours

and my conversation with Bear, and I couldn't remember now the last time I'd eaten.

Bear and Chance were collapsed on either side of me. Chance had dark stubble coating his cheeks, soft red scratches on his chest and sides, and chapped lips. Bear's dark circles under his eyes had grown, and his lips were bruised too, his normally tidy beard a little unruly around the edges.

I'd worn them out. And with a quick glance at myself—beard burn over my chest, my inner thighs red and abraded, my sex still swollen—I realized I'd worn myself out too.

Which would be fine, except that...

My cunt clenched as my stomach growled, twin cravings pounding through me, and I swallowed my whimper.

The heat wasn't over.

I crawled to the foot of the nest, searching for the snacks Chance had stashed, but all I found were empty bags and wrappers and bowls. Behind me, my men continued to sleep soundly, bodies weary. I knew if I woke either of them, they'd press me down into the bed again, feed at least one of my needs for the moment. But they looked so exhausted.

Bear's words from hours or days ago echoed through my head.

Just a few more pieces to put together.

I wasn't sure what all of them might be, but I was confident about at least one.

Tentatively, I parted the curtain in front of me, wincing at the bright sun streaming through the window. The air outside of the nest was a little fresher, but still comfortingly familiar, and my eyes widened at the sight of a cooler sitting in the corner.

Reinforcements!

I grabbed Bear's shirt up off the floor and slid it over my head, crawling over to the cooler. Inside were apples and a jar of peanut butter. Crackers and cheese slices. A can of the sparkling water Bear knew I loved too. I helped myself to a small feast, feeling a little like a scavenger, sitting alone on the floor, stretched and sore and starving.

I could just see inside of the nest from where I sat, Chance's slack body, chest rising and falling with weary breaths.

Bear was trying to make me a pack, but he couldn't convince King to be my alpha while he was busy fucking me through oblivion. I recalled the icy stare of the other alpha as Bear had carried me out of his office, and my body responded immediately with fresh arousal and a demand for more attention.

I glanced at the door of the room. I hadn't walked around the clubhouse on my own yet. The idea felt both illicit and dangerous, like I might be snatched by Omikron the second I stepped outside on my own.

But Omikron hadn't found me yet. And the risk might be worth the reward. I needed a pack, and a pack needed more than one alpha.

It was time to catch King on his throne.

I'd considered changing rooms at least a dozen times since the omega had arrived at the clubhouse. I wasn't sure if I was imagining it or not at first, the gentle bleed of her scent down from Bear's room and into mine, but I knew for certain now that the walls, the carpet, my sheets, and the very air of my suite was infected with her perfume.

I woke with my cock hard every morning, already leaking, knot swollen. This morning I closed my eyes, allowing myself a brief moment of listening to them above me.

The moans, now hoarse after *five days* of fucking constantly. At least at night it seemed constant. I spent my days—and late evenings, and early mornings—in my office, escaping the evidence but not the knowledge of what was taking place in the omega's nest. I could've, or should've, slept on the couch in my office too.

Weakness dragged me back to my bed. My lungs craved her scent. My ears...

Above me, the delicate woman cried out in relief and I groaned in denial, wrapping one hand around my erect cock, squeezing hard on my knot, before pulling away.

Release meant nothing. I'd be hard again in minutes listening to her.

I rolled out of bed, hissing at stiff muscles and aching joints. Why did I feel older than ever these days, sore and tired like I'd been riding with the others?

This was hell.

And hell was the icy water of the shower striking my feverish skin, my brutally stiff cock, providing only a temporary reprieve from the angry desire lurking in my chest. Hell was the pit in my stomach, the ache in my jaw from clenching my teeth. Hell was the way I grew twitchy as I marched my way down the hall to my office, my body protesting the separation of proximity to *her*.

It would've been impossible to believe that Bear and Chance had survived the heat, if I wasn't painfully aware of their continued efforts. Their nuts had to be shriveled raisins by now.

Except that I'd jerked off more in the past week than I had when I was a teenager, and I was still as swollen and trigger-happy to come as I was on day one.

I'd fucked Katie the night we found the omega, thought I'd just been itching for a little relief. But the sex had left me craving more rather than satisfying any urge, and now, with the club girls out and the real object of my interest locked away...

I fell back into my desk chair with a groan, pressing the heel of my hand over my half-hard cock.

Hell was answering emails and texts and calls with a cock that just wouldn't quit, reminding me that I hadn't gotten what I wanted yet.

I settled into business, almost used to this tortured state by now, let the mundane tasks eat away at the hours. Guys like Rider wanted my crown, wanted pussy and power and the reputation that came with being prez of a good club. What they didn't realize was that the reality was fucking bureaucracy and tedium, negotiating with pricks who thought they were better than you every bit as much as they were afraid of you.

There were a few exceptions, at least, I decided as my phone rang.

"Waylon," I greeted, relaxing slightly.

"Hey, King. Got a good crop for you when you're ready," the man drawled.

Waylon Deans was a rancher northwest of Dead End whose land I'd looked into buying. What I'd found instead was a small pack of men I actually respected—rare for me—and a ready-made facility for the exact purposes I'd been planning. Rather than buy the land, I'd struck a deal. Waylon used Last Chance Ranch to grow me a good clean crop of weed, and I helped keep him floating along, holding onto his land.

"Guys will be back in a few days. I'll arrange the pickup," I said. "How's...how's your pack?"

I trusted Waylon and Hank, who ran the bar I used for neutral territory conversations. I didn't know the others in their pack well, but I had a feeling they had that same noble thread running through them as the two alphas I worked with. They might be a good fit for the omega upstairs...if there was a chance Bear would give her up.

"You making polite conversation now?" Waylon asked, low voice chuckling.

I grunted but pushed. "You guys start looking for an omega?"

"Shit no," Waylon laughed. "We can barely keep the lights on —and no, I'm not asking for more work or more help. We're fine as we are."

I might've offered, like he suspected, but I'd just caught a lick of sweetness on the air, my cock kicking in my pants in eager greeting.

"Better off without, in my opinion," I muttered, but my tongue went dry in my mouth at the soft, shuffled footsteps from the hall. "I gotta go. I'll call you when I get the guys assigned."

"Sure thing," Waylon answered, a note of curiosity in his tone.

I hung up and glared at the open door.

"Go back upstairs, princess," I snarled.

My voice had the opposite effect as I'd hoped, and my hips bucked into nothing as her perfume bloomed and floated in my direction, like she'd shot a arrow directly to arouse my cock.

She appeared in the doorway, hair a long, dark tangle piled

high on her head, a baggy black T-shirt of Bear's slipping off one tan shoulder.

"Please," she whispered, eyes pointed to the floor. I wanted to grip her jaw in my hand and tear those eyes up to mine.

"Where the hell is Bear?" I asked, only slightly ashamed as I backed my chair away from my desk, trying to keep space between us.

She walked fearlessly forward.

"Sleeping. I...didn't want to wake them."

"Well, you better—"

Her eyes lifted, all fawn brown as they met mine, cutting through my warning. She brushed a hand over the back of the chair in front of my desk, walked slowly around the corner. "I want you. Please."

There was a little crack in her voice, and for a moment I was almost fooled by that one note. But there was a wariness in her gaze, like she was waiting for me to bark, to throw her out on her ass.

I stood from my chair and watched her steps falter, not sure if I was pleased to see the hesitation or if it made me vaguely queasy.

"I know what you're up to, girlie," I growled. I would not bark at this woman. I wasn't fucking Preston Bowers. But I'd remind her that I was alpha. "You come any closer, and what you'll get is a punishment, not a reward."

I realized suddenly that I'd made two rather large mistakes. One was that by moving back from my desk, I'd put myself against the wall and made room for her in front of me, an empty space she slid into easily, suddenly just inches away from my twitching hands and throbbing cock. The second was the warning I'd given her. She didn't look scared at all. Her eyes lit up, cheeks flushed.

"What kind of punishment?" she breathed, red tongue sweeping out over swollen lips.

Fuck.

"Princess—" I growled once more, wondering if maybe a little bark *wasn't* in order.

"Faith. My name is Faith. Please, just let me—"

Her knees bent, eyes lifted to mine as she started to drift down. I realized with a hungry horror what she would do, what she wanted, and how *badly* I craved letting her have it, how good it would feel, what a relief it would be to finally give in.

I grabbed her shoulder and her eyes widened in excitement. But I pulled her up and twisted her around, only half-aware of my actions, regretting every one of them as they happened. She was small in my hands and so easy to push down onto the table, her breath puffing out of her in a shocked gasp and a low answering moan. Bear's shirt rode up just enough to offer me a glimpse of rounded flesh, and then my free hand flipped the gray fabric up. She had fingertip bruises on her ass. Her thighs flexed as she rose up to her toes, hands spread and planted on my desk.

Heat blazed on my palm before I realized what I'd done, the noise cracking in the quiet room.

Faith, her name echoed in my head. *I'm sorry*.

Faith moaned, lifting that ass into my palm where I'd spanked her. Her perfume exploded, leaving me dizzy, and I watched cum and arousal slip out from between those red and glossy lips.

"More," she gasped.

If I were a weaker man, I'd lie and say I was helpless in that moment, drowned in her scent and my own self-denial for so many days. In truth, I was relieved she begged, because I didn't want to stop now. Not after finally feeling her skin in my hands, her warmth near mine.

My hand rose and fell as a dark glee bloomed in my chest. Her ass jiggled as I smacked her and a bright, muffled cry was pressed to my desk.

"I told you," I said.

"I want this," she whispered, turning her head and pressing her cheek to the smooth surface, gazing back at me with serene eyes.

"Good."

I struck quick, once on each cheek, and she rocked into the force of my hand as if it were my cock filling her. I groaned as she moaned, outraged and delighted, not sure of what directions the feelings were coming from.

I didn't make her beg again, working her quickly, spanking her ass red under my burning hand, keeping her pinned in place by her shoulder. She sounded like I was fucking her, little shouts and gasps and whines. She sounded like she had in the nest over my head, driving me mad at night, and I found a sick retaliation as I snapped my palm over her giving flesh. A grateful relief too.

"Oh fuck!" she cried, and I paused, but she wiggled her hips and begged through gritted teeth. "Don't stop! I'm so close."

Fuck. Fuck me, she was going to come from a spanking. It occurred to me to deny her, to really punish her. The only one learning any lesson right now was me. But I wanted the power that came from making a woman come, wanted to watch her and hear her and know that this time it was *me* undoing the omega.

I alternated one side for the other, back and forth, staring at the quiver of her thighs, the slip of her toes against the carpet as she arched for more, a hypnotic focus forming. She called my name, chanted praise, and I watched the mark of my hand form and fade and form again on her skin with one smack after the other.

"Oh god, yes! Ah-ahh!"

I stared, mouth hanging open, breath coming hard as Faith suddenly bucked and writhed, legs quaking and release spurting out in a little dribble. I reached for the fluid and she trembled, nails clawing against the desk. She pressed her pussy into my scorching palm, ground herself against my fingertips, and I watched her coat my skin in that release.

I was hard as stone in my pants, the zipper biting uncomfortably against my cock. My back and arms were tight, saliva coating my tongue and teeth. The hand that had been holding onto her shoulder was suddenly in her hair, dark and thick and knotted from days of fucking. I formed a fist, and she moaned and rutted against my palm as I lifted her head from the table. I needed to drag her up and toss her out the door.

But I wouldn't.

"Fuck me, alpha," Faith said, voice low and throaty and deeply feminine, the sound of a satisfied woman.

Asking for more.

I pulled my hand away from her sex and she whined. I hissed

as I unbuckled my pants, pulled the zipper down, and shoved the fabric to my knees.

I yanked on her hair to draw her gaze back over her shoulder to me. Her pupils were black, pretty face flushed. I wanted to bite those full lips, seal them with mine and keep her from speaking. But the damage was already done now.

"Please," she whispered, eyes wide. There was no wariness now, no hesitation. She looked at me like she did at Bear or Chance, pleading for their touch, needing them.

I watched her as I found her silken, soaked pussy with two fingers and guided myself inside. Dark eyelashes fluttered, but she held my gaze as I sank in, releasing a slow, soft sigh and moan.

I wasn't a romantic idiot. Every woman's pussy felt like heaven after a stressful week or two with only your hand for company. But Faith was plush and burning hot and dripping all over me. She was desperate and relieved and a little victorious too as I kept sinking and sinking and sinking in. God, she took my cock as if she'd been molded to me once and I'd simply lost my way till now.

"You need this cock, princess?" I asked, pressing my hip bones to her flushed red ass.

She nodded, mouth hanging open. It was a shame I couldn't fill that too. If Bear found us now... Would he tear me away from her, or step up to the edge of the desk and join me?

"I needed this cunt," I admitted, narrowing my eyes at her. "But you knew that, didn't you?"

I was surprised that she nodded, but at least she was honest.

"Then you'll understand that I'm not gonna go easy on you," I whispered, drawing slowly out.

She licked her lips and blinked slowly at me, almost drowsy. "Good."

"And when I finally give you my knot," I continued, trying to force the tremble in my voice out of the words, "it's gonna stay there for a long time, until we're both good and done with one another, princess."

Faith smiled, sly and sweet and wicked. And I knew then, just as she did, that my words were a lie.

Done with one another. Like I could have her once and not again.

I slammed in again, hard and fast, smacking against the marks I'd made with my hand, filling her to where my knot swelled and waited for its time. Faith cried out, the smile vanishing, and I was the victor for the moment, before surrendering to what we both demanded.

King fucked me with that same resentful force he'd spanked me with, like he was punishing me for his own desire. I craved that punishment, wishing it would absolve me from manipulating him. Maybe he wouldn't have been able to resist much longer. Maybe he would've come to me eventually, at Bear's bidding or his own.

We'd never know now.

He held me in place, one fist in my hair, another hand wrapped around my hip, and fucked me with simple and rough command. He didn't touch me or pet me or offer me pretty words. He and I both knew this was enough, his breathless grunts and growls and moans, his thick cock pounding in my hungry core, feeding all the pressure and stroke I was trapped in craving. His hips were hard against my ass, reminiscent of the quick, hard smacks of his hand.

"Oh god, King, it's so good," I whined, speaking to his desk as he worked in and out of me. He growled in response, his hand tightening on my hip.

I didn't know this man, had barely spoken to him, only heard little scraps of his character from Bear and Chance. But I needed him. Not just for Bear's plan of a pack, but my own plan too. I needed his scent in my lungs, his grip on my skin, his cock inside of me. I'd needed it for days, and there was a sense of settling now, the rightness of having him even in all his anger.

"I ought to leave you wanting, deny you from coming," King hissed. "But that isn't fucking possible, is it, princess? No, I can feel you already, sucking on my cock, begging me to join you. Not fucking yet."

He stilled as I came, kicking and riding his cock as much as his grip on me allowed me to move. It wasn't enough, a kind of frustration mingling with the release. He laughed and I shivered at the sound, at the low aftershocks trembling through me until I was still again.

And then he resumed his hard, drumming rhythm.

King thought he was finding his revenge, fucking me until I came, making me thrash as he stilled and refused me his knot, his own pleasure, before starting up again as I settled. And it was true that Bear and Chance had given me everything I'd wanted, begged for, even as Bear claimed it was all selfish.

The truth was that I wanted this too. I wanted King's punishments, his pleasure and my own. I wanted to be denied, laughed at, and then driven to a new frenzy.

I wanted the sounds of his ragged breath, the sweat of his palm on my hip, the stretch of his knot pushing and then retreating, stretching me and pulling away again.

"Goddamnit, princess," King growled, fucking me with his knot at my opening, making me wild and weak all at once. "Goddamnit, I can't."

I sobbed as he pulled away, misunderstanding the words for a solitary moment. And then he was thrusting in and deeper in, the knot making its home in me easily after all his teasing of us both. We both howled, King's stomach flattening over my back, tickling me with chest hair and sticking with our sweat.

Heat flashed inside of me as he released, and I remembered vaguely about contraception and condoms, and then those thoughts evaporated as he ground against my ass. We groaned in unison, King's forehead on my shoulder.

He never stopped moving again.

———

I'D ASSUMED his claim of not stopping was a little exaggerated.

But he fucked me on his desk, working his knot in me until I nearly passed out from delirious pleasure. He dragged me into his lap on his chair, bucking softly until I was too limp, stripping off Bear's shirt and teasing my breasts and nipples until they were sore. He hobbled us over to that leather couch, spread me out beneath him, and just fucking kept going. He propped me up against the back cushions, my cheek against the wall, stroked my stomach and thighs with his hands, dragged his lips over my shoulders.

Kisses. Kisses on the back of my neck. I hummed at their softness, and King purred in my ear.

The heat died out in those hours, fucked out of me at last.

I grinned at the knowledge, and then King's face appeared over mine and I realized suddenly he wasn't inside of me anymore. I blinked and stretched, shivering on the couch, my skin sticking uncomfortably to the leather.

"Drink, princess," King rasped.

He was wearing his jeans, but they weren't buckled. I hadn't gotten a good look at him before, but I helped myself now, distantly aware of how clear my vision was. His chest was broad, lines and muscles softer than Bear's but fuller than Chance's, blond curls running down to his belly button. He had scars on his skin, puckered and shining, and I wondered where they came from. The lines on his forehead dug deep, but the ones around his eyes were softer. Gray was eating up the edges of his blond hair and all through his beard. His nose was a little crooked, faintly scarred in the middle, evidence of an old injury. He stilled, watching me as I reached up and touched the spot with shaky fingers.

The plastic mouth of a water bottle touched my lips and I gasped, tilting my head and letting him soothe my parched throat.

His eyes were a deeper shade of blue than before, and the anger on his face was gone.

"I guess that's what I fucked out of you," I murmured, splashing a little water on my chin.

His brow furrowed at the declaration, but he didn't ask me what the hell I was talking about.

"You okay?" he asked, eyes trailing down and over my sprawled form.

There was sort of a gaping, hollow sensation between my legs I was electing not to examine further, and my ass was still hot from his palm, my breasts tender too.

"I've never felt so good," I said honestly.

King looked away, but not fast enough to hide the twitch of his lips in a smile.

"What about you?" I asked. I was too sex drunk to wrap my head entirely around the situation, but I knew that he'd told me to leave and I hadn't. Maybe he'd changed his mind. Maybe my perfume had.

King let out a long sigh, capped the water bottle in silence and set it on the floor, combing one hand through his beard. His mustache was rumpled, and he smoothed it with an absent gesture of thumb and middle finger. Then he turned to me, sliding his hand under my neck, bending down to hover his face over mine.

Blue eyes flashed over mine, trailed over my nose, down to my mouth and back up again.

"Never fucking better, princess," he said solemnly. Then his mouth was on mine.

His beard was soft on my face, mouth confident as it folded over mine in a kiss, opening me up for his stroking tongue. I wrapped my arms around his shoulders and his free arm scooped around my back, lifting me up to deepen the kiss. There was something in the steady confidence of him, or the almost mournful way he'd spoken, that made me want to cry.

Or maybe I was just strung out and exhausted, still hungry, overwhelmed.

King didn't relent, even as he lifted me from the couch, cradling me to his chest. He pulled away slowly, walking toward the door and into the hallway.

"Bear came looking for you while I had you facedown in the

cushions," he said, and I caught the pride in the words. "Told him I'd bring you back to the nest when we were done."

Was Bear angry or pleased? I couldn't tell from King's expression and I didn't want to ask, so instead I tucked my face into his throat and breathed him in. With my back to his chest while knotted, there'd been something more animal than intimate between us. I rubbed my cheek against his shoulder, and his steps faltered.

"Will you sleep with me?" I asked.

Or had he done what he said he would? Fucked and knotted me until he was done with me.

King didn't answer at first, carrying me up the stairs with a careful steadiness, like he was trying not to jostle me in his arms.

"Somebody's gotta keep an eye on things," he said.

I tightened my hold on his shoulders as his steps slowed.

The door to Bear's room was cracked open, and King pushed it open with his bare foot.

Bear was standing inside, fully dressed, smile calm and—I suspected—carefully controlled. "Chance is cleaning up. I'm gonna sort us out a fucking buffet of food. Keep an eye on her?"

King stiffened, still holding me. I thought for a moment he might drop me to the floor and go marching out the door, washing his hands and everything else clean of me. His head jerked in one brief nod, and Bear gave him a pat on the shoulder as they passed one another in the small space.

Bear snuck a kiss to the top of my head and a squeeze of my elbow, then shot me a surreptitious wink as he skirted out the door, shutting it behind him.

I glanced nervously to King. His face was impassive, watching me, and he lifted one brow slowly.

"I guess the princess gets her wish," he said, dry or flat, I wasn't certain.

I reached up slowly, slipped my fingers into the short hairs at the back of his head, and watched his lids lower slightly, the silent vibration of a purr soaking into me.

"Thank you, King."

He sighed and walked to the opening of the nest. The curtains were parted and the sheets had been changed, although the scents were still just right. Bear had known before I did that the heat would end.

King set me on my feet and watched as I crawled into the nest, fixing a few pillows and dimming the lights. When I had settled, he pushed his pants down his hips. His cock was large and dark, the shade of curls around his base and sac deeper than those on his chest. He kicked his pants away and then knelt down at the foot of the bed, bracing his hands on either side of my knees, ignoring the space I'd left for him at my side.

"Don't feel like sleeping yet," he said, eyes on mine as he bent his head. His lips met my knee as he watched me. His tongue flicked out, circling briefly. He raised up slightly and shifted, moving to the other. "You wanna rest, you can do it with my mouth on you."

I wanted King curled around me, holding me like Bear or Chance did, kissing me until we fell asleep together. There was something beautiful and tender as he brushed his lips over my knee, up my thigh a little and then down my shin. It was gentle and reverent, but cold and removed too.

But he'd given me my choice, so I relaxed, accepting whatever King would offer.

———

"LET ME OUT! LET ME OUT!"

The heels of my hands were sore from pounding on the cage, my voice hoarse from screaming, my heart aching from knowing it was useless. I knew what happened to omegas.

"Adam!" I screamed.

Had they caught him too?

"Faith."

"She's been howling the whole way."

"Of course she has. They all do. Ready?"

I would kick and claw and bite and scream when the doors opened. I would fight every day. I would give Omikron hell. I would try to escape at every chance. Until I was free, or Adam had found me.

"Adam! Let me out! Let me out!"

"Butterfly, wake up."

I sat up with a start, sucking in a rough lungful of air, ready to scream again. But with the breath came the scent of the nest, of Bear at my side, his arm wrapped around me. Chance's arm was over my lap and he shuffled up, turning to face me in the nest.

"That's it," Bear soothed, stroking my back as my racing heart started to slow, as I caught my breath as though I'd been running from my own nightmare.

I'd dreamt of the first night. Of the girl who thought she could stand up to Omikron, survive whatever they had in store for her, be a fighter to the end.

The truth was that I'd grown weary too quickly, frightened and ashamed. I hadn't always fought.

The door of the room banged open, and I jolted as Chance scrambled for the nest's opening. But King's scent arrived before he did, yanking back the curtains and standing broad and powerful in front of us.

"What happened?" he asked, words sharp.

"Nightmare," Chance said, and King's shoulders sagged, the sharp edges of his face softening.

He'd left quietly earlier, as Bear and Chance had returned with food. But he'd come now, all ferocious, ready to fight. I must've been screaming in my sleep, echoing the dream. I reached out for him and he was already sighing, a weary resignation as he climbed into the nest.

"Faith," Bear murmured, drawing my gaze to his, dark and warm. "Who is Adam?"

I swallowed under Bear's stare, trying to keep the secret down. Except now I wasn't sure it needed to remain a secret.

I was surrounded by these men. They'd hidden me away from the gang who'd bought me, helped me heal physically, built me a nest. Even King had helped, aside from that horrible alpha he'd called in to try and get me out of his hair. Could I blame him? I knew how much trouble I had hunting me. If I'd been more concerned about these men's safety than my own, I would've left by now.

King's rough hand reached out to my jaw, turning me to face him. He was cold and angry by default, never giving anything away in his expression but his own strength. But there was a possessive focus in his touch, and it made me feel almost as connected to him as I did to Bear, forgetting that he was, by his own admission, reluctant to be involved with me.

"You're safe," King said, and there was no refusing the weight in his voice. "If he hurt you, we'll find him."

My breath hitched, and my eyes widened. "No! Adam is..." I glanced at the others, drew my knees closer to my chest. They needed to know the truth. I'd been hiding here for weeks now, but nothing would change if I just kept myself locked up in the nest. I licked my lips and confessed.

"Adam is my brother. We were separated the night Omikron captured me. I need to find him."

Bear's hand tightened on my shoulder, Chance's fingers linking with mine, and King answered my stare with his own. The truth was out now, for better or worse.

"I can't find shit about this," King muttered, the lenses of his glasses reflecting the bright screen of his laptop. It didn't matter; I knew he was glaring.

"Were you expecting to find information about a global sex-trafficking ring on the internet?" I asked. Not that I hadn't done a little searching myself.

His lips twisted in a deep scowl and he tore his glasses off, massaging his temples with white-knuckled fingers.

"We knew it had to be fuckin' big if she was too scared to go to the Omega Center or a hospital," I pointed out.

King heaved a sigh and dropped his glasses and hands to his desk. "I was hoping she was just...terrified."

Maybe I had been too. Maybe part of me had thought it'd been some shady, but small-scale ring we could sweep out of our territory. But the facilities Faith had described—trembling in my hold—had medical staff and surveillance and hormonal drugs to try and induce her heat. Maybe one of those things would've been believable. All of it combined, all the information she'd offered, led to a huge conspiracy-level organization.

"You think...Preston..."

King scoffed and shook his head, sagging back in his chair. Then he paused and groaned. "Fuck, I don't know. Maybe?"

I'd walked in on him and Faith earlier. She'd been mindless, and he hadn't been much more lucid, a shattered moan hanging from his lips as he'd fucked her like he would die the moment he stopped.

He was back to his usual self now, or close to it, at least. But I'd seen that control snap for once. I wasn't entirely sure if King would crumble or if he really did have the willpower to walk away from Faith. The last thing I wanted was for him to break her heart, but I'd seen enough signs in the past few weeks to guess he wasn't half the cold bastard I'd seen in him before now.

"At least not at an organizational level. Potential customer, maybe," he admitted, brow tangling. I released a soft growl, and King shook his head. "I'm not saying I thought he was the kind of guy who'd buy an omega, I just can't see him higher up the food chain than that. Obviously, I didn't—Never mind. Mistakes were made."

"So we've got the Wasted sniffing around for her," I said, raising one finger, and then adding a second. "This big box store of omega traffickers. Think Preston will become a problem?"

"He's the least of my concerns on that list," King said.

Which wasn't a no. Fuck.

"We have to figure out how to handle the club," he continued.

"Handle them?" I asked.

He arched an eyebrow at me. "I've ordered fucking cleaners to help breeze out some of her scent, but you don't seriously think you can keep an omega under wraps in this place, do you? We need the guys back if we're gonna stand a chance against even the Wasted. And as soon as they realize she's here..."

"Molly or I can get Faith mild suppressants, enough to chill her scent out," I said, trying not to laugh as King wrinkled his nose. Fucker was already addicted to her, I could tell. How fast had he run upstairs when he'd heard her screaming in her night-mare? "We can try and pass her as a beta, but..."

King's jaw clenched. "But?"

"But she'll need to be mine," I said, feigning calm, holding his stare. "She's not going to be club ass. And you're right. I can't hide her in here, and I can't be here and worry about her hiding somewhere else. Hell, we can say she's a beta and my old lady, if she's willing to take stronger suppressants."

King was quiet, eyes flicking back and forth over my face. "And Chance and me?" he asked.

Caught you, I thought, but I refused to savor my victory, at least not in front of King when he might get the urge to punch me in the face.

"You'd have to back off," I said, shrugging. It was the biggest fucking bluff I could come up with, and Faith would probably bite me again if she'd heard it. She and Chance were completely smitten with one another, one-hundred percent wrapped around each other's fingers. She'd never let him slip out the door. I rolled my eyes up to the ceiling, feigning thought. "Or..."

King growled.

"Or we tell the club the truth about her. That she was what we grabbed in the truck raid. That she's an omega, and that she's the exclusive property of the three of us," I said. "And that if anyone has a problem with it, they can take it up with us."

King twisted in his seat, glaring daggers at the wall, probably daydreaming about strangling the shit out of me.

And I felt a bit guilty. I was telling him he either had to jeopardize angering the rest of the club, attract more negative attention, and probably give Rider a leg up in his campaign...or admit that now that he'd touched Faith, he didn't want to fucking stop.

King's worst feelings about pack and omegas were true. My loyalties had shifted. I had sworn myself to the brotherhood of the Dead End Devils, and now that bond was fracturing in favor of a new one, all biology and instinct and hindbrain. But Faith was mine in all but bite now, and I would not give her up.

"Get out," King muttered. "I need to think."

I rose from the chair immediately, pausing to stare down at him. If I was wrong, if he refused to acknowledge any connection to Faith, it would only be a matter of time before we had to leave. King had brought the Devils up from the ashes, and it wasn't a guarantee that he would lose his grip on the club if Chance and I took off, but it was likely.

I'd backed him into a corner, challenged his principles, and dangled the one thing almost no alpha could resist in front of him. But King wasn't most alphas or most men.

I didn't know what he would choose. I could only have faith.

I gripped the handlebars of my bike a little tighter, added gas, savoring the roar of the engine and the vibration of the beast of machinery between my legs. The rest of the club grew small in the circular rearview mirror to my left as I sped ahead on the dry barren road, sun blazing down, baking me through the black leather vest on my back.

Most of the guys had groaned when King's official bidding came through on mine and Rider's phones, as if the crew had fooled themselves into thinking the ride would go on forever. At one point, I would've done the same.

I loved rides as much or more than any of my brothers, couldn't resist the urge to bolt ahead, explore the horizon first. I even loved the puzzle of repairing a bike in the middle of nowhere with nothing but my tools. I was road captain for a reason.

But this time, I'd been chomping at the bit to get back, and the order from King to return had come as a relief.

First order of business would be church, of course, but then the agenda was clear. Get my dick wet, get drunk, probably fuck *another* pussy 'cause the girls would be so excited to have us back, and then...

See what Chance thought of that request of his after two weeks stuck in the club without me.

I'm asking you not to knock.

Because nothing felt as good after I'd gotten loose and sated at Chance's hissing voice in my ear as he stripped me down of all my ego and fucked me into a worthless heap on his mattress.

It'd been the first ride in years Chance had missed, and while his absence was a quiet and small void in general—he was surly and silent, lingering at the edges of our club—it was an irritating and impossible-to-ignore loss for me. A blank space at the corner of my eyes I kept searching for.

Little speckles of Dead End, all but dust on the wavering horizon, appeared at last, and I grinned under my bandana, leaning into the speed of my bike as I charged home.

Roars echoed behind me, the others catching sight of our decrepit little town. And those in Dead End would hear us too. I didn't know if locals would be relieved to hear the club returning and bringing our business with us, or mourn the end to the weeks of peace. But Dead End accepted us for what we were, visited our bar, used the laundromat and the other businesses King owned. Maybe we were their only option, or maybe we were part of the fabric of the town. I didn't care. It was home.

I beat the others back, but only by a few minutes, pulling my bike around the motel and into the vast garage King had built for me to work in and for us to store our bikes. In the morning I would come back, tune everyone up, spend a day in grease and metal and wearing out my body, but tonight I'd enjoy the sparse comforts of the clubhouse.

I crossed the yard to the back of the bar, slowing down at the sight of a bright yellow inflatable pool waiting in the middle of the open area. The water was clear, just freshly used, or would be soon. Gift for the girls? Or a gift for us to watch the girls in, maybe. I grinned and yanked open the door, marching into the relative dark, relying on muscle memory to guide me.

But my steps slowed as I entered. The club smelled...clean. My nose wrinkled at the blank-slate quality of the air, all the surfaces and furniture sterilized.

Had King really taken the trouble to clean the goddamn club

out while we were gone, or had shit gone down to make it necessary?

My eyes adjusted enough to see into the dark, at the same time that sweeter notes reached my nose. Two figures were nestled into a booth near the door to the large conference room we used for church. I recognized the man immediately, all the traditional and poke and stick tattoos, the shaved sides of his head. My body tensed at the sight of him, then relaxed just as quickly in an instinctive relief to be near him again.

What I didn't recognize was the way he was holding some-one's face in his hands, the low sounds he made as he kissed the woman on his lap, the way his mouth stroked hers, deep and possessive. I didn't recognize the slack expression on his face as she pulled away, gasping for air. I sure as hell didn't recognize the way his cheeks swelled and his lips stretched and curved as he stared back at her.

I did recognize her, though, just barely.

"I thought the plan was to get rid of her," I said.

The omega on Chance's lap stiffened, eyes flashing to mine, and I grit my teeth as her hands dug into his shoulders. And that smile on Chance's face, the one I'd never seen before—so foreign I could barely believe I was staring at the right man, as if maybe he had a cheerful twin I'd never fucking heard about—that smile dropped.

Suddenly, I knew it was him because that dark, pissed expression taking over his face was absolutely Chance. It softened again as he turned back to her, leaning in and whispering in her ear, their cheeks nuzzling together, my stomach turning at the sight. She pressed her lips to his, and I couldn't decide if I wanted to tear that smile right off his face or take a picture of it. Because it was *beautiful*, painfully so, and I hated that it was for her, that it existed and I'd never known before now.

Chance helped the omega off his lap, sliding out of the booth before her, blocking her from my sight for a moment before she darted through the meeting door. The air was mild and sweet, her perfume pleasant but not overpowering or mouthwatering.

"The plan changed," Chance said as the door to the bar banged open.

I cringed at the sound of the others arriving, so much I wanted to say—to shout—now trapped in my throat.

Chance glanced over my shoulder, the smooth-as-glass serenity he'd been sporting tightening to his usual scowl. Or maybe not quite as dark as before. He turned on his heel, following after the omega without another glance or word to me.

I wanted to chase after him, grab him and prove to him, and to her, that he was as obsessed with me as I was with him. I wanted to turn around and march out of the club, go to the garage and work on the solvable puzzles and problems of machinery. I wanted to start a fucking fight, get punched in the face and knocked down to the ground.

Rider clapped a hand on my shoulder, nose up to the air. "Jesus, King wash off all the good funk out of the place while we were gone?"

He'd washed the omega's perfume out of the air, I realized, grunting in answer to Rider and letting him carry me along with the others toward the meeting room. My eyes found the omega immediately, sandwiched between King and Bear, and at my side Rider's steps slowed.

"The fuck?" he muttered. "You know about this?"

I shook my head, unable to find my own voice, too busy locating Chance in the corner, back propped against the wall, arms and legs crossed.

King stood from his seat, and the omega leaned into Bear's side, but she gazed up at our prez. She looked almost nothing like the creature I'd seen in the van. She was slim and pretty, with a pile of chestnut brown hair on the top of her head and a natural smile on her lips. Her eyes flicked to the back corner of the room where Chance stood, and I understood that flicker of longing on her face. She was exactly the sort of woman I would distract myself with, then discard when her interest peaked. I hated her.

"Quit gaping and take a seat," King called to us, as a murmur of interest and chuckles rose up behind me.

"Didn't know we could bring club ass to meetings, Prez," Skid joked.

King and Bear just scowled. In her seat, the girl shrunk as we rounded the table. I was at Bear's right, and her scent was clearer, a touch sweeter. Something was muting the intensity of it, but it was a poor disguise, and it covered Bear too, like he'd been dipped in syrup. If the others didn't realize she was an omega, she would still be a tempting as hell beta.

Trouble.

The look on her face—on Bear's and King's and Chance's too —said she knew as much.

"Who's the treat?" another man called.

"Sit," King snapped, and even without the command of a bark, out of the corner of my eye I caught the omega twitching.

The Devil's prez glared out over us with the last scrape of chairs and muttered remarks.

"This here is Butterfly," King said, and he didn't have to point to the woman or even glance in her direction for us all to know exactly whom he meant. "She was sold to the Wasted. We found her in the raid."

King waited for the stir of interest and revelation to sweep around the table. I watched my brothers' faces. There were those who relaxed—the ones Rider and Skid had been stirring up suspicion in on the ride—who were grateful to finally have the explanation for what had seemed like a phony bust weeks ago. And there were those who now stared at "Butterfly" with intrigued hunger, who would easily snap her up for the same purposes the Wasted would've.

"She's club property now, by her own choice," King said, expression hardening as a few hoots of excitement rose up. "What she is *not* is club ass."

"Unless by her own choice, right, Prez?" Rider called, grinning easily up at King with narrowed eyes, drawing up more laughter from his cronies.

Bear had her hand in his on his lap, and her fingers were white as she gripped him.

"She's an old lady. As such, she has our protection," King said, flat and hard as ever, ignoring the slathering grins and stares pointed in the woman's direction. Only half the expressions sobered at the announcement.

"Whose?" I asked, my eyes physically aching with the urge to twist and stare in Chance's direction.

"Mine," Bear said, voice barely stifling a growl.

Now at last the laughter died. There weren't many who would risk pissing off the club enforcer, or any man of Bear's size and reputation.

"And mine," King added, grinding the words out, looking like he was chewing glass as he spoke. But his hand reached for the omega's shoulder, and when her own fingers brushed over his...he didn't soften, but some of that tension turned down.

Silence fell at last. Was it respect or resentment? I wanted to check on the others, but I couldn't pull my eyes away from *her*. She twisted and arched, and her gaze traveled in the same direction mine always wanted to. The small huddle of betas and prospects parted, and I knew the moment Chance stepped out of the shadows, because she smiled and Rider stiffened.

"And mine," Chance said, a quiet warning daring anyone to object or argue. He walked forward to her back, almost within reach of me, and I wrapped my hands around my knees and squeezed there until my legs and arms hurt.

"You're fucking packing up in the club?" Rider hissed, starting to rise from his seat. The movement was quelled with one glare from King.

"I am not," King bit out at his VP before looking around the table. "This is not the first time club members shared an old lady, and it won't be the last. All I need to know right now is if my men, my *brothers*, are going to be loyal to this club and its property. Or if any of you think it'd be clever to give the *Wasted* exactly what they fuckin' want."

"If we'd raided guns or drugs, we'd've gotten an equal cut of the returns," Skid pointed out, a dangerous look in his stare on the omega. "This just doesn't seem to work out so fair."

Bear snarled but King raised a hand, silencing them both. "There's no fucking money. And if it's pussy you want...you'll see plenty of it around here. Called in some friends. But, and mistake me if I'm wrong, we deal in ladies' fucking choice around here." For the first time, King looked down at the woman at his side. "You wanna fuck Skid, princess?"

She was staring up at him, pale and visibly nervous, but she didn't whine or tremble, just shook her head, eyes dropping at the laughter that echoed around the table.

"There you have it," King said, arching an eyebrow. "And if I see any of you fuckers shooting your shot, you'll have the three of us to answer to."

Their expressions were grim, their broad bodies surrounding her. It'd been a long time since anyone had claimed a new old lady, and it certainly hadn't been met with this tension.

Was it that the club knew she was a war prize, snatched from the hands of the Wasted? Or was it all the shit Rider was stirring with King, fissures of resentment and distrust crackling along the surface of the club's loyalties?

King twisted and nodded to Chance, who took the signal to tug Butterfly to her feet. That sure as shit wasn't her name, and she didn't look like some airy carefree creature to me as she tucked herself into Chance's side and followed his lead to the door.

"Now let's cover the rest of this shit with the trip and the Wasted and get you gentlemen into better company," King declared, feigning cheer, gaze tracking Chance and the woman's progress to the door.

I tracked them too, his arm around her shoulder and hers around his waist. A fucking old lady for Chance? Just weeks after he'd fucked me and told me not to show up at his door again?

I called bullshit. At the very least, I wasn't fucking accepting the change. I wasn't giving up Chance.

I stretched my arms over my head and lifted my face into the spray of the shower. I was alone for the first time in days, using Chance's shower instead of the one in Bear's room, which still smelled strongly of the heat and all of our scents.

And for the first time in months, I was on suppressants again. It was almost like getting myself back. I'd spent years on suppressants, living as a beta while on the run with my brother, and going off of them had been like discovering a foreign animal inside of me. The brand Bear had brought was milder, a relieving compromise between the muffled cotton of heavy suppressants and the extreme sensation of being an omega.

I could breathe again, be *me* again.

There was a knock on the bathroom door, and then Chance's head appeared through the foggy distortion of the semi-sheer shower curtain.

"Brought the fluffy towels and shit from Bear's bathroom. You good?"

He didn't approach the shower, and I wasn't sure if I had to invite him in with me...

No. No, I didn't *have* to, but I could if I wanted to. I sighed at the reminder, brushing damp fingers over the ceiling as I stretched to my toes.

"I'm good," I answered.

"'Kay. I'm gonna go steal a couple pizzas from downstairs before the guys get out of church. I'll lock the door."

"Thank you, Chance."

"You got it, old lady," he said, warm and light.

I grinned as the door clicked shut. The words *old lady* didn't mean much to me, but Bear and Chance had lit up when they said it, murmured it as they peppered my skin with kisses. And I would be lying if I said the way King forced it out in the meeting hadn't thrilled me. He held himself at arm's length from me, but wasn't apparently willing to deny himself the claim in front of the others.

Pack, the sedated hindbrain whispered in my head. I was claiming them in my way.

But no bites yet.

I took my time in the shower, and the glass mirror was fogged as I stepped out. Chance had brought the best towels and all of the lovely skin creams and hair nonsense Bear had gotten me. The kinds of products I'd never in my life dreamed of owning.

I wiped the mirror with a washcloth and stared at my own reflection. I'd lost weight while trapped, but I'd started gaining it back. Eating was less of a trial of will now, and I'd stopped gagging on pills. I trusted my environment, trusted the men who were taking care of me.

I am safe, I thought, staring at my own reflection, hands braced against the cool linoleum counter. *Safe and protected and cared for*. I'd been surviving on the first point for so long. It was nice to add new markers to the list.

I reached up to pull the towel from my wet hair and scowled at the mess on my head. My long hair had grown wildly tangled during the heat, and Bear had tried brushing it a couple times, but I'd just whined and then ended up wanting more sex anyway. Now it was fully matted at the back, tangled to my waist, ends ragged and tired.

I dug through Chance's bathroom drawers and found a buzz clipper kit with a pair of scissors inside.

It was time for a change.

———

WITH A FULL BELLY of pizza and a lighter head, Chance led me through the halls of the club. I'd grown used to the quiet recently, and I was grateful for the suppressants now that the rooms were full again. Full of heavy scents, and of alphas letting out growls and belly laughs and sexual grunts of satisfaction.

My steps slowed as we neared the bar. Dim hanging lights made soft spotlights on small scenes in the large room. A group of men stood playing pool, guns strapped to their hips. A pair of women knelt on the surface of a table, kissing and groping one another for an audience that sat in a circle around them, catcalling and laughing. A couple was in a back booth, woman bent over the surface of the table as a man fucked lazily into her.

A few eyes drifted in my direction, and I sucked in a breath and looked away as Chance steered me into King's office, the door swinging open. My heart leapt into my throat at the sight of the man behind the desk.

King looked almost exactly the way he had when I'd walked myself into his office in only a T-shirt and begged him to fuck me. His eyes sported exhausted dark circles below, lips pressed in an annoyed scowl. He was terrifyingly handsome. His brow furrowed now, just as it had then, but then his lips quirked.

"What happened to your hair, princess?"

I ran my fingers through my shorn locks. My hair still reached my shoulders for the most part, give or take a few places where I'd been a little overenthusiastic in the trimming. Chance had laughed as I'd emerged and ruffled the strands before wrapping me up in his arms and kissing me breathless. I wasn't sure what King or Bear would say.

"I cut it," I said, wondering why all my powers of speech seemed to want to evaporate in this man's presence.

He arched an eyebrow, still faintly smiling, but didn't say anything else.

"Thought you might want me out on the floor," Chance said. "And Bear said you sent him out to call in a few favors."

King nodded but didn't take his eyes off me.

"Well?" King said, leaning back in his chair. "You gonna stand there, or come over and sit on my lap like a good girl?"

Chance covered his laugh with a cough, and my breath hitched at the question. I turned, pulling Chance in for a quick kiss before he could step away, and he pressed his forehead to mine in answer. When I turned and hurried to King's lap, the alpha had already pushed his seat back, leaving me room.

"Uh-uh," King said, stopping me with a hand on my hip as I started to sit on his thigh. "Face me."

My cheeks warmed as I turned in place, and the office door clicked shut behind Chance. King's thighs were spread wide, and he was languid in his chair, staring up at me from those heavy-lidded, ice-chip eyes. He scooted in so his knees touched the drawers of his desk, trapping me between them. Meaning I had to raise my legs up one at a time to climb over him, an act which he watched with determined fascination.

I was wearing silk sleep shorts and a shirt that almost completely covered them, with slits along the hips to make movement easy. King's hands slid up under the shirt, grasping hotly around my waist as I settled on his lap. The fabric of my outfit was thin and cool and did little to disguise the hard lines and rough contrast of King as he pulled me into his chest, the patches and leather vest he wore rubbing through silk to my skin.

I arched my neck, preparing for his mouth to start rooting for skin to bite or lick, but instead his nose pressed to my throat. He breathed in and out, slow and deep, the sigh sagging his chest beneath mine. His hands slid down to my ass but he didn't grip, just held me in place.

"Can't decide if I'm glad these suppressants stifle your scent or if I hate them for it," King muttered into my throat, the scruff of his beard tickling and drawing a shiver out of me.

I shimmied on his lap, and he grunted but didn't take the bait, so I simply pressed my own face into his shoulders.

"They dull my sense of smell too," I admitted.

This isn't arm's length, I thought as King held me against him, seemingly content to breathe me in. And the longer we remained wrapped up like this, the easier it was to believe King wanted me here. Not just on his lap nearing midnight while a party raged in the bar, but in general. That I hadn't used our biology to lure him into fucking me.

"What you said earlier about pack—"

King sighed, but this time the sound was weary and his face lifted from my skin, head falling back against his chair. I sat up a little to stare at him.

"What makes claiming an old lady different from claiming an omega?" I asked, pleased with myself for not whining. It felt like the sound had been constantly trapped in my mouth during the heat, and if there was anyone I wanted to show that I was more than a whining, needy omega, it was King.

"You know what," King said.

I chewed on my lip, holding his stare, not feeling the cold prick of it at the moment. Not when he was so close and quiet and his hands were still cupping my ass. "Old ladies never get bonds?"

King's gaze skirted away briefly, jaw ticking, but it returned and he was relaxed again. "Princess..." he started. My eyes rolled automatically and he stilled. "Oh, you got a problem with that pet name, huh? Butterfly and birdy are fine, but—"

I huffed, face hot, but I wasn't the terrified, trapped creature in the cage now, and I wasn't the bundle of sex and hormones from the heat either. I was *Faith*, and I could argue with this man sensibly. I could tell him the truth too. He'd proved as much so far.

"I'm an orphan who was passed from foster home to foster home until I ended up in the equivalent of a holding cell for breeders. I ran away with my brother. I've been living on the road, out of cars and abandoned buildings and people's couches. I've been dumpster diving for food and conning gas station attendants for twenties," I blurted out.

King blinked at me. He'd gotten the story about Omikron, the omega trafficking network Adam and I had been spending years chasing and being chased by, but not the whole story. Now was as good a time as any to tell him.

"I've stolen and I've begged, and I've been caged and treated like an animal," I said, holding that crystal clear stare. "So I need you to listen and know I am *not* a princess."

King's head tipped. "You could be. Right pack of alphas, and you'd—"

"Still be completely traumatized and fucked up from a lifetime of running and hiding and knowing I was *livestock* to so many alphas," I snapped back before he could finish. "What makes you think, after everything I've been through, that some asshole alpha like the one you brought me, and all the shiny bullshit he would come with, would ever make me feel safe? That you could find me a nice house and nest, and suddenly I'm going to get over the past decade of my life and *heal* into a happy little omega?"

And maybe part of me asked King that because I'd been fooled by the same fairy tale for so many years. It was what Adam had promised for me, the pot of gold at the end of the tired rainbow I'd been chasing with him. Except we weren't chasing a rainbow after all, we'd been running for our lives. And I was tired now.

King didn't balk at my words, just lifted a hand to cup my face, thumb stroking over my chin.

"You will heal, princess. Just like your eyes healed, you *will* heal too," King said, so gentle and sweet. And I fell for those words, believed them immediately, thought he was making a promise. Until he opened that mouth of his again. "We find you the right pack, and your head will heal and your heart will heal. But Faith, I am not your medicine."

The bubble of hope in my chest burst, and I remained frozen and stunned as King leaned in, soothing his words with a silky kiss. Bastard. I pulled away, bracing my hands on the back of his chair, and his gaze dropped from my face down to my breasts.

Because he would not claim me—not in earnest, not with a bite, just false words to keep me temporarily safe until he could find someone else to lob me off to—but he would fuck me if I offered him the chance. If I begged.

King grunted as I struggled off his lap, one hand grasping my thigh briefly as if to hold me in place.

"I'm going out to sit with Chance," I said.

King scowled. "Gonna be messy out there. Guys are all wasted by now. You should stay—"

I shrugged, and King didn't fight me as I swatted away his hands. I wasn't sure if I was grateful or annoyed by how easy it was to push him off.

"Chance can take care of me," I said, bucking up my chin.

King huffed and crossed his arms over his chest. "You gonna be a brat every time I tell you the truth?"

I growled softly at him, and his lips twitched again. "Probably. Just a princess, after all."

King waited until I'd reached the door before his chair creaked. "Faith, wait."

The music was blaring as I opened the door, and King didn't continue. Just "wait." It was a fair request. He'd only just finished my heat. He was protecting me, sheltering me even when he knew the threat I potentially posed. "Wait" was simple. He deserved a little patience.

But I was selfish. Or maybe I just didn't want him to have the pieces of me he wanted and let him reject the rest.

I marched into the belly of the beast, the bar in high and sloppy spirits, the scents churning my stomach for a moment before I remembered to breathe through my mouth. Alphas' stares fastened to me, and a few with lewd and obvious interest in their gazes. King was standing in the hall behind me now, his shadow stretching almost to my bare feet. His warning to them was fresh.

I scanned the room, and it was easier than I expected to maintain a straight face and ignore the obvious debauchery taking place in the room. Chance was sitting in a booth near the bar, almost out of sight aside from the long stretch of his legs. And across from him was the same sweet and spicy alpha who'd interrupted our kiss earlier. The alpha was leaning across the table, speaking to Chance, and my beta's eyes were drifting over the crowd, almost ignoring the other man.

King's shadow was approaching, and I bolted forward before he could draw me back. Chance's stare snagged on me, and he straightened in the booth. For a moment, I could almost imagine myself on a tightrope between King and Chance, running from one end to the other, a narrow line of safety beneath me and any number of dangers I might fall into if I failed to keep my balance.

Chance had barely started scooting to the end of the booth when I arrived, and I pushed him back into the cushions, ignoring the stare of the alpha across from us.

"Birdy?"

"Do you want me?" I asked, and Chance's eyes crinkled at the corners with laughter. I shook my head. "Here, I mean. To stay."

His humor cleared, eyes flicking over my shoulder and then back to me. His hands reached for my hips, and I slid one leg over his to scoot closer.

"I do," he said, leaning in and kissing my jaw. His scent mingled together with the alpha's across the table, and I suddenly recalled the whiff I'd gotten on his shirt that first day I'd pulled him close in the closet nest. "Is King misbehaving?" Chance whispered in my ear.

I ignored the question, wrapping my arms around Chance's shoulders, aware of the stare fastened to us. I hadn't gotten much of a look at the alpha earlier, only enough to know he was handsome with dark curly hair and a dense beard. He'd marked Chance with his scent at one point, and glared daggers at me earlier.

"Are you mine, Chance?" I asked, just loud enough for the alpha to overhear us.

Chance tensed, but he never drew his stare away from mine, and his hands stroked up my back to my shoulders, drawing me down on his lap, pressing me to his chest. His grin was slow and a little oily, something soft and cruel in the expression, but it brightened and cleared as he stared up at me.

"Yes, all yours, birdy," Chance said.

The alpha's scent thickened as I ducked and crashed my lips

into Chance's, dug my fingers into his shoulders and wrapped myself tighter around him. The bar had been clean and quiet this morning, but it was already filled with the scents of booze and sex and pheromones. I didn't care.

Jealous alphas watched Chance and me kiss, and a few grew brave, whistling in appreciation. King could refuse me or refuse himself, but I would bite him myself before I let him keep Bear or Chance out of reach.

"You tryin' to start a fight?" Chance whispered, kissing the lobe of my ear and then pulling it between his teeth.

My breath hitched, and I rocked on his lap. "Between who?" I asked.

Chance released my lobe with a final nibble, leaning back against the booth. He glanced at the alpha in the booth with us but his stare didn't linger. "Us and the world."

I grinned. He wasn't really wrong. "Do you think we'd win?"

Chance grinned back, and this one was pure and just for me. "Oh, absolutely."

"In that case, yes," I said, and I fell back into him, swallowing his laugh with my kiss, swallowing the groans of pleasure that followed too.

There was a breath of warning—leather and bite on my tongue as Chance and I pulled apart—and then a warm hand grasped around my arm.

I squeaked and Chance laughed as King pulled me bodily off the beta's lap.

"What the he—"

"No games, princess," King snapped, tugging me close and pressing his lips against my ear. "If I go chasing you down a hallway in front of my club, you better believe my old lady will get what's coming to her."

I swallowed hard and dropped my gaze to his chest to hide my glare. Or to hide from his.

"Chance, you comin'?" King said. "Little thing is a handful tonight."

A roar of laughter went up from the nearby tables, and I turned to look at Chance. But the other alpha was the one who caught my gaze. He looked *angry*. More than angry—he looked like he wanted to hit King, or me, or Chance. I wasn't sure, but the force of that dark stare sent me stumbling back into King's chest, and his hand came down on my hip, soothing the spot with more care than he put in his words.

Chance stared at us from the booth, expression blank, and then glanced around the room, shaking his head. "I'll meet you up there later."

"But—" I started, and King squeezed my hip, silencing me.

"Can't guarantee I won't wear her out before you get up there" King said, shrugging behind me, still stroking my hip as my face went hot, thrilled and embarrassed in equal measure.

Chance smirked and nodded, the motion stiff. An eyebrow arched at me, and I let out a breath. If I begged Chance to join us, he would. And I wanted to, not just as a buffer against King, but to drag Chance away from that alpha who'd turned that hateful glare on me again, stretched out in the booth as if he were relaxed, calm, tipsy even, his eyes saying the exact opposite. But King was already guiding me back to the hallway and Chance had said he would stay and my head was muddled.

"Who is that?" I asked King, staring at the alpha.

King's arm tightened around my hip as he answered. "Ghost, our road captain. *Not* for you."

I jolted and shook my head. "Wasn't asking like that."

"Call us if you need an extra hand, prez!"

"Or another knot!"

"Don't see why the fuckin' beta should get to slide into that ripe piece."

"He ain't even fucking interested."

King's jaw was ticking by the time we made it to the hallway, clenched so tight I wasn't sure he'd be able to speak. But when he did it sounded calm, even.

"They saw you go into my office, princess. Saw you storm out, run to Chance. We don't look like the happy couple, like I'm your good old man, when you put on a scene like that."

"I'm sorry," I started.

King shook his head. "You don't need to be. You just need to know why I'm gonna be a possessive brute in front of the club."

I released the breath I'd been holding and leaned into King

until he nestled me into his side. His treatment of me was a confusing mix of possessive and cold, tender and commanding. I wanted all of it, if I were honest with myself, and enjoyed the way he tied me up in knots and then unraveled me. I just wished there was actual solid ground beneath all the turbulence, reassurance that King wouldn't drop me for good.

I'd been trying to push against him, direct him into position. It had worked, to an extent—I'd gotten him in my bed, his protection and promise he wouldn't immediately pass me off to a pack of strangers. Maybe it was time to follow his lead for a little while.

We were about to cross over into the motel area of the building, still in view of those in front of the hallway. I pulled us to a stop and rose up on my toes, twisting into King and kissing under his beard.

"I just want you to want me," I murmured, ignoring the hum of interest floating down the hall from our audience. King's arms wrapped around me, pulling me flush against his chest.

"Wanting you isn't the issue," he muttered.

"Fine," I said, nipping at his skin and then arching back to stare up at him. "Then I'm just going to be a brat until you decide to keep me to save yourself the hassle."

King growled, but there was a purr in the sound and his fingers dug into my back. "I ought to send you up to the nest alone."

"I thought we had to keep up appearances," I said.

He huffed, and then he was tugging me up into his arms. I wrapped my legs around his hips and my arms around his shoulders.

"I'm too goddamn tired to fuck you for four hours straight, princess," King said.

I laughed and rested my chin on his shoulder, closing my eyes and breathing him in. "I'm still a little sore from the heat," I admitted.

One of King's hands squeezed my ass, but I thought it was more in response to my statement than in interest.

"Will it mess with appearances if we just curl up in the nest?" I asked.

King sighed. "Quit rubbing my nose in my own words."

I wasn't sure if that was a yes or no until King put me down to unlock Bear's room and then led me to the nest, our hands linked. I was already dressed to sleep, and I watched from the mattress as he took off his leather cut and folded it carefully, resting it on the roof of the nest. He undressed down to a pair of black briefs, and his motions were weary and automatic.

He paused, hands reaching up to brace against the roof of the nest, body stretched out in display for me, although more by coincidence than design. I'd never really been around a man like King. He was older than me, comfortable in his skin and body, and so absent of self-consciousness I couldn't stop myself from staring now that I'd started.

"Ten years ago, I had a good grip on this club. My road name suited me, and my brothers loved me for leading the Devils in a new direction." He turned his head and narrowed his eyes. "I suppose all kings wear out their welcome eventually."

I didn't know what to say, so I scooted back in the nest and King took the invitation, ducking under the curtains and crawling in. I lay back, and he moved to balance above me, thick arms on either side of my shoulders, knees braced outside of mine.

"Ten years ago, I would've accepted the consequences of biting you, princess, and known I could weather the storm," King said, frowning down at me. "But that was ten years ago. Nowadays, you could tear this club apart by being here. You get that?"

I wanted to break his stare, roll onto my side and ignore the words, the refusal yet again. *Follow his lead*, I reminded myself.

"I get that," I said, nodding.

I was bringing the threat of the Wasted closer. Plus the added potential threat of Omikron. I was the dangled ripe fruit in front of alphas who were being refused a bite. I was a blatant lie told to suspicious ears. I was a risk.

"Why didn't you tell them I was just Bear's?" I asked.

King groaned and fell to my side, bundling me against his warm, bare chest. "'Cause I'm a fucking idiot who hated the idea of not getting to touch you again. I *can't* offer you a bite and keep the club, and I can't deny myself this," he said, squeezing me.

I squirmed just enough to drape one leg over his hips and get my arms up out of his grasp so I could touch his neck and shoulders and hair.

"You mad at me for that, princess?" King murmured, even as I scratched my fingertips gently into the short, fine strands of his hair.

"Yes," I said.

King purred and stroked his hands over my back. "Good. You stay mad, and I'll stay mad. This won't go too far."

Liar, I thought, but he was comfortable and warm and we were both tired. We could fight more, be angry again, on another day. Right now, I wanted to enjoy the little he would offer. It was more than the last time we were in the nest together, and that was enough for now.

"He's pushing his luck."

"Ehn, can you blame him? Pretty little piece like that?"

I tensed as spice and syrup shivered down my spine. I was seated at the bar, and a warm chest pressed up against my back, using the crowded area as an excuse for proximity.

"Would you fuck off?" I hissed, my neck too tight to turn, not that I wanted to see his face.

"Missed you on the ride," Ghost answered, soft in my ear while his hand clapped on my shoulder in some feigned friendly affection.

"No you fuckin' didn't," I snapped back, trying to shrug him off, but instead only letting his hand rub over my muscles, familiar and not as unwelcome as I wished it were.

Faith was perfect. She gave me everything I'd needed with Ghost, but in a sweeter and more honest package. I should've been able to rinse my hands and mind of this man now that I had her. If only he would leave me the hell alone, get that rich scent of his out of my lungs.

"Whaddya think, Ghostie? That new catch of Chance's as sweet as she fuckin' looks?" Buck asked from my left.

My hand clenched around the now lukewarm bottle in my hand, and Ghost leaned more heavily into my side, his arm hanging casually over my shoulders.

"Gotta be honest, she's got a funk to her up close," Ghost answered.

"Bet that's just how stuffed full of spunk she is after a couple weeks of getting railed by Prez and Bear," said Natalie, club ass and part-time bartender, cheerful as ever.

I didn't mind Natalie, in spite of the three-week run she'd had a while ago of riding Ghost's dick any time he snapped his fingers. She was funny and as disgustingly foul-mouthed as any of the guys. And right now, I wanted to smash my beer over her head.

"You have a lot of fun pulling your dick and watching that girlie get railed, Chance?" Buck asked, grinning and winking at Natalie as he pulled a slug of his beer. "Bet he had to wait till the alphas were asleep to get his dick wet, poor guy."

"You see the way King pulled her right off him?" Natalie laughed and winked at me.

I ignored them. I could get pissy with Buck, start a fight, but the other alphas would pile on me or pull him out of reach. I could tell them all about the way Faith had made me fuck her first thing this morning while Bear watched us and jerked off. But the last thing I wanted was any of these fuckers thinking about her more than they already were.

"Oh, if I know our Chance, I know he's already learned all the ways to turn that girl into an absolute worthless heap," Ghost said.

I pushed my bottle across the bar and jerked myself out of Ghost's hold, shoving the chair into his hip as I exited from the right to avoid him.

"You're all happy to run your mouths until Bear walks in the room, I bet," I said, reminding them that while they may not have respected me, they sure as shit weren't gonna talk about our girl while the club enforcer was within earshot. It did the trick of shutting them up, and I headed for the backdoor of the bar.

It was tempting to go hunt down King and Faith in the nest,

take out my frustrations in a way that would—in fucking fact—leave Faith a worthless heap. But I was riled up and angry, and I *knew* the club would be talking shit about King tonight in certain circles.

If only I didn't have a fucking *Ghost* attached to me.

His scent followed me out into the backyard, where Danielle was entertaining a few guys at the picnic bench with her multi-tasking skills of hands and mouth.

"Join in, Ghost!"

I scowled at the confirmation of being followed, and Ghost answered them, "Later. Got something to catch up on in the garage. Come on."

His hand landed against my back again and I spun, fists clenched at my sides. Ghost was smart, stepping out of reach immediately, and only his expression stopped me from swinging. Ghost was not a serious man. He was more like a sponge, soaking up all the attention he was granted, all the humor and energy around him. He soaked up my frustrations and rage too when we were together, and instead of infecting him, they seemed to just run through him, leaving us both limp and relaxed for brief moments.

So seeing him staring back at me, sober and tense, tipping his head in the direction of the garage gave me pause. He moved to lead the way, and after a brief internal struggle I followed, ignoring the slurping and the low, almost aimless grunts we left behind us.

The garage was cool and quiet as Ghost opened the door, and he switched on a table lamp rather than the overhead lights. The bikes were lined up into their places, still dusted from the road. Tomorrow, they'd be cleaned and tuned up, mostly by Ghost, who fussed over machinery like a nursemaid over her charges.

"The fuck is your problem tonight?" I asked.

"What the hell is King thinking?" Ghost asked, leaning up against a counter with his arms crossed over his chest.

His tools were organized in tidy rows behind him. Before Ghost, the Devil's road captain and head mechanic was named Busted, and the garage had been a greasy, chaotic nest just waiting to give a man tetanus. By comparison, Ghost kept the place as clean and organized as a religious sanctuary.

"It's not a pack," I said automatically.

"I don't give a fuck, it *looks* like one," Ghost answered.

I sighed and moved to one of the tool benches, sitting down to face Ghost. "What do you care?"

Ghost snarled and looked away for a moment before turning back with a blazing stare. "My problem is that King has you sniffing around the club—which I get, he needs someone—"

"Wait, what the fuck?" I asked, a bolt of shock running through me.

Ghost rolled his eyes. "Please. You think I don't notice shit? You're spying for King. Spying on fucking *Rider*."

Ghost arched an eyebrow, as if to encourage me to argue the point. His head tipped as we stared at one another and his face relaxed, a faint smile curving his lips.

"You think I don't notice *you*, Chance?" he asked, pushing off the counter. He stepped forward, words turning low and silky. "That I just spontaneously find my way to your room at a random whim, like I'm not fucking watching and waiting for every possible opportunity to get alone with you?"

For a moment, Ghost's spell worked. He craved me, I craved him. We were a perfect and ugly pair. And then I remembered the way Faith had thrown herself into my lap, kissed me in front of the club and demanded to hear that I was hers, with Ghost sitting directly across from us, perfectly capable of overhearing her.

"Stop," I said, sharp and sudden, realizing Ghost was just about to reach out and touch me. I glared up at him, and his smile grew wider. "Does Rider know?"

Ghost blinked and shrugged. "Doubt it. I haven't said shit."

"Are you going to?" I asked, because I didn't know where Ghost's loyalty was, or if he was even capable of any.

"To Rider? No," Ghost said, frowning. "I know what he's up to, but I don't have skin in the game. King or him, doesn't mean shit to me. But King shouldn't have you doing his dirty work, not against your own brother."

I scoffed and stood from the bench. "Doesn't mean shit to

you. Doesn't make a difference to you what alpha top dog is in charge of the club. It matters to *me*, Ghost. You think I wanna be a nobody under Rider's rule? I went to King in the first place."

Ghost blinked in answer, silent for a beat as he absorbed the information. "And dragging you into what is *as good as* a pack, the one thing he swore up and down would never have shit to do with the club? What? So you can play guard dog for the omega while he and Bear are busy?"

Simple question. Same one all the other alphas were probably asking themselves. What was the beta doing in the mix? Playing guard dog.

I had a short temper on the best of days, but even I didn't expect the way my fist flew up through the air. My shoulder burned with the sudden movement, clumsy and urgent, and Ghost's eyes widened as he jumped back out of the way, even while I pulled back.

We stared at another, panting hard, at my aborted punch, still hovering midair as I considered whether or not I wanted to try again, in earnest this time.

"I am not your business," I ground out through clenched teeth, forcing my arms back down at my sides. "And *she* is not your business. I told you to back off before you left, and I'm telling you the same now. I will not say it again."

"Chance."

I stiffened and spread myself wider, feet planted and vibrating with tension. Ghost had that rasp in his voice he got right before he begged for my cock, but I'd had enough. He'd already proved what he thought of me. If he wanted to slum it with someone who would treat him like garbage, he could find someone else. Because I was sick of joining him in the muck.

He stalled, eyes flicking over me, brow furrowing. "You can't be serious about her."

"How would you know? You wouldn't have a fucking clue what serious feelings looked like," I said. "Stay the fuck away from me. That's it, that's all you get."

We were only a foot away from each other. If I licked my lips I would taste him, even when it'd been weeks since we touched.

I didn't know if it was just muscle memory at this point to want him, but I wasn't giving in.

I moved for the door, slow and cautious and determined, half expecting him to reach out and grab for me. What would happen if we touched while we were alone like this? Would it be too much? Would I fall into the magnetism of him like King had with Faith?

I opened the door to the garage and sucked in the fresh air, moving faster now, refusing to run and refusing to stop. I would listen in on everyone tomorrow; the gossip wouldn't die down overnight. For now, I needed to clean out the little threads of Ghost that still lingered in my veins. I knew my cure.

I ignored the muttered remarks and openly hostile jabs of rude humor directed at me as I moved through the bar. The party was starting to die down, pairs and groups heading for private rooms for more thorough release. I heard their grunts and fleshy slaps and lewd moans as I passed by doors.

Would King be hoarding Faith to himself? I almost didn't care. I meant it more than he did when I called her mine. I would force myself into the nest with them if I had to, if only because I was too terrified to go alone to my room, too certain Ghost might just turn up there...or too afraid he wouldn't.

But there was nothing to interrupt in the nest but peace, and somehow it was worse to see King and Faith cuddled tight on the mattress than it would've been to find them fucking. I hesitated at the entrance, wondering where I fit in, even as an open place at Faith's back waited for me.

She stirred, rolling in King's arms, and paused, blinking at me. Her mouth curved, eyes falling heavily shut.

"Chance," she murmured, patting one hand on the bed.

I sighed, leaned against the edge of the nest and stared at her for another minute as the poison of anger leaked out of me.

One eye opened, and I grinned as she pouted.

"C'mere."

"Just enjoying the view, birdy," I said, shrugging out of my cut, folding it and placing it next to King's.

"Better up close," King said, huffing and scooting back, dragging Faith to his chest again, leaving more room for me.

Fuck the others, fuck Ghost, fuck my own head too. This was what I wanted. As I crawled into the nest, sliding in and facing Faith, her lips grazed my clavicle. As we settled together, the rest of the world faded to the background and the noise in my head turned down. This was the shit worth keeping, and I wasn't going to lose sight of that.

The bed rustled behind me, daylight already crawling into the nest from the window, sharp and golden. The body behind me was too large and their scent too sweet to be King. I rolled over with a smile on my face as Bear sat up, looking rumpled and barely rested.

"When did you get back?" I asked in a whisper, Chance still fast asleep on my other side.

"Few hours ago. Gotta head out again," Bear said, glaring at the sunlight.

I frowned and propped my head up in my hand. "Again?"

Bear's gaze slid down to me and his expression melted warmly, lips curling up. It was still such a delight to see these men clearly, more than any other part of having my sight repaired. Mostly because they were just so freaking good-looking. Bear's features were even bolder and stronger than I'd guessed by touch, expressive and direct. I stretched under that stare of his, inviting him closer, and the corners of his eyes crinkled in response.

"Got a few people to hunt down, collections to make, and need to ensure the Wasted are still coloring within the lines King granted them," Bear said, drinking me in, his smile widening as

Chance's arm coiled around my waist. "You're in good hands till I get back, and it won't be late. I'll bring you another surprise."

I squirmed at the suggestion of a present, cheeks warming. "You don't have to keep giving me gifts, you know. You did more than enough already."

Bear grinned. He and I both knew I was excited at the suggestion. His head ducked, and I stretched my chin up to receive his soft, pressing kiss.

"Alpha has to court his omega. Those are the rules, Butterfly," he rasped.

My mouth dropped open, but Bear was sliding out of the nest before I could think of an answer, rising huge and broad and handsome at the opening.

"I'll be back this afternoon. Rest up, and stay safe," Bear whispered, patting softly on the roof of the nest before ducking out of sight.

Courting. I grinned and collapsed down to my pillows, tucking my beaming face away. I'd daydreamed about courting *before*, although it'd been hard to believe in a happily ever after while on the run. I'd given up the idea while I was trapped by Omikron, and even after the Devils had found me. It was more important to secure bond marks than worry about courting presents from prospective alphas.

I'd been so determined to trick or trap or chase Bear and King into biting me, claiming me, and protecting me. But they'd offered their protection without a bond, or at least a full one, in Bear's case. I'd spent my heat with them, chosen them, and they'd only given me what I'd begged for—aside from that bite.

They were good men. Good *alphas*. And as much as that made me more determined than ever to claim them for my pack, it also only seemed fair they be allowed to choose me too. Bear had, but King...

Chance stretched at my back, groaning and burrowing his face into my shorter hair, puffing and tickling my neck with his breath. His morning wood prodded cheerfully at my ass and he sighed, grinding against me briefly and then relaxing.

"Morning, birdy," Chance mumbled into my hair.

I sighed, placing my arm over his, tangling our fingers together where they rested against my stomach.

Chance had chosen me too, although I had some questions for him after last night.

"Tell me about the alpha," I said, and Chance's fingers tightened around mine.

"What alpha?" he asked, the words clipped.

I sighed and pushed my shoulder against his chest, pulling my hand free and rolling over to face him. There were three little lines between his eyebrows and I pressed my fingers over them, but they only tightened.

"Ghost," I said, using the name King had shared with me. "He was the one I smelled on you before they all left."

Chance remained tense, his eyes squeezing shut, jaw clenching. I leaned down, kissing the muscle in his cheek, and he released a huff of breath against my ear.

"Birdy..."

"You said you were relieved they were leaving," I said, sitting up again.

Chance's eyes opened, searching mine.

"Did you miss him?" I asked. "Did I interrupt last night?"

He growled and started to twist away from me before going limp, all the tension bleeding out of him. "No. Or yes, you interrupted, but I didn't want him there anyway."

I rewarded Chance's confession with a kiss, and for a moment he remained still. Then all at once he was around me, on top of me, tongue thrusting between my lips and hips settling between my thighs, kissing me like he was starving for touch. I held him every bit as fiercely, answered his hunger with all of my eager acceptance, and Chance groaned into my mouth, rocking against me. I expected it to escalate into a frenzy, but he slowed and softened, turning a ravaging kiss into gentle pecks and pulls and nibbles, hands stroking up and down my sides.

He pulled away, and I caught my breath only to have it stolen again.

"You know that you're everything I've wanted," Chance said. My eyes flew open and he smiled down at me, all of that anger and stress missing from his features now. "What I've *needed*."

My eyes welled up, and Chance stroked his cheek against mine as I tried to find the words to answer him.

Then he flopped to the side, an arm over his face. "Ghost and I fucked around for...years."

My eyebrows bounced. "*Years?* Chance! I can't—Did I—"

"In secret," Chance muttered. "Far as I know, no one caught on."

I gaped for a moment and then remembered to shut my mouth. Our legs were tangled and I shifted, moving to settle over his lap. His arousal was fading, but he moved his arm from over his eyes and rested his hands on my thighs, gripping me as if to keep me from moving away.

"He and I were... I can't even call it fuck buddies, because we weren't friends," he said, glaring up at me, even as his thumbs stroked my inner thighs. "You didn't break up a love story, Faith. You gave me a reason to walk out of a shitty situation."

"Did he hurt you?" I asked, wondering if I was capable of tearing the alpha limb from limb.

"He used me. I used him. Maybe it could've been something more, but it wasn't," Chance said. "He never hurt me. He liked... Don't tell anyone this. I dunno why I'm being loyal to him, but he liked me talking down to him, pushing him around. Being rough. It was like we switched designations when we were alone."

I sighed and fell forward, my heart breaking at the idea that Chance saw being a beta as being talked down to and pushed around by alphas. Chance's arms reached up, circling my back, the pair of us holding one another.

"He still wants you," I said. It'd been obvious the night before.

Chance grunted.

"Do you still want him?" I asked, trying to sound calm and not make it super obvious that I would go hunt Ghost down and tear his throat out if Chance said yes.

"I meant what I said, birdy," Chance murmured, stroking my back. "I... You know my brother is an alpha."

I blinked, tried to sit up, but Chance held me fast to his chest.

"Same alpha dad, same beta mom. Rider got my dad's alpha gene, and I didn't," Chance said. "And I wasn't the only one disappointed. My dad took it...personally. And Rider thought it was fuckin' funny. He'd always be on top where we were concerned. Always stronger than me, better."

"I don't believe that for a second," I said.

Chance ignored me. "Ghost set my temper off one day. We fought, and...he fucking loved it. Liked me chewing him out, throwing him to the ground, and it escalated at first. I thought I was really going to beat the shit out of this alpha, feel powerful. And then he kissed me, and the whole thing just...went sideways into fucking. But I still felt powerful.

"He didn't want to put me down in my place in the dirt, like Rider and the others. He wanted *me* to put *him* there, and...so did I." Chance's arms loosened enough for me to push up on my hands and study his scowl. "I was high on that. I'd never felt like an alpha's equal. Or their superior. It was clear from the start that was just private for him. He acts like the rest of them, fucks all the beta club ass—"

"Rude name," I said, and Chance's smile flickered out.

"Ignored me when we were around the others," he continued. "Blind idiots."

He grinned up at me and sighed. "He kept showing up. I kept chasing the high, craving it. Until one day, a little omega in a closet held onto my wrist like she needed me."

"I do need you," I said, jutting my chin out.

"I know," Chance said, smile bright, all relaxed again.

He was moody, shifting his expression like changing winds, but I knew how to make the sun part the clouds and the reward was *divine*. Chance shone when he smiled.

He pushed himself up on his elbows until our faces were inches apart, eyes bouncing back and forth over mine. "I can't decide if you make me feel *like* an alpha, or like it doesn't matter either way."

"It doesn't matter. You're as important to me as Bear," I said, brushing silky strands of hair back from his face.

"I know," he said again, stretching up to steal a kiss.

But he hadn't answered my original question, and I sat up,

just out of reach. "Do you still want him?"

Chance froze, blinking at me.

"I want you *and* Bear...and King. And I haven't had...almost any opportunities for relationships, but I know feelings don't just evaporate," I said.

"Part of me does," Chance admitted in a rush. He sighed and sagged, collapsing beneath me. "Physically. But the idea leaves a bad taste in my mouth. What he offers isn't enough now."

"Good, you deserve better," I said.

Chance arched an eyebrow. "You deserve a pack who's beating down the door to be yours, thinking of courting presents, like Bear said."

King...

"I come with a lot of baggage," I said, shrugging.

"No, birdy. You're being chased by a lot of horrible people, and you've been treated cruelly up until now. That's not your fault. King needs to—"

"I don't want to talk about King," I said, pressing my palms on Chance's shoulders, staring sternly at him. "You meant what you said last night? You're mine?"

Chance searched my face for a beat, then nodded slowly. "I'm yours, birdy."

I dipped down briefly to nip at his lips and then sat up again. "Good. Then make me yours."

Chance's brow furrowed. "Make you—I can't—"

"You can. However you want," I said, hovering over him.

Chance stared up at me, but I smiled as I watched the ideas pass over his face, flickering in his eyebrows, twitching his lips. His hands slid down to my hips and I wiggled on his lap, bouncing my eyebrows at the same time.

"That's a good start," I said.

Chance's eyes narrowed. "You've got those alphas wrapped around your pinkie finger, and you think you can lead me around on a leash too, don't you?"

His voice was lowering, gaining an edge that wasn't an alpha's growl but sharper, more dangerous. It made me shiver in anticipation.

"I'm willing to try," I said, tipping my head.

Chance laughed, that beautiful, bright and joyful sound, and then he leapt up, holding me in his arms and flipping us over, throwing me down into the mattress. I found myself flat and limp beneath him, his knees trapping my thighs and hands braced on either side of my shoulder.

"You forget that I know exactly how easy you take all of me, birdy," Chance rasped, moving one hand to slide up under the hem of my rucked-up sleep shirt, tweaking a nipple to a sharp tip. "My cock," he said, and the hand swept back down my chest and into the waistband of my shorts. I tried to open my legs, but he held them pinned shut and his fingers could only wedge between my thighs, rubbing dully against my sex. "My fist," he added with a feral grin. "Which is your favorite?"

"Both at the same time," I said immediately.

Chance laughed. "Of course. Thirsty cunt. So eager to be stuffed."

I nodded, squirming and using the friction to stimulate my now throbbing clit.

"Well, you're not getting either of them," Chance said, pulling his hand away abruptly, sitting back on his heels and yanking my shorts down my hips, only moving enough to pull them off my kicking legs.

"Chance!"

"Hold yourself open, birdy," Chance said, pushing my knees wide. I reached for the backs of my legs, and he shook his head. "Not there. Here," he said, and he flicked his thumb and forefinger against my clit, making me cry out. I wiggled as Chance pushed my knees back toward my chest. I reached down and spread my lips open.

He stared down at me and I blushed, catching my breath from the sudden filthy assignment.

"I can literally *see* you getting wetter for me," Chance said, his own breath thin.

I whimpered and squeezed my eyes shut, aware of the gasping clench of my cunt, and how easily Chance would be able to see every quiver and tremble like this. The bed jostled, and I gasped at his breath on my exposed sex a moment before a hot, eager tongue swiped up my center.

"Oh!"

"Mmm," Chance hummed, helping himself to two more quick strokes, tongue wet and catching my arousal, spreading it over me, right up to my fingers and around my clit. "Good little slut. Open a little more, down to your cheeks."

I whined and obeyed, pulling at my inner thighs and down to my ass, hands splayed and skin spread taut.

"Oh, yes. Pretty as a picture," Chance hissed.

I squealed as he tongued me, slow and thorough, prodding at every fold and hole, ass to clit and back again.

"Ohh, birdy. Every little bit of you is just begging me to fuck you."

"Yessss!"

Chance pressed at my asshole and it pulsed and puckered, begging just like he said. His tongue probed at my cunt, and I could feel my muscles trying to suck him in, claim that tongue and use it for my pleasure. I laughed with him as he pulled away, but mine was desperate and sobbing and his was smug.

I understood why Ghost had glared at me last night, why he didn't want to lose that sense of helpless possession Chance could wield over you. But I wasn't stupid enough to hide how much I wanted Chance, and I would never let him doubt that his designation meant next to nothing to me.

"Chance, *please*," I gasped, rolling my hips into his teasing tongue.

He groaned and I got my wish, in a perfect and punishing way. Chance latched his lips onto my clit, circling my asshole with one gentle finger as he sucked on my sensitive flesh like he was trying to draw my soul out with my orgasm.

And when it hit, I almost believed he'd succeeded. I arched, howling, my hands abandoning their post to clutch his head closer as electric bolts of agonized pleasure laced through me. It grew to be too much faster than usual, my sopping sex panting and begging to be filled. I tried to wiggle away from his mouth, but he latched an arm around my hips, holding me in place. Just before I thought he might force me to come a second time, Chance pulled away, caught one desperate and ragged breath, and then dove down.

I screamed in earnest as he bit at the inside of my thigh.

For a delirious, orgasm-soaked moment, I believed I was being bonded. But the pain was dull and muscular, not a clean cut of teeth into flesh but a bruising pressure. Chance swiped his thumb against my clit, and my scream transformed into a shuddering moan as I came, my flesh clamped in his ferocious jaw, fingers gently teasing and tracing over my sex.

He released me and lifted up enough to meet my eyes. "It'll leave a bruise, that's all," he said.

A mark. Not a bond, but a mark. He'd given me that first, before the others, before even Bear. And if he could've, I was sure it would've been more. My eyes watered and Chance bent down, kissing the spot he'd bitten softly.

"Give me more," I said.

He lifted his head again, smile smug. "Where?"

I licked my lips, and his thumb on my clit stroked down and slid inside of me, not remotely enough but a start.

"Everywhere."

Chance grinned and shifted, kissing up the thigh he'd bruised, across my belly. His thumb was pushing in and out of me, keeping me at a simmer of arousal, and his eyes met mine as he sucked a kiss on my hip. No, a hickey, I realized as I shivered at the rough suction and the way it pulsed through me. I combed my fingers through his hair, rolling my body into that tiny stimulation of his thumb inside of me.

Chance's jaw opened slowly, letting me feel the drag of his teeth over my skin, and I forced myself to relax as he rested his bite against the soft curve of flesh above my hip. He growled as he bit down, slick thumb slipping out of me as I whined, circling over my clit.

I didn't know if it was the illusion of the bite—what it meant to my instinct—or if Chance was especially good at reading my body, but I came again, gushing on his hand, leaning into his teeth, and he held his grip on me until my whimper of pleasure became one of pain.

"Feel that, birdy?" Chance asked, reaching back and pulling one of my hands from his head down to my hip, tracing my fingertips over the rough indentations from his teeth.

"I love it," I said.

He kissed the mark, my fingertips, my palm, and then moved those grazing lips to my ribs. "I know you do. I can feel you soaking the bed again. Slick and so, so hungry for my cock, aren't you?"

"Yes!" I squirmed beneath Chance as he tickled my ribs with kisses and soft touches, working his way over to my right breast.

I moaned in understanding as he started to tongue and kiss at the mound, lapping and licking and slurping at my nipple like it was my clit. It might as well have been, for the way the treatment seemed to echo in my cunt.

"Please, I need you," I gasped, arching into his mouth, trying to wrap my legs around his hips. But his cock was too far away to catch, and I'd set this game into motion. I only had myself to blame.

Chance was quick this time, biting hard around my breast without warning, snarling and flicking my nipple with his tongue while he held me still. My feet kicked against the mattress, and I let out a strangled yelp through gritted teeth. This one fucking hurt.

And I clutched him closer, pressed myself into those cruel teeth until they softened, his lips apologizing gently over the mark.

"More," I pleaded, stretching my throat.

Chance's breath hitched, and he sank against me, his cock finding my entrance and sliding in easily, both of us groaning.

I was lost, riding him from below, my breast and hip and cunt and thigh all throbbing. I was as animal as I'd been in the heat, as desperate and shameless. Chance's stare on me was a caress as I moved, his body resisting the pull of my hands to draw him down to my throat.

"You want my mark, birdy?" he asked.

"Yes, fuck, please, yes. I want *you*," I cried out.

"Fucking beautiful," Chance murmured.

His chest was hot against mine, body heavy, and he took over the motion of our fucking, smoothing it into a steady glide and grind, hypnotizing and calming me into following him.

"They'll all see," he said.

"Yes," I answered, twisting my head further, offering him every bit of me. "Claim me."

I didn't think about what it would look like to other alphas, Chance's bite as a bruise on my skin. I wasn't even aware of the difference in that moment. I *needed* him.

Chance kissed and licked every inch of my throat and shoulder until his breath rushed over the slick skin, drawing out goosebumps. He was thrusting harder, faster inside of me, our bodies slapping together, a moan dragged out of me with every beat.

I didn't need a knot, didn't need Bear's or King's scent. Just needed the pressure of rising chaos to break in me, and for Chance's teeth to claim me once more.

No, it was the other way around.

Chance dove down, biting hard and unrelentingly at my throat, and the tether snapped, my orgasm booming through me. A scream vibrated in my throat, but my pulse was too loud to hear or the cry was silent. For a moment, I thought Chance and I had fused together, his cock so deep inside of me I lost track of the division between us.

Our arms were knotted around one another, his teeth trying to bury themselves in me, my cunt trying to suck him down to join me.

And then the roar of the orgasm softened, leaving us both weak in its wake. Chance's bite on my throat ached, and he sighed and groaned, unclenching his teeth. My heart sank a little as he pulled away. There was no tangible bond, he hadn't even broken skin, and we were still two people, although as close as possible.

Then Chance kissed my throat and warmth flooded me. Affection.

"Thank you," he whispered, kissing the mark again, rubbing his cheek against mine.

"I'm yours, Chance," I said, turning my face to catch his mouth with mine.

He hummed in agreement. "Oh I know, birdy. And I'm not letting anyone fucking forget it."

Creeping around in Wasted territory—the tiny pocket north of the border that King had granted them—when we were undoubtedly on the brink of war with them was not the safest place to be. I'd almost considered calling in Chance. King was right that he was suited to be a spy and was less conspicuous than me, but someone needed to stick to Faith like glue now that the club knew about her, and I wasn't sure King deserved the time with our girl when he insisted on acting like every minute was a burden.

I'd parked my bike safely away, my cut packed into the saddlebag, and walked to the Wasted's home base on foot, keeping an eye and ear out for anyone around.

The text message I'd received this morning was running through my mind with every step.

Wasted got raided last night. Team looked like some kinda black ops spy shit. Busted shit up and left.

I wasn't sure what I could find out hours later, but I had a bad feeling about the news. King had a plant named Gizmo, an old drunk MC dropout who lived on the edge of the Wasted territory and was willing to let King pay for his habits in exchange for the supply of information. Generally, Gizmo was an unreliable witness, especially to specific details, but I doubted he was likely to be left confused on something as dramatic as a black ops raid.

Black ops sounded about right for the kind of operation Faith had described Omikron as—highly connected, exceptional resources, military-like efficiency. Except what was Omikron doing raiding the Wasted? Even those fuckers couldn't have been so stupid to have messed with an organization like that.

Unless they'd decided Omikron was to blame for them not receiving Faith.

If that was true, the Wasted might manage to eliminate themselves before they became a bigger problem for King.

The sight of the Wasted's warehouse compound didn't promise such an easy out. I'd found an old abandoned general store with a ladder up to the roof and a clear view, and I crouched at the ledge facing the Wasted, peering through binoculars. The only evidence I found of any kind of raid was a busted window at the front. There'd be no way to tell any real damage unless I got inside or Gizmo sent us pictures, but I wasn't gonna push the old man to take that kind of risk.

Maybe something had happened and Gizmo had exaggerated. Maybe there was a new fucking gang coming our way and they'd decided to tackle the easy pickings of the Wasted first.

A few men rounded the side of the building into my view, and I fought my own grin. Bruised faces and busted lips, one arm in a sling.

I didn't know what exactly had happened to the Wasted last night and what consequences might ripple in our direction, but I knew that it was satisfying to see those little shits beat up.

I watched for a while longer, just enough to see there was a chaotic and panicked energy from the club, before packing away my binoculars and heading back toward the ladder. I had one more errand to run before I headed home, but I was already itching to get my hands on Faith again. The sooner I knew my little Butterfly was safe and surrounded by us—her old men or her pack, whatever the fuck King wanted to pretend we were— the better.

I FOUND Faith and Chance at the laundromat next door to the club, after a bit of frantic searching and a clue from one of the club girls. My heart rate slowed back down as Faith beamed at me, curled up on Chance's lap on the bench, a bunch of food wrappers and to-go cups at their side.

She was a whole new girl. With a haircut? When the hell had that happened? I didn't care; it was just one little difference of the myriad that had come since we'd found her. Her cheeks were flushed, her skin was clear and bright, and fuck me if she wasn't getting sexier every day. Happier. More at ease.

She knocked her head against Chance's as he whispered something in her ear, and her hair slid back over her shoulder, revealing the oval-shaped growing bruise on her throat. I stopped dead in my tracks, nearly dropping the shopping bag in my hand, and a brief, startled growl rose up from my throat.

Faith and Chance both stiffened, their eyes turning back to me as I swallowed the sound and glared at the mark. Chance's arms were wrapped around her, crossed over her stomach. His chin rested on her shoulder, and he glared right back at me, daring me to object. I didn't want to object. I wanted to dive forward and sink my teeth into that bruise. I knew it wasn't a real mating mark, but it had the intention of one and I—I—I fucking wanted it to be *mine*.

"King see that yet?" I asked.

"No," Chance said, arms tightening around Faith, her hand stroking over his forearms to soothe him. "But...others did, so he'll probably hear about it sooner or later."

My mouth twisted, teeth aching.

Chance's chin lifted. "I'm not apologizing."

"You better fucking not," Faith said.

My smile cracked as Chance nuzzled his cheek against Faith's shoulder. Betas didn't have much scent to mark, but Faith painted her perfume over Chance like she was trying to disguise him as an omega, and they touched enough that I occasionally caught whiffs of him on her. I definitely did today.

"I'm not mad. I'm jealous," I admitted, and it made the

simmering possessiveness in me calm a fraction. Faith's gaze slid to mine, and I held it with my own until she nodded slightly.

I hadn't bitten her yet, although there was no longer any doubt in my mind that I would. The trick of it was *when*. Was I waiting for my sake, or King's? I stroked the bite she'd given me on my hand, searching for that delicate thread between us, finding the echo of understanding from her. We'd talk about it later.

"How was work?" Faith asked.

The laundromat was empty aside from the three of us, and the air conditioner was running high. The space smelled clean and sterile, probably a relief for Faith now that the clubhouse had refilled with alpha pheromones. Every so often, some of the guys would send the girls who hung around the club out with all of our laundry, but otherwise the laundromat tended to be pretty quiet. There weren't enough locals in Dead End aside from the club to fill it up. I wasn't sure if Faith had met any of the girls yet —or how that meeting would go, given her circumstances—but at least this place was private, somewhere for her to retreat to in the meantime.

I groaned, passing the snuggled pair and dropping the shopping bag onto the large counters meant for folding and laundry baskets, before pulling myself up and lying flat on the surface. "Mostly easy. Got some news we need to cover with King in a minute."

Out of the corner of my eye, Faith stretched on Chance's lap, trying to get a peek into the bag. I grinned at her, arching an eyebrow. Would she ask to see it, or wait for me to share it with her?

She rose from Chance's lap and stepped between my knees, leaning forward onto my thighs. Little minx. She crossed her arms over my hips, and I reminded myself I was a grown-ass man, not a teenage boy who needed to get hard at every provocation. But my body didn't listen as she rested her chin down on her arms and waggled those delicate brown eyebrows at me.

"Do I have to earn my present first?"

Tempting, but the news about the Wasted lingered in the back of my mind, and the laundromat wasn't *that* private. "You more than have already, Butterfly," I said, propping myself up on an elbow and pushing the bag her way. "Go on."

Faith grinned, grabbing the bag and flopping it down onto my chest, drawing out a grunt from me. Chance laughed and turned on the bench to watch. As soon as she tipped the bag over and looked inside, that giddy smile went slack and her breath caught.

"It's too much," Faith whispered, staring at the box inside, a laptop computer displayed on its side.

"You needed it," I said, shrugging.

Her teeth sunk into her bottom lip, and that thread between us was tangling and twisting up with too many emotions at once. "I don't even know if I could set the server up by myself. I'm not as good as Adam."

Chance rose from the bench, stepping in behind her, his hands resting lightly on Faith's shoulders. "King had a computer, but I guarantee it has some kind of virus on it. He's constantly bitching about getting spam emails and pop-up ads."

"And I only really use my phone," I said, studying her face and what I could find in that partial bond between us. She was relieved and scared, grateful and embarrassed. Nothing bad that wouldn't pass. "We figured you needed something fresh and more powerful than the cheap shit we've got lying around here."

"We?" Faith asked, looking back up at me, eyes growing glossy.

"Group effort, birdy," Chance said, kissing her temple.

"Was actually King's idea," I admitted, catching her gaze. "Not that he deserves extra credit."

"He also happens to have the best internet signal in his office," Chance pointed out.

Faith glanced between us. "Is this a set-up?"

Chance's lips twitched, but I didn't flinch. "Was it a set-up when you walked into his office in the final throes of your heat?"

She rolled her eyes. "Fair enough. But..." I sat up as she hesitated. Did she regret drawing King in? They'd been tightly tangled up together in the nest when I'd gotten home the night before, but maybe that was at his insistence. Faith was tucked between us now, and she sighed and blinked up at me. "I don't want to push him anymore. Never mind how much you've all already done for me, and the risks he's been willing to take to keep me here—I just don't want to...*bully* him into accepting a bond."

"He's being an idiot, bothering to resist," Chance muttered.

"But he *is* resisting, and it's past time for me to accept that," Faith said.

I was silent, staring at her, eyes reading her face like a written page, catching the little notes of emotion I could gather. She was reluctant and determined at the same time. Reluctant to give King up, I suspected, and determined to give him his choice. He didn't deserve her. Or maybe he did, and she was right. I had a feeling that if she backed off, it would spook him into chasing after her, but I didn't want to make her think I was still calculating the pair of them.

"Okay. I'll quit goading him too. Although I'm not sure that plan will work out the way you expect. Now, you gonna take this thing for a spin or not?" I asked, patting the box.

Faith rose up on her toes and I bent, lips meeting hers for a soft kiss that tasted like sugar and blue raspberry slurpee. Chance pushed her freshly shorn hair aside and kissed the back of her neck, and Faith shivered between us.

"Thank you," she whispered, smiling at me as we parted. "Yes. But I'm serious when I say I don't know if I'll make it work."

I shrugged. "Gotta try, Butterfly. Now, I need to talk to King, and I think you should be there too. No set-up, just news."

THE NEWS DID NOT GO OVER WELL.

"It's Omikron," Faith whispered, eyes wide and all the color in her features washing away.

I'd be lying if I said I hadn't known how much even her posture had changed over the weeks, but it made me sick to watch her crumple in on herself again.

"Butterfly, it's gonna—" I reached for her shoulder, a tentative touch, but she immediately dove into my arms. I let out a sigh as she burrowed into my chest, happy to draw her closer, pull her legs over mine. Chance slid across King's office couch, staying close, and one of Faith's hands reached for him, gripping tight. This was pack—this settling sensation in my chest as we huddled together, Chance and I offering whatever support we could to our omega.

I glanced up and King was there watching us with an almost wild stare, his hands tight on his knees.

He felt it too, or at least he was struggling not to throw himself forward. An easy purr rose from my chest, a sound to soothe the shaking woman in my arms, and King joined me a moment later, brow furrowed with concentration.

"What would Omikron be doing raiding the Wasted?" Chance asked.

"They wouldn't," King said stubbornly, eyes on Faith.

I licked my lips and debated sending Chance and Faith to the nest to avoid stressing her out further, but if it did have anything to do with Omikron, it involved her first and foremost.

"I've been running through it in my head. Coulda been a drug raid, although I doubt Gizmo would miss enormous DEA initials if it was. Might've been a new or rival gang. Wasted's sure to be pissing off other people," I suggested.

"What if...what if they did something because you stole me?" Faith asked, lifting her face from my chest.

"I considered that," I said, nodding. "It's the only thing that made sense to me, but even so, I don't think it's the only answer out there."

"But if it was them, we have a heads-up," King said, leaning forward and catching Faith's eye.

"They could already be on their way," Faith murmured.

King's lips pursed. "You know we aren't exactly good men, princess." His eyes flicked up to mine. "No church. Tell our best to be armed. Club is closed to strangers. Hell, close it to the girls who aren't already inside too."

I nodded. "You wanna tell 'em the truth, or just that we might have trouble coming?"

"Blame it on the Wasted," Chance suggested. "It's true enough."

"But they'll be expecting the wrong thing," Faith said. The three of us all turned to stare at her, and her cheeks pinked. "It's just...I watched the pair that came here that Chance dealt with. Maybe the Wasted are dangerous, but they're not exactly stealthy or hiring mercenaries like Omikron. It's a totally different kind of attack...don't you think?"

King purred again and nodded, his eyes slitted and focused on Faith. Apparently, her strategizing mind did it for the club president. I couldn't blame him.

"You're right. But I also agree that the whole story will kick shit up with the others. So give folks the rundown on what happened to the Wasted. A threat to one MC warrants caution from us, and planning. We may want to take advantage of the Wasted at their weakest," he said.

I nodded and rubbed my hand over Faith's shoulder. "Whether those fuckers come for you or not, you're staying safe right here, Butterfly. I promise you that." She twisted on my lap, nibbling on her bottom lip and gazing up at me, worried. I shook my head. "Nothing's happening to *any* of us. Now, you wanna go up to the nest with Chance?"

She took a breath to answer, but King beat her to it.

"Stay here."

Faith blinked at me, and I caught the ripple of confusion and surprise in our connection before she turned to face King again.

He was staring back at her. "You're safe no matter what, but I..." He struggled, gaping at her and his brow tangling, and I wanted to laugh as he searched for an excuse as to why she should stay in the office.

"You've got work to do too," I said, saving him.

Faith looked down at the unopened computer box on the floor and nodded, straightening. "Right. Okay."

She stood with me, stopping me with a gentle hand on my chest. Her face was lifted, large dark eyes aching with worry, and that beautiful bite mark vivid on her throat. It took everything in me not to haul her up into my arms and drag her back to the nest to place another more permanent mark on her too.

"Be careful," she said, soft and serious.

I wrapped an arm around her waist to haul her up against my

chest, slanting my lips over hers. I hadn't had much time alone with her since the start of the heat. It might be time for me to ask Chance and King to politely fuck off for the night. But first, I needed to make sure we were locked down and secure.

"Be good, don't push yourself, and wear the glasses Molly gave you," I said, dragging myself away from those plush and tempting lips, leaving Faith all soft and panting as I set her back on her feet.

She swallowed and nodded, turning to Chance next.

I pointed my finger at King as they embraced, and he arched a silver eyebrow back at me. *Be nice*, I mouthed, glaring at him.

He scowled back at me, but I knew the reminder would stick in his head. I was learning King's weak spots lately. And they just so happened to be the same as mine.

I bit down on the inside of my cheek, distracting myself from the urge to scream and throw the computer across the room. Adam had made me watch him anytime we had to reconnect the server to a new computer, and he'd definitely lectured me on the steps or sat over my shoulder and instructed me in the process. Doing it on my own was a lesson in trial and error and giving myself seven headaches in a row.

I was on day two of working, and I'd already needed to start from scratch twice.

Luckily, the project was the perfect distraction from the news Bear had brought back yesterday afternoon. There'd been no sign of Omikron around the club so far, and I was holding my breath that it remained that way. I was too close to reaching Adam now, too attached to these men who'd saved me, to be ripped away again.

I pushed the computer to one end of the couch in King's office, tearing off the glasses Molly had found for me, and collapsing back against the other end, glaring up at the ceiling. I knew I was close on the server, but close wasn't good enough when dealing with source coding.

Across the room, behind the desk I'd been avoiding looking at for most of the day, a throat cleared.

"I'm fine," I said, a little too sharply.

King's rolling chair squeaked as he pushed back from his desk, a loop of keys on his hip jangling as he approached me. My knees were bent, feet planted on the couch cushion, and he lifted them and my computer together, sitting down and stretching my legs out over his lap.

"Shit. This is gibberish," King muttered.

I smiled and tipped my head to look at him. He was wearing a pair of glasses too now, the sight of which did outrageous things to my insides, and he glared at the laptop screen like it was playing tricks on him.

"Did you come over to help?" I asked.

King grunted and continued to squint. I slid one leg out from under the laptop and rubbed my foot against the side of his thigh. He reached for me absently, fingers wrapping around my ankle like a cuff.

Do not get horny right now, I scolded myself, even as my body heated at the simple touch.

"Thought I'd take a look but...now I'm afraid of touching anything," King said.

"Mm, better not. I know I'm nearly there. I think I'm just switching a few of the strands around." I reached for the laptop and King passed it back to me, but he didn't get up to leave. I rested the computer on my stomach, and his hands stroked over my calves.

"Gotta be pretty smart to figure that kind of thing out," King said.

"Adam *is* smart. I didn't build any of this. I was just supposed to remember how to get in. Which, obviously, I failed at." I let out a long sigh as my next attempt failed. But it was easier to stay calm with King working his fingers into my muscles like that. Harder to focus too.

"You need to take a break, princess," King said.

"Not yet."

"Faith—"

"One hour!" Over the top of the laptop, King raised his

eyebrows at me. I raised mine back. "One more hour of trying, and then I will take a break and you can make me go take an omega nap or whatever coddling it is you and Bear think calms me down."

"Princess, I *know* what calms you down," King said, smirking and sliding one hand high up my leg, teasing my hips forward without touching and then retreating again.

I almost scolded myself again before I realized that, *no*, this was definitely King flirting with *me*, and while I'd sworn to myself that I would stop pushing him, I'd made no vow on responding to his advances.

"The massage is helping," I said, waggling my eyebrows. "I know you're busy, but—"

"I've got a little time," King said.

I hid my smile behind the computer and got back to work as King moved those magical hands down to the soles of my feet. I couldn't decide which I liked best—when he was being gentle with me, or when he was spanking my ass hot and red.

"So if you're not the computer genius, what are you?" King asked.

"Hmm?"

"You said your brother was the one who set this...service thingy up?"

"Server. Yeah. Adam did...most of the work, honestly. Made the plans, hacked into the companies to find the information we needed. I just made sure to do whatever he needed. Be the lookout, open the right door at the right time, smile at the right security guard in a bar while Adam swiped the badges."

King laughed at that. "Pretty little bait. Bet it worked every time."

I frowned and glared at the screen, nodding.

"Did you like it?"

"Like it?"

"Fooling them?"

I scrunched my nose up and shrugged. "It was just what Adam needed me to do. He did it himself when he could. Coached me on what to say and how to move when he couldn't."

"What made you decide to leave the foster home with him?"
King asked.

I blinked.

"You must've been pretty young."

I had still been a teenager. Underage. Adam and I ran *hard*
those first few years.

"Was the house unsafe?" King asked.

"It wasn't... Not exactly. It was just what would happen when
we turned seventeen. Straight into the system for a pack. A year
of courting and then that was it, we'd be bonded and settled."

King was quiet for a few minutes, and my head was in a far-
off place. Years ago. When I was fourteen and Adam was making
plans to leave for both of us and it was *impossible* to not go
with him.

"Why didn't he come back for you?" King asked.

I sat up, pulling my legs out of King's reach and glaring at
him. He was relaxed, lounging in his seat, face easy and
thoughtful.

"Omikron had me. He didn't know where to look!"

King blinked and shook his head. "Not that. When you were
a kid. Why didn't he let you stay at the home for a few more
years? Come back for you when you were seventeen and about to
be shopped around to packs?"

"I didn't want that."

"Mmm." King nodded. "Woulda been hard. The two of you
were all you had. No other family, no friends."

I'd had friends. Friends in the home and at school. And I'd
wept at night at the thought of leaving. But I'd wept at the
thought of staying too.

"What are you asking me?"

King shook his head. "Dunno. Just trying to figure you out. If
your brother is the mastermind, the one with the plans, who are
you?"

"His sister," I said, shrugging. King's head tipped to the side,
eyes narrowing, and my skin was hot and uncomfortable. "A
helpless omega! The idiot little sister who got caught—"

"Hey," King said, catching one of my flailing hands in his,
tugging me across the couch cushions, and ducking his head

until he caught my eye. "Enough. What was your favorite subject in school?"

I gaped at him. "I..."

Adam's had been math and drama. He'd even starred in one of his high school plays before we ran away. But King wasn't asking about Adam.

"I liked the easy classes," I admitted, staring back at King, snagged in his trapping gaze. "Umm, art and gym. I didn't really want to be in school."

King grinned at that, his arms stretched out over the back of the couch sliding down so his fingers could toy with the ends of my hair. "Me neither. Shop was my favorite, and I learned to like economics after I got lucky on an investment project."

I sighed, sliding the laptop away from me and helping myself to King's chest, outrageously pleased when his arms circled me. "Before our last home, we spent a couple years with this family that had a bunch of property, and it was all wooded, and...the woman ran a Girl Scouts program, and I just remember spending all of my time, when I wasn't in school or sleeping, outside in those woods." I still missed them, actually. Missed the smell of the air and the cluttered quiet of sounds that made up nature. I blinked and shrugged. "Not that that's something useful, really."

"Joy doesn't have to be useful, princess," King said, digging his fingers into my hair and scratching gently. "I didn't join this club or run for prez because I love the thrill of micromanaging. I find my joy on the road. On my bike. In the hoard of us together, moving like one."

"You don't have to be president for that," I murmured.

"No, that comes down to being ambitious, I suppose," King said, and he sounded weary. "And wanting to make sure the club survived, grew stronger."

"Adam is ambitious. He wants to take down Omikron, dismantle the market of putting omegas directly into the hands of wealthy packs," I said.

"Good for him." He sounded nonplussed, and my lips twitched.

"I'm not ambitious," I admitted. "I want what Adam wants, but I..."

I was tired of running, tired of being in danger. I wanted my nest and my pack and the reassurance of keeping both and remaining safe.

"You don't have to be ambitious, princess. You don't have to be useful to matter."

My face was hot, but King was too comfortable to move, his scent cloaking around me, its intensity almost defensive, like armor.

Who are you? King's words echoed in my head.

An orphan. A sister. A little helpless. Able to identify over two dozen types of trees and almost as many birds by their songs. A bad con artist. A dismal cook. An omega.

"I need to get back to work," I murmured, but made no effort to move.

King's beard whiskers brushed over the top of my head, and I thought he might've grazed a kiss there. "Me too."

"What *do* you do?" I asked.

King laughed. "Answer questions, mainly. Send emails. Make sure all the businesses we own in part are running smoothly, all the loans we give out return with interest. There's feet on the ground for all of it, I just have to keep the facts straight." He groaned and stretched his legs out, toes reaching toward his desk. "Landed myself in a desk job somehow."

I grinned and twisted to face him, my back to his desk, his arms around me keeping me balanced on the couch. His hair was dirty blond and silver, kept short enough and styled in a simple swoop. Unlike the others, he had no visible tattoos when he was dressed, and with the glasses perched on his nose, it was harder to tell how many times his nose had been broken.

"Bet if we put a suit on you, you'd look more like a CEO than a biker prez," I said, combing my fingers through his beard and smoothing his mustache.

King growled in response, eyes narrowing, "You trying to earn another spanking?"

I rose up to my knees, prepared to turn and plant my elbows on the arm of the couch, giving him the perfect pose to do exactly that, and King barked out a laugh, his hand landing on my shoulder and pushing me to the opposite side of the couch again.

"Get back to work, princess. You have one hour," he reminded me, rising up from the cushions and heading for his desk. "Then you can demand a distraction of your choice."

With a promise like that, it was hard to remember that I'd been dead set on working until I'd cracked into the server. Focusing on anything other than ideas of what to do with King seemed next to impossible.

But the conversation had shaken loose old cobwebs in my head and unwound the stress from minutes ago. I tweaked aimlessly, more interested in wasting time now than confident I'd succeed.

Until suddenly a familiar frame took over my screen, rudimentary and old-fashioned, almost clumsy-looking. I gasped, fingertips still hovering over the keys, prepared to continue editing the code even after I'd finally pieced everything together. The login box waited for me, cursor blinking.

"What is it?" King asked from across the room.

"I did it," I said, staring dumbly at the screen.

King rose from his chair and I shook my head, diving into typing again, hands trembling and mind blanking over my password.

Shit, I'd managed to rebuild the server on a new computer after months away from Adam, and I couldn't remember my—

Oh, right!

The couch cushion sagged as King joined me, and I blushed as he huffed next to me.

"Well, would you look at that," he said, leaning in to squint at my username. *RunawayPrincess*.

"Shut up," I answered. "It's from a video game..." It was not, and King scoffed. "I was sixteen," I mumbled.

King chuckled, and my finger hovered over the enter button. "He might not even be safe," I said, frowning at the screen. "I don't know that Omikron hasn't had him this whole time. He could be auct—"

King pushed my finger down and my breath hitched, but I didn't tear my eyes off the screen.

The server has moved.

"What?" My voice was air, my lips numb.

There was nothing else. Just the four words in the center of the screen.

"What?" I repeated, scooting forward, hovering over the words and then frantically around the box, searching for a link. "No. No, no, no."

A warm hand landed on my back at the same moment that the words dissolved, a strand of code flashing across the bottom.

"Fuck! No. I—Adam—"

"Faith, it's—"

"It's not okay!" I shouted as the server froze, one error message after another popping up. "It was hacked, or—Oh fuck, it could be—Fuck, fuck, fuck!"

I scrambled at the keys, trying and failing to close the server. Adam would know what to do.

The server has moved.

My one fucking link.

Adam would never have closed the server. Would he? Had he given up on finding me after Omikron snatched me?

I let out a wild yelp of frustration, throwing my hands forward to knock the laptop away, but King was fast. He caught it as it clattered off my lap, snapping it shut and tossing it onto his desk in one smooth motion.

I couldn't breathe. My head was pounding and my chest was ice. King's hands caught my wrists in hot iron-tight grips as he knelt down in front of me.

"Omikron must have them," I gasped out.

"No. You don't know that," King said.

"But—"

"The night you got caught. Why were you and Adam there?"

"Because we'd gotten information from—" I blinked, and the room straightened around me, the vibration in my head settling.

"From the server?" King asked.

I nodded, and his hands loosened slightly. I set my own on his shoulder, anchoring myself by the force of this alpha. He reached for my waist, tugging me closer, and my legs had to part to make room for him.

"You think there was someone in the server who set a trap for me?" I asked.

"And Adam. But that doesn't mean they caught him," King soothed immediately, hands slipping under my shirt to stroke my back. "And that doesn't mean he wasn't the one who decided to move the server."

I bit my lip and stared over King's shoulder at the laptop. "If he did...he knew that was our only way to get in touch, King."

One hand caught my chin, pulling my eyes back to his. "Your brother is the one with the plans, right, princess?"

I sucked in a breath and nodded, and King mirrored me, his thumb reaching up and pressing to my bottom lip briefly.

"Then how do you know he doesn't have one now?"

"And if—"

"If he doesn't, you're safe here," King said, voice lowering to a purr. "You're safe with us. And *we* will come up with our plan too, how about that? I've gotta be good for something, don't you think?"

I released the breath I'd been holding, King's smile so confident and at ease. And when I leaned in he didn't push me away, didn't warn me that he wasn't the alpha for me or tell me I was misbehaving. King let my arms twine around his shoulders and slanted his lips across mine, swallowing my worries with deep kisses. I pulled him into me, drew him over me like a security blanket.

Good for something indeed. King was just *good*. Maybe he didn't see it, or maybe he didn't want me to get my hopes up. It was too late for that. With the server gone and no way of contacting Adam, I had nothing else to cling to. King, Bear, and Chance were it. And I didn't care what King thought was good for me—I wasn't giving him up.

"You see that fuckin' joke of a mark he planted on her?"

"Kid's got a complex."

"What he's got is some serious fuckin' knot envy," Skid spouted, cackling at his own shit humor. "Struttin' around the club with her on his arm like he thinks we don't see what a joke it is. Like he's not there to do more than lick her clean after Bear and King are done."

Rider grunted as I all but slammed the wrench down on the cement floor, livid and tense. A growl sat trapped in my throat at the thought of Chance having anything to do with another alpha.

"You jokers mind?" I asked, barely restraining my bark. "Trying to work, and you're sitting around gossiping like the club ass."

"Someone's tense," Rider said, low voice slinking under the body I was working on.

It was just a shitty little crotch rocket project for an alpha a few towns over who had more money than sense and taste. Any other day, I could've done the work in my sleep. Rider and Skid were throwing me off.

"Someone's been playing boy scout since we got back from the ride," Skid said.

Rider snorted as I tried again—and failed again—to ignore them. "When's the last time you got laid, Ghost?"

When your brother fucked me into his mattress and then told me not to come back, I thought, grimacing at the engine in front of me.

Skid feigned a whisper. "I know what's got his balls all bunched. There's new pussy around, and he's not getting a piece of it."

I nearly burst out in laughter, but Skid misinterpreted the hitch of my smile and ran with the joke.

"Pretty little thing, the whole group of them pretending they ain't dangling ripe omega right in front of us," Skid said. "You ever knot an omega cunt?"

Rider started to hum, pretending to think, and I rolled my eyes.

"Don't be a dickhead, we all know we've never been within feet of an omega before. Not one with a perfume, who wasn't already bitten and claimed," I said.

"And now here we have one all but in our laps," Rider mused speculatively.

And I happened to despise her. Or was at least burning with a jealousy that pooled acid in my chest. Even so, I didn't like the direction of the conversation.

"Ass is ass, cunt is cunt," I said, looking up from my work as Skid chortled. "And hers isn't worth three of my brothers wanting to rip my balls off."

"Don't chu know? Ghost prefers betas," Rider said, low and sinister.

My eyes didn't know where to look. Was I imagining the pointed hint in his voice? Did he know about my relationship— no, it couldn't be called that, could it—with Chance? My back was so tense, it was starting to drive daggers of pain up into my head.

"I'll take my chances with whatever cunt I can get," Skid said.

Rider snorted. "We *know*."

"Can you two fuck off so I can focus?" I asked, sharper than before.

Quiet followed and my jaw ground, adding to the growing

headache. I was not this guy, pissy and defensive, telling my friends to fuck off. Rider had once told me that I had the walk and attitude of a man who was perpetually getting his dick sucked. *Maybe that's what I need*, I thought, lying to myself.

"Man, what is your—"

"Sure thing, brother," Rider answered me before Skid could jump down my throat.

The work bench creaked as they rose, and my fist clenched around the wrench, muscles coiling tighter, just *wishing* one of them would reach for me, start a fight.

I imagined the clamp of a hand on the back of my neck, fingers digging in, and I held my groan behind my lips, head dropping forward as Skid and Rider's boots marched away.

I needed Chance. It wasn't those dickheads' fault I couldn't focus. I wasn't tense because they were disgusting idiots. I needed to be fucked, dismantled from the persona I wore every day, exposed for the truth. Weak. Worthless. Desperate. Disgusting.

I released the breath I'd been holding, sucking in a fresh lungful of grease and hot concrete and metal. Boots crunched over stone, and I rolled my neck on my shoulders, preparing for whatever private chew-out Rider was bringing.

"Don't tell me, Skid left his dick behind again," I said, bracing.

"Uhhh, I hope not. For his sake, whoever he is."

I stiffened, dropping the wrench and rising, turning to face the unfamiliar voice. The man standing in the open entrance of the garage was tall, handsome, with long brown hair tied back in some kind of artful man bun that would've gotten him eaten alive in the club. He was a civvy of some kind, and not a face I recognized.

I stepped forward, glancing over his shoulder to see the yard between here and the club clearly. This guy didn't look like a member of the Wasted. His hair was too long, and he was too... pretty, really, in a masculine way. But he definitely wasn't a local.

"Can I help you?" I asked, crossing my arms over my chest.

He grinned, all easy and cheerful, and stepped forward. His boots were right for riding, and they looked dusty, like he'd been out on the road with them, but there was something off about him that made the hairs on the back of my neck rise up.

"Gabe Cleary. My Triumph has a broken carb," he said, nodding his head to the left. "Station down the way on 78 said you'd be the place to take it."

"Didn't hear the tow."

"I walked it," he said.

That was a solid five miles away, which explained the hair bun, and also the sunburn on this guy's face and shoulders. I moved forward and he walked back, leading me out of the garage. His scent was juicy, almost alluring, but there was a sharp bite underneath the sweetness, enough to warn me this was an alpha in sheep's clothing. Not that I'd been likely to let my guard down with everything going on with the club.

But as promised, sitting just out of sight, was a dusty Triumph 900 Thunderbird. It looked to be in decent shape, an older model than I'd expected. It was the kind of bike I would've coveted for my own collection, really, a biker's beauty. There was no real rule of thumb when it came to who rode what, but I couldn't resist eyeing this guy over, trying and failing to imagine him on the bike.

"What do you think? Can you fix it?" he asked, still smiling.

Too friendly, bad timing, my head warned.

"Definitely. But I'm booked up for a couple days, and it'll take that long to get the part anyway," I said.

Gabe Cleary shrugged. "Not a problem. I'm staying in Huberville."

Two towns north. And right on the route of 78 he'd mentioned. I chewed over my suspicion, the club's current policy on outsiders, and nodded slowly.

"Lemme check this beauty in, then. I have some paperwork for you to fill out, got ID on you?"

Mr. Chipper nodded and kept smiling.

"Follow me," I offered, turning back to the garage. I'd get the bike, file and copy his ID, and take it all to King.

"Any chance of me getting a beer at that bar when we're done here? Just while I wait for a cab?" Gabe asked, digging into his pocket for a wallet as I dug out the pages for paperwork I didn't usually bother filing. I glanced up at him, and he plucked at his sweat-stained collar. "It was a long walk."

"Bar's closed for a while. Renovations," I said, noting the slight tightening of his eyes. "Best bet is the convenience store. I'll walk you over when we're done here."

The little plastic ID card clicked against my counter.

"Great," the alpha across from me said, and I tried not to smirk at the snap of frustration at the back of his voice.

———

KING GLARED at the photocopy of Gabe Cleary's ID. "You watched him get in the cab?"

I nodded. "And I watched the cab leave town."

"This look legit in person?" Bear asked, plucking the paper from King's fingers.

I shrugged. "It did, but it's not like we wouldn't know how to get a good one, right?"

"And you're sure he wasn't—"

"Skid and Rider left the garage right before he appeared. They would've seen him around the back if he'd been snooping. He looked like he'd just walked the five miles."

Bear hummed. "Could be true."

"Might not be," King countered, leaning back in his chair, hands steepling over his stomach. He looked to Bear. "Where is she?"

"With Chance," Bear said. "They made some dinner."

"Probably riling up the club," King said with a sigh. "Does Chance have to rub it in with those hickeys and bites?"

Bear's chuckle was low. "She loves it. She eggs him on."

I cleared my throat, drawing their attention back. I'd seen the marks on the omega's skin, and my own nerves had prickled with envy.

"Look, I... Some of the guys are talking," I said slowly, my brow furrowing.

I did not spread shit in the club. I didn't get involved in the little politics between Rider and King. I just wanted to ride, to fuck, to drink, and to work.

"Talking," King prompted, staring at me over the rim of his glasses.

I hated that omega. Envy was scorching running through me. I wanted her gone and my time with Chance back. But I wasn't so much of an asshole that I wanted her being preyed on by someone like Skid, who would push past a "no" to get what he wanted.

"No one has crossed the line with her yet, but the longer she's here, the more they'll think about it, test that boundary. Your warning is only gonna hold up so long," I said. "She gets comfortable, ends up alone with the wrong person..."

Bear growled lowly, but he and King both nodded.

"Understood," King said.

"Would you keep an eye out?" Bear asked, head tipped and eyes narrowed at me.

I frowned, considering the question. "I don't want anything to do with her. But...but I wouldn't let anyone hurt her either. If I was around."

Just get her out of the club, I wanted to beg. *Get her away from Chance. Or get them both out of my sight. Or...*

"Fair enough," Bear said slowly, the pair of them staring at me speculatively.

I had the sudden urge to squirm under those gazes, an uncannily similar sensation to the understanding I was being watched by an unseen observer. What were Bear and King seeing that I hadn't intended to reveal?

"Keep me posted on this guy," King said, tapping the paper on the desk. "He comes back, text me and stall. I wanna see him face-to-face."

"You got it," I said, digging my hands deep into my own pockets, backing up toward the door.

"You see Chance and our girl, send 'em upstairs," Bear said.

I gritted my teeth but nodded, praying the pair had already cleared out of the bar. The music was blasting, and the air was thick with alpha pheromones. We only had about half the girls that hung around still on hand, and I had a feeling shit was about to get ugly as brothers jockeyed over them.

I'd meant what I'd said to King and Bear about keeping the

omega safe, but it wasn't just her. The guys could be rough with the beta girls too, and I didn't stand for it. I was no prince, I knew that. I cut myself loose from the women I fucked around with, left bruised egos in my wake, hurt feelings, but I made sure they were enjoying themselves every bit as much as I was, if not more, while we were together. Competition over women led to bad behavior with a lot of the others, and I wasn't sure King really realized the strain the club had already started to take since he'd brought that woman home from the raid.

I debated going directly to the bar, searching out Chance and sending him and the girl away, if only for the excuse to speak to him. But I needed a moment to breathe before diving into that mess. I headed for the bathrooms, only needing to nudge the door to the men's room open a fraction before letting it slap shut again. Literally disgusting. It smelled like one of the toilets was backed up again.

I sidestepped easily to the women's instead. Most of the idiots in the club wouldn't be caught dead walking into the women's, too afraid they'd get heckled. But I was a regular in here, although usually with a...*friend* in tow.

I smirked as I opened the door. The women's restroom in the bar wasn't the freshest ladies', I was sure, but it was world's away from whatever had happened in the men's. It even smelled all sweet, and—

A soft gasp sounded from the stalls, an obscene wet clap of skin.

I grabbed the handle of the door before it could slam, guiding it shut and grinning as I listened to the girlish whine and low grunt of the couple.

"Filthy little thing, aren't you?"

I froze at the familiar rasp and the answering feminine keen.

"Slutty, slick hole," Chance growled.

"Chance, please—"

"You'd take two cocks here if you could, wouldn't you? And another here—"

I didn't know where the fury came from. Envy, not worry for the girl. Shock that he would say something like that to her, an omega, and not just a worthless shit like me. The final snap of tension after a day of winding me up. But whatever the trigger was, the anger shot free, lashing off my tongue.

"Hey! Get out of there. Now!"

I hadn't used my bark in years, and the last time had been to keep some fool prospect from burning his skin off on a hot welding iron in my shop. The sound was rusty but effective, and heat flashed through me, shame and anger and arousal burning up to my cheeks and down to my groin as I clenched my hands at my sides.

Two figures came stumbling out of the stall, the door banging hard behind them. Chance's arm was around the omega's shoulders as she cowered, her face pressed into his chest. His pants were barely hanging onto his hip, rigid cock not yet tucked away, and my mouth watered at the sight of him. He was livid, face red and flushed, chest panting, gaze as sharp as the tip of his throwing knives.

"*What* the *fuck*," he snarled as the girl he held trembled.

I gaped at them. I hadn't been thinking, and realizing I'd walked in on them fucking had split my head in two. He spoke to her in that same dark, mocking promise he'd used with me, and I wanted to shove him away from her for her sake, or tear them apart for mine.

"Don't play those games with her," I said, half-begging. "She's not—That's not—You're a beta, and—"

I knew the mistake I'd made as soon as the words came out. Chance's face went cool and impassive, his body straightening and stiffening, free hand reaching to tuck himself away. We'd never talked about my designation or his, but I knew how Chance felt about being a beta and what it would feel like to have me, of all fucking people, remind him.

I was too busy staring at him, shock spiraling my brain into careless mush, to notice *her*.

The snarl was low at first, soft and velvety, but it grew in warning and I flinched as she straightened, turning to face me. There was the creature we'd found in the van, the wild beast of a woman, tiny and dangerous all at once.

"Come on, birdy—" Chance started.

"No," she growled, stepping out from the shelter of his arm. "What did you just say?"

I shook my head, trying to swallow my own tongue since it was determined to be a bastard today.

"Say it again," she dared, eyes narrowed to slits, shoulders high and hands shaped like talons.

She was wearing a too-large T-shirt, and it skimmed around her mid thighs. She looked like a biker chick, actually, with black boots on her feet and that careless attempt at clothing, hair a mess, neck marked up.

"I didn't mean—No," I said, shaking my head again. "I fucked up, Chan—"

"You don't fucking talk to him," the omega snarled.

My eyes widened, and for a moment, I almost made the mistake of laughing, but she let out that low warning growl and my brain was finally catching up with my mouth. I bit the sound off, tensing, preparing for her scratch. I hoped she drew blood.

"You aren't fucking worth a tiny fraction of him," she continued.

"Birdy," Chance called softly, almost reverently.

I stared over her shoulder, saw the way he gazed at her back with that hunger he'd shared with me and the tenderness he never had.

"I know," I said.

She glared at me for a moment, tense and prepared to strike, and I relaxed, hoping she tore right through my chest to my heart. Eviscerated me.

"Lock the door and get on your knees," she said instead.

I gaped at Chance, but his eyes were only for her, as unreadable as ever. She turned her back to me, draped herself into Chance's chest. They were loose and soft and decadent together, perfectly beautiful and tempting. I didn't know if I was about to be absolved or slaughtered, and I realized I didn't care.

I turned, reaching numbly for the latch on the bathroom door, listening to their murmurs at my back.

"You sure, birdy?"

"I want him to see how good you fuck me. What it really takes. I want him to know..."

The lock clicked shut, and I turned back as she guided him to the sinks. There was a ledge there, the perfect height. I'd used it myself with girls plenty of times.

Chance lifted her to the counter and her legs spread, a brief and shadowy glimpse offered before he filled the space. Over his shoulder, that pretty, dark gaze studied me.

"I want him to know how perfect *we* fit together," she whispered, holding my gaze.

I shuddered and sank to my knees, and the pair of them grew larger in my view, vaulted above me, divinity in a dingy bar bathroom. Did she understand what she was doing to me? I pressed my lips flat to keep my thanks bound in silence, spread my knees wider to play the supplicant and relieve the ache in my cock as it fought against the constraint of my jeans.

They kissed, slow and deep, Chance's arms circling around her waist as she melted into him. I bit my lip, waiting for it to bleed.

He pulled away from her gaze, one lazy hand drifting down between them, slipping under the hem of the shirt. "You're just too desperate to wait, that's what it's really about, isn't it?"

He called her "birdy," and she sang as he sank his fingers inside of her, body arching, the slack open of her mouth as explicit as if I could see every inch of her.

I'd been around the debauchery of the club long enough to know that voyeurism was no special treat. What the fuck did I want to watch the others going at a woman for when I could be sinking into a pussy myself?

All of that changed when it was Chance I was watching. I could see almost nothing, just her face and his in the reflection of the mirror, his eyes fixed down at where he touched her. I didn't matter. Their scents cloyed together, sweetness clinging possessively to his freshness. Their breaths snagged and gasped and caught on the air.

And then he spoke.

"You need a knot, birdy?"

"No," she moaned.

"You want my fist?"

Fuck. Did he touch her that way? With everything he had? I didn't doubt it, only wished I earned as much.

"I want *you,*" she whined, draping her arms around his shoulder, swaying forward with her lips tipped up in offering.

"You want cock," Chance corrected, and my chest burned at that cocky, careless smile on his lips for her.

"Yours," she vowed sweetly.

"Your pussy seems plenty wet for just my fingers," Chance teased.

Her breath was ragged, body nudging forward onto his touch. I twisted, shifted quietly on the floor, and stifled my moan as I finally found a view between them. Chance's arm was corded with muscle, tattoos flexing as he worked his fingers inside of her.

This was torture, to watch and not touch, not be the recipient of that probing, stretching touch. And I loved being tormented. I deserved to be left wanting, to be ignored and abandoned on this dirty bathroom floor for what I'd nearly said.

Because I knew better than anyone, anyone but *her*, how little it fucking mattered that Chance was a beta.

My own chest heaved with hers as Chance's fingers slipped free, then rose between them, gleaming with her slick and poised in front of her mouth. Her eyes caught mine as she darted forward, wrapping pink lips around his skin, moaning eagerly as she sucked him clean.

I hated her, and now I realized I liked her too. She was mean and sweet at the same time, unafraid of me, adoring Chance. A feral smile—nearly a grimace—spread across my lips. I shifted one hand from where it clutched at my thigh, rubbing over my groin, and her eyes flicked briefly down to the spot before returning to Chance.

"Do you know why he wants to watch you fuck me?" she murmured, ignoring the way I was stroking myself through my jeans.

"'Cause he's a worthless piece of shit who can't find satisfaction," Chance muttered.

I barked out a laugh and Chance flinched, but she caught his face in her hands and shook her head. "Because you're fucking perfect. And he'll never know what that feels like."

I moaned, bucking into my own palm as they dove into one another, arms tightening and fingers clutching, grappling with clothing and skin until she was shouting as he plunged inside. Chance's face fell forward into her shoulder, a bellow of pleasure buried into her skin that I coveted and memorized in one. His surrender was brief, and in the next moment his hand was wrapped around her throat, stretching her back, her eyelashes fluttering. He surged between her thighs in that beautiful sinuous thrusting that made womens' toes curl.

"Fuck, Faith," Chance muttered, his brow furrowed. "Your little cunt won't stop strangling me."

It took me a moment, in the haze of need, to realize he'd said her name. Faith. Pretty and hopeful.

She keened, knees raising, body bowing to press into Chance's thrusts. The mirror wiggled behind her head, distorting Chance's crazed expression, but hers was clear, eyes fixed to the point where they joined.

I reached for my zipper, unable to resist the urge to join them, to involve myself in some way, be a part of the moment as more than the invisible observer.

Chance's head whipped to the side, glare fierce on mine.

"No," he snapped.

Faith's lips were an *O*, and he didn't pause fucking her, didn't spare me another second before his focus returned to her, to her face, watching the way he made her feel. I could've ignored the instruction, but instead I leaned into the pain in my cock, in my fists, letting it rush through me. It was heady agony, as fierce as the pound of my heart.

"Tell me, birdy. Tell me whose pussy this is," Chance rasped.

"Yours," she cried eagerly, throat arching.

"That's right. Whose omega are you?"

She shuddered and sagged, a limp thrill I knew well. "Yours, Chance."

"Mmhm. What wouldn't you let me do to you, birdy?" Chance murmured.

Her eyes opened, a wild light in her gaze. "Nothing."

Chance growled, hips snapping, and her hands clutched at his back as he bowed over her, tucking his face into her throat, nuzzling gently.

"Oh, god, yes. Bite," she gasped.

My teeth suddenly ached and my knot grew hard and stiff at that plea. I hated her. I liked her. I fucking *craved* her.

Chance held her tightly, and I knew the moment he dug his teeth into her throat because she tensed and howled and trembled. The room grew terrifyingly sweet, all her scent flooding the air, and Chance bucked wildly. My cock throbbed and my heart broke as his knees bent and bobbed, weak at the release he'd shared with her.

Their lips met as they caught their breath, stroking and dragging kisses that echoed in the silence. Chance cupped her face like she was made of porcelain, and her gaze was honey as she stared at him when he pulled away.

What I'd never had.

"Time for the nest," Chance said, a velvety warmth in his voice that made me shiver with longing.

She nodded, cheek rubbing against his palm, all soft and sweet, no sign of the snarling woman I'd drawn out. They soothed and tidied one another, and Chance lifted her from the counter as she giggled, his arms wrapped around her hips.

His eyes were up as he turned away from the counter and walked by me like I was just a bit of trash on the ground. Her gaze found mine, still soft from pleasure, but there was something else too. Victory.

She'd taught me her lesson.

She'd given me a gift too.

They left me on the floor of the bathroom, the door bumping shut behind them.

I groaned loudly, shaking hands tearing at the closure of my jeans, rising up on my knees and shoving my pants down to pull out my painfully stiff cock.

I was immediately close, at the edge of release with nothing but shame and jealousy to credit.

Faith and Chance.

I swallowed hard on their names, pulled my cock with a

clammy hand, and bucked into my own rough palm. I hauled their scents into my lungs, moaning recklessly, aware of the unlocked door at my back, the empty counter in front of me.

I didn't hate her now. I craved the mix of them on my tongue, thought of crawling after them and begging to lick her cunt. I ignored the fluid pooling at the head of my cock, punishing myself with my own uncomfortable grip. Nothing would stop me from finishing.

I'd told Rider and Skid the truth hours ago. I had less interest in the omega than any of the other girls at the club. It would be a lie now to say the same.

I'm sick, I reasoned to myself, shuddering at the cruel declaration of my own thoughts.

She was as perfect as Chance. I needed them both. Needed them staring down at me, leaving me weak. I needed that softness they shared too, wanted it stroking down my back when I was ruined from their words and touches.

That wish, those fantasy touches, drew out the sharp crack of release, bowing me forward as I spurted in hot, thick ropes over the floor. I fell to one elbow, still milking my own length, gasping and growling and fucking into my palm.

The aftermath was cold and filthy—the bitter reality of being left behind on the floor of the bathroom. But I had a new goal now. One sweeter and even more necessary than before.

Chance was mine. And soon Faith would be too.

I paced the familiar living room, cataloging the little changes Molly had made since the last time I'd been here. New couch, curtains over the windows now, missing photo above the mantle. Little pieces of our relationship erased. I didn't blame her. I'd never kept evidence of her in my office or my club bedroom. Her house didn't need to remain a tribute to what had long since crashed and burned.

I paused in front of the window that faced the street, checking the road again. No sign of anyone watching Molly's house. I pulled my phone from my pocket to glance at the time.

There was work I should've been doing, calls to make, people to check up on.

"You don't have to come," Bear had said, frowning at me.

I'd used the looming threats as my excuse, as if someone else like Chance couldn't have been called in. But Bear was right—I didn't need to come.

A door clicked shut behind me and I spun around, waiting for Faith and Bear to reappear, but it wasn't either of them. Molly entered the living room, pausing on the threshold and arching one of those all-too-knowing eyebrows at me.

"Almost done?" I asked, too gruff, abrupt.

Molly's lips twitched. "Yep. Running late?"

I cleared my throat and shook my head. "It's fine."

Molly's arms crossed over her chest, and she leaned against the doorway. She was still beautiful, still sporting that glint in her eye that made it apparent she'd already made a mental checklist of all my bullshit. There were times when I'd wondered what it would take to get Molly back in my bed. But our connection had been built out of a mutual weariness and understanding. The spark had never been a blaze, and it'd faded long ago. She could do better, I figured.

"She's doing well," Molly said, taking pity on me at last.

"Good." I couldn't keep my eyes from drifting over her head to watch the hall.

"Results are all clean, and I was able to get my hands on a birth control they offer to newly bloomed omegas. Will last her a couple years," Molly said. "Stress hormones are still high, but they may stay that way."

I stepped forward. "Wait, what?"

Her eyebrows rose and she shrugged, but her voice gentled. "She went through an extremely traumatic experience. Omegas develop a defense under those conditions where their hormones try to mimic that of an alpha. Added aggression, extreme temperaments, increased fight response."

"But when she finds a pack..." I said, hiding my clenched fists behind my back.

Molly snorted and rolled her eyes. "Maybe it will help, maybe it won't. There's not a lot of research available, from what I could find. Considering the extended period of her duress, I would assume it's going to be a long time before she levels out again, if ever. Considering the current circumstances, it's not bad for her body to still be ready, as long as she isn't under constant threat."

I thought of Faith splayed out on my desk the night before, limp and sweaty and satisfied as I licked her flavor off my fingers.

"We try and keep her relaxed," I said.

Molly's smile flickered out again. "I'm sure you do."

I resisted the impulse to grin. I'd be a lying bastard if I said that Faith's presence in my life didn't leave me swinging on a pendulum between coiled tension and weak-kneed, smug satisfaction. Luckily, the door down the hall opened and closed once more, preventing me from blurting as much out to Molly.

If her smirk was anything to go by, she already knew.

Bear's massive hand was cupped over Faith's shoulder as they appeared. She was wearing a leather jacket he'd gotten her, as well as a pair of thick jeans and solid boots. She looked every inch the old lady we claimed she was, but worse, she looked like *Bear's*.

I should've been relieved. I should've kept my mouth shut when Chance and Bear claimed her in front of the others. I should've tossed her out on her ass when she'd slipped into my office, all poison and sweetness.

But I'd made myself a liar dozens of times already. What was once more?

"You're riding back with me, princess," I said.

Bear rolled his eyes; Molly hid her smirk behind her fist. Faith just smiled and shrugged, reaching a hand out for mine.

"Okay."

And fool that I was, I reached back, clasping her hand in mine, running my calloused fingers over her smooth ones before tangling them together.

"Thank you, Molly," Faith murmured as I headed for the door.

"Anytime. I'll check in with you guys soon."

Bear rounded in front of me, opening the door for us. "Same route back?"

"It's the fastest. You think it'll be an issue?" I asked.

Bear shrugged. "We're at the edge of our territory, near theirs."

He was thinking of the Wasted. I was worried about the phantom of Omikron that haunted Faith.

"Then I'd rather be quick getting out," I decided, and Bear nodded, smiling at Faith and passing me her helmet.

Faith and I stopped in front of my bike, and I plopped the helmet down on her head. Her hair was braided back, and she tucked the ends into the collar of her jacket as I zipped her up.

"You like riding?" I asked. I'd watched her on the back of Bear's, learning to lean into the curves with him, relaxing gradually.

"I do, actually," she said, smiling. "It's hot, though."

I nodded. "We head north for the mountains a lot. It's fresher there. But we can ride year-round out here."

"How come you don't wear a helmet too?" Faith asked.

"Helmets are for precious cargo," I said, offering her a hint of a smile in exchange for her blush. "Now hop on."

She followed me onto the bike as I held it steady. She was less awkward getting on my bike than she had been with Bear, and I was pretty sure she'd have the hang of riding in no time.

My bike roared to life and Faith's thighs squeezed around mine, her arms wrapped around my chest as we rolled smoothly forward.

The vision of her on the back of my bike as the club rode out together was a tempting one, but Ghost's warning from a couple nights before lingered. The longer she stayed, the more restless the others would grow.

I'd wanted to believe they'd grow used to her, used to her place with us, but Ghost was probably right. Faith couldn't stay on suppressants indefinitely, and when her next heat came, there'd be no pretending she wasn't a buffet of temptation to all the alphas on the premises.

I had enough money saved to buy the kind of house an omega dreamed of, somewhere to tuck her away safely, but who would stay with her there when Bear and I were swamped, when I needed Chance's ear on the club?

She's a complication, the cold part of me reminded.

Everything was already complicated, the other half of me answered.

Both halves were right, and all it meant was that the scales were unbalanced, trouble heaped high and heavy.

Behind me, Bear's engine snarled, and my focus was drawn back to the road, to our surroundings. There were small figures in the rearview mirror, more motorcycles chasing our heels.

"Shit."

I twisted, nodding briefly at Bear to let him know I'd seen

them. I reached down, pulling Faith's arms tighter around me, patting them in place, trying not to be so goddamn pleased with myself as she pressed herself against my back. I remembered Molly's words and my own in tandem—my promise to Faith that she would heal in the right hands, and Molly's claim that she may have been changed permanently.

As I glared into the rearview mirror at the approaching enemy, adding gas and speed to my own bike, I decided I was proud of my princess. She'd survived and came out a fighter. I knew what that was like from clawing out of my old home, climbing my way to the top of the Devils. I would protect her from the worst and respect what she'd already lived through.

I signaled to Bear a new route, narrower, forcing us but also the Wasted to ride in single file. Bear backed off just enough to slide in behind me, guarding Faith's back, as we made a sudden sharp left turn down an alley.

Faith's grip tightened over my stomach, but she didn't fight the turn.

We'd reach the edge of town soon, and the open road would give the Wasted too much opportunity to surround us. I needed to gain as much room as possible between them first, if not send their bikes crashing off the road.

I rushed through back alleys and side streets, backyards and broken down cars and dry pools blurring out of the corner of my eyes. My grip on the handlebars was brutal, my fingers aching, as I spread my focus for any sign of a civilian stepping out. I didn't know if I imagined the pound of Faith's heart against my back, or if I was aware of my own, my pulse pounding in my ears.

A crack sounded, and Faith jerked behind me as a burst of plaster on the corner of a house hit our sides and dusted the narrow, pocked alley. Another crack, more gas, and I snarled into the rushing air. Faith's grip remained tight around me, and I couldn't risk looking back to check on her. If it weren't for her on the back of my bike, I would've pulled over so Bear and I could fire back. But I wasn't risking Faith getting hurt in the mix.

The gunshots were going to attract police attention, and I needed to get Faith out *now*.

I cut down a side drive, checking my mirror as Bear twisted in place, turning to face the Wasted.

"Bear's gonna buy us time," I shouted back to Faith, skidding out onto the road, cutting off an ancient pickup driver and grimacing against the blare of their horn.

There was no sign of the Wasted or my enforcer behind us as we raced out of town and onto the highway that would lead us back to Dead End. I wasn't sure if that was a good sign, or if I had just left one of my men behind in danger or worse.

They would strip me of my crown for certain if I did, if Bear met an unnecessary end at the hands of the Wasted, but there was no muscle in my body prepared to turn back while Faith was still wrapped around me. I would get her back to the clubhouse, and then bring Ghost and Chance and Rider back with me.

Faith was trembling by the time we shot into the front lot of the clubhouse, screeching to a stop under the eaves of the old motel entrance. I didn't know if it was fear, if she was back in her feral state, or if she was just shattered from riding like hell on wheels with all that tension. I had to push and nudge her off the bike to rise up from the seat myself, and my own hands were shaking as I pulled her helmet off.

"You okay, princess? You get hit anywhere?"

There was plaster dust on her jacket, and her pupils were blown black, gaze unfocused as I tipped her chin up.

"I gotta get back and see if Bear needs help, princess, but you have to tell me if you're hurt," I said, searching her again, twisting her to check her back.

"He's not hurt. He's coming," Faith murmured.

"I think so too, but I need to—"

"He's coming back," Faith repeated, more determined.

Fuck. If Bear was hurt, what would it mean for Faith? I couldn't be good for her the way he was, but I would sure as hell try.

"Okay, baby, but—"

Her hands flew up between us and I braced myself for her strike, but it never came. One gentle, clammy hand cupped my jaw, and my eyes followed the other as it landed over her chest, pressing into the zipper of her jacket.

"I can feel him, King," she said, eerily calm with those full black pupils, her scent all ragged from stress. "He's on his way back."

Anger, *jealousy*, blazed in me, my gaze scorching over her in search of the mark. "He bit you?" I growled.

And the dangerous, beautiful, perfect woman in front of me blushed and smiled. "I bit him, the day you all found me. It's not a bond, it's been fading, but—"

Her stare whipped away from mine, and my hands twitched to drag it back. There was an engine purring on the road, growing louder with every second. Bear was back, just as she'd promised.

She had bit him. Could feel him. And fuckin' Bear hadn't said a goddamn word to me about it.

Faith's gaze was on the road as the words slipped out of my mouth. "I never stood a chance of getting rid of you, did I?"

She blinked and glanced back at me, and I cursed my own mouth. But she didn't shove me away as I gripped the back of her neck and dragged her lips to mine. She was safe. Bear was safe.

I didn't give a shit about their bond aside from wanting...

I growled against Faith's lips, licked them open and stroked my tongue to hers. She melted into me so beautifully, and I wasn't sure which of us was surrendering as we tangled closer. I'd never had a sweet tooth until this omega showed up, but now I couldn't get enough of her delicate sweetness.

My hands tightened on the back of her neck and her waist as Bear's bike made the ground under us thrum, but she pulled free of me. Her gaze was shy and it left me too quickly. She stepped out of my arms and ran for Bear's bike, not allowing him to stand fully before she was throwing her arms around him.

Bear turned off his bike, the sudden silence a roar in my ears. He swung one leg over and scooped Faith up off her feet, into his arms.

"You're bleeding!" Her hands came back red from his jaw, and she struggled in his grip, searching for the wound.

"It's a scratch," Bear answered, marching over to me, a brutal scowl on his face.

"You good?" I asked.

"Fine. But I'm fucking done with this old lady nonsense," Bear snarled at me. Faith froze in his arms, her face slack and stricken in response until he continued. "She is my omega. Don't care what that means to you. It's just fact, and I'm not pretending otherwise."

"We need to talk to the—"

"I am taking Faith up to the nest. You'll see us tomorrow," Bear said to me, the words gritty—a warning.

I swallowed. I didn't want to have a church meeting anyway. I wanted to follow Bear, strip Faith down to nothing, and kiss every inch of her just to reassure myself she was safe. But he was marching past me, her face pressed to his throat.

The club is your life, I tried to remind myself. *Your vow is to your brothers.*

Bear's loyalty had shifted. I tried to drum up anger, but all I had was envy.

I sighed, wiggling away from Bear's tiptoeing fingers on my side, my head falling back against the bathroom mirror as his tongue ran up the center of my throat.

"Quit distracting me," I said, but my voice was too breathy to be stern and my nipples were prodding sharply against Bear's palms in encouragement. "Just let me put the liquid stitches on, at least."

Bear wrapped his teeth around my throat, dragging them over my skin, and I moaned, my thighs falling open. Tricky alpha. He knew me too well now.

"Bear...did you mean what you said to King?" I rasped, scooting my hips forward on the counter until they pressed to his as he loomed over me.

"I did, Butterfly," he purred, lips kissing down from my throat, hands now busy lifting the hem of my shirt.

"You're sure?" I whispered.

He paused at last, standing straight and soothing his hands down to my waist. Every time I looked at this man, I marveled at the strength of him, the pure power illustrated in every inch of his body, and the way all that came with such incredible gentleness and care.

"I'm sure, Butterfly," Bear said, smiling softly. "Are you sure?"

I grabbed up the little tube of liquid stitches and Bear rolled his eyes as I leaned in, but he lifted his jaw for me. It was just a scratch, as he said, and I'd already managed to clean it, but I didn't want to take any chances. Bear saved all his gentleness for me and I needed—wanted—to be the one to do the same for him.

I thought over his question as I smeared the glue in place, but there was only one answer running through my head over and over again. I capped the tube, set it aside, and cupped Bear's face in my hands, blowing gently over the scratch.

Bear didn't look nervous as I leaned back again and stared up at those warm whiskey eyes. He knew my answer too.

"You are my alpha, Bear," I said, tracing my fingers up the back of his neck and then running them into his curls. "I'm absolutely certain of that."

His answering purr was rich and heady, hands scooping back to grip my ass and tug me closer. "No going back."

I thought of what King had said to me before Bear arrived, before he'd sweetened the cruel words with a hungry kiss. "There never was," I said, shrugging.

I dropped my hands to my hem and lifted my shirt off over my head. I was wearing a lacy bralette underneath and Bear licked his lips, studying me as I arched and reached back for the end of my braid. I liked his eyes on me, the little ways his purr changed as he stared at my mouth or breasts or bared sex, different notes of appreciation for every part of me.

He caught my hand before I could pull my hair free, and his fist wrapped around the end of the braid, tugging slightly. He grinned as I gasped.

"Leave it, you like it," he said.

I nodded and then Bear dove forward, hauling me off the counter and over his broad shoulder. I cackled as he carried me out of the bathroom, and even to my own ears the sound was a surprise. A wave of gratitude rushed over me for this alpha, Chance and King too, for what they'd found me as, and the ways they'd already transformed me. I kissed Bear's back and he grunted in surprise, stopping in front of the nest with me slung over his shoulder.

I was jostled lightly, the sound of a buckle coming undone, and I watched from my bird's eye view as Bear shucked his jeans and underwear off, the round globes of his ass especially delicious from this angle.

"Hey!" I cried as he yanked me back down in front of him. "I was admiring..." I trailed off as I realized he was standing naked before me. His hands reached out to my hips, and I danced back out of the way. "I *am* admiring you. I didn't get to do that enough at the beginning."

Bear was enormous, muscles thick, and there were infrequent scars decorating his frame, including one puckered round that I suspected was an old gunshot wound on his thigh. It made me ache, a confusing mixture of worry and sorrow and heat.

"You're okay?" I asked, my eyes traveling slowly back up, lingering on the softened planes of his chest while he was relaxed. They would turn to carved stone as he fucked me, flexing and straining into the need between us. He was built by biology and circumstance, beautiful in all the instances of flaws and perfection.

"I'm fine, Butterfly, aside from how fucking badly I need to get inside you, hold you, make you mine," Bear purred.

Which was as convincing an argument as I required to join him in his nudity.

Bear grappled with me as I worked to undo my jeans, his hands joining mine, making the effort clumsier but more urgent with every scrape of his calloused fingers on my skin. His hand thrust down inside my open jeans, cupping me through my underwear, and I shouted, arching and riding that touch for a few weak thrusts before returning to the task of undressing.

I laughed, gasping as Bear ducked down, kissing my breasts through my bra as I tried to kick down the tight jeans and squirm out of the fitted legs. One arm ended up around his shoulders, and I wasn't sure if I was straining for balance or holding him to me. Probably both.

I'd never been with anyone often enough for them to really know me, know my body and how it responded. Bear, Chance, and King had learned more ways to get me desperate or make me come than I had on my own.

I ignored my socks and jumped free of my pants at last, Bear ready to scoop me up and hold me against his chest. He turned us toward the nest, one arm under my hips and the other reaching for the curtains.

"Leave them open. I want to see you," I said.

Bear grinned, waggling his eyebrows. "Don't have to ask me twice."

I squeezed my thighs around his hips as Bear ducked down, holding me steady and climbing into the nest. I took advantage of his focus being elsewhere to study his face and that milky, homey, sweet scent surrounding me. I closed my eyes and recalled the warmth of him the first night, the closeness and relief of him as he pet my back and let me ride him in the dark.

My instincts had driven me right into Bear's arms, the perfect shelter, the most worthy alpha.

"I love you," I said.

Bear's eyes widened and then we were falling over, landing in a heap on the mattress. He squashed me, and a laugh burst out with my *whoof* of breath.

"Shit, Butterfly, I—you—what?" Bear stuttered in a panic, tipping us over and then wrestling free of my arms to brace himself over me. His hair curtained down around his head, and he was stiff as I reached up to pull it to one side so I could see him.

"I love you, alpha," I repeated, a little shy of the words but determined to offer them, in spite of him practically dropping me. "You smell and feel and taste like home to me. You *are* my home, and you have been since the beginning."

Bear's breath rushed out of him and he sagged slightly, just enough for me to stretch and press our skin together. I still had my bra and underwear on, but I figured wrestling out of them at the moment would be a little distracting for Bear.

I raised my eyebrows in his answering silence. "Is that...okay?"

Bear shook himself, blinking. "Okay. Okay? I—"

He blinked once more and then dove down, mouth crossing

over mine, hands traveling everywhere at once, squeezing my ass, petting my side, hooking my leg up around his hip, shoving my bra up to expose one breast.

"Love you too, Butterfly," he rumbled against my lips. He sat up just long enough to beam at me, let me catch my breath and start to smile back, and then he was sliding down, mouth latching onto my breast.

I moaned and arched into his lips, the soft scratch of his beard on my tender skin, the intense suction and flick of his tongue over my nipple. My fingers combed into his curls again, holding him in place. His hands tried to tug my underwear down, but with him lying between my legs there was no budging them out of the way, and I laughed and whined as he growled against my breast.

"Bear. Bear...Courtney!" I cried at last, catching his attention long enough for him to lift off my nipple, staring in a daze at me. I grinned. "You have to move if you want those to come off," I said.

He stared at me for a long moment, lids growing heavy and a slow, sly smile stretching over his lips. "No, I don't."

His fingers twisted in the sides of my underwear and the edges pinched against my skin for one breathless moment.

Riiiip.

I gasped, my eyes growing wide, and then Bear raised his hips just enough to shove the torn fabric aside. The crown of his cock kissed against the lips of my sex as we stared at one another, one brief and tender warning. And then Bear was plunging inside of me in one steady stroke.

A high, aching note rose up unbidden from my lips, and I bowed up, pressing my stomach to Bear's as his cock filled and stretched me, my body eager to accept what it loved at the basest and most primal level. Bear rocked, thrusting deep and long a few times before I felt the first hint of resistance, his knot thickening at his base. I dug my heels into the bed, trying to push onto him, and above me Bear chuckled.

"You get my knot when you get my bite, Butterfly. And I wanna fuck you for a bit first," Bear purred.

I glared up at him and he grinned back. I whined as he sat

up, but the sound died as I watched the sunlight running through the window and into the nest kiss his honey warm skin, lighting up his smile. He shifted until he was kneeling, my body splayed out and pinned on his cock. It was explicit and exposing, and I reached for him.

"You're too far away," I murmured.

"Mm, for now. But I've thought a lot about this. Don't wanna steal Chance's spot on your throat," Bear said, brushing his fingers over the bruises Chance had left, marking me as his. I warmed at that, pleased that Bear would consider the beta's feelings on the matter, just as I would want. "And I know I told King to fuck off downstairs, but he's coming around. So it's gotta be a little private. Something to taunt him, but not the others."

"Bear," I said, nudging my hips forward, reminding him that I was naked aside from my rucked-up bra and his cock was still thick and throbbing in me, and in spite of his claim, I was currently being fucked neither a little nor a lot, as I would prefer.

"So I'm gonna bite you right here," Bear said, holding my gaze and running his finger down from my throat to the breast he'd sucked to a point. He circled there, just around the puckered skin, using the edge of his nail as if he were drawing a line. "But you're little, and I'm tall—"

"Enormous, and a tease to boot," I said, grinning and surging my hips in little swirls since he wouldn't move. The friction was slight but decadent, and the tipped angle of my body left his cock dragging against the best places.

"—and it's gonna be a bit of a challenge for me to knot you and bite you at the same time. But I think I figured it out," he said proudly.

"Share with the class, baby," I answered, my breath growing short as I worked myself up.

Bear purred, his hands grasping my hips. He rose up on his knees, carrying me up with him, and I groaned at the stretch, adding to it by reaching my arms back. He was holding me in place, my toes barely grazing the bed, leaving me helpless, and I liked it more than I maybe ought to have.

Bear dragged slowly out of me, watching me squirm, wetting his lips as he glanced down at where we were joined, before pushing slowly back in. I moaned and my eyes fluttered shut, but he squeezed my hip and drew me back.

"You're beautiful, Butterfly. My sweet omega," Bear purred.

"Alpha," I answered without thinking, the primal effect of him using my designation making me hot and quivery all over. "Bear, please."

"Patience," he groaned, although his head fell back briefly as he drove into me again, a little faster than before. But where my breath was ragged and my chest was heaving, Bear's was steady.

His hand shifted on my hip, circling the front, thumb stretching to press and swirl over my clit.

"Oh, fuck, yes," I hissed.

"You're gonna come on my knot, Butterfly. Need you to get it nice and wet first so it slides right in for you," Bear purred.

I actually liked the pressure and stretch of a knot pushing in, but I wasn't about to dissuade Bear from his current pursuit. Nonsensical praise flowed from my lips as he worked my clit and kept his slow and torturous pace of fucking.

I was close—too close, probably—and I should've warned Bear, but I was greedy. I knew he could make me come and then knot me and give me a second—and third, and fourth, and however many he was in the mood for—orgasm.

He knew my body too well now, and when I started to flutter and squeeze on his length he slowed to a stop, lowering his ass down to his heels. His thumb pulled away, and I whined and tried to press my feet back to the bed, use leverage to move. Bear tutted, scooping my legs up and over his arms.

"Not yet, Butterfly. So close," Bear murmured, leaning forward, folding my legs with him.

"*I'm* so close," I whined.

He grinned. "I know you are. And I know you can wait just a little bit longer, omega."

The word worked its magic again and I preened. Bear had somehow sweet-talked me into liking being called omega again, at least by him, in these tender, private moments.

His head leaned down and I twisted his hair back, gasping softly as he littered kisses over my shoulders, my ribs, circling around my breasts, slowly working his way closer. I hummed as he kissed a wet line up between my breasts, grazing his mouth over one, licking the nipple, before returning to my left.

"That one's your favorite?" I asked.

Bear chuckled against my skin. "Maybe. She's just a little more sensitive."

Was that true? I hadn't even noticed, how had he managed to—

"Ohhh," I groaned, bucking my chest up into his mouth as he kissed my nipple and then sucked it gently between his lips. His teeth circled around the wet tip and I tensed, bracing for his bite, waiting too long before I felt the gentle tremble of Bear's laughter.

"Quit teasing me!" I said, swatting him on the back, trying to resist joining him in laughing.

"Don't tense, Butterfly," Bear said, lifting his head just enough to rub my breast with his beard as he smiled at me. "I won't hurt you."

I nodded, relaxing again as he purred for me. He held my gaze, kissing my nipple once, twice, a third time until I was giggling and melted in his arms, over his lap. He released my eyes at last, hips flexing, mouth enveloping my breast, and I sighed at the wet suction, his circling tongue.

His knot pressed to my opening, and he stroked out of me just briefly enough to rub against my clit. I moaned and then he was pushing in, filling me with a firm stroke and thrust. His bite mirrored the pressure of his knot, the force of them together creating an immediate and electric current that ran from my chest to my cunt. I came in a sudden velvety wash, my twisted and tense and needy body turning liquid in Bear's embrace. Warmth pooled in my chest as Bear purred into my breast, his sharp teeth digging and fitting into my skin. The bite was hot— stinging, almost—and then it was heavy and soft, a rush of gentle hands running from head to toe.

Bear's arms adjusted, letting my limp legs fall, his body crouched over mine as he started to gently buck.

The sweet enveloping sensation continued. I gasped as I realized the bond was forming, soaking into my chest with a creamy warmth. Bear groaned, his arms circling my back, body rocking in tiny shifts, tongue swirling around his teeth.

This was no thin thread—this was like being dipped in the honey sweetness that *was* Bear, being surrounded by him. And he was wilder and bigger and more eager than I'd even realized, his affection fervent and love fathomless. His pleasure was predatory in its hunger, consuming and greedy, and I laughed in relief at the selfish joy he found in claiming me, knotting me, and biting me. Because I knew the animal inside of him, and its exact match lived in me.

Bear released the bite slowly, soft whimpers and whines running freely from my lips as he lapped at his mark, shivers of syrupy pleasure drawing one release after another from me.

"That's it, omega. You're mine now. Soak my knot. Let me fill your greedy little cunt up," Bear rasped. His hand slid to cup over his mark, his knees unfolding to pin me beneath his body.

I gripped his face and drew it to mine, tasting my blood in the kiss, and Bear rutted on top of me.

"My alpha," I murmured.

He growled once, purred next, and I came, burying the cry into his throat as he joined me, filling me with more of that decadent heat, love clawing through me like a storm.

———

"I THINK...I think you don't need to keep, um...oh, god—licking it like that," I said, panting even as I thrust my breast against Bear's tongue.

"Nursing the mark is important," he rumbled.

He'd been tending it for hours already, and I was slightly crazed with the nonstop *arousal* that it caused. It was like a mini heat, but all for Bear. He'd fed me from the stash of snacks in the room, bathed with me, fucked me twice more, and *still*, he was tracing a circle on my breast with his tongue.

Just when I thought I might *scream*—for a break or for his cock, I wasn't sure—he sat up, hair tangled and a bright boyish grin on his face.

"Done for now," he declared.

I huffed and collapsed, flopping an arm over my eyes.

Bear laughed. "What? I can *feel* you now. I knew when to stop."

My own smile stretched in response, the joy buoyant between us. There was *so* much of it, just running circles around the bond, that I thought it might suddenly come flooding out of me, illuminating the nest.

"I was a little kid the last time I was this happy," I said without thinking.

Bear purred, settling at my side, bundling me up in his arms. A little sliver of sadness cut through the joy, and the contrast made the moment more beautiful, more precious. I savored that memory, in the woods with Adam, a rare day in childhood when he'd agreed to play the knight to my princess.

"Won't be so long in between from now on," Bear rumbled in my ear, tucking his legs against mine.

I nodded, my chest aching with relief, with missing Adam. The light show in my heart dimmed, still warm and tender, and I breathed in the scent of my alpha, one deep inhale at a time, until I fell asleep.

I liked the clubhouse as the sun rose. Dawn entered through the front doors of the motel, cutting through the posters on the bar windows to beam rosy stripes of light through the filthy space. I was meant to have one of my men with me at all times, but Bear and Chance were heavy sleepers, and King was usually gone before I woke.

There was broken glass on the sticky floor this morning, and I sidestepped it carefully in my flip-flops, roughly counting the bottles left on tables and planning my attack on the room.

The bar's kitchen was surprisingly tidy, and I suspected the beta girls ran it without much interference from the bikers. I'd learned from Chance how to set up the industrial coffee carafe that was kept in pristine condition, and I'd developed a routine of prepping the coffee and cleaning the bar while everyone else slept.

I was bent down in front of the sink, digging for the giant trash bags, with the carafe whistling, when I was caught.

"You're not supposed to be sneaking around alone."

I jerked up at the warm voice, cracking my head against the sink's edge. I cried out, cupping my head, squeezing my eyes shut as flashes of pain pounded through my skull. In one breath, I knew whose boots were stomping against the cracked tile floor of the kitchen, heady spice and sweet syrup on the air. Rough fingers caught my wrist, and I opened my eyes to find Ghost standing in front of me, scowling.

"I'm not sneaking around," I said, glaring at the startlingly handsome face in front of me, recalling it twisted in agonized desire as he'd knelt on the bathroom floor. I searched for a sense of shame at what I'd done with Chance, but there was none now, just as there'd been none the night it had happened.

Ghost's green eyes flicked over my shoulder to the coffee brewing and then back to mine, the contact startling. His scent was calmer now than it had been in the bathroom, so rich and cloying as he'd watched us, but I was still grateful for the suppressants because even dulled, his pheromones made my mouth water.

"Club ass picks up after us. That's not your job," he said, frowning.

"Don't call them that," I said, my voice too thin.

His eyes narrowed, lips pressing thin but curving up at the corners. "What do you think you're doing, slick?"

My face went hot at the nickname. Ghost was standing too close, and somehow I'd found the sink's edge against my back. He pulled my hand down to my side, and he was tall enough to look over my head simply by looming closer, leaving my nose directly in front of his throat. I told myself not to breathe, but my lungs rebelled, greedily capturing whatever they could.

"It's not their job, either, they just do it for you 'cause..." I trailed off, frowning, not really sure *why* the women who hung out at the club agreed to do so many chores.

"'Cause we pay them. King covers some of their tuition if they wanna be in classes, or pays them to work at the bar or clean the place up," Ghost said, leaning back just enough to arch an eyebrow at me.

His beard was longer than Bear's or King's, dark hair curling at odd angles on top of his head. He had intricate but slightly faded tattoos running down both of his arms, and I tensed as those muscular arms braced against the sink on either side of me.

"You tryin' to get caught by an alpha down here, slick?"

"Don't call me that."

"Why not?" Ghost grinned at me, feet shuffling closer, pinning my hips with his. His gaze grew hooded and hot on my face, scanning over every visible inch of me. "I've seen it myself, smelled it. Haven't tasted it yet, though."

His hand skimmed up my thigh. I was wearing a pair of Chance's boxers, but they were loose and Ghost's fingers slipped easily up under the hem, stroking the front of my thigh, moving toward my center. I stiffened and rose to my toes, words rushing out of me.

"You're trying to get back at Chance."

Ghost blinked, hand freezing, and his head shook slowly. "I'm trying to get Chance *back*."

I snarled, the frozen and somewhat eager prey version of me vanishing in an instant. Ghost laughed as I shoved him back, my body tensing and preparing to fight.

"I am *never* giving him up, especially not to you," I growled.

Ghost only laughed, head tilting to the side slightly, eyes grazing over me. "Never said that. I want you too, slick. Want the pair of you crawling all over me, pinning me down, just like you did in that bathroom."

I blinked at that, relaxing slightly. Ghost's smile grew, but there was something false to it, too charming, all greased up and confident. He'd been more honest on his knees.

"You hurt him," I said, watching with a cruel kind of pleasure as that smile fell apart, and the man before me was stripped down with a slow ripple of shock.

"I never—"

"You're never going to get Chance back by being ashamed of him."

Ghost's eyes widened, tan skin paling. "I'm not ashamed of him!"

The coffee carafe beeped, and I turned away from Ghost with a sigh of relief, retreating to my morning ritual. I hadn't started cleaning the bar, but I believed Ghost was telling the truth about the girls getting paid, so I supposed I could leave them to it for this morning.

"I'm not ashamed of Chance," Ghost repeated, his warmth hovering behind me as he approached.

"How many other people aside from me knew the two of you were ever together?" I asked.

"That's not about being—You and I both know that Chance doesn't want to be seen as an alpha's beta," Ghost said, voice lowering.

"Why would that be what anyone saw?" I asked, frowning, watching the coffee rush into the mug.

"Because I—I don't know how—"

I turned, and for a moment I did feel a kind of sympathy or affection for the floundering man standing in front of me. His fingers ran through his hair, gripping at the roots. There were dark circles under his eyes, lips slightly chapped. Handsome, yes, but haggard too.

"You're ashamed of yourself," I said.

Ghost's eyes bounced to mine, widened, a hint of fear in the growing pupils.

"Or you're ashamed of what you want from Chance. But that's not so different than being ashamed of *him*, right? Because that dominance we love from him is part of what he needs and who he is," I said, shrugging. "He will never be less to me than Bear or King. I don't care what your so-called brothers think. I will try and make that obvious to them at every opportunity."

Ghost swallowed, and I decided he needed the mug of coffee I was holding more than I did. He took it from my outstretched hand, blinking down into the dark surface as I poured myself another.

"Do you think...he's going to forgive me?" Ghost asked.

"Do you think you'll earn it?" I asked.

His smile returned, smaller and private. "Dunno. He has you now."

I bit my lip. "I think for Chance, designation is...everything, and he's wrestling to make it nothing. The fact that I'm an omega matters to him. And I'll never be an alpha, so..."

Ghost's gaze searched the kitchen, like he was looking for

Chance as he sipped his coffee. Suddenly, his brow furrowed and he turned back to me, still smiling.

"You want me," he said, with all that cocky alpha confidence from minutes ago. But I knew now how easily it was stripped away, how hollow he looked beneath the surface.

I rolled my eyes, turning and filling another mug. "You have me curious."

"Maybe Chance isn't the only one who'd like to put their boot on an alpha's throat," Ghost said, voice growing deeper.

I lifted my chin in response. "Maybe you should stop leading women on and let them hold the reins for once."

"Oh, but slick, you *know* how much I liked it when you took the reins," Ghost purred, and I tried to hide my shiver at the unexpected sound. "You can probably still find how much I liked it on the bathroom floor."

Well, that cleared my head. I snorted and headed for the door. "Gross."

"Wait," Ghost said, following me. "I meant what I said. You shouldn't be wandering around here alone. Never know when one of the others might appear. I'll walk you back."

And in spite of the way he'd cornered me earlier, Ghost was gentlemanly as we walked back through the bar together, remaining at my side but with space between us. There was no sign of the rest of the club, aside from some growling snores behind closed doors, but Ghost was quiet and watchful company.

I drew to a stop in front of Chance's bedroom door. He'd stopped by the nest briefly while Bear was still teasing me, and then left again and not come back. I wasn't sure if the bondmark would be a sore subject for him or if he'd just wanted to offer us our space, but I'd find out now. Ghost stared at the blank door with an open longing. An idea bubbled up and I hoped I wasn't making a mistake.

"Hey. Give me your scent mark," I said softly, nudging Ghost's hip with mine.

I had a mug in each hand but I held them aloft, standing straight and arching my head to the side, offering the opposite side of my throat from where Chance's kissing bruises were.

Ghost's eyes bounced between mine and my throat, and he licked his lips twice. "Are you sure?"

"No, but—"

He didn't let me change my mind, ducking down. I stiffened as his dense beard and soft cheek rubbed against my throat. His hair tickled my nose, rich with that spicy scent, something playful and bubbly under the surface. His nose stroked over my pulse, and I sucked in a breath as his lips grazed over my throat.

"You're pushing it," I whispered.

And then his tongue was flat and hot against my skin. My knees wobbled and my legs threatened to fold as he lapped one long stripe up the side of my neck. My cunt throbbed its immediate approval of the mark. I pressed my lips flat, refusing to make a sound, but my eyelashes fluttered closed as a shiver of pleasure ran through me.

Sneaky bastard.

My eyes opened again to find Ghost staring down at me, smile soft, green eyes gleaming.

"You're messy," I said.

He laughed and nodded. "Yeah. Well, I've watched you come, and you're not so tidy yourself."

My cheeks blazed, and then Ghost reached out and turned the knob of Chance's door for me before stepping back. His eyes flicked to glimpse inside the room and then he was retreating, licking his lips again.

I pushed open Chance's door with my shoulder, bracing myself. Instinct had led me right so far, and it seemed in favor of Ghost, but I hoped that didn't backfire. I debated cleaning up a little in the bathroom, but Chance's bedsheets rustled as I entered, and he sat up in a direct ray of sunlight, all pale and exquisite.

"Birdy? Where's Bear?"

"Sleeping. Missed you last night."

Chance smiled, squinting at me, looking young and rumpled and soft. "Wanted to give you a little space, but I missed the nest too. You sneakin' around making coffee in the morning again?"

I nodded, and Chance grinned and patted the bed. I walked forward, holding my breath as if it meant that if I didn't smell the evidence of Ghost, Chance might not be able to either. But his face changed as I sat down, all that peaceful morning ease tightening into a slight frown as he leaned in.

"Ghost came in while I was there. It's okay. I'm okay, we talked," I said quickly.

"You talked as he rubbed himself all over you?" Chance spat.

"He's kind of obsessed with you," I said.

Chance's jaw flexed, teeth gritting briefly. "Doesn't smell like it's me he's obsessed with."

I set the coffee down on Chance's bedside table and tentatively scooted closer. I braced myself for him to pull away, but instead Chance snatched me up and dragged me closer, twisting and pressing me into the bed, arching over me, burying his face into the marks he'd left. I moaned as he bit, gentle now, careful with the bruise.

"Sorry," Chance whispered in my throat. "You're okay?"

"Don't be sorry," I said, reaching up to smooth my palms over his shoulders. "I'm okay. I think... I mean, don't you think we kind of owed him a conversation after what happened the other night?"

Chance groaned, but his arms tightened around my waist. His skin was warm from the bed and I mapped it greedily.

"We literally never bothered with much conversation," Chance mumbled into my skin. "He didn't deserve to watch you."

"Watch *us*," I corrected.

Chance lifted his face finally, glancing briefly at the other side of my neck before meeting my gaze. "What did he say?"

"That he wanted you," I said, and then decided to admit the rest. "And me." Chance scowled, and I slid my hands up his back and to his face. "Told him he didn't deserve you. But I think he might...attempt to try."

Chance was silent, staring back at me for a long time, still as a statue.

"Would you want that?" I asked, my voice small.

He hauled in a breath and then grimaced, reminded of Ghost's mark. "Birdy, you and I...we talked. I'm *yours*, you're mine. I will keep that mark on your throat every day until—"

I surged up, pressing my mouth to his, swallowing the protest, kissing him until he was kissing me back, until the tension bled out of him.

"I'm not going anywhere, Chance," I said against his lips, slowly relaxing back into his arms, stroking his cheeks. "But would you want a relationship that was honest and public and, you know, positive, with an alpha? With Ghost?"

Chance went quiet again, eyes flicking back and forth as he thought. And he *was* considering it. I'd heard the quiet ache in his voice the last time we talked about Ghost, felt the urgency and excitement that had run through Chance as he'd fucked me in front of the alpha. The pair was broken, there was no doubt, but maybe the pieces left behind might be worth reexamining, finding a new way to put them together.

"I don't know," he whispered, brow tightening, eyes on mine again.

I nodded. "Fair enough."

"Do you want him?" Chance asked.

I didn't want to tell Chance how the omega in me was excited by Ghost, so I stuck with the part I knew he would understand.

"I liked making him kneel," I said, my cheeks growing hot. "Him watching us. And I...have thought about what you said about the two of you. Watching you together."

Chance relaxed at last, face smoothing and lips smirking. "Horny little omega."

I squirmed at the words, thinking of Ghost calling me "slick."

Chance's hand reached up and cupped over the scent mark left by the alpha. "Shower with me?" he asked, and I nodded eagerly. The mark had been a calling card. But I'd have even more questions to answer if Bear smelled it, and this was between Chance and me first and foremost.

"You wanna suck my cock to make up for the surprise?" Chance asked, arching an eyebrow. "Nice and deep, like I know you can."

My breath hitched and my eyes widened and I nodded eagerly.

He grinned, pushing up, the sheet slipping back to reveal him pristine and naked and growing hard. "Good girl. Follow me."

I was sincere in my apology in the shower, and Chance was generous in his forgiveness, fucking me against the wall and gifting me a new bruise over the spot Ghost had licked. I wondered if he wanted Ghost to see the mark. I knew I did.

"Whatcha think of Ghost?"

I flinched at the question as Bear landed heavily in the seat next to me at the bar.

"I don't," I lied, leaning just far enough back to see that Faith wasn't at Bear's side. With King, then. Unless... I twisted on the barstool, searching the room quickly, ignoring the snag of my stare against Ghost's, where he sat in the corner with my brother and the usual crowd. No, she was safely away.

"Thinking he might work for pack," Bear said.

I blinked. For pack? I straightened and glared at him as it settled in my head. "Are you insane?"

Sure, Faith had already put a little worm of the idea in my head, but considering a relationship with Ghost was different than thinking of him as pack, a concept I was still adjusting the view of in my mind.

"He's the least consistent bastard in here," I said. "You wanna let him near Faith just so he can vanish out of her life again in a couple weeks?"

"You really think he could?" Bear asked, a serene smile on his face.

I laughed, and the sound wasn't as rough as I expected it to be. I actually liked Bear, as it turned out. And he was here talking to *me* about this, not King. Considered me pack, my opinion important. But he was so soft for our omega, he had rose-colored glasses on when it came to the whole damn club.

"She say something to you about him?" I asked, an uneasy slithering sensation circling down from my chest to my gut.

Bear shook his head. "No, but he came to King and me, worried about her safety. Just thought if he's decent enough to say something, maybe..."

That was news to me. "Why was he worried?"

Bear's cheer darkened at last, and his eyes narrowed in Ghost's direction. "Your brother and Skid were talking shit. Sure they're not the only ones."

My fists clenched at my sides, glaring at that corner table where my brother was huddled with his cronies. Ghost was sliding out of the booth, shaking his head and scowling, marching away from the group, and I realized suddenly I should've been heading in their direction, listening in on the conversation. I'd been neglecting my duties for King recently, wrapped up in time better spent with Faith.

Ghost was heading in my direction and I jerked my stare away, over to the hallway where King had appeared, Faith slung up in his arms, her face tucked into his throat. They were both sporting loopy grins, and King was strutting into the room like the rest of us weren't perfectly aware he was eating pussy for dinner every night of the week now.

"Hey. We've got trouble."

I twisted to face Ghost, startled by his nearness and also the hard fix of his expression, none of the humor and cocky smirk I used to strip him of.

"What trouble?" I asked.

But Ghost didn't get a chance to answer before it all became clear.

"Oh look, pack daddy decided to grace us with his presence tonight," Rider called from the booth, rising slowly up.

"Shit," Ghost muttered, stepping to my side.

Most of the room laughed, turning to eye King, whose grin

drizzled away as he set Faith on her feet and whispered in her ear. She gripped his arm briefly, staring up at him, but he nudged her in our direction and she hurried over, Bear's arms open and ready.

"What is this?" I asked Ghost under my breath.

"Mutiny," he whispered back.

"You been missin' me?" King called back, a sharp and false smile on his lips.

"Been wondering when you'd actually take the fucking time to see your club," Rider called back.

"Fuck," I breathed. A heavy hand pressed against my back briefly before retreating again.

The line drawn in the room was foggy, a few faces turning in confusion toward Rider, more smirking up at King. And yet Ghost was here, standing with me, with Bear, calling Rider trouble. And I fought against the relief that burned through me, wrestled down the gratitude, and focused on King.

"I see more of you fuckers than I sometimes care to," King said, arching his brows, drawing out fewer chuckles than he'd typically get for the joke. "You got something that can't wait for church, VP?"

"I've got something I want added to the docket," my brother said. He was marching slowly forward, one step for every taunt. Fewer of the brothers looked surprised than the ones who were eager to hear Rider speak.

King glanced in my direction, our eyes meeting briefly. This had been building under our noses. Rider had taken advantage of our distraction, the focus on Faith. Maybe he'd even taken advantage of the club's ride together.

"How long?" I asked Ghost.

"He brought it to me on the ride and I told him to fuck off. We were drinking—I didn't think it was serious," Ghost answered back.

I tried to recall every conversation I'd overheard, if Ghost had ever been present. But no, Rider must've realized where Ghost's loyalty would lie. *And why was it with King?* I wondered. Rider was his friend.

I turned to look at Ghost and he was already staring at me.

There was no obvious answer in his expression, and I wasn't brave enough to go digging for one.

"My door is always open," King said. Which even I knew was the wrong thing to say.

"Not lately," Rider said, with an exaggerated stare in Faith's direction.

"What is it then?" King asked, sharper.

Rider straightened and Skid and Nutso flanked his back. "I'd like to make the case for the impeachment of our club president."

King's smile returned, jagged edges and snarling lip. "You wanna present the case? Not ready to put it to a vote?"

"I wanna do things by our laws," Rider answered immediately, chin lifting. "I made a vow to this club to follow those laws. I take that seriously."

The implication was obvious. King had broken his vows.

I never intended to speak. That wasn't my role. Not for King, not in the club. But staring at Rider, at his confidence in his case, knowing what it would mean for me in the club, for Faith and King and Bear, I was up off my chair before my brain caught up with my mouth.

"One of those vows was loyalty to the president of the club. Not fucking whispering behind his back, trying at every chance to turn a brother's loyalty," I called.

Rider's stare turned slowly in my direction, and the open confusion at hearing me speak out, the obvious amusement, made me want to launch myself across the room and shove my fist into his teeth.

"Another was no fucking pack," Rider said, glaring at me, over my shoulder to Bear and Faith. "Every brother equal, no bonds, no fucking omegas."

"There's no pack," King said, but even I thought he didn't sound very convincing.

Rider laughed, holding my stare. "Maybe you can't call it that with a beta in the mix, gnawing on the piece of ass like a dog with a bone."

He looked like our goddamn dad. Sounded like him too. My

fists were clenched and I was moving forward, aware of the laugh in his gaze, how eager he was to have me swing a fist, to make a mess, to give him a reason to bark at me and prove which of us was really powerful. I didn't care. I'd keep his mouth busy with punches for as long as I could.

"Chance has more alpha bark in his dick than the whole lot of you combined."

The fuck?!

My steps stuttered to a halt so fast I actually felt dizzy. I didn't have to turn around to see who had said those words. I knew that voice, knew the teasing arch, the lazy drawl.

Rider barked out a half-laugh, stare sliding over my shoulder as his brow furrowed. "What?"

"I said," Ghost continued, words slowing in mock patience, "that Chance's *cock* is more of an alpha than you are. Any of you. All of you."

No one was looking at me, but I felt like I was standing under a hot spotlight, fully exposed.

"The fuck would you know about Chance's cock?" Rider asked, still trying to laugh, to grin, but the sounds and shapes were all wrong, too many teeth bared, too much panic.

"Repeated personal experience," Ghost declared, careless and proud.

Rider's eye twitched, and I thought maybe I was passing out while still somehow remaining standing.

The ripple of shock was an actual flavor in the air. Battery acid. Everyone was still, time suspended, and then Rider was running forward, growling. I braced myself, my hands limp at my side, and I wondered if he would kill me. His shoulder struck mine roughly, and I stumbled back, but it wasn't me he was charging toward. The impact spun me and I stared in a trance, watching Rider barreling toward an utterly calm and smirking Ghost, watched Rider's arm pull back and Ghost's smirk stretched. The punch cracked, and Ghost's head snapped back and the spell broke.

I ran for the pair at the same time Bear leapt up from his seat. He grabbed my brother, yanking him back. Ghost surged up from the barstool, teeth stained with blood, lip split. His eyes were wild and he lunged forward, chasing Bear and Rider. I caught him, banding my arm around his chest, shoving him back onto the stool.

I hissed at him as Rider growled and wrestled against Bear. "Stop, you fucking idiot, that's not—"

Ghost's hands grabbed my face and drew my mouth to his with stunning and clumsy force, mashing our lips together without any finesse. He tasted like spice and soda and blood, and for some reason that flavor lit me up from the inside. I clawed briefly at his chest and back, drawing him in, claiming the upper hand because it *was* mine. Ghost moaned into the kiss, sagging into me, mouth opening for my tongue to thrust in. Power was the explosion in my veins, the weak note of surrender from the alpha in my ear. It was the way he clung to me, melting in my hands. Familiar and heady, and...and sanity came in the soft, feminine gasp from my right.

I pulled back immediately and the room returned, watching, baffled, maybe disgusted.

"Fuck," I muttered.

Ghost grinned, teeth red. "Fuck *yes*."

A small hand caressed my elbow and I spun to face Faith, her eyes wide, bouncing around the room.

"You okay?" she asked.

I'd fucking kissed Ghost right in front of her. *He kissed me first*, a weak part of my head chimed in, as if it mattered when I'd immediately leapt into the action.

"Rider, Bear, my office. Chance, take her up," King ordered.

"I want you fucking out, King!" Rider roared.

The room held its breath, and I thought my heart stopped beating for a moment as Faith slid under my arm, tucking herself against my chest.

"You'll make your case," King said cooly, eyeing my brother with all that icy command he'd held for years. "For now, you're still my VP. And you'll join me in my office."

"We should get Ghost out of here too," Faith whispered.

I blinked, frowning down at her. "What?"

"He's bleeding," she said, shrugging. "And everyone is staring at him."

"I'll be fine," Ghost rasped from behind me.

I was tempted to leave him here. I was tempted to turn around and strangle him for just fucking *announcing* to the whole club that we'd been fucking, for kissing me in front of them all. He would survive whatever heckling or harassment the others wanted to give him better than I would. But Faith was staring up at me with those huge eyes of hers and those full lips pursed.

"No, she's right. You're acting crazy, you're gonna get in a fight," I said, glancing at him over my shoulder. "Come on."

He grunted, rising at my back, and I tried not to look back at the others. Bear was marching Rider out of the room, and there was no shield for me and Faith as we headed for the hall.

"If I'd known you liked it up the ass, I woulda found a blindfold and helped you out, Ghost," Buck called.

I tensed, but Ghost just huffed. "You and I both know you wouldn't need the blindfold. I'm too goddamn pretty."

"Just walk," I muttered.

A few others heckled Ghost, and every time he responded with a laughing answer. I was queasy with an irrational jealousy, furious with his ability to roll with the jokes. Faith's hand slipped into mine, our shoulders brushing with every step, and that anger was snuffed out as quickly as it had spiked. I was mad at her for how easily her presence calmed me, but relieved too.

Ghost's room was on the first floor, but Faith tugged me toward the stairs. I was putting her in charge, my own head tossing on stormy seas, incapable of making a decision that wouldn't lead to a fight.

"I'm sorry," Ghost said.

Faith glanced back at him, but neither of us answered. My steps slowed as we neared my door, but she tugged me along to the end of the hall.

"Not the nest," I murmured.

"No, not the nest," she agreed, squeezing my hand.

I wasn't sure I even wanted to let Ghost *near* the nest, but it was hers, and she made the decisions about who was allowed in and when. She unlocked the room and led us directly into the bathroom.

"Shit, it smells good in here," Ghost breathed, pausing in the doorway, pupils dilating and gaze losing its focus. He licked his lips and then winced, finding the open wound and turning for the bathroom. His eyes widened again. "The fuck? Why is Bear's bathroom so fuckin' nice?"

"'Cause he gives a shit," I answered, sitting down on the edge of the soaking tub. I'd used the tub during Faith's heat, and it was enough to convince me to embrace the finer things in life, if I could get my hands on them.

One of those finer things was the gorgeous omega currently crouched down in front of me, digging in a drawer through all the bubble bath and CBD oils for the first aid kit.

"Sit on the counter," she ordered.

"Yes, ma'am," Ghost purred, a little rumble in the words, his cocky grin ruined by the sight of blood.

If I hadn't known Faith so well by now, I would've missed the slip of her shoulders, the instinctual effect of that purr.

I wasn't sure if I could do this. It was one thing to share her with Bear or King. I'd never felt the need to challenge their role as alpha, and they'd never rubbed my face in it. But Ghost was... mine, in a way. Challenging him was a shared thrill. Watching him alpha Faith, knowing I never could do the same...

Faith stood, staring up at Ghost with a disgusted wrinkle of her nose. "You're a mess," she muttered.

"You know it, slick," Ghost answered, a little drip of blood running down his chin.

She gripped that chin and pressed an antiseptic swab to Ghost's bottom lip, drawing out a hiss and growl of discomfort. I smiled.

"I'm going to leave you two to talk, but I just want to say that what you did was not only stupid, it was really disrespectful," Faith said, holding Ghost's gaze. My heart hammered in my chest, stare flicking between her firm and steady confidence and his bravado crumbling.

"You said I had to show him I wasn't ashamed," Ghost mumbled as she cleaned him up.

I sat up straighter. She'd said that?

Faith huffed and scowled. "I said show *him*, not the whole fucking club at the most volatile moment. Can you honestly tell me you thought that moment through?" Ghost answered with silence, and she arched an eyebrow at him. "I didn't think so."

All the unease, the anger, the jealousy was slowly puddling together and melting away as I watched them. Faith didn't fall into Ghost's chest like she did with Bear, seeking shelter. She didn't bat her lashes and tempt him like she did with King. She saw Ghost for the charming but ignorantly insensitive idiot he was.

"Open your mouth," Faith snapped at Ghost, lifting up a tube of antibiotic ointment. He obeyed, shoulders slumped and body slouched to make it easier for her reach.

He was staring at her with something like awe, not that hooded and hungry look he got when I started to snarl at him and put him on his knees. This was vulnerable and sheepish and a little scared.

Faith had said she was curious about watching Ghost and me together, and I understood now. Seeing my two lovers together, learning how they looked at one another and spoke to one another, learning the way Faith could strip Ghost down as effectively as me, but with something sweeter and sterner all at once, was *fascinating*.

"Hey, birdy," I said as she capped the tube.

She glanced over her shoulder. "Hm?"

"You love me?" I asked.

Her eyes lit up, lips curving, and Ghost gaped at us.

"You know I do," she said softly, transforming just for me. "C'mere."

She dropped the tube, forgetting about Ghost entirely, and took the two steps to reach me on the tub, stepping between my legs. Her lips were tipped up in offering, and I plucked at them gently with my own in a series of soft, quick kisses. My hands rested around her waist, and I watched her with my eyes open as she softened with every peck.

"I got it from here, okay?" I said, pressing a final kiss to the tip of her nose. She nodded, blinking drowsily at me. "Wait for me in the nest?"

"'Kay." She drifted toward the door and then paused, glaring back at Ghost. "Behave."

He blushed and nodded.

Faith shut the door behind her, and for a moment Ghost just stared at the spot. I accepted the pause, organizing my thoughts in the silence.

"I am her pack," I said finally.

Ghost's eyes whipped to mine.

"I don't care what King says or what he thinks, Bear and I are Faith's pack. I don't get to bond her, but that doesn't mean I haven't decided to stand by that woman from now on."

Ghost smiled, bracing his hands on the edge of the counter, studying me. "Okay."

I frowned at him and shook my head. "No. Don't make it sound easy. I'm telling you that whatever it is you think you want from me now, it can't change that I am going to follow her first. She chose me, right from the start."

Ghost's eyes slid away, and he nodded. "Heard. You and Bear thinking about leaving?"

"You think Rider and the others are going to stand for us staying?" I asked.

He raised a hand, pinching between his brows. "Fuck."

"Yeah."

"You'd really leave the club?" Ghost asked, pulling his hand away, frowning at me.

I tried to give it some thought, but the answer was easy. "Yeah. I would. Even with King in charge, I barely feel like this club wants me here. If Rider has his way..."

Ghost blew out a breath, shaking his head. "He's too obsessed with the way it was when he was a kid."

"It was a shit show when we were kids. He just listened to my dad's bullshit stories too many fuckin' times," I muttered.

Ghost grunted, fiddling with the remains of the first aid kit Faith had left out. "I never wanted you to feel shitty about what we were doing, Chance."

I swallowed, and it felt like my tongue went down my throat.

He looked up, locking gazes with me. "I didn't know that you *did* until you were fucking telling me not to come around."

I grit my teeth and gripped hard at the porcelain ledge I was perched on. "How was I supposed to feel?"

Ghost shrugged. "I dunno. I'm not saying my behavior was on you. I just wish I'd known, so I could've done something about it."

I was used to locking alphas out, keeping my feelings to myself so I didn't give anyone room to harass me for them. I'd never complained to Ghost about keeping me a secret, and I'd done the same to him.

"Figured it was just the same as how you were with the girls," I said.

Ghost groaned and scrubbed his hand through his beard. "I never went back to any of them."

I stood from the tub then, Ghost's expression brightening until I crossed my arms over my chest.

"Do you want her?" I whispered, nodding toward the door.

He didn't pretend not to know who I meant. "Yeah. Both of you. Not her more than you, just...yes."

"Then you have to be serious about it," I said. "You can't treat her like a queen for two weeks and then not look her in the eye the next day."

Ghost winced but nodded. "I deserve that."

"You deserve a lot more than that. But not from me. From Lilah and Krissie and Beth and the rest of the girls."

"I'll apologize to them too," Ghost said, leaning forward, catching my eye.

My eyes narrowed. "You will?"

He nodded again. "I used them and I tried to pretend I was less of a dick about it by being sweet, when really I was being more of an ass by leading them on. I get it, Chance, I hear you. I can't be that guy with Faith or you," he said.

"I won't let you," I said.

Ghost tipped his head. "You think she would?"

I smiled in spite of myself. "Probably not."

He smiled back, and the feeling in my chest was as uneasy as it was warm. This wasn't us. This wasn't how we talked—we barely talked—or how we looked at one another. I didn't *not* like it though. Which was scary as fuck.

"I'm not gonna fuck it up," Ghost said, voice low, velvety, but not in that fake way he sometimes used. "Just...can I have one thing?"

"What?" I asked.

He stretched his neck, tilting his head back, looking down his nose at me with hooded eyes. "Gimme a bite like you do her."

My mouth watered as I glanced at his throat, the muscle taut. I fucking wanted to. Would the rest of the club laugh at the mark on his throat the way they did with Faith's? Somehow, I didn't think so.

My mouth was dry as I spoke, stepping forward until his knees brushed my hips. "You have to earn it first."

Ghost let out a soft groan, sliding off the edge of the counter, and it took me a moment—his body brushing against mine as his knees bent—before I realized he was trying to kneel.

"Not like that, dickhead," I hissed, laughing, pulling him back up. The idea was tempting, but I wanted to talk to my omega first. "You can't suck cock with a split lip."

"Oh, I definitely can," Ghost said, grinning, the lip in question growing fat and the cut shining with whatever Faith had smeared over it.

I shook my head. "Get out of here."

"One kiss," Ghost urged, eyebrows waggling.

"You had your one kiss in the bar," I grumbled.

"One *more*," he said, reaching for my hips.

I caught his hands and slammed them back to the counter, glaring at Ghost just for looking so goddamn pleased by the move. He pressed his hips into mine, still grinning, and I gave in.

I caught his upper lip with my teeth, dragging it between both of mine. Ghost moaned, leaning into me, knees bending in order to give me the upper hand. I licked his lip, sucked on it, offering him a softer kiss than we usually shared. His breath gusted against my chin, and I pulled back a fraction before snapping my teeth briefly on his busted bottom lip.

His hips bucked into mine as he gasped and I pulled away, backing up until my calves hit the tub. My hands ached, empty and wanting to grab at him. My tongue was numb from not tasting him, the old memory of his hands holding my thighs as I thrust into his mouth scorching my skin.

"I will earn your bite, Chance," Ghost vowed, gaze dark. He flashed a grin. "Hers too."

I swallowed at the thought of watching Faith sinking her teeth into Ghost's skin, snarling in her heat. Thought of her working herself on his knot as he moaned beneath her. And it wasn't jealousy racing like lit gasoline through me, burning hot.

"Not tonight," I rasped.

He sighed and nodded. "Fine. Not tonight."

We stared at each other another moment before he smiled and turned for the door. I ignored the urge to draw him back, shadowing him to the front door.

"Night, slick," Ghost called at the door.

"Night," Faith called back from inside the nest.

"The scent in this room really is insane," Ghost whispered to me, eyebrows bouncing.

"It's thicker in the nest," I said.

He let out a purr, blinking in surprise at the sound, and then shook himself. He reached for the door with one hand, and I jumped as the other caught my fingers briefly.

"G'night."

I watched, too struck to move, as he opened the door and left the room I now thought of as the pack's, rather than just Bear's.

"You two make up?"

I turned and smiled at the sight of Faith's head leaning out of the nest, sideways, with her hair dripping down.

"I don't know what just happened," I admitted.

She smiled back at me. "But you don't hate it."

I wet my lips and shook my head. "I don't hate it."

"Good. Now come to bed."

If I could've purred, I would have. Instead I just ran toward the nest, Faith giggling and diving back inside as I rushed to undress. I wasn't going to think about the club's reaction to Ghost's insane declaration. I wasn't going to think about whether or not he would live up to his promise or fail. I was going to tackle the woman I loved into the mattress and kiss her until she couldn't catch her breath. The rest could wait till morning.

I stayed out of the way for the next couple days, and even tucked away in the nest, or catching my breath by hanging out with Chance and occasionally Ghost—who was funny and careless and too handsome for his own good—I could still taste the tension in the club on the air every time I walked through the halls.

It was morning now, not so early that I was the only one up, and I kept my eyes on the floor as I passed one of the alphas. I didn't know if he supported King or Rider, but he stopped and watched me walk by without speaking, his stare prickling against my back.

King's room was directly below Bear's. It'd been him with someone else that I'd heard that first night, and I had no right to be as jealous as I was over the knowledge. I still was, though. I knocked now, biting my bottom lip. I hadn't seen King for more than a couple hours since Rider had challenged him in front of everyone, and he hadn't come back to the nest at all. Church was taking place in an hour, and I didn't know if I'd come to his door to try to talk him into declaring me his omega or denying any connection between us so he could keep his position. I just needed to look at him—maybe talk, if I managed to think of any words.

"What?" he snapped from inside.

I had to clear my throat twice. "It's me."

The door was opening before I finished speaking, and the only thing to reassure me was that King didn't look angry to see me at his door.

"Get in here, princess," he said, reaching for my arm.

He pulled me into his chest, swinging the door shut behind me, and his hands dove into my hair, lifting it in his hands as he bent over me. I nestled my nose against his throat and he breathed, letting out a long purr.

"Been too fuckin' busy, missed the smell of you," he said.

I sighed and wrapped my arms around him. He was being sweet. I couldn't stand it, and I couldn't get enough.

"I should be there today," I whispered against his throat.

King pulled back abruptly, and I cursed myself for ruining the moment. "No way."

"This argument is about me," I said, looking up at him and frowning. "It's my fault."

The last thing I expected was for King to smile at me. "It isn't, princess. Rider's been itching to unseat me for years."

"But I've created the excuse."

King sighed so heavily, it ruffled my hair. "Come relax with me for a bit."

We didn't have long before he would have to appear before the others and let Rider spin a bunch of bullshit together to try to convince the club to impeach King from his position. But I couldn't refuse him. I was still greedy, and I hadn't had enough of his time in the past couple days.

But King led me into the bedroom area and my steps slowed, my face growing tense and pinched.

He laughed at me. "What?"

I glared back at him. "It smells like other people."

King's smile went slack, his eyes wide. "Huh? Still? Princess, it's been since..."

"I know when it's been since," I said, scowling at the bed and thinking of the noises from the woman I'd heard moaning the first night. "You haven't washed your sheets?"

King cleared his throat and scuffed his hand over the back of his neck. "I...didn't—Sorry. I can't smell them," he offered as a weak defense.

I walked slowly closer to the bed, sniffing. The smell didn't get any stronger the closer to the bed; it was just a stale remnant in the air. If anything, the bed smelled more like King than anyone else.

"You jealous, princess?" King asked.

"Yes," I bit back, shooting him another glare over my shoulder for sounding so pleased with himself.

He laughed and walked past me, falling back onto the bed and patting the mattress at his side. "Serves you right, for everything I heard during the heat," he said, pointing above his head.

Damnit, now it was my turn to blush. I hadn't really considered that if I could hear King and whoever he was with the first night, he definitely would've heard me, Bear, and Chance plenty. Which made me wonder if hearing us had done the same to King that it had to me. Over and over, for days.

I stared down at my own feet and mumbled out the words, "I'm sorry I was so determined to...to have you fuck me. To make you get involved during the heat, and—"

King sat up, scrambling to the edge of the bed, ducking his head to meet my eyes. "You regretting things between us, princess?" he growled.

I blinked, my eyes stinging and my head shaking. "Not like that, but if I...if I hadn't come to your office, would you have...ever—"

"God, I hope so," King whispered, drawing my words to a halt.

I stared at him, aware of the guilty tear rolling over one of my cheeks. He reached out, hands circling the backs of my thighs.

"You did me a favor, princess."

"I didn't care what it would mean for you or the club," I admitted, breathless and nervous. "I was being selfish."

King smiled. Why was he so damn calm today? "I know."

"So it's my fault. It's my fault that Rider has a reason to make a case against you today."

King didn't disagree, and I didn't fight him as he pulled me in, lay down on the bed and drew me over his chest like a blanket.

"Here's what's gonna happen today," King said, stroking his fingers through my hair, running his hands down my back, and then starting the process all over again. "I've got a few things on the agenda, some stuff to butter everybody up, and I'll get through those first. Then Rider is gonna try and make his case about the laws I've broken in the club. He'll say his piece. Present any evidence he has. You being in the room is only gonna make things stickier, and if he drew you into it, I wouldn't keep my cool. So I need you to sit it out, okay?"

"Okay," I murmured.

"There's a process. He presents his case today. We both have two weeks to campaign," King said.

I blinked at that. "Campaign."

"Mhm. I've known this was coming. I'm sure he's got bribes and threats he can make to gather votes, but so do I," King said. "In two weeks, we'll take the vote."

Two weeks felt like a long time. It'd only been two weeks since the whole club had returned and discovered my presence. If King could turn the men's opinion in that time, whatever damage I'd done would disappear, or at least be shoved into the background.

"Now, I don't want to hear you talking about us like I was helpless," King said, continuing the strokes of his hands through my hair and down my back. "You didn't break my self-restraint by walking into my office smelling like candy and just begging for my knot. I very eagerly threw that restraint out the window. I knew exactly what you were up to, and I was desperate for the excuse. I might owe *you* an apology."

"No," I said quickly. Going after King had been a gamble, but I'd been thrilled by the risk.

"Okay then," King said.

His touch was hypnotic and my eyelids sagged as he carried on, soothing both of us with the petting. I wanted to ask if he was calm because he knew he would never cross the line of biting me, or because he didn't care about that stupid "no pack" rule anymore, but I was afraid of the answer. I liked King too much now. I hadn't hooked him into a bite. Now I wanted one, not for protection, but because I needed to know King was as possessive about me as I was him.

He rolled to the side and I burrowed into his chest, afraid of what might come next.

"I gotta get going soon," he said.

I breathed him in, ignoring the words.

"Think you're right that this room shouldn't be smelling like other women though, princess." I grunted, and he shook with laughter. "Got a change of sheets around here. Wanna do me a favor?"

I stretched my neck to tip my head back. "What kind of favor?"

He glanced around. "Fix it up in here for me?"

My eyes narrowed. "You want me to *clean* your room?"

King snorted. "Not clean. Perfume," he said, waggling his eyebrows. "Thinking maybe you should stay here in my bed. Touch yourself. Get yourself off. Make it smell like you so I get hard every time I walk in. *Especially* when I get back from this meeting. Could probably use the distraction then."

My blood heated in my veins at the invitation, King smiling down at me as I squirmed into the bed.

"Can I use the toys Bear got for me?"

"You can use whatever you want, princess," he said, bending down and kissing my forehead. "You should start with my pillow." My breath hitched and King's hands squeezed my hips. "Would you do that for me?"

I licked my lips and nodded. "But you have to find your other sheets. I'm not your maid."

He laughed, all grit and gravel. I arched my hips, pressing myself into him. "Deal, go on then." His hand slapped my hip once and he sat up.

I scrambled off the bed and then turned back, lunging forward to press my mouth clumsily to his. He pressed back, his purr vibrating into the kiss, and pulled away smiling.

"Hurry."

"Yes, Prez!" I answered, darting away at his huff.

It occurred to me as I ran back to the nest, grinning and ignoring the stares of the club, that King was doing this more for my benefit than his. Or at least that was what he thought. I would make sure it worked out best for us both.

"And do you deny" —my eyes ached from not rolling, and Rider's repeated use of that phrase made my entire body want to twitch— "that you alienated a long-standing and beneficial relationship with Preston Bowers on behalf of the omega?"

I stiffened, and Rider's mouth fought an obvious smirk as he stared back at me. Neither Bear nor Chance would ever have told Rider about Bowers. Which meant Rider had taken the initiative to talk to him himself.

"I don't deny it," I said slowly, a crackling growl trapped at the back of my throat.

An answering murmur stirred around the table as Rider turned away from me to face his audience.

"This club was founded on the principle of brothers before all else. We're not white knights meant to be on hand to rescue stray omegas. We're sure as hell not meant to see our prez and enforcer packing up like their loyalties won't be split away from the club."

I reminded myself for the hundredth time to unclench my jaw. My eyes circled the room as Rider spoke and I studied the faces of my men, watching the ones who nodded, the ones who listened, the ones whose eyes rolled. The room was split in Rider's favor now. I had to remain seated, silent as Rider made his case against me.

"King's energy has been waning for years now. We've all seen it. He's grown complacent. The Devils need to keep the fire under our wheels," Rider continued, voice growing.

I scowled and stared down at my hands, at the rings on my fingers, the scars there from fights and working on my bike. Was Rider right about my energy fading? Those words struck harder than the rest. I had built the club into what it was today, saved it from ruin from the last generation. Rider wasn't what was best for the club, but maybe I wasn't either now.

"Case rested," Rider said, feigning solemnity. Bastard was smug as fuck right now.

It was a good case. He had more little flaws—minor financial slips in the past couple years, a few business losses, decline in club growth—than I'd been expecting. I had a week to prepare my own rebuttal, and two weeks before the vote for both me and Rider to make and break alliances behind the scenes.

"Case heard," I answered, nodding my head in his direction, refusing to show anything on my face.

I had one anchor in the hour-long parade of my sins, and I held onto it now. Faith was in my room, working herself into one little whimpering frenzy after another, making my room rich with the scent of her satisfaction, waiting for me.

I rose slowly from my seat, trying not to appear too eager to escape this extended judgment.

"You'll all hear from me next week. In the meantime, listen to your own counsel, and consider your experience here in this club, under my presidency. There is no bond that comes before ours," I said, holding the gazes of a few men I thought I might need to sway back.

If I want to win the vote, a small hiss in my head whispered.

"Church dismissed. Potluck and club-only party tonight," I said.

I remained in the room as the men filtered slowly to the door, shaking the hands of the brothers who offered immediate support. There weren't enough of them. Five years ago, no one would've even considered challenging me, doubting my leadership. Had this started when I'd declined to sweep the Wasted out? When I'd offered Rider a consolatory place at my side?

"You want to plan?" Bear asked, still standing at my side.

"Later, after the party."

I had someone waiting on me. Maybe Rider was right about my loyalties. Or maybe I just needed a less bitter pill to swallow before I faced the club again. I'd told Faith I wasn't her medicine, but perhaps she was mine.

Bear cleared his throat and glanced at me. "Warning would've been nice before I sat through that meeting feelin' her getting ready for you."

Unclench, I coached myself, relaxing my jaw again. Bear had a bond. He'd been feeling Faith following my instructions. Lucky fuck.

I shrugged and left the meeting at last, marching for my bedroom.

The attack against Rider was running through my head, formulating with every step. Lean on the connections I'd built, like Waylon and the ranch, the local sheriff. Preston was obviously out of the question now, but he'd be unreliable for Rider, who lacked any finesse. Money mattered to the club, no matter what kind of anarchist party lifestyle Rider thought he could pitch to the others. Money was what I was good at.

It was a relief for the thoughts to stop running as I reached my door. Sticky sweetness and floral lace edged the simple frame. *Good girl*, I thought.

I unlocked the door and groaned as I stepped inside. No sign of those quick one-night releases now. The air was infused with Faith. I leaned back against the door and reached down, palming my own thickening cock through my jeans. There was a buzzing sound coming from the bed and I was a coward, too afraid to see Faith, that I might fall to my knees at the end of the mattress and beg her to...

What? Destroy my promises to the club? My willpower to resist biting her?

"King?" Breathy, weak. I loved the sound of her when she was orgasms deep. The buzzing noise cut off.

"Don't stop, princess," I called, my voice thick with a purr.

It started up again, and she let out a high cry. Wet, slick licking sounds joined the buzzing, and it wasn't bravery but hunger that drew me forward.

"Fuck," I moaned at the first sight of her.

She was spread out on the bed, the mattress decorated with a startling collection of toys—vibrators and plugs and squat dildos with glittering knots and nubs. What did omegas need with alphas when they had a spread like that?

My spare sheets were black and Faith glowed on their surface, her skin dewy, the curtains drawn shut, and the mounted lamps on either side of the bed kissing her skin golden. She was sweating, upper lip dewy and eyes partially closed, fucking herself with a long, thin wand that glimmered with her release and fresh arousal.

"Did I do good, King?" she whispered, her motions jerky as she leaned into the vibrating wand, pumped it inside of her and then drew it out to circle around her clit.

Wicked creature. Beautiful and dangerous.

I leaned into the bed, bracing my hands on the mattress, staring at the darkened wet spot she'd made at the center, right where her red and swollen cunt was gasping at me.

"You did very good, princess," I growled, leaning in, licking up the length of the wand, groaning at her flavor on the silicone, nudging it with my tongue back down to her entrance. Faith moaned as it sank easily back inside of her, and I joined the sound with my own voice as my tongue reached her folds, lapping up to her clit.

"Oh, fuck, King, I—"

I grinned against her soaked skin as she shook on the wand, helped her fuck herself when her hands grew limp and weak, and sucked kisses on her clit until her slippery hands were in my hair. I mourned the fact that I would have to wash her scent away before the party. She should've dressed me like cologne. Fuck Rider. Fuck that stupid rule I'd made for the club.

"I need you, need to suck you," Faith gasped, wrestling me away from her sex.

She shoved the still-vibrating wand aside, sitting up and flopping weakly in my direction. I stood at the edge of the bed, reaching for my shirt, and her tongue was on my stomach as I started to strip.

"Gonna fuck you, princess," I said, not sure if it was a warning or a promise.

"After," Faith gasped, wrestling with my belt. She sucked at the skin of my hip, and I helped her wrestle my pants down my hips.

Her lips were clumsy, tongue eager as she pulled my length free from my pants, and the lack of shyness, the pure hunger, drew a shout from me. Her mouth was hot and hungry, and she was so fucking *determined* to suck me down. My hands were in her hair, hips thrusting without thinking, head thrown back. All the tension from the meeting was transformed into this moment, as I held myself back from fucking her face, failing entirely.

The head of my cock hit the inside of her cheek, both of us moaning, and the sound of her rattling into me sent me thrusting to the back of her throat. Faith gagged and I nearly drove in farther, the flex of her around me a cruel siren call. I pulled free instead, holding onto her by her hair, laughing as she tried to dive forward again.

"Wait, princess, lemme help." I stroked a hand down to her cheek, then circled her lips with my thumb until her eyes lifted up to mine. "Roll over onto your back."

She blinked at me for a moment, lost in a lusty fog, and then with a little nudging from me, she was rolling over onto her back, my cock poised above her face. My bed was high and I tugged her to the edge, her head falling back and breath hitching.

"You wanna take me deep?" I asked, standing back and watching her nod eagerly, reaching for me. "I'll be gentle. You swat my hip if it's too much."

"Yes, alpha."

I ignored the shudder that ran down my spine, kicked my

jeans off, and dragged the small bench that had come with the room over to the edge of the bed. It let me kneel to the perfect height, and the sight of Faith's waiting open mouth, lips spread for me, was enough to make me dizzy. I clasped my length, circled it around her lips, coating them selfishly in my precum, and then guided myself in. She hummed like I was feeding her chocolate cake or some other kind of feminine wishlist treat, the kind of thing I should've been bringing her.

"Fuck, you're such a greedy little angel," I muttered, watching her lips purse, her tongue lapping hungrily as I slid in and out of her mouth a little deeper every time.

The vibrator was nearing the edge of the bed, still rattling, and I reached forward, sinking deep into Faith's mouth, a little farther as she groaned appreciatively. I snatched the toy up, licking at it once more—better than any lollipop—and then brought the tip down to her breasts, pointed high and arched prettily from this position.

She howled on my cock, breasts thrusting up, lips sinking down, nose nuzzling at my balls. I joined her cry, moved the wand to the other breast, and started to fuck that moaning mouth.

"Oh, fuck, that's good," I rasped.

Faith whined, hips wiggling up from the mattress. I laughed at the silent order, continuing to tease her breasts with vibration, rocking into her lips, gasping as she swallowed my tip once. She deserved her reward for that. I slipped out of her, letting her catch her breath as I licked her breasts and moved the wand between her legs.

And like the talented, perfect little creature she was, she reached her hands back, filling them busily with my cock and balls.

"Fuck, baby, yes," I said, sucking on a nipple, rubbing her clit with the wand.

"Cock," she whined, drawing me closer.

"Not much longer. You know I want my knot in you," I said.

She hummed, either ignoring or agreeing; it didn't matter. I was getting my way, and she'd be howling with gratitude when it happened. I let her play a little longer, my eyes all but crossing as she sucked me down, her throat flexing around my head until I was tempted to finish there first. Her nails dug into my ass as I pulled out again, but her ragged gasp of air proved me right. I pulled her claws free of me and tossed the vibrator aside again, grinning down at her red and sweaty face. She was a mess, and she was perfect.

"Present for me," I purred.

Her mouth hung open and a whine released, but there was no argument from her now. Here was her hindbrain state, the sweetest part of the feral edge that lingered. She rolled back onto her belly, turning and crawling to face the head of the bed. And there, peeking out between her cheeks, was a glittering pink plug, right above those slickened red lips. I'd missed it earlier, hidden away from my view.

A pleasant surprise, and my knot pulsed in approval, fresh precum pooling at my tip.

"Is this for me, princess?" I growled, pressing my finger into the plug.

Faith's back bowed, and she let out a pretty cry for me. "Yesss."

"You want me to wear you out today, don't you? Fuck you and knot you and fill every hole?"

Faith trembled, arms stretching in front of her, fingers digging into the mattress. "Yes. I want..." She trailed off, face lowering to the bed, head turning so I could just catch her eye.

"Tell me."

"I want to make it so you can never get rid of my scent in your bed," she whispered. "I want it so the next time you leave my nest, you come back here and you're still surrounded by me."

I stared at her, holding my breath, tying my own tongue to keep words I wasn't ready to commit to from falling from my lips. I gripped my length, squeezed my knot once, and then guided myself into her, just poised at her entrance.

"You want me obsessed with you, don't you, princess?" I asked.

She nodded.

"Say it."

"I want you obsessed with me. Thinking about me. Wanting me," she said, voice a little hoarse, face trying to hide in the bed.

"Look at me."

She turned her head, gaze wary.

"You've already won, princess," I said. Her eyes widened and then I thrust in to the hilt, my knot barely resisting. Her expression went slack for a moment and then tightened, a kind of tortured relief written in tense lines. Her eyes fell shut and mine followed suit as she bit at my knot, squeezing around me with an immediate release.

It was easier like this, blind to her beauty, pretending the pleasure was selfish, knowing I would give in to her every demand but one—at least for today. Resisting her was a series of battles won or lost one day at a time. Her score far outweighed mine, and I wasn't sure whether or not I was looking forward to the final surrender.

———

BEAR'S GAZE was wary as he sat across my desk from me.

"You should get up to the nest," I said, going over the list once more. All the phone calls that needed to be made, all the new promises to offer, the favors to call in.

"Promised her I wouldn't leave you in your office all night," Bear said.

I smiled one second, grimaced the next. I was fucking tired. The party had gone late. In spite of spending most of the day fucking Faith in my bed, it'd been torture to avoid her in the crowd, to play dutiful king to the club rather than desperate supplicant to my princess.

"You know you're going to win the case, right?" Bear asked.

I blinked, lifting my head slowly as if it weighed a hundred pounds. It felt like it did these days.

"Sure, some of the guys are wobbling. They've had Rider in their ear more than you lately, and maybe you've faltered. But this club *wants* to follow you. You just have to renew their faith a bit," he said.

I flinched at her name, just the word.

"Good to hear," I said, the lie thick on my tongue.

Bear nodded, his hands resting on his stomach, body slouched in the chair. "You can squash Rider's temper tantrum, Prez."

I cleared my throat, nodded.

"Do you want to?"

The club was eerily silent. I'd made sure the alcohol was supplied liberally and brought back some of the girls we'd been missing—the easiest way to soothe rising tempers. Everyone was sleeping the party off now but me and Bear.

"Do I want to?" I asked, frowning.

"Do you want to win the case?" Bear asked. "Do you want to keep the crown?"

I don't know, I thought immediately.

I could tell Bear to fuck off, or go back to the nest with him, or go back to my now decadently perfumed room and probably fuck my fist just like Faith would've wanted. I could tell him the truth: that the likely cost of the crown was starting to feel too high to pay.

"You come from a pack?" I asked instead.

Bear shrugged and nodded.

"My parents were betas. I assumed I would be too, till puberty hit. But I knew the world they saw, the one built for packs. My dad bitched about the slack betas picked up for alphas and omegas. He took that resentment out on my mom. And I think she resented just being...left outside of that world too," I said. "I knew she did. She resented me, my dad, her life. I never understood why they acted like they couldn't build themselves something just as good as a pack. Why we had to be lesser-than."

"So you rebuilt the Devils," Bear said.

I nodded. "I meant for it to be as good as a pack—stronger than one, even. I thought it was, but I...went wrong somewhere."

"You didn't go wrong," Bear said. "You just don't understand that pack is more than omega and alphas and heats. I mean...I'm gonna be honest with you, King. The Devils *are* a pack, except we just don't say so. And there's probably too many alphas for good balance."

"What do you mean?"

"I mean it doesn't take bondmarks to make a pack. We were a unit. We supported one another. The community keeps all of us alphas from going feral." Bear shrugged. "It was sort of a cold, toxic-masculinity version of a pack. It's gotten worse since Rider talked you into that big prospect crew a few years back." I glared at Bear, and he shifted and sat up, combing his hair back with thick fingers. "Right, so historically, like centuries ago, packs would grow steadily, add in more and more alphas to help protect the omega, until eventually tensions rose and they would split. Over time, omegas have become more common—still rare, but less impossibly so. Now packs tend to stay small."

"How do you know all this?"

"Pack history stuff gets passed down," Bear said. "You're what would be considered a new line, or a latent line, if there were alphas further back in your family tree. Your parents were right about the way our world is skewed, but that has more to do with alpha prevalence in leadership than it does with pack dynamics. A pack is just a family, whether it has bonds yet or not. I didn't stay here with the Devils because I wanted a life outside of a pack. I chose you as a kind of...pack leader."

I was stiff in my seat, stumped and startled by the earnestness in the words. Bear stared back at me, and I was struck by the meaning. I'd taken every prospect who'd sworn into the club as an honor, as a piece of my pride surrounding the Devils, but it'd been our club as a whole on offer, not just me. Bear had chosen *me* to follow. Me to be loyal to.

He cleared his throat, brow furrowing. "I don't want to leave, but I do think I could be Faith's head alpha if you need us to go."

The refusal was on my tongue, immediate and sharp, but the sudden bright crackling of glass shattering interrupted us both.

Bear and I stood at the same time.

"Front door?" he asked.

"I'll check the bar and meet you there," I answered, opening my bottom desk drawer and retrieving my gun from its case.

Bear pulled his own from the holster on his hip as another warning sprinkling of glass sounded.

We were just reaching the door when I caught a whiff of the gas, saw a whisper of it in the hall.

"Fuck, Bear—" I hissed.

But a massive figure in black shot forward from the bar, tackling Bear with a growling grunt. We were under attack, and the sight of the tactical gear, the bulletproof vest strapped over the broad chest even as I fired, gave me an easy guess as to the source.

They'd come for her.

My body curled around Chance's back as we lay in the nest. I teased him with little traces of my fingertips, the pair of us nearly dozing under the dim twinkle lights, just waiting for Bear and hopefully King to arrive for the night. I was tipsy from the party, overstuffed on casseroles and bratwurst. In spite of the tensions within the club, I'd finally talked to some of the betas and other alphas. With one exception—an alpha called Trick, who'd made sly remarks about Chance until we'd walked away as a group—I'd liked everyone I met.

"The nest is gonna be crowded with Ghost in here too," I mumbled into Chance's hair.

His hand reached up and covered mine. "You gettin' ahead of yourself, birdy."

Ghost had followed Chance around the party like a puppy, stretching out on a bench and laying his head on Chance's thigh at one point. He and I had developed a unique kind of flirting that basically consisted of us competing for Chance's attention. I had a feeling my packmate liked it more than he was willing to admit.

"Maybe," I said, kissing his head.

My eyes were falling shut, eyelids too heavy to keep open,

and I reached down the bond, searching for Bear to try and coax him to hurry to bed. I had a feeling that even if King went back to his room, he would end up in the nest. There was no way he'd be able to stand sleeping in his bed after the work I'd put into perfuming it. It was my revenge for all the times he'd left the nest while I was sleeping, and he'd sanctioned it himself.

Bear brushed back softly, a gentle reassurance that made sleep slide even closer. I was giving into the floaty sensation that came right at the edge, our bond still open, when a sudden spike of alert and worry shot through me like lightning.

I gasped, sitting up, and Chance grunted, flopping over, his face mashed into the pillow.

"Birbthy?"

"Something is wrong," I whispered, scrambling for the end of the bed.

"Wait," he called, hurrying after me, hands catching at my hips.

I cried out at a sudden blast in the bond, a bolt of caution, a boom of anger, the tension echoing from Bear to me. "Someone is here. Bear's downstairs, I need to—"

Run, hide, fight.

I fell out of the nest, Chance tossing blankets aside. I needed to dress. I grabbed for the first thing I could find, but it was the dress I'd worn to the party, the one Ghost had kept slipping his hand under when we'd gone to the kitchen together to fill up our plates again.

A bone-rattling strike from the bond hit me, and I fell to my knees.

"Hey, hey, slow down," Chance hissed, wrapping his arms around my shoulders. He pulled the dress from my hands, throwing it across the room.

"Bear's hurt," I whined. The room was too small, and my heart was swelling and hammering in my chest, at the brink of exploding.

"Shirt," Chance said, standing and pulling one down from the roof of the nest. He shoved it over my head, and I pulled my arms through the holes. "Jeans."

I managed those on my own, breathing through my teeth,

forcing myself to block Bear out just enough to function. Chance was dressing out of the corner of my eye, jumping into his own jeans, sliding on his vest. There were knives strapped to the inside. Good.

"You need to stay here, birdy," he said. I was already heading for the door, running in bare feet. "Wait! Faith!"

"They're here. They have Bear."

"Bear can handle himself!"

But Chance's voice was growing short, faded, and I was already out in the hall. His footsteps pounded after mine, an echo of fists against the wall signaling his path.

"Wake up! We got company," Chance bellowed.

"Bear!" I shouted, running for the dim light of the stairs.

"Faith!"

There was smoke on the stairs—a fire? Was Bear in the fire? The steps weren't hot, but my lungs and eyes stung as I rushed down.

"Gas! Faith, no!"

"We got her."

They had my alpha. Black shadowy figures reached for me, familiar silhouettes down the hall. There wasn't enough gas or fire or smoke to keep me from reaching Bear and King.

"Don't fire!" a male voice shouted. "Honey, come here, we got y—"

A long arm stretched toward me and I snarled, grabbing and twisting it, relishing in the bark of surprised pain.

"Faith! Faith, stop!" a familiar voice called.

"Don't shoot!"

"Let her go!"

The voices and shouts layered until every noise was a threat, every figure an enemy.

"Bear!" I screamed, voice already hoarse, the world watery and red, hot fire streaming down my cheeks.

Another body, bigger than the first, grabbed me around my waist, lifting me off the ground. Iron arms were banded around my own, but my legs were free to kick, and I bit blindly at the arm to my right. My heel connected between the man's legs, and I was released with a surprise grunt. I reached for the black mask covering his face, ripped it away, and fell backward with my own force.

"Fuck, she's feral."

"Faith! Faith, get back."

"Bear! King!"

I ducked as another black-clad figure dove for me, landing hard on my knees, and crawling through the smoke.

"Eve, I swear to god, *don't shoot!*"

"Enough!"

My arms and legs gave out beneath me, dropping me to the hall floor like a pancake. The bark was incredible, an inarguable order to *cease*. Even some of my anger and fight fled me with that single word.

"Someone open a door," the woman continued, and I whined, getting ready to turn and obey when all I wanted was to reach the end of the hall.

"Faith?"

I blinked and my eyes ran with the tears from the gas.

"Faith, it's me. Adam."

Adam.

"Bear," I whined.

"Eve, quit pointing your guns at them."

Oh my god. Adam.

I sat up, flinching at the blurry figure in front of me, dressed in black like the others.

"Here," he said, reaching forward. "I've got water."

"Put the knives away," the woman ordered.

"Don't fucking bark at him," Ghost growled from near the stairs.

"Faith, it's me," Adam whispered.

"Adam." I reached for him then, and the shape of his shoulders was familiar in my hands, his voice weak and muffled.

The air was clearing, and I held still as he tipped my head back and poured water in my eyes from a bottle. It rushed over my cheeks, down my throat, cool and surprisingly calming.

"Omikron found you," I breathed.

"No. Well, yeah, a couple times. But no," Adam said, taking away the water.

He pushed the mask off his face and there he was, blurry but startlingly clear too. I knew the cut of those cheekbones because I had them too, that same dark and unruly hair. He smelled like warm vanilla and sugar.

"Oh my god. It's you." My eyes were watering again, but this time the tears were earnest, the sting harsh but welcome.

"Found you," Adam said, a wobble in the words.

Found you, kiddo. As if we'd been playing a months-long game of hide-and-seek.

I sobbed and Adam gasped, crashing into me, his arms circling my shoulders. Cookie warmth and sweetness hung in the air, his embrace strong enough to squeeze heartache out of my chest.

"You're safe now," he whispered. "I'm here, you're safe."

I wept, clinging to Adam, because it had been months and I'd lost hope of seeing him again. But the truth sat uncomfortably in my chest. I was safe. I had been safe. And I wasn't sure what Adam being here would mean for the future.

———

I KEPT CHECKING the door of King's office. Adam was on the couch at my side, four alphas lined up in front of us.

"It's okay. You're safe," Adam whispered, his arm around my shoulder, squeezing.

I licked my lips and nodded. Bear was pacing in the bond, trying to hide his own anxiety under reassuring waves sent in my direction. They didn't work.

"I *am* safe—that's what I've been telling you," I said, but my voice was faint.

Eve, the slender and gorgeous female alpha standing at the center of the pack, glared down at me with her arms crossed over her chest, smelling like the air after an explosion. She was terrifying. She was the one who'd barked and made my limbs betray me.

"Is there a bond mark?" Eve asked me.

I nodded, and Adam's breath hitched at my side. "Bear's. He's the one who pulled me out of the van, took care of me, got me to see a doctor after...everything," I said to Adam, because he was easier to look at than that row of unfamiliar alphas.

"Bear?" Eve echoed, dry as the desert.

"His legal name is Courtney, and he is my alpha," I said, a bright flare of temper giving me the bravery to turn and face her again. "And I want to see him and the others."

Two of the other men looked at Eve, both wearing slight smiles. The third, a huge man with a permanent scowl and a white stripe on his short beard, glanced toward the door.

"She doesn't seem coerced and captive to me," Garrett said. Adam had introduced me to the alpha as one of his bondmates. Garrett was handsome, with bright green eyes and long hair. He was also surprisingly calm about the fact that Chance had managed to cut his arm with one of his knives, although Eve took the injury as personally as if it had happened to her.

"Why didn't they take you to the Omega Center?" Eve asked me.

"The Omega Center isn't safe," Adam and I said at the same time. I glanced at my brother with a quick and grateful smile and then turned back to her. "Bear wanted to, but I begged him to keep me here with him, and he listened to me. Please. I want to see him."

"They are cooperating," Jamie said, standing at Eve's side and nudging her lightly with his shoulder. He shot me a warm smile, and I relaxed slightly.

When they *weren't* attacking my loved ones, Adam's pack seemed okay. Aside from Eve.

Adam's hand found mine at my side, squeezing my fingers and catching my attention. "I wanna talk with you alone."

His face was a surprise all over again. He was the person I'd seen almost every day of my life, and then he'd been ripped out of reach. Sitting next to him was a strange kind of dream. His scent was different now, notes of Eve and Garrett in the mix. His face had even changed in tiny ways, and there were shiny, healed bite marks glittering all over his throat.

"Let her check in with them, and then you can interrogate them to your heart's content while my sister and I catch up?" Adam asked Eve. There was a note of teasing in the question, but he still had to ask, and I couldn't help but glare at her out of the corner of my eye.

She glared back for a moment, our stares clashing, before nodding once. The big alpha, Rory, marched to the door without orders, opening it as I jumped up from the couch.

Bear, King, Chance, and Ghost were all waiting outside in the hall, and I launched myself into the mass of them, Bear's arms snatching me up off my feet.

"I'm fine," he and I said at once, my face buried into his shoulder.

I helped myself to a moment of his purring before finally lifting my gaze. King was sporting a swollen and quickly blackening eye, and Ghost's nose was bleeding, but Chance looked like he was unharmed.

"I'm going to talk to Adam for a bit," I said.

King's uninjured eye glanced over my shoulder. "We'll entertain the intruders," he said.

Bear set me down on my feet and I slid around his side to King, whose expression softened as he drew me into his chest.

"I'm sorry," I whispered.

"Coulda gone worse," King said. He was tense, but he was rubbing his beard against the top of my head.

"The others?" I asked.

"Confused, annoyed, but it was wrapping up before most of them even put their pants on," King said.

I glanced in either direction but didn't see anyone. I had a feeling King was lying for my sake. There was no way Rider wouldn't use this to his advantage. King pulled away, reaching up to lift my chin. He studied me, scowl deepening.

"Was the tear gas fucking necessary?" he growled, glaring over my head.

"Apparently not," one of the alphas answered. The voice was gruff and I figured it was Rory.

Chance checked me over just as King had, letting me interrupt his study with a series of kisses. "I'm fine. You?"

"Fine," he said, nodding to the right. "Look at Ghost, though. If he keeps getting the shit kicked out of him, he's not gonna be so pretty soon."

I grinned at Ghost, who laughed. "You'll have to work on your personality," I teased.

"Very cute," Ghost answered, rolling his eyes. "Anyone care to fuckin' catch me up?"

"I will," Chance rasped, kissing my cheek once more. "Go on. Talk to your brother."

But Chance held on to me, Ghost stepping slightly in front of us as Adam's alphas filtered out of King's office.

"Bar," King said to them. He arched an eyebrow. "It's a bit breezy. Someone broke the window, but it will have to do."

"Try not to let anyone get stabbed or tear-gassed," I said to Chance.

Eve snorted as she passed us. "No promises."

I tensed, but Adam was there in the doorway, smiling sheepishly at me. "We really weren't expecting you to, uh...be here voluntarily. She's sulking," he whispered.

Hands stroked my sides as Chance and the others followed after Adam's pack, and my brother and I were left standing in the hall.

"Sulking?" I repeated.

Adam nodded toward the office, and I took one last glance at the mix of packs before following him in. He shut the door behind me and I was surprised by how nervous it made me. Adam let out a heavy sigh and then rushed to me, arms snapping around me.

"I'm so sorry," he breathed. "Oh, god, Faith, I'm so sorry."

He was shaking, starting to cry, and it didn't matter that he smelled slightly different, or that I was still wired and tense from adrenaline. I had my brother back, and all the wrongness of the night and his military-grade badass pack could wait for another minute. I grabbed onto Adam, tightening my arms around him too.

"I'm so sorry that I put you in danger. I'm so sorry. I'm so sorry." His voice cracked, and my heart followed suit.

I couldn't say it was all right. That it worked out for the best. I had Bear and Chance now, hopefully King and even Ghost. But there was no band-aid for what I'd been through with Omikron.

"I'm so glad you're safe now," Adam said, voice thick with tears. I sagged into him and nodded, my own rising quickly.

"I thought you were Omikron. I thought they'd found me," I whispered.

Adam stiffened, sucking in a breath, and he had to loosen my own grip enough to pull back. We were both a mess, snotty and teary and red-faced. His eyes were wide, staring down at me, lips parted. His head shook slowly.

"Faith. They're not coming."

I blinked up at him, and his smile wobbled into place.

"We killed the head of Omikron," Adam whispered. "And, umm...a few other officials on the way down here. The FBI is chasing the organization's heels. They're falling apart."

"You what?" I whispered.

Adam grinned. "They sent Eve to kill me. I got her to bite me instead. It's a long story, but the ending is, Omikron is crashing down on itself. They're not chasing after you, Faith. You're safe."

The room tilted and Adam caught me by my elbows as my knees gave out.

"What?" I repeated, but there was no sound in the words.

"Shit, sorry, your alpha's gonna worry," Adam muttered, guiding me to the couch, joining me there. "It's big, I know."

"Omikron is *gone?*"

Adam's face scrunched and he shrugged. "Not gone. Not yet. But there's infighting, we think. People are going underground to run from the FBI. We're, um...hunting some of them."

My eyes widened, my brain still spinning like a top over everything he'd said. "Eve was sent to *kill* you?"

Adam laughed. "Yeah. She probably almost did a couple of times. Definitely wanted to. I won her over in the end."

I gaped at him. Was he joking?

"She's an acquired taste," Adam said.

And he looked so...happy and strangely smitten as he said the words.

"When you said you were going to find the biggest and baddest alpha..."

Adam melted slightly, his perfume floating around him like a sugary sweet cloud. "She's perfect."

I should've tried to hide my skepticism, but I was too deep in shock to bother and Adam's love-drunk daze faded as he stared back at me.

"I mean, she's perfect for me," he said, blushing and clearing his throat. "I know we haven't made the best impression as a pack tonight, but the guys are way more normal and nice. You'll like them. And once Eve gets over the whole rescue mission gone sideways thing, and we like...make sure you're safe—"

"I am safe. I've said I'm safe," I snapped.

Adam blinked. "I know, but... I mean, this wasn't exactly what you wanted, right? A biker bar is not a wrap-around porch and an attic nest," he laughed.

He was right. The bar wasn't ideal, even if I was slowly finding my footing. But it set me on edge.

"I have a nest, I have an alpha who loves me—"

"You have bruises on your throat too," Adam said, dropping his smile.

I blushed, a hand rising to cover the marks from Chance. "Ones I asked for from my beta."

Adam blinked and relaxed slightly. "Okay. That's cute. It's not like I'm not asking for bites." He stretched his throat for me, displaying the marks I'd already tried and failed to count.

He looked like a chew toy. Apparently, considering killing Adam had eventually turned into a possessive need to mark the shit out of him. I didn't find it "cute," though.

Adam settled and we stared at one another, siblings and now somehow strangers too.

"I just want you to be happy," he said, frowning. "To have a good pack that will take care of you."

I blew a breath out of pursed lips and leaned forward, resting my forehead against Adam's shoulder. "Thank you. I want that too."

"We'll figure it out, kiddo," Adam whispered. "We're together now."

I nodded and tried to quell the doubt that curdled in my chest.

My heel jiggled against the floor. Faith's emotions were flipping too fast to track. I didn't know if it was the shock of the night, the attack, her adrenaline throwing her back into her feral state, or Adam pulling her out again, but she hadn't settled on one feeling for more than a second yet. I wanted to rise from the booth, march to King's office, and wrap myself around her like a safety blanket. But if I did, one or more of Adam's alphas was sure to chase me down. And if it was the woman, Eve, I'd get my ass handed to me.

She sat across from me, also at the edge of the booth, looking cool as a cucumber, staring at each of us in turn. Garrett, on the inside of the booth, kept frowning and staring over Ghost's shoulder to the hall, as if checking on our omegas. I assumed he was in touch with Adam like I was with Faith, and it was interesting to me how impassive Eve managed to remain.

All four of them were military at some level, that much had been clear from the start of the attack. I was too, but apparently I was out of practice. And now privately humiliated.

"So you're saying she's not in danger from Omikron?" King asked.

"Not necessarily," Rory said. He sat across from me, huge and equally stony-faced.

"They're chasing their own tails, and we're picking them off," Eve said.

Rory shot her a glare, and she returned it with a silky smile and a bat of her thick, black lashes.

"It would be *unlikely* at this point in time for them to organize enough to worry about tracking down an omega they've already been paid for," Garrett offered.

Glass clinked at my back, Chance and the final member of their pack, Jamie, working together to clean up the broken window they'd launched the gas canisters through.

"There was some kind of trap set up on the internet for Faith," King said, and the three alphas across from us squinted in unison.

"On the server Faith and Adam used," I explained.

"Oh! Right, sorry, that was Adam and me," Garrett said. "We knew Omikron had gotten in once, and we didn't trust that they wouldn't again. We set up a fishing bot for logins, gathering IP addresses. It's how we found you when Faith tried to log in."

"And you came and dropped off your bike with me to check us out?" Ghost asked Garrett.

He shrugged and nodded. "There's a camera on the back of the bike, but it didn't get much info."

"All of our surveillance only proved that you had Faith and that she wasn't free to leave the compound without escorts," Eve said.

King growled. "We weren't holding her captive, we were protecting her. We've got the Wasted on our ass, and we thought we had an international trafficking ring coming next."

"It's a good thing you didn't," Eve said cooly. "If tonight proved anything, it's how ill-prepared you are to protect an omega."

King and I both growled, but behind us, Jamie called out, "Eve, be chill."

"Luckily for you, my pack insisted we only aim to retrieve Faith," Eve continued.

"Which you failed at," Ghost muttered under his breath.

There was a jerk on our side of the table, King kicking Ghost quiet again.

"How often does she go feral?" Garrett asked me.

I shrugged. "When she's threatened or feeling protective," I said. "Not that deep since before her heat."

Garrett and Eve glanced at one another, and Eve's eyes were slits as she turned back to me. "She's been through her heat?"

I nodded slowly, my muscles bracing for an attack even as the threat sat loosely across from me. "It started coming in when we hid her here. I was...a service alpha for omegas before I joined this club. I made sure she had everything she'd need to ride the heat with or without an alpha."

Eve pinned me with that stare a moment longer before blinking, all the tension seeming to vanish at once, a fire snuffed out. "She and Adam are uncomfortable around one another. Why?"

"Is he okay?" Rory asked Garrett, who waved a hand in the air in response.

"Happy, sad, anxious, he's all over the place," Garrett said.

Rory's frown deepened, and then it was his turn to glare at me.

"Faith is the same. It's probably because there are unbound alphas in the mix," I said.

All together, the rest of the room turned to stare at me. I sighed. I had extra training from my time servicing, but it wasn't as if most of this wasn't taught in high school health classes. Not that I'd paid attention in those, either.

"Multiple omegas in a family isn't that common. Generally, when omegas reach an age to start gathering their pack, they find other omegas a threat. Faith and Adam remained on suppressants together while they were on the run. We got her some light ones to help with the club environment, but they're not meant to mute her instincts. Adam is a potential rival. Not personally, but at a base, biological level," I explained.

"His heat barely ended, we hurried here when we got the log-in alert," Garrett said, frowning.

"I don't even like his scent," King said to me.

I shrugged. "Doesn't matter. There's no bond to reassure

Faith of any of that. He could steal you. She could steal him," I said pointing to Rory.

"She could not," Eve said calmly, and Rory turned to her with what could only be deemed a reverent gaze. I didn't know any other alphas with a bond, but I hadn't met many female alphas, either. "But I understand. We'll stay nearby, but give them both their space in the meantime, until we decide what to do."

"What do you mean, *decide?*" King asked, and he barely fought the growl out of his voice.

Eve blinked at him. "Do you intend to keep an omega here surrounded by dozens of alphas who are not her pack?"

"Are you saying you intend to take her with *you*, who is also not her pack?" King snarled.

"It's not up to either of you," Chance said, appearing at my side, and it was King he was staring down at. "Bear and I are Faith's pack."

"Adam is her brother," Eve said. "He's not going to let us leave her here in an uncertain environment. And I'm not inclined to, either. I know what happens when you put too many alphas together and dangle a toy for them to fight over."

I opened my mouth, tensing to fight, when a weary wave called to me through the bond and reason settled back into my head. "It's late. Faith is exhausted and needs us. I'm sure Adam feels the same. Come back tomorrow and talk more, but I agree with Chance. Faith's fate is up to her, and he and I will stand behind her decision."

"Adam's made enough decisions regarding her safety up till now," King said in a low mutter.

I stood as the other pack shot King a series of looks—a dark glare, a confused glance, even a more thoughtful study from Jamie. Before anything else could be said, the door from the hall opened with a squeak. Eve rose, stepping out from the table, and I turned toward the hall.

Faith and Adam were walking hand in hand, but neither one looked entirely at ease. I held my arms open as they neared, and Faith slid away from her brother and into my side without hesitation. I spared Adam enough of a glance to see him do the same with Eve, Garrett rising to join the pair.

"You good, princess?" King asked, following me out of the booth.

She nodded, and I couldn't resist the wicked thought, *If you'd bond her, you'd know she was lying.* Now wasn't the time to say so.

"Are we staying here?" Adam asked.

"No, you need your nest," Eve answered, and even to me, her tone was hypnotic and velvety. Vicious and cold as she seemed, there was obvious warmth in the woman when she spoke to Adam. And she was concerned for Faith, which meant I could tolerate her long enough to prove that I would take good care of my omega.

"If you're comfortable with it, we'll come back tomorrow," Jamie said to King.

"We'll come back tomorrow," Eve said to Adam, smirking slightly.

King grunted but had the sense not to argue.

Adam stared at Faith, eyes widening, and I could almost taste the bitter panic on the air. He'd been separated from his sister for months, only just found her again, and tonight was probably not quite the reunion he'd had in his head.

"We'll take good care of her in the meantime. I promise," I said.

Faith squeezed me, and then slipped away and Adam threw himself in her direction. My own chest clenched, watching their embrace, desperate and relieved and nervous as they clung to one another. Faith whispered something in her brother's ear and he sighed and sagged, nodding.

"Tomorrow," he murmured.

Chance caught Faith before I could as she and Adam separated again. The window of the bar was boarded over, the glass cleared away, just a faint residue of bitter gas still lingering in the air. King would have the wreckage of the night to deal with in the morning, more to explain and justify to Rider and his ilk. For now, we walked to the front door in two groups, Adam's pack and Faith's, if I counted King and Ghost. Which I did, even if they didn't.

"Love you, biggo," Faith said as we reached the door.

Adam released a ragged laugh, and Eve purred. "Love you,

kiddo," he said, but he stood still in the door, staring back at her.

Eve reached out and stroked his jaw. "Come on, sugar."

Faith sighed as they walked out and King locked the door behind them.

"I'm sorr—" Faith started as King turned back.

"Don't." He shook his head and stared at her. "Busted windows and black eyes aside, tonight was good news, right, princess?"

She didn't answer right away, and her nod was small. She was bubbling with nerves, and I wanted to tell her about how angry King had gotten at the idea of Eve taking her away.

"I need you all in the nest with me tonight," she said, holding King's gaze.

He nodded. "You do. And I need some fuckin' sleep, so let's go."

Anxiety floated away in the bond and I smiled.

"Me too?" Ghost asked.

I'd seen Faith and Ghost together more since he'd made his fairly surprising announcement about Chance in front of the club. I couldn't tell yet how he and Faith were together without Chance, but the idea of another alpha in the pack was a relief, and I had my fingers crossed.

"You too," she said, nodding wearily, dragging Chance and I toward the stairs with our hands linked to hers.

It was too close to dawn, and I would need to help King with the work and conversations that needed to come in the morning. King was a mess, and Ghost was a little bloodied, but the club was quiet and we made it back to the nest in whole but weary pieces. I undressed Faith as the others stripped, bent my head to sniff her hair.

"We'll wash in the morning," she muttered.

I took off the shirt I was wearing and then dropped it down over her head, lifting her chin to see her answering smile.

"You in first," I said.

Faith blinked over my shoulder at the three other men waiting on her to get in the nest. It was too dark to see if she blushed, but I chuckled at the little bubble of sexual interest that popped into nothing as she let out an enormous and noisy yawn. She ducked and then slid into the nest.

"Dunno how we're all fitting," Chance muttered, but he followed her in.

I did the same, and we claimed our spots on either side of her, Faith's hip warm against my stomach. Ghost was next, blinking briefly into the dim glow of the nest, breathing deeply.

"Whoa," he whispered, eyes hooding.

"Here," Chance instructed, patting his other side.

Which only left one man. King stood in the open curtains, watching Ghost squeeze himself between the padded nest wall and Chance's back. He glared down at us like a puzzle he wasn't in the mood to solve. There was barely any room at my back, and I was going to have a hard time not laughing if King tried to spoon me.

"King," Faith murmured, and her legs spread a little bit.

He nodded once, a quick, decisive jerk of his head, and then he was climbing in, reaching for her knees and drawing them up around his hips as he draped himself on top of her. Her breasts were his pillow, legs curled around his back, and I drew one of the blankets up over us.

Faith sighed, one arm wrapping over King's back, another reaching to clasp my hand.

"This is it," she whispered, barely giving sound to the words. And she was sinking happily into the bond, settling and letting the rough edges of the night fade away.

We are it, I thought. *We are her pack.*

I dimmed the lights and joined her in the thick comfort of the bond.

Chance's ass was hugging my cock. The nest smelled like home and epic sex and top-shelf pussy, and I was wedged between the hard wall and the edge of the mattress I was barely hanging onto. Half my body had lost sensation, and I'd been awake for an hour, just wishing I could roll over or stretch in any direction. I was in heaven.

Finally, as the sun rose high enough to glare into the nest from Bear's bedroom window, there was rustling from the other side of the bed.

"Gonna shower," Bear whispered, and it was King who answered with a grunt, one man crawling carefully out of the nest.

I waited for King or Faith to budge, hoping for a little room to maneuver myself out of the crevice of bed and wall, but for a moment, nothing changed. Fabric rustled, breath deepened, and I shut my eyes, surrendering to perfect discomfort, Chance's scent tickling my nose. Then a soft, wet suck echoed in the nest, answered by a breathy, feminine moan.

My cock twitched.

I peeked one eye open, and heat spiraled down to my length as I watched King burrow against Faith's breasts, the shirt she slept in pushed up only far enough to give him room to kiss and suck. He was still lying on top of her, offering a glimpse of creamy skin before it was swallowed up in his beard, but Faith's slack expression of teased pleasure was enough to leave me riveted.

She was so goddamn pretty, lips full and parted, lashes thick on her cheeks. Her knees bent up, exposing tan thighs clamping around King. If they started fucking I was going to have a full boner burrowed between Chance's cheeks and absolutely nothing I could do about it, and yet I kind of hoped they would. Faith's scent was blooming, coating down my throat like syrup with every breath, and she was rubbing herself against King's stomach as he continued to suckle and nibble.

"King," she pleaded, reaching for his head.

He rose up suddenly, and I caught a sweet and brief glimpse of a rosy, wet nipple begging for his return before he tugged the shirt down to her belly button. He was grinning at her, wicked and handsome in a way I'd never noticed on King before, looking genuinely and rarely happy.

"Gotta go clean up too," he whispered to her.

"Bastard," she hissed, baring her teeth at him. He was half-hard in his boxer briefs, and he tweaked her nipple through the shirt before diving out of the nest.

"You've got plenty of playmates left to keep you occupied, princess," he said.

Faith groaned and rolled over onto her stomach as King dressed, and I stared openly at her ass in the precious pink cotton underwear she was wearing. Chance followed her, and I wasn't sure if he was asleep or not as he cuddled up to her hip again. I gasped as I was finally able to make room for myself on the bed, and then grunted as I rolled directly onto my now stiff cock.

Blood shot into my immobile left arm, and I groaned at the flood of pin-pricking sensation. I flopped limp limbs until I was on my back and found Faith sitting up on her side, studying me with a soft smile. She'd been spooked and quiet last night. It was good to see her looking at me again with that knowing, amused, and vaguely impatient expression, like she was still waiting for me to get my shit together.

Her gaze ran over me and her eyebrows bounced as she reached my hips. "Well, good morning to you too."

King shut the door to the bedroom and Bear was humming in the shower, and I was rock-hard, lying next to Chance for the first morning ever. I didn't want to interrupt the peace, afraid I might be tossed out now that Faith was feeling better.

"Morning," I croaked.

"May I?" Faith asked, hand lifting from the bed, hovering over Chance's back toward me.

May you what? I thought, but her eyes were on my erection in my underwear. *We haven't even kissed yet!*

But my head was nodding. "Uh-huh."

Faith's smile grew, and she hummed thoughtfully as she reached across Chance and helped herself to groping my length through a thin layer of fabric. Her hand was warm, grip sure, and I bucked against her palm as she studied my girth and length. The waistband of my underwear was gaping over my stomach as my cock kicked for freedom.

Faith granted it, and I stopped breathing as she pushed the waistband down, letting the elastic bite under my sac, putting me on display. Her touch lightened, teasing with her fingertips as she circled my tip and then tapped her way down my length.

Chance grumbled into the pillows as I lifted my hips into her hand again. "You hornballs."

Faith grinned at me. "His dick is pretty."

Her hand looked good on my cock, I thought, tan from the desert sun, fingers almost long enough to circle me completely.

Chance rolled over, bumping her arm and making her run her hand up and down my length as I moaned. Chance barely blinked before he was joining her, scooping his grip down to grab my balls, making me yelp and creating a liquid dribble at my tip.

"Taste him," Chance rasped.

"Fucking fuck," I muttered.

But Faith just sat up and leaned over Chance's lap, ducking down until her tongue was licking at the fresh precum. "Mm!" Her eyes widened, and I tried to breathe through my teeth.

"Good?" Chance asked.

She nodded and smiled at him. "You wanna try?"

I somehow felt like I wasn't present, even as they pawed and stroked my length. I wanted their eyes on me, and yet I loved the simple use of my body, like I was a toy to be shared.

"Get it for me," Chance said, folding an arm back for his head to rest on.

He squeezed me and Faith worked my length as she took me between her lips again, sucking forcefully.

"Oh, god!" I thrust up between her lips, and then Chance's tug guided me flat on the bed again. Faith pulled on my cock like I was a fucking milkshake straw. My eyes crossed and I gasped for air.

She popped up without warning, lips swollen, and then she released me from her hand, twisting to Chance and offering him a kiss laced with my flavor. He licked into her, their tongues briefly visible, and his grip on my balls held me in place. They moaned as they kissed, softening into one another, all while I lay panting and needy at their side, neglected and thrilled.

"It is good," Chance murmured as Faith pulled away. "You want more?"

Faith's eyes slid to mine, and I was about to beg her to say yes. "I want to watch you two together."

Chance's hand tightened briefly, and I let out a bellow, rocking into his grip. "'Kay. Pull me out for him."

I was released, abandoned, and I scrambled up to my knees, already eager to have Chance in my mouth again. He and I had kissed since I'd started earning my forgiveness, but he'd always returned to Faith's side. I'd stopped being jealous of her and instead found myself jealous of them both, that they got to hold one another at night, sleep in the nest together, and I had to return to my shitty bedroom. Until last night.

I needed to make sure I earned my invitation back *every* night.

Faith pushed Chance's boxers down with a brief lift of his hips, and I found myself licking my lips at the sight of him. It'd been weeks. I sighed as I rolled and scooted down. Chance's fingers caught my beard, tipping my face up to meet his gaze.

"Don't finish me. You're both getting fucked this morning," he said.

I turned my face into his palm, breathing deeply, catching my own scent there from where he'd gripped me, kissing the flesh in front of me.

"I've missed you," I whispered.

Chance was quiet, and I looked up warily, struck still when I caught the warmth in his stare, the soft smile on his face. That fucking look. And it was mine now.

"I missed you too," he said slowly. "But this is better now."

I nodded, swallowing hard, and Chance tugged on my beard again. This was better, and I needed to earn it, to keep it permanently.

I bent my head, reaching for his cock, running my tongue up its length and groaning with pride as he started to stiffen in my grip.

"He's so eager to please," Chance whispered to Faith as I lathered his length with sloppy kisses and long licks. "So pathetically desperate to suck me. I've been wondering what he'd be like eating you out too."

I was panting as he spoke, stroking him in one hand, gripping his balls gently in the other. I wanted him hard as iron as I choked him down.

"Would you want his knot?" Chance asked her.

"Would he know what to do with it?" Faith asked.

I moaned at her question, at the teasing speculation. Did she instinctively understand this game, or had Chance explained it to her? I didn't care. Bear was laughing to himself as he left the shower, and the door to the apartment opened and closed once more as I slurped and sucked on Chance's dick.

"Do you know how to use your knot for an omega?" Chance asked me.

I stuffed him between my lips and mumbled into his length, licking and shaking my head slightly.

Faith tutted. "You'll have to teach him. It looks like he doesn't know how to suck dick, either," she said, her fingernails stroking through my hair. Then she tightened her hand into a fist, pulling at my roots, and thrust me down on

Chance's cock. I gagged and Chance groaned, finally bucking into me.

Fuck. Perfect.

"That's better," Chance praised—her or me; it didn't matter.

I was a mess, just like Faith said. An alpha who didn't know how to fill the shoes the world had fitted him for. Faith's hand loosened and I whined, but she only petted me once more, letting me draw back for breath before she was clasping the back of my neck, forcing me to bob on Chance's shaft, fit him back to my throat as I swallowed eagerly.

"Yes, like that," Chance panted. "Push him deeper."

Faith's fingers twisted in my hair, but she didn't push. She didn't have to. I *did* know how to swallow Chance, to let him fuck my throat even if it made me gag more from this angle. My eyes watered, and Chance's thumb stroked the wetness of my cheek. Faith forced me up for air again, and I opened my eyes to find them staring down at me with twin fond expressions.

I didn't know if this was love or obsession or my twisted head, but I had to keep them, to make them keep me.

Adam's alpha Eve had said that the unbound alphas in the pack were making Faith anxious. Chance's words about not being able to form a bond with Faith were ringing in my head. A terrible and perfect idea was forming in my stupid fucking head.

I ignored Faith's grip, my mouth wide and lips working hungrily down Chance's length, tongue squirming against his slick skin until I was nuzzling into the dark hair over his groin. He moaned, and the sound was so rare and beautiful I grew dizzy.

"Stop," he gasped.

I pulled away immediately, caught my breath, and then kissed all the skin I could reach—his thighs, his balls, his length, his belly. Chance caught his breath and both he and Faith were petting me, the approval from them both and the idea in my head mingling into a nervous energy.

My hands and mouth fumbled and trembled as I stroked his thighs and kissed over his hip bone.

"He's sweet," Faith whispered.

Chance laughed, but he was still running his fingers through my hair in a softer touch than I was used to. His legs spread for me as I sucked a mark on his inner thigh.

"Quit messing around," Chance said, voice all warm.

So I did. Faith's breath hitched as I opened my mouth, a note of shock escaping as I sank my teeth into Chance's flesh. He yelped, hand tightening on my hair, trying to pull me off, but I wrapped an arm around his leg and held on. I licked around the inside of my teeth, moaned at the flavor of his blood.

"What the fuck, Ghost?!" Chance yelled.

And anger spiked in my chest, a knife blade connecting directly to my heart, an electric charge running from him to me. I'd expected anger, and I shivered at the excitement that was there too. Chance's grip remained firm, but his leg relaxed in my hold as I licked him again.

A gentle hand cuffed the back of my neck and then squeezed. "Release him," Faith said.

It was too late now. The bond was in place, confusion and curiosity, frustration and disappointment. I unlatched my teeth and then sucked at the bite mark, licking it rapidly. Out of the corner of my eye, Chance hissed and his cock bobbed.

"Ghost," Faith snapped.

My shoulders hunched as worry wormed from Chance to me and back again. I licked him once more and then looked up at them. They were pale with shock, and Faith's glare was fierce.

"You need bonds," I said to her. She blinked and Chance groaned. I licked my lips and glanced down at the mark. It was red, still fresh, and starting to swell around the torn flesh. I turned my gaze to his. "You want a bond with her."

He stiffened, shock taking over from the anger. Hope. Excitement again, annoyance too.

"Oh, you fucking mess," Faith breathed, rolling her eyes and shaking her head. "You didn't think you should ask for permission?"

"I did, but I didn't want you to say no."

Their lips pursed in tandem. I lowered my head slowly and Faith's eyes narrowed, watching me as I lapped at the mark. It needed nursing. I may not have been much of an alpha, but I did know that.

Chance was mine now. His emotions were rioting, anger flashing forward and then fading again under more promising emotions.

"Are you all right?" Faith asked Chance.

He was sagging back into the bed, chest heaving with deep breaths. "I can feel him."

That was right! I thrust the mess in my head in Chance's direction. All the envy, the longing, the craving to be in the nest, in the pack, with *them*. How badly I wanted to be accepted, to just be *touching* them. I nursed the wound and shared what I could, relieved as his emotions shifted.

"Fuck, that feels good," he muttered. "Trying to stay mad, but he's just so..."

"Pathetic," I mumbled into his thigh.

"Sweet," Chance whispered, and I froze.

"Sweet?" Faith asked.

"And greedy, like you," he said softly. "It's permanent."

Mine. Pride and determination swelled in my chest. I licked my mark once more and looked up again. Faith was still glaring at me. She was seated on her knees at Chance's side, and she glanced at him once more, at the mark I'd been nursing, before reaching down and peeling her underwear off. Her scent was heady, and my mouth immediately watered as she slid down onto the mattress and parted her thighs.

"Make mine match," she said.

Chance groaned and laughed as giddy victory rushed through me. "Just 'cause you're getting your way doesn't mean you're not getting punished," he said to me.

"Not that he cares," Faith scoffed, but her lips were twitching now.

I knew full well what I really deserved was being kicked out of the nest. I'd taken what was absolutely not mine to have, at least not without Chance begging. But I would *earn* this moment. Every fucking second of every day, I would figure out how to make these two glad to have a bond with me.

"Kiss first," Faith said.

I gave Chance a final lick before hauling myself up and crawling around their legs until I was braced above Faith.

Chance rested on his side, watching us, his finger tracing aimlessly around my mark.

"Are you sure about me?" Faith asked as I started to lower my head. Her brow was furrowed, teeth nibbling on her bottom lip.

"I am, but I should be the one asking you that."

"Why start now?" Chance mused sarcastically.

Faith blinked at me, reaching up to comb through my beard. Her eyes skimmed over my face, studying me, seeing too much. "I am too, actually."

How could you be? I wanted to ask, but the words were too wonderful to make her take them back, and I swooped down, clasping her mouth in mine before she might change her mind. Her lips were sweet, and she hummed as I kissed her, searching eagerly for Chance's flavor. Her hands cupped my throat as she guided me. I'd kissed dozens of women, but this one felt new and confusing, like I was starting from scratch.

She was confident where I was nervous. I knew how to kiss, for fuck's sake—I'd been doing it since I was twelve—but it was more important than ever to get it right, and the knowledge made me clumsy.

"You're such a shit," Chance said on a sigh, and for some reason the insult relaxed me.

I stroked my tongue against Faith's and ran my hand up under her shirt, arching her back into my chest. I recalled the sound she'd made for King as he'd sucked on her nipple and earned it for myself as I did the same to the tip of her tongue before moving back to her lips, over to her jaw.

"Give me your bite, Ghost," Faith whispered in my ear as I nibbled on her jaw.

"But be gentler with her," Chance added. "Fucking hurt like a bitch."

"It can hurt, I don't mind," she murmured.

I sat up and she peeled out of the shirt. I paused at the picture of her, at ease in her nest, a nearly healed circle of teeth marks around her left breast, hair rumpled around her head. She'd seemed scrawny and starved when we'd found her in the van, but all the slopes and curves of her belly, breasts, and thighs were on display now, lush and blushing the longer I gazed down.

And between her thighs, she was shining.

"Slick," I said, grinning as I stared down.

"Your turn to taste," she said, stretching provocatively.

I groaned. I was half-hard, neglected after her earlier study, but as I shifted down onto my belly, face hovering in front of those dark pink lips, the hooded folds wet and glossy, my cock bucked in protest against the mattress. Every breath drew her perfume in, my head growing hazy. Why was I here? What was the plan? None of it mattered except getting my mouth on—

Faith gasped as I wrapped my lips around her, and I joined her in her moan as I tongued her sex, burrowing eagerly deeper into her, wanting to drown myself in that flavor, needing it to coat my mouth and beard and lungs and nose.

Chance's laugh was in my ear, cutting through the fog, and then his hand ran warmly down my back. Hungry growls and purrs and sloppy, obscenely wet noises joined his laugh and her breathy, high gasps.

"Guess we know where messy works best," Chance said. "Keep him busy, birdy. I have a plan."

My scalp ached as Faith gripped my hair, her hips bucking into my mouth. I worked my tongue inside of her and purred as she fucked my face, shameless and noisy and sweet, her flavor running onto my tongue and down my throat.

Okay. So *this* was the omega thing. I wanted to tell Rider and Skid what absolute *bitches* they would turn into if they ever were lucky enough to fuck an omega, except they didn't deserve to know what this felt like.

When a familiar probing touch appeared at my ass, I moaned into Faith, resurfacing for air.

"You've got her close," Chance said, and I blinked and found Faith wild-eyed and blushing from forehead to tit. Her sex was swollen and flushed red, probably from my beard, and she was humping the air, begging for my return. "Make her come when you bite her."

I nodded, diving back down, slurping and licking and groaning as she immediately started to clasp tightly around the two fingers I'd thrust into her. I kissed her clit as she humped her hips into my hand, licked a circle around it, and then pulled away, panting as Chance coated my ass in cold lube.

"Gently," he reminded.

I wanted to extend the moment selfishly, have Faith coming on my tongue and riding my face for hours, but Chance was urgent in the bond, determined, and I needed to prove how good I'd be for them. I kissed her thigh in the same spot I'd bitten Chance, pumping my fingers in Faith, sucking at the skin like I was trying to make one of Chance's hickey marks. She was whimpering and riding my hand, her fingers slipping in my hair like she was losing her grip. That was good. I needed to hurry.

I opened my mouth, wrapping my teeth around her flesh, and Faith keened, a sudden gush and spray of release wetting my hand. And then Chance's fingers were pushing forcefully into my ass. My jaw tightened on reflex, teeth digging briefly before tearing. I growled into my bite, forcing myself to hold still as Chance stretched my ass and Faith whined.

She was lighter than Chance somehow, and there was so much happening at once, it took me a moment to really feel the bond. I shuddered as it floated in. God, she *was* sweet, silky in my chest, tangling around me like ropes and tightening with a possessive promise. It was a grip I'd run from in the past, a woman clutching onto me, but I'd given Faith the access myself, permanent and deep, and I surrendered into it now with something like relief. She was mine and I was hers, and there was no changing that now, no running.

And then they found each other. We shouted together, lightning and satin tangling, drawing tighter. The bond was suddenly flooded with heat, and...

Oh, god.

Love.

I moaned, teeth unlatching, mouth circling the wound, nursing it hungrily as they met between me, drawing me into the emotions that were meant to be for each other. I squeezed my eyes shut, but it couldn't block out the intense happiness, the eager connection. Mine. Not for me. It didn't matter. Tears pricked in my eyes and then there were hands in my hair, rubbing down my back, comfort from the pair of them. Comfort I probably didn't deserve, but which swarmed me with the affection all the same.

"I can't breathe," I hissed, pulling away from the wound.

"Shh, yes you can, come here," Chance said, pulling me up onto my knees. It just pushed his fingers deeper in my ass, and my cock dribbled in excitement as Chance wrapped his free arm around my chest. "Relax," he said, but the soothing touch in the bond came from Faith. Her cheeks were red, brow sweaty, and she smiled up at us.

"You're going to knot our omega," Chance murmured in my ear. "I should let you fuck her a little first, but you did pull a whack move on us. Anyway, I want to teach you how to make her feel good. You need that, don't you?"

I groaned and nodded, and Chance patted my chest. How he could fucking think straight with the bond just ringing like a church bell, all joyous and bright and—

Love, and it wasn't even fucking mine.

"It's the only thing that'll distract him," Faith said, sitting up and reaching for me.

They maneuvered me between them, Faith cupping my cheeks and drawing me into a numb kiss, Chance pushing me down to lie on top of her. But no one needed to guide my cock. That fucker found his way like Faith had a homing device just for my length.

"Fuck," I gasped as I sank into her opening, slick and hot enough to burn. I started to pull out, to pump on instinct, and Chance's hand pressed to my back.

"No. All the way in," he said, and when I hesitated, he appeared at my ass.

And all the way in we went, him into me, me into her. I'd never knotted anything but my own goddamn fist, and suddenly I had a velvet chokehold surrounding me. I bellowed, and Faith fluttered and swooned under me, rising into the pressure.

My punishment for biting Chance was that they were planning on killing me, I realized. Like this. Perfectly, heavenly, blissed-out murder.

Chance's cock made my ass sting. It'd been too long, but it

was a relieving contrast to the drowning pleasure of Faith squeezing my knot, riding me from below, eager and confident. Chance thrusted, pushing me into her, and Faith gasped and shuddered, washing me in heat. Their hands were everywhere on me, stroking and gripping, pulling my hair, pushing my hips.

I was the object between them, the charged rope for them to express their love through, the body to fuck each other with. I anchored myself with a hard grip on Faith's ass. My mark on her inner thigh was bleeding against my hip, as if she weren't already slippery enough. I groaned as Chance's lips brushed over my shoulder.

And then he bit me.

I howled, stiffening, even as he fucked me into Faith, making my knot circle and grind inside of her, forcing another orgasm out of her and ripping one directly out of my soul.

You have to earn my bite.

I sobbed into Faith's shoulder and she kissed my jaw. The affection bloomed, the rope grew thicker, and the warmth was in every stroke of their hands over my skin, Chance's lips on my shoulder, Faith's on my face.

Chance's hands ran down my arms, finding my own on her skin, loosening my grip and moving it to the bed, our fingers tangled together.

"Mine now," he said.

"Mine," Faith murmured, nibbling my jaw.

I rocked, mimicking the motion Chance had described, making him groan and Faith whine with pleasure.

"Yes, keep going," Faith begged. Such a pretty sound—an omega's imperative to my alpha instincts.

"Let's ruin her," Chance coaxed, kissing the bite on my shoulder, the one with and without a bond.

Chance's hips flexed and I moved with him, the pair of us moaning, Faith crying out.

And it wasn't a cord running through me, it was a knot with three ends. They loved each other, and they were mine. I'd claimed them, and I'd claim their love too. I'd fuckin' earn it. Every second, starting now.

I reached into the cardboard box, pulling out the last ice cream cone and unwrapping it before Adam realized I'd gotten four to his two. It was his own fault. He wouldn't stop talking.

"And then Eve *made* him film a last testament leaving all his money to the women we'd just set free and literally talked him into—"

"Is that legal?" I asked, pausing his story before he delivered another horrifically gruesome tale of victory.

Adam snorted and waved the melting ice cream cone through the air. "Not remotely, but it worked. We checked up with one of the girls. There's no one to contest it now."

I hummed, and Adam took a breath and a pause, biting the cone.

I watched our packs mingle together through the open garage doors. Ghost had been very excitedly discussing Eve's car with Adam's pack, and he'd just started to show off his own collection of bikes in the shop, when the woman drifted away from the group, heading in our direction.

It helped a little to see Adam's pack out of the black military-grade garments—in fact, they almost fit into the scenery around the club—but there was no disguising the lethal prowl of a predator. Even when the predator was wearing a T-shirt, Daisy-Dukes, and high top sneakers.

"Save me any?" Eve asked, arriving at our picnic table.

I froze, but Adam just shook his head and grinned up at Eve. "But I'll share." He held up the bottom half of the cone—the obvious *best* part—and Eve returned the offer with a sultry grin, leaning in and taking a bite.

"Rory is bored out of his mind. Go sweet-talk him into taking you to the convenience store for more provisions," Eve said.

Adam laughed and I stiffened as he stood from my side. "Deal. Any requests?"

Eve was almost bashful as she shrugged. "You know what I like."

"Spiciest thing I can find, got it," Adam said, strolling away, leaving me behind with his alpha. He paused, spinning on his heel and pointing his finger at Eve. "Best behavior."

"Scout's honor, sugar," Eve purred.

And then she swayed into the seat across from me, cinnamon-warm eyes sliding in my direction. My mouth was dry, and I was trying to keep the instinctive alarm blaring inside of me muffled before any of my bondmates grew worried. I didn't want Adam to leave me alone with this woman, not while everyone else was so far out of reach. Not that I thought any of them being closer could really stop her from killing me as quickly and efficiently as she had so many men in the stories Adam had been filling my head with this afternoon.

Eve's eyes blinked slowly and her gaze reminded me of a cat, the pretense of trust in that brief shuttering of her lashes.

"I like a fresh bond and a good fuck after a fight too," she said.

Ice cream dribbled down my hand as my face flushed hot. Eve rested her elbow on the picnic table and set her chin on the heel of her hand, a serene smile stretching over her lips. Bear had scented Ghost's bond right away too, surprisingly calm. It was still fairly fresh, and I'd worn a skirt rather than something that might rub against the spot before Ghost had time to finish healing it.

"It's centering," Eve continued. "Reassuring, even."

"Is that why you've bitten my brother, like, seventy-five times?" The words snapped out of me, and I sucked in a breath in their wake.

Do not goad the international hitwoman, I shouted in my own head.

Eve just laughed. "That, and that he tastes like candy," she said. "But I restrained myself last night. Bit Rory again instead. He begs almost as prettily as your brother."

My eyes widened at the idea of the huge, tattooed, scowling alpha begging for this woman's bite. Then again, he looked awfully relaxed today.

"I bit Bear the day we met," I said.

Eve blinked. "You bit *him*?" I nodded, and her eyes strayed to where Adam and Rory were walking across the back lot toward the convenience store.

"It made something like a bond—fainter, though." It was a bizarre conversation, but I hoped Adam got the chance to sink his teeth into Eve for a change.

"Intriguing," Eve murmured. "Do you know why you bit him?"

I stalled, thinking and lapping up my melting ice cream cone. "I don't remember it exactly. He smelled like home, or—you know, not *my* home that I knew, but what it feels like to be home? Anyway, I was scared and angry, and he was reaching into the cage for me..." I frowned. "I dunno if I was biting him because he felt safe, or because I felt threatened, actually."

"Both, probably," Eve said, her stare too intent to hold for long. "I was feral for a long time growing up. I learned to control it, to put the instincts away when I needed to work. To draw them out again when I needed the extra protection. They always served me better than any rules or logic I'd been instructed with."

"Is that why you bit Adam?" I asked.

Eve snorted. "I bit Adam because he is a sneaky little con

artist who put me in a rut to keep me from killing him. So, yes," she said, grinning. "I suppose it was instinct."

"And you don't regret it?" I asked, thinking of Bear and King, and even now Ghost.

Eve sighed, a heavy, weary sound, and my heart ached for Adam. "Don't tell my pack, but...no, I don't regret any of the many times I've bitten my packmates," she said with a smug smile, which faltered a moment later. "Well, aside from one inconveniently-placed bite on the ass. Garrett whined for *days*. It was very annoying."

My laugh caught me off guard, and so did Eve's shy smile in answer.

"You like it here?" she asked.

I looked around at the dry, sparse landscape, the paint chipping off the plaster walls of the buildings, the garage overflowing with machinery and grease, the burn barrels glittering with beer bottles. Ghost's laugh was loud, and heavy metal music had just started pouring out of the windows from the kitchens—the girls starting to clean or cook for the evening.

"I like my nest, my...my pack," I said, smiling at the word on my tongue. I had a pack now, small as it was, still missing King in the mix. "It's not what I'd imagined, but it's nice to just...be somewhere, and not plan for where we have to run next."

Eve's nose wrinkled, and I recalled all of Adam's excitement over his past few weeks of travel.

"Adam talks about the Charger like it's a mansion," I said, surprised by my own impulse to offer a compliment to the woman. "Like it's the world's best nest."

"You're different people," Eve observed.

I opened my mouth to argue and then shut it again. Of course we were different people. We always had been.

"We have a house in the suburbs," Eve said slowly, gaze distant. "I do think we prefer the Charger, but it's there for us when we need a break. But does it feel permanent here for you?"

I licked my lips and they were dry from the desert air. I had a nest built from plywood and soundproof foam. I was surrounded by alphas that seemed to simultaneously want me out or want a piece of me. I'd been told from the beginning that I was only staying until I found a good pack, but the good pack was here, and I didn't know what that meant for the future. King was a coin toss in the air right now, and I was still waiting to see which way he would land.

"I don't know," I admitted. "I want...them. I want my pack."

"You're afraid of asking for too much," Eve said, and then before I could digest that, she added, "Adam still is. We're working on it."

She loves him, I realized. She was terrifying and deadly and cold and a little mean too, but she loved my brother. And that did a lot to win me over.

"Want to play a game?" she asked, and it took me a moment to realize the question was directed over my head.

I felt a cool tug in the bond and then a warm, familiar hand settled on my back. I looked up into Chance's sharp, studying stare, and my smile spread instinctually, his own hinted at in the corners of his eyes.

"I noticed a target board," Eve said to Chance. "And you could use the practice."

"She's acting up 'cause Adam and Garrett aren't here to stare disapprovingly at her," Jamie said, following Chance to our table, rounding it as Eve glared at him.

"That's not your job too?" I asked him.

His smile was silky, even in the force of Eve's dangerous atmosphere. "Never."

If she preened in response, it was too subtle to say for certain.

"Sure," Chance answered her at last. "I suppose you might have something to teach me."

"Humility," Eve answered, grinning. "My knives are in the trunk. I won't coach you, but if you watch carefully, you might learn something useful."

I probed the bond, and Ghost circled me curiously, following along as I found a mix of amusement, annoyance, and interest in Chance.

Adam and Rory returned, armed with an excessive array of snacks, as we moved around toward the back of the garage, where the desert spread out like a warm blanket past Dead End.

Chance's targets were makeshift, red and white nearly circles hand-painted on plywood boards. There were more tables here behind the garage, more barrels filled with old beer bottles with sun-faded labels and flies buzzing wishfully. We dragged the tables into the shade as Eve and Chance appeared, black cases filled with gleaming knives in hand.

"I hope your packmate's not a sore loser," Adam murmured, and Garrett laughed and elbowed him in the side.

Ghost and I exchanged a brief uncertain glance. Neither of us was sure how Chance would respond if bested by an alpha. By *this* alpha.

Ghost's side pressed to mine, and we were clumsy together in the bond. It was impulsively formed, premature, but I liked the almost nervous flavor of him in my chest, so at odds with the cocky persona he shared with his club brothers. His hand landed in my lap and my thighs snapped together reflexively, but he wasn't teasing me. He grinned, content with his fingers clasped between my legs, a giddy happiness extended to me in the bond.

"You first," Eve said to Chance.

I'd watched him before, the ease and expertise in every step and flex, the flick and toss of the knife toward the target. Ghost and I both flinched as it hit, right of center, wide from the goal for Chance. He was nervous.

Eve made no remark, just waited as he stepped aside and then took her own place.

He moved back far enough to study her head-to-toe, and I wasn't surprised when her knife struck heavily, centered in the slight oval of the bullseye.

"Again," Chance said, taking a few steps closer.

Eve didn't argue, just nodded. "Next ring up," she declared, and then the knife was catching sunlight at every whipping turn in the air, lodging exactly straight above her first, just one ring up.

"Ring below," Chance said, tipping his head.

She threw, and it landed, perfect again. "Ready now?" she asked, arching a brow.

Chance was quiet for a moment, gaze distant.

"He'll get it," Ghost murmured, his fingers squeezing my flesh just a little.

"Ready," Chance said, nodding.

"Rory, grab mine," Eve said.

The alpha pulled Eve's knives from the board and stepped aside as Chance positioned himself. He shifted briefly, and then before I knew it, the knife was tossed. I barely had time to catch my breath or brace before it landed.

Ghost was booming in the bond, but I waited, watching Eve study the target.

"Good," she said, head dipping once. "Let's get a better target."

Chance showed almost no reaction, an equally brief nod of his head, but I beamed for him and Ghost whooped once, grinning as Chance flicked a roll of his eyes in our direction. He was proud of himself, and we would show it, even if he wouldn't.

———

THE KNIFE-THROWING contest attracted the rest of the club, one member at a time, until the area behind the garage was blaring rock music out of speakers, the grill was pluming smoke into the air, and someone finally bothered to empty the old barrels so they could be filled anew.

Garrett had staked a large, branchy plant to the target, and Eve and Chance were taking turns telling each other which branch to cut off. He missed occasionally by tiny margins. She never did.

Every few turns, one of the other club members would get it in their head to join Chance and Eve, only to be promptly humiliated and heckled from the sidelines by those of us who knew better than to challenge the real experts.

"It's a good thing you bonded him," Garrett said to Ghost where our packs were clustered together at one table. "Eve likes to collect pretty and deadly people."

Bear and Ghost sat on either side of me, and I was comfortable between their heat as the sun set and their scents sharpened.

"She'd have a fight on her hands if she tried to take Chance," I muttered.

Rory, who'd brought plate after plate of food to the table until none of us could eat another bite, flicked a smile in my direction. He was nicer than I'd initially thought, he and Jamie quieter than the rest of their pack, steadying forces. I'd never seen alphas look at another alpha the way they did at Eve, covetous and proud at the same time, but they clearly cared for Adam too. An unusual pack dynamic, but it worked.

I searched the crowd as another alpha was booed away from the target board after a knife wobbled wildly left and into the desert. King was yards away, talking with one of his club members, their faces relaxed but attentive. He was using the night to work on his alliances, and it made me squirm in my seat. I didn't want to tear him away from the life he loved now, but I hated the thought that his position as president might prevent him ever actually making me his omega. I would lose him. One or both of us would eventually pull away. Maybe I would even leave with my pack. The thought of it made my stomach turn now. I wasn't ready to give up on King, and I didn't want to think about the moment I would be.

A warm arm draped over my shoulder at the same time as a large hand grasped mine. Ghost pulled me into his side as Bear drew my hand onto his lap, the pair of them offering silent comfort and a wave of warmth in the bond. The combination was as powerful as the heartache in my chest, and all together it just made the tears in my eyes swell into fat, hot drops. I turned my face into Ghost before they spilled over and he nuzzled against me, wiping those tears away with his beard. He smelled like cheap beer and smoke from the grill and that spicy sweetness that made my mouth water.

"Whatever it is, I've got your back, slick," he said softly.

I laughed, wiped the last of the wetness on my cheeks onto his T-shirt, and turned back to the game, only to find Chance watching us. He echoed his support in the bond as he rolled his wrists, knives at the ready.

"Here," Eve said, reaching through the tangled and trimmed

branches staked to the target to point at a tiny and hidden branch.

Chance laughed and shook his head, arms shrugging. It was a nearly impossible target, hard to see in the shadowy night and difficult to reach, tucked behind other branches. But he didn't refuse as Eve stepped away, just shifted into position.

Bodies jostled at the edge of the crowd, rearranging to get a better view. I frowned as I watched Chance's brother, Rider, move toward the front. Ghost sucked in a breath, sitting up straighter at my side, and I reached over, resting my hand on his thigh.

"Chance can handle him," I murmured.

"Doesn't mean Rider doesn't need his nuts kicked," Ghost muttered.

I snorted but then Chance was in motion, slight and subtle as it was. I held my breath, ignoring the *thunk* of the knife hitting the board, watching Chance's shoulders tense slightly.

"Your baby brother is getting his ass kicked by a girl, Ride," Skid called from the other side of the crowd.

"Are we surprised?" Rider asked.

At my side Ghost growled and tried to rise, my hand on his thigh struggling to hold him down. Eve didn't turn, but I caught the quick flick of her hand, the knife tossed clumsily back behind her.

Or not clumsy at all, I realized, as the hilt struck at Rider, directly between his legs. He grunted and she turned slowly in his direction, eyes scanning him with false innocence. Garrett and Adam were snickering, Jamie shaking his head, and Rory watched with tense readiness.

"Whoops," Eve said, glancing down at Rider's crotch. "I missed. Small target, I guess."

Chance ignored them all, throwing again, and his knife struck the board once more, snuggly against the first. But this time, the tiny branch Eve had chosen tipped to the side, cleanly cut. A cheer rose up, louder and fuller than any laugh Rider and Skid had managed to get from their insults. Chance ignored the cheers with the same tense stillness he'd ignored the heckling, and he leaned toward Eve, speaking softly in her ear. She nodded, and the pair of them moved to our table in unison.

Adam yawned widely as Eve approached, and he was sagged against Garrett's side, eyes heavy.

"Ready to head out, sugar?" Eve asked him. Adam glanced in my direction, and she smiled briefly at me. "We can come back tomorrow."

Adam nodded eagerly this time. "Deal. I am tired. You're good?" he asked me.

Chance draped his arms over my shoulders, pulling me back to lean against him. "I'm good," I said to Adam. If anything, I could've used a day alone with my pack to rest. *That's not right. You haven't seen your brother in months*, I reminded myself.

Still, there was a little flicker of relief as we finished our goodbyes for the night and I watched Adam and his pack walk to their car.

Bear's hand stroked down my arm and I turned to him. My own eyelids were growing heavy too. We hadn't gotten much sleep the night before, and my new bondmark was itching for attention.

"You're...you're keeping me, right?" I whispered to Bear, the worry strange but persistent. Chance's hands tightened on my shoulder, and Ghost startled at my side.

Bear didn't look surprised by the question, as if he'd already read it in the bond. "Wherever we go, we go together, Butterfly," he answered.

I sighed and relaxed.

"How about we make that the nest for now?" Chance suggested.

"Yes, please," I said, reaching for Ghost's hand, finding it easily.

We rose from the table together to slide through the still mingling crowd, and I searched for King once more. He'd disappeared, probably to his office to work or hold a more private conversation. But I had three bondmates at my side and I took comfort in their solid support, the strength in my chest, and the affection. It was time to start embracing the future within reach, rather than the one that didn't want to be caught.

I ran my finger around the oval mark I'd found on the inside of Faith's thigh. She hummed in her sleep, her perfume swarming my head.

Ghost had bonded her.

A week ago, he hadn't even been in the picture. Now he had a bond.

The nest was dark, the four of them tangled together and snoring when I'd arrived after finishing all my haggling and hand-shaking and promises. Bear was right—I would have the votes against Rider.

Do you want them?

I'd managed to worm my way back into my spot between Faith's thighs, and she'd welcomed me sleepily, stroking her hands through my hair as I rested my face on her stomach, my legs hanging out of the nest. I was exhausted, mentally and phys-ically, but I couldn't sleep.

She had two alphas now, and Chance, who'd proven to be as good as one, if not better. She didn't need me. Omikron was falling apart. I could handle the Wasted, and she would be safe. She would have a good pack.

"King," Faith whispered, squirming under me.

I hadn't stopped touching that damn mark on her thigh, but my finger was trailing closer to her center. She was sweet and creamy and airy, and I wanted to guzzle her, treat her taste on my tongue like a good vintage of whiskey. I shifted onto my side and tugged on her opposite thigh, pulling her closer, twisting her in the bed.

"King, they're sleeping," Faith hissed, voice soft.

"Let them. You know what I need, princess," I answered, voice low and rough. *And I know what you need. I just haven't decided if I can give it to you yet.*

Faith whimpered but she rolled, knees braced in the bed, her pussy hovering above my face. Out of the corner of my eye, Ghost's fresh bite taunted me. I ignored the goading in my own head, reaching up and pulling Faith down with a tight grip on her ass. She moaned into her own pillow as I seated her on my mouth, tongue vicious and hungry, lapping at her without preamble.

I grinned as she ground against me, rubbing her clit against my nose. She could smother me, and I would die happy like this. I sucked at her flesh, thrust my tongue into her cunt, and pretended this was a dream that morning couldn't break.

I DRUMMED the pen in my hand against the list Bear and I had made. Every item was crossed off. Church would take place in the morning and I was ready. I could even call for the vote early if I wanted, really thrust it into Rider's nose how easily I'd won back the club's favor.

There was a roar of laughter from the bar, and I glared at the partially opened door of my office. I was meant to be approachable, but lately I just wanted some fucking peace.

That's not all you want.

I scowled at the list, scorned the victory I'd all but won, and wondered if Faith was busy with her brother or if I could—

The door creaked and my stare only grew ruder as Eve walked in.

I wasn't too big to admit that another alpha—a *stronger* alpha

—in my territory set my teeth on edge. The fact that this woman had tried to rip Faith out of our arms only made me dislike her more.

"I'm busy," I said.

Eve shut the door behind her. "I don't care," she said, shrugging.

I didn't bother stifling my low growl, but Eve looked undaunted. Not that I expected her to be intimidated. She'd already proved her bark was as good as her bite, and I wasn't in the mood for either.

"We only temporarily incapacitated the Wasted when we realized they didn't have Faith," Eve said.

I sat up, head clearing. "The Wasted are our problem. But I can't say it wasn't good news when we heard about you hitting their club."

Eve helped herself to the seat in front of my desk, her movements sinuous. "Adam would feel better knowing they would never pose further threat to his sister. As I'm sure Faith would, as well. I don't want to overstep. Faith told Adam about your current upset in the ranks," she continued. "I'd like to offer our help to your club. As an apology for our rude arrival. And to see the matter dealt with before we move on."

I chewed over the offer in my head. It would be good to take this to church. A further point in my favor. And I couldn't say I'd mind seeing the back of this woman and her pack, even if it did mean Faith parting with her brother again.

"I appreciate that," I said, nodding. "I'll take it to the club tomorrow."

Eve nodded once, turning and glancing toward the door, and I itched for her to leave my office. Her scent was aggressive, and it left me tense and bracing.

"I should express gratitude on Adam's behalf," she said, turning slowly back to me. "In spite of my suspicions, it's clear you did take good care of his sister."

I grunted, but before I could think of what to say, she continued, "Adam will be glad to have his sister back at his side. I hope losing some of your club members doesn't backfire for you."

I stiffened in my seat, my hands gripping hard at the arms of my chair. "Excuse me?"

Eve blinked and shrugged. "Adam has his pack now, but he and Faith were close. They were fighting Omikron long before the rest of us showed up. I think he's excited to go after the last of them, now that he and Faith are reunited."

Anger boiled in my veins, sudden and swarming, the room going foggy aside from the sharp vision of this alpha sitting in front of me.

"No," I growled.

Eve arched an eyebrow. "No?"

"No," I repeated. "No, you're not fucking taking Faith. No, you're not putting her on dangerous missions. No, you're not sending her out to chase after the organization that kept her in a cage."

"Says who?" Eve asked coolly.

"Says fucking me!" I snarled back.

And I hated her with a ferocious strike in my chest for how unflinchingly calm she remained. "I'm not sure your opinion matters in this case."

I jumped up and my chair skittered backwards, and still she was loose and relaxed in that goddamn chair of mine. "Like hell it doesn't. Faith might love her brother, maybe too much to say no, but I don't give a shit about him or you or frankly, anybody but her. She's been through enough. And I would eat your little box of knives before I let you put her in danger again."

Eve's eyes narrowed slightly as I tried to loom over my desk. "You're not—"

"You're not fucking taking my omega!" I roared, the bark startling in my throat, but clear and determined.

My eyes were wide, hands clenched on the desk. Eve's lips were curved, and even though I suddenly understood the trap she'd laid for me, it was as if I was suddenly breathing fully for the first time in...years.

"I see," she purred.

"Fuck you," I spat, but my eyes were on the door. They flicked back to the alpha in front of me. "Would you really put her back into that life?"

Eve rolled her eyes. "I don't know if you underestimate women or omegas, or just Faith in particular, but I'm sure she's capable. She doesn't deserve an ivory tower."

I huffed. "No, she deserves a fucking pack that's going to make sure that she's living the life she wants. Not the one everyone keeps trying to..." I growled again, reaching up and scuffing my face with my hand.

Goddamn it.

"Adam wants his sister to be happy," Eve said, rising from the chair at last.

I bit back my answer, a new urgency building in my chest. I stared down at the list on my desk, every note crossed off, and listened absently as Eve left the room. I thought about Rider's accusations, about Bear's question that I couldn't shake from my head like a poppy song lyric, and the nest upstairs that I barely fit into. I thought about the stares Faith received from the other alphas in the club, the way they sniffed the air of my office, a flicker of hunger in their eyes every time.

This club was no place for an omega. And Faith *would* leave eventually, although I ought to have known better than to fall for Eve's trap. There was no way in hell Bear would put Faith in harm's way.

But what if, my head whispered poisonously.

Do you want the votes? I did. I wanted to know that the club would keep me, that I hadn't fucked up so badly I might be voted out of my position. I knew I had those votes now, and the victory was a faint satisfaction.

My omega.

I growled once more, but it was worthless with no one to hear me, and my feet—and the drumming animal in my chest— were already leading me out of my office. The bar was barely occupied, just a couple of my men drinking beer and staring out into the dark gray clouds outside of our windows.

A storm was coming. Which meant I knew exactly where Faith and the others would be.

"Ready for tomorrow, King?" Skid called from the bar.

I flashed him a rough grin, too big and manic, and he jerked back on the stool. "Almost," I said, and then I threw my shoulder into the back door.

The storm was coming from the west, a gray sheet far in the distance, and I found Faith easily in the lineup of my club and our few visitors, her small frame tucked in the huddle of her pack. Ghost had his arm around Chance's shoulder, and Faith held Bear and Chance's hands in each of hers. I knew where I wanted to be, and I stepped up to her back, my arms circling her waist. I swallowed hard at the catch of her breath, the way her head fell back to rest on my chest.

My omega.

She twisted, trying to face me. "Hey, you're—"

"Come with me," I said, suddenly too impatient.

She blinked. "The storm's coming."

"We can watch it together." I tugged at her waist, backing away from the crowd with her.

Her brow furrowed. "King..."

I leaned in and kissed the lines digging into her forehead. "Come with me, princess."

Her lips were parted, eyes flicking back and forth over my face, but she followed as I tugged her away from the others. Bear's expression was smug, and Ghost was grinning at Chance, who looked...well, not pissed off, at least. Not that any of them mattered half as much as the woman before me.

"Is everything okay?" Faith asked, jogging to keep up with my long strides as I dragged her away from the others, behind the garage to the picnic tables out of sight.

"Tell me what you want, princess," I said, stopping us, shrugging off my leather cut as Faith watched with wide eyes.

"I want...to know what's going on," she said, staring as I laid the leather down on the rough table. "King?"

She was wearing a short little sundress, one that slid against her skin as I drew her to my chest. She hummed as I kissed her, softened and forgot her questions, her arms twining around my shoulders. Her lips were my favorite fruit, tender and sweet, and I feasted on them now. The short skirt slid up, and I cupped her ass in both hands, drew her hips to mine and held her there as I licked her sighs from her lips, soft little notes of confused pleasure.

The wind was rushing toward us, the air charged and heavy, a rare humidity wetting my lungs with every deep breath I took of Faith.

"Tell me," I said into her mouth, pulling away and biting at her jaw. She shivered as I ran a fingertip around the edge of her panties, over one cheek, and down to where she was hot and as wet as the coming rain.

"King, what is this—?" Her laugh was muffled against my mouth as I swallowed her question once more, kissing her until she was clinging and soft against me.

"Tell me what you want."

"You," she breathed, rocking her hips into me.

I purred, and she swooned back in my arms as I lowered her to the table, draping her down over my cut. There was a small line of buttons down the front of her dress, and they gaped slightly as she caught her breath. I unbuttoned them as the roar of the storm approached, exposed her breasts in the pretty green lace bra that made her blush even rosier.

Faith's eyes were hooded as I lowered my head, kissed around her bra and then tugged the cups down. Bear's bite shone at me and I licked the mark, groaning at the answering soft whine from Faith. I fumbled with my belt and pants, needing to be ready for her.

"I want you, King."

I purred into her breasts, slipped my hands under her skirt, and pulled her underwear down until she was lifting her ankles free. I tucked the fabric into one of my pockets, sucking on Faith's nipple as she clutched me closer.

My pants were slipping down my hips and I shoved them out of the way, stroking my cock hard. Faith's hands were tangled in my hair and I reached up, stroking her palms until they loosened. I knelt on the picnic bench, bracing myself over her, finding her gaze again.

"Tell me, princess," I said, smiling down at her.

"I want your cock," she whined, hitching her hips closer.

The first cool, wet drops smacked against my back as I

notched myself at Faith's silky wet pussy, tucking easily into her body, a perfect fit. She moaned and a raindrop hit her cheek, and an enormous smile stretched across her face. She laughed, blinking up at me.

"I always had a fantasy about this," she murmured, glancing at the sky. "Sex in the rain."

I grinned at her, watching her face go slack as I slid deep inside of her, right up to the slow swell of my knot. "Is that so?"

"Mm... I'm going to get your cut messy, King," she said, pressing her hips into mine with a soft lift and push.

I lowered to my forearms, let my chest press to hers. She liked the friction of fabric against her nipples, and I could undress us both fully later. I bent my head to her ear, circling my hips to pull slowly out and glide smoothly in.

"That's the point, princess," I purred in her ear, nibbling the lobe and sucking it between my teeth as she gasped and arched into me.

The rain arrived in a roar and I sat up again, letting the drops strike against her chest and lips, watching the answering moan slide out of her mouth as her eyes fell shut. I fucked her slowly, my jaw clenched and my knot throbbing, her body trying to pull me deeper.

Rain soaked my shirt and plastered my hair down until I swept it back from my eyes. It made our skin stick together, washing her arousal away only for it to pool anew. Faith's hands slipped under my shirt, nails digging in to catch me and draw me closer.

"You have to beg for it," I rasped, waiting for the words she'd never asked but had always sat between us.

"Your knot," she gasped. "Give me your knot, King, please."

I growled but I wrapped my arms around her shoulders, pulling her closer, pressing hard at her opening. I thought I might just fall into her, give her what we both wanted and I refused to share until she told me the truth.

"It's not enough, princess. You have to tell me everything. You have to beg."

Faith stilled beneath me, her eyes blinking against the rain. It had turned her hair into inky strands, covered her face in a running dew, and made the shirt dividing our chests a second skin.

"Tell me what you *want,* princess," I hissed, pressing my knot to her opening but not letting it sink in.

Her mouth opened and closed a few times, and a kernel of doubt chewed into my thoughts. Had she never asked because she didn't want me?

But the words poured out, as hard and fast as the rain had arrived.

"I want you to put me before the club, to love me, and to be in the nest with me every night. I want you to be pack, and I *know* I can't ask because that's breaking your vow, and I know everything you built here is too important—"

I covered her lips, groaning, her tongue hungry in my mouth. It wasn't a battle, but there was a fight in the kiss, one to claim each other, and she was desperate. She thought she was facing losing odds.

I pulled away, and she sobbed briefly until I cupped her face in my hands, wiping the rain away and maybe a tear too.

"Tell me," I said, one last time.

Faith sucked in a deep breath, terror warring with hope in her gaze. "I want your bite, King."

I groaned as I pressed in, her body resisting the knot briefly —the tension of pushing her to open up to me—until she sighed and gave way. She came, clenching and gushing on my knot, and I finally loosened my jaw, diving forward.

Her throat was pretty, Chance's bites on the right slightly faded, but I found the curve of her left shoulder with my teeth. I loved this tender muscle, the soft slope, loved running my tongue over the spot, tasting her sweat as I fucked her, loved the way her perfume gathered there, the way her hair curled to brush against it.

And I fucking loved sinking my teeth there as she cried out, arms clasping around my back, cunt squeezing on my knot. Her skin gave easily, blood sweet and thick on my tongue. I swallowed a mouthful, and my purr was as rough and ragged as the drum of the rain on the picnic table.

"Oh, god, King," she gasped, muscle flexing in my teeth. Her fingers dug into my back at the same moment the bond floated into my chest, nervous and thrilled and baffled.

I laughed into her skin, drawing my teeth out carefully, quick to lick the beading blood away and wrap my lips around the wound.

"Why didn't you *say* so? What about the club? What are we going to do?" But even as she ran through her questions, her hand slid up into my hair, stroking through the short strands. Her neck stretched and arched and she sighed, the nerves fading slowly. "You're sure?"

My purr was steady, and I spoke through the rattle, keeping my chest pressed to hers, rocking my knot inside of her. "I'm not an impulsive man, princess. I've been making this decision in small steps ever since I realized what a fucking mistake it was to call Preston."

She grunted, and I soothed the reminder of the alpha with a stroke of my tongue over the bite. Arousal was hot and silky in the bond between us, but the rain was slowing and my clothes were heavy and abrasive and it was going to get cold soon. I needed to get Faith into the nest. Preferably both of us into a hot bath first.

"You have a plan?" Faith asked.

I licked at the bite, grinned at her hiccuping moan, and lifted my head. "I do. Starts with this," I said, sitting up enough to reach between us, rubbing damp fingers over her slippery clit.

Bear had offered instructions on how to disengage a knot without hurting the omega when I'd mentioned worrying about sudden emergencies or interruptions. There was no emergency now, but I didn't want to have Faith knotted on a picnic bench. Rain might be a romantic fantasy for her, but the cold reality of the wind afterwards would be less so.

"King," she keened, rocking into my touch.

I pulled at my knot slightly, gritting my teeth against the pressure. Faith keened and shifted, trying to push me in deeper. I pressed at her clit harder and she gasped, eyes flying open and a noisy cry rising from her lips. The others would hear her. I bucked in, rewarding her with a rough thrust, and then finding her a little looser as I pulled back again.

"Come for me, princess. I need my omega to come again," I growled.

I lowered my head and licked at the bite mark, growing dizzy in the swarm of need and pleasure and joy, and as Faith came—abrupt and loud and messy and beautiful—I pulled my knot free. I yanked myself away in order to watch the sudden spilling of slick and cum between her thighs, onto the leather of my cut.

"Oh my god, oh, fuck," she groaned, shaking and starting to roll away.

I pushed her hips down with one hand, pressed two fingers inside of her, and scooped gently, more messy fluid on my hand. She sat up on her elbows, eyes wide, and watched as I rubbed it all into the leather.

"What are you doing?" she murmured.

I sucked my fingers clean and then reached to her dress, buttoning her up slowly before pulling her in by the neck and kissing her roughly as she gaped at me. She followed my mouth as I pulled her up from the picnic table, setting her on wobbly legs and then picking up my freshly christened cut, sliding it back on over my wet shirt.

"King?"

"We're making a statement. Come on, princess," I said, taking her hand in mine. "Gotta do one thing before I get you back on my knot in your nest."

She blushed and stumbled along at my side as I wrapped an arm around her shoulders. I marched us back to where we'd left the others. The club was soaked and laughing, drinking, someone passing out beers from the cooler, and no one gave us a second glance as we approached. Not until I slid my arm back across Faith's shoulders, scooping up her wet hair and pulling it away from her neck to expose my red, bloodied bite.

"Everyone listen up," I called.

Faith was frozen, eyes wide and cheeks flushed, but it was a booming excitement in the bond, a heady thrill that made me grin.

I stared out at the crowd as one by one they turned, caught sight of the fresh wound on Faith's shoulder, and smelled her release on my cut. "I know our laws, my vow. But there's nothing in this fucking world that would make this woman anything but *mine*. There are changes coming in the club. I am marking my omega with pride, and if anyone takes issue with that, you can speak tomorrow at church. Until then, I don't want to hear from a fucking one of you. Understood?"

A few alphas scowled, others laughed, a few loyal friends even clapped. My pack, and Faith's brother's pack, all cheered. I found Rider's stare and released Faith's hair from my grip, grabbing her hand instead and pulling her back to my side.

"One last thing to say and we're done. You angry, princess?"

"You know I'm not," Faith said, eyes bright and wild with happiness.

I marched us over to Rider, who seemed divided between smug victory and sullen suspicion.

"Guess you made your decision," Rider said, glaring briefly at Faith.

"I did. You and I both know that even now I could win the vote tomorrow," I said, drawing that stare back to me. "Meet me in my office an hour before church, and we'll settle this."

He frowned, puzzled, but nodded. I was still prez, and he would report to my orders until otherwise.

I pulled Faith away from the crowd at last, running into Bear on our way to the back door of the bar. "Give us an hour or so," I said.

"Long as you need," Bear said, grinning. "Glad to have you as pack, King."

The word still sat oddly in my head. I could more easily accept my role as Faith's alpha—it was necessary and *right*—than being part of a pack, but it would come. I liked Bear and Chance, and Ghost was an unlikely but not unwelcome addition now. And we all loved the same woman.

I drew Faith's fist to my lips as we walked into the bar.

"What you said to Rider is true? You have the votes?" Faith asked.

I nodded. "If I want them."

Her eyebrows rose as we hurried down the hall. "Do you?"

I stopped us in front of my office door, resting my hands on her shoulders, smiling down at the flushed, wet, beautiful woman in front of me. "What you said before I bit you, about what I've built here...how was that going to be finished?"

Faith's eyes rolled up as she thought. "Um...that, that what you've done here with the club was too important for me to tear it apart for a bond," she said, wincing.

I leaned in, cupping her chin and lifting it for my kiss. Her eyelashes still had water droplets caught in them.

"Nothing changes what I built. I don't fail because I decided to move on."

"Move on?" Faith whispered.

"Mmm, you're shivering. Come on. You can show me what your favorite bubble bath is."

"King," she huffed, but she followed along at my side.

"It's time to build something new, Faith," I said, and this time it was her turn to pull me to a stop.

She was uncertain, a question tugging in my chest, but I answered it without words. Was I sure? Yes. I was. I would've been certain sooner or later, and as annoying as it might be to admit—even to myself—I was just grateful Eve had made the decision clear before it was too late.

Faith's smile bloomed, and I hummed at the sudden bubbling sweet swarm of emotion flooding through me.

"Love you too, princess," I whispered.

Faith giggled, and when she jumped, my arms were ready to catch her, scooping her off her feet, my legs returning their march toward her nest.

"Love you," she echoed, the words already spoken in the bond.

"Now...I want you to tell me all the other fantasies you have. We can check them off one by one. I love a list," I said, grinning.

Faith laughed and tucked her face into my shoulder, the joyous sound bright and sweet in my ear.

My foot jiggled, and King's hand landed on my knee, calm floating down the bond from his direction, the rest of my pack all hiding their twitching smiles.

My pack.

I had a pack. I'd fallen into their laps and chosen them out of a determination to survive. I'd been more concerned with whether or not they could protect me than make me happy. I'd been selfish, deceitful, determined, and frequently so out of my mind with terror, I'd acted on feral instinct.

And they were perfect for me. Maybe not for the girl before Omikron, or at least the one I'd been before Adam and I had started running, but they were certainly perfect for the woman I was now.

"It's going to be fine, princess," King murmured, resting his lips over his bondmark, tickling the tender edges with his beard and mustache.

I fought the dizzy rise of arousal. Every bondmark I had now was outrageously sensitive, and especially so when touched by the maker. King was taking eager advantage.

"You're gonna work her up and make Rider crazy when he

walks in here," Bear said, catching my eye and winking at me as King settled.

King caught my chin between his thumb and forefinger, pulling my stare back to his, those ice blue eyes bright and glittering with promise. "I'm sure, princess. Not giving up anything but burdens today," he said softly. I sighed and nodded, closing my eyes and soaking up the confidence from Bear and King.

"Go stand with Bear so I can focus," King said, patting my hip.

I rose and King's hand swatted cheerfully at my ass just as the knock sounded on the door of his office. Bear's arms wrapped around me as Rider walked in.

I searched for the resemblance to Chance and found it in small doses, like the color of his eyes but they were surrounded with milky red the high arch of his cheekbones. Rider's frame was heavier, his hair a few shades lighter and several inches longer. He was handsome, but not beautiful like Chance, and he sneered when he caught sight of me in the room.

"Pussy at official meetings now?" Rider asked.

"Sit," King said, cold and firm.

I wanted to laugh at Rider's scowl, the clear impulse to resist King's order written in the sour twist of his mouth. He dragged his feet and scraped the legs of the chair against the carpet. Petulant. He would make a bad prez, and I suspected his rule over the club might be shorter-lived than he imagined.

"I'm willing to announce my resignation at church today," King said.

All of Rider's scorn, all his bravado, evaporated at once into open shock, a new and almost clumsy version of the man now sitting before us. "*What?*"

"My records are good, if you want to use them to keep up the runs and the contacts. You'll be able to find everything you need," King continued.

Rider raised his hand, cutting in. "You said *willing*, so I'm assuming you want something first."

King leaned back in his chair, lips curving up. "To wipe out the Wasted."

Rider barked out a laugh, eyebrows rising. "Now? Now you

want to run them off? Wasn't it your idea to give them their little corner?"

"It was a mistake, you were right," King said with a syrupy magnanimousness. "And we've never been in a better position to clean them out. Eve's pack is offering their help. We take it, as a club, and I will hand the presidency to you."

"And take our road captain, enforcer, and my brother with you," Rider said, glancing at my bondmates surrounding me.

King shrugged. "You're better off building your own cabinet anyway. Coke is as good in the garage as Ghost."

"I don't need your *advice*," Rider spat, leaning forward, his face growing red. "I grew up in this club!"

King just answered him with a smile. "And now it can be yours."

Rider's gaze slid in my direction as he slowly sank back in his chair. "She must really be something in the sack."

King's voice lowered. "Do you want to antagonize me, Rider? Or do you want to accept the position you and I both know you would never have earned on your own?"

Rider's hands clenched at his side, fists growing white for a moment, before he exhaled and settled. "If you want to give up on the men who swore themselves to you, give up on the work you put into this club, and pass on the crown you've been clutching for years...then yes, we'll wipe out the Wasted and I'll take your place."

I swallowed hard, but King was calm and steady in the bond. He had no doubts as I held my breath and waited for them to pop up.

King nodded his head once and reached his hand across the desk. Rider's reached back and they shook solemnly. "See you in church," King said.

Rider glared at all of us as he rose from his seat, but he turned his back and left the room in silence. Bear's hands were working at my tense shoulders, and the bond was watchful.

"I feel a little sorry for the others," Bear admitted.

King spun in his chair and shook his head. "They'll vote him out in a year or two. Buck or Cubby will put it all back together."

"How do you know?" I asked.

King smiled at me, warmth stirring in my chest. "I told you, princess, I've been making this decision slowly for a while now. I did what I could for the club. And moving on looks a lot sweeter with you on the horizon."

Bear kissed my head and then I slipped back to King's lap, lifting his face to mine. "That was smooth," I murmured, dipping my head, grinning with him as we kissed.

———

"So where will you go?" Adam asked me, brow furrowed.

I shrugged and lifted the drink Ghost had made for me to my lips. It was sweet and syrupy, and there was enough spiced rum to warm my chest with every sip. "Dunno yet. King says not to worry."

Adam rolled his eyes slightly, and I kicked him under the table. "I just can't imagine those guys in, like...you know, a nice house with pretty shutters, like you want."

"Is that what *you* want?" I asked.

Adam blinked at me. "No, I like being on the road with my pack. Eve says we'll always find somewhere to settle for my heat."

"Well, I don't need that house either," I said, shrugging and scowling. "I don't need any house, unless it has my pack."

Adam stared at me, lips slightly parted, and I lifted my chin before he could challenge me again. A rap of knuckles on the table interrupted us, Jamie wearing a sly smile.

"We need to get Eve out of here before she hustles all the bikers and we end up in a fight," Jamie said, nodding back toward the pool tables.

"Not again," Adam sighed, sliding out of the booth and then pausing to turn back to me. "See you tomorrow?"

Adam and his pack had come to the club everyday, so much so that some of the Devils had started to accept their presence as a welcome given. It still gave me a slight pang to watch Adam leave, and I understood that uncomfortable question in his tone. Would we be separated again? Had our bond broken somehow when Omikron stole me away?

"Tomorrow," I said, nodding and reaching out to grip his hand in mine.

With our own packs now, we would never be what we were to each other before. Our universes had split to revolve in new directions, but something was growing easier between us every day.

I searched the bar as Adam walked away with Jamie, a note of vague panic calling to me in my chest. I'd seen my pack briefly after their club "church," but King, Bear, and Chance had left with Rider and a few others to do some scouting on the Wasted. Ghost had been assigned my babysitter for the night, and he'd been attentive while still leaving me and Adam to ourselves.

I caught sight of him at the bar to my left, his back to the counter so he could keep an eye on me. The beta club girl, Deedee, was at his side, leaning into him and batting her lashes as Ghost tugged on our bond. He shifted to rise from his seat and Deedee reached, grabbing his arm. I arched my eyebrow at Ghost, and his panic flared anew.

"You better watch out for that one."

I turned and found another of the girls watching the exchange with me. Chance and Ghost had caught me up on Ghost's history with the women of the club. There was a feral, possessive part of me that clawed and roared at the sight of Deedee's hand on Ghost's arm, but the feedback from Ghost in the bond made it too obvious that I had nothing to worry about. And he needed to figure out how to turn women down on his own. I wasn't starting a cat fight.

"I don't need to worry," I answered the girl at my side, and she blinked at me and shook her head, wandering away.

Sure enough, Ghost patted Deedee's hand, prying her fingers up and offering her a sheepish grin as he slipped away from his barstool. She pouted slightly, rolling her eyes, but moved on easily, and by the time I met Ghost halfway, she looked well on her way to finding company for the night.

"Should I be offended you didn't come to my rescue?" Ghost asked.

"You're a big boy, I knew you could handle it," I said, patting his chest.

He beamed at me, and I wanted to dig and probe at the pride in his chest. I knew him the least, and even with the bond on my thigh and the eager attention he paid me, we still felt halfway up in the air sometimes.

"Wanna get some fresh air?" he asked at the same moment I said, "Wanna go back to the nest?"

"Either," he said.

I chose quickly, grabbing his hand in mine. "Outside."

His fingers tightened, a warm and solid grip marked with callouses that I'd already learned to love brushing over my most sensitive skin. The yard was empty tonight, and I led Ghost to the table with the best view of the full moon. He sat down and pulled me between his thighs, nestling me with my back against his chest.

"I wasn't flirting with Deedee," Ghost murmured at my back.

I closed my eyes, the round moon blue behind my eyelids, and stroked a hand over his arms where they crossed around my waist. "I know."

"I just don't want you to think that I'm going to...to ghost you," he huffed.

My eyes opened and my lips curved, my head falling back onto his shoulder. "I won't *let* you."

He sighed, and I sank into him further. He was comfy, a little clingy, and frequently nervous, even when he wore that silky smile of his. This man wore layers of masks, but the bond cut through most of them and I would learn to peel away the rest.

"What's your real name?"

"Gavin."

"Oo, that's a sexy name," I said and shook with his chuckle. I tested it out on my own, slow and smooth. "*Gavin.*"

The alpha wrapped around me purred, the sound vibrating through us both. "Well, I don't mind it when you say it."

"You don't like it?" I asked, twisting halfway to face him.

Ghost kept his arms around me, holding me close, studying my face. "Gavin Moore, Junior. It was my dad's name," he said, wincing. "My single inheritance from a drunk asshole."

I reached up, tangled my fingers into the dense beard, and smiled as Ghost's eyes fell shut when I tugged. "Was he an alpha?" I asked. Ghost nodded, brow creasing with tension, a turmoil of anger and shame and self-loathing circling in the bond. "Is he still alive?"

"Dunno," Ghost rasped.

I tugged his beard once more, pulling him down enough for me to stretch up and kiss his furrowed brow. His eyes blinked open, startled, and I softened my touch against his jaw.

"Tell me about you and Chance," I said. Ghost's eyes widened, and I continued, "You like when he talks down to you."

"During sex," Ghost added.

I nodded. "Right. I like it too. It's like he's giving me permission to enjoy the things I'm still afraid of," I said. "I can pretend I can't help myself, and I can enjoy the shame and the pleasure all at once."

Ghost was quiet for a moment, eyes bouncing back and forth between mine before he finally licked his lips and spoke. "It's him seeing the worst in me, and still wanting me," he whispered.

I leaned in, and Ghost's eyes fell shut again as I pressed my mouth softly to his. "You are not perfect, but neither Chance nor I think you're unworthy. Whatever you think the worst is, I promise that isn't what we see in you," I said, sealing the words with another kiss.

Ghost moaned and licked into my mouth, his tongue sweet and searching, the bond eager and anxious all at once.

"You're ours now. You'll be good to us," I mumbled against his lips, catching my breath and kissing across his cheeks and over his nose as he nuzzled into Chance's bite bruises.

"I will," Ghost whispered, arms tightening to a vise around me. "I'll be so good. Promise, slick."

There was a thick and demanding need in the bond, and it took me a moment to realize it wasn't sexual. I wrapped my arms around Ghost's shoulder, shifted until I was straddled over his lap, and held him tight.

"I know, alpha," I said.

Ghost shuddered and let out a slow exhale, lifting his face. "Part of what drew me to this club was that we were always brothers. It was never alpha or beta. My dad spent my fuckin' life telling me what an alpha was and wasn't, but he was just so fucking...awful. I never wanted anything to do with it. Either it meant I was growing up into a monster, or the pressure of living up to it was impossible."

I combed my fingers through his hair, watched those thick eyelashes flutter. "Hmm, want to be my bondmate instead? No alpha and omega."

Ghost's smile grew at last. "Makes Chance and me equal."

I nodded. "You and I need to have a bond, a relationship. But I don't ever want Chance to feel less-than."

Ghost purred and I slid my hands down to his chest to soak up the sound. "Agreed. He and I are lucky you showed up, slick."

I hummed and smiled down at Ghost, lowering my head slowly, hovering my lips above his. "That's true. I am too."

Ghost's kisses were as disarming as his smile, skilled and charming, but when I nipped at his tongue and his fingers dug into my hips, the need grew earnest, his flavor sweeter. He didn't push for more, and there was lovely simplicity in just kissing, wrapped around one another under moonlight. We stayed like that until the rumble of bikes sounded from the road, headlights streaking over the yard.

Chance was probing curiously at the bond, a careful question calling down the line. Ghost and I answered it together, tugging at our bondmate, luring him to us. He came, boots crunching over the dry yard, a secret smile in his eyes, and Ghost let me slide from his lap to sit at his side on the bench.

"You two get up to any trouble?" Chance asked.

"Nope, we waited for you," Ghost answered as I reached out my hand for Chance.

Chance's eyes lit up. "Good. Because I've got plans for you both."

Excitement raced through the bond, sizzling arousal circling the three of us.

"Inside," Chance rasped. "Now."

Shivers licked up and down my spine as King's fingertips spun circles over my back. Sweat was cooling on my skin, and Ghost and Bear had already started snoring for the night. Chance's eyes blinked slow and heavy, his lips softly curved as he watched King tease me while I lay limp on top of the pile of us.

"You said it was time to sleep," I murmured, and King hummed. "Touching me like that doesn't put me to sleep."

His chest shook with silent laughter, rumbled with a smooth purr, but his hands flattened on my shoulder blades and the shivers settled. I was still learning to pick out the notes of the bond, who was who when we were all gathered together. Sex was especially potent, dizzying when they surrounded me with mouths and cocks and hands. With Ghost and Bear asleep and Chance mellow at my left, King's slow churning was easy to pick out.

"What are you thinking about?" I asked.

King's chest rose and fell beneath my cheek, his sighing breath rustling the crown of my head. "Next week. Next month. Next year."

I stiffened, but his hands rubbed at my shoulders, the swirling of his thoughts stilling to a steady warmth in my chest.

"I'm not worried, princess. Just planning," King whispered.

I wrinkled my nose and turned my cheek, resting my chin over his breast bone, his eyes crossing slightly as he stared down his nose at me.

"Care to clue me in on my future?" I asked.

King grinned at me, and Chance muffled his laugh in a pillow.

"Next week—running over the plan. Make sure it's gonna finish the matter, but not land any of us in hot water. Keep you safe and know not one of those men will ever get their hands on you," King said.

"They haven't, and they won't," Chance rasped, eyes falling shut. "That's what we're here for."

I smiled at my drowsy beta and King nodded, continuing, "Next month—setting up all the pieces to leave the club in the best shape I can. Figuring our route out of here, how we're gonna get your nest all packed up with us."

"I have a license. I could drive," I said.

King frowned in thought. "Noted. And the last of it is just... where do we go, and what do we do when we get there?"

"We could travel, like Adam's pack. You love to ride. You could have that without the weight of a club," I said.

King's hands lifted, stroking my hair back from my face, and I caught my breath at the sudden pounding of affection in the bond. My muscles turned to honey and my eyes watered, closing at the force of King's appreciation and gratitude for me. I whined and he chuckled, releasing me from the overwhelming sensation.

"We're gonna put roots down, princess. I can always ride. But we're gonna find a home, build you an even better nest. I've got some ideas I think you'll like. Might make it a surprise."

I nestled into King's chest, still swimming up to the surface of the depth of feeling King had revealed to me. "I trust you," I said.

King brightened with pride, hands running paths through my hair, twisting the ends around his fingers, lulling me to sleep.

———

"WHAT DO YOU THINK?" Bear asked, arms crossed over his chest as he glared at the four men standing at attention in front of Adam and me.

Two betas, two alphas, all of whom had been polite and ambivalent towards me.

"If we need guards, shouldn't it be our packs?" I asked Bear.

He turned toward King, scowling, who then turned toward Eve and arched an eyebrow.

"For the record, we don't think you need guards," Eve said, raising her palms. "However, if we are wrong and the Wasted or anyone else has their eye on you, they're not making a move while we're on hand to protect you."

Adam groaned at my side, and I bounced my stare between our packs and my brother.

He rolled his eyes at me. "They want to use us as bait."

"We want to provide you as a temptation," Eve corrected smoothly.

"I hate this plan," Bear growled.

"If you're comfortable with this crew, they'll be here to protect you," King said, catching my gaze. "If you aren't, we scrap the idea."

I bit my lip, nerves jangling in my chest, flicking my eyes over to the group of men standing and awaiting judgment. I looked at Eve next. "How confident are you that Omikron is out of the picture?"

"Eighty-seven percent," Eve said, and I wasn't sure if she'd chosen the number at random or had diligently weighed the odds. "But I'm ninety-three percent sure they aren't equipped to manage the work of kidnapping you again effectively."

"*I* will protect you myself," Adam said to me.

"No," Rory corrected. "DID protocol."

Adam gaped at the alpha. "No! Come on!"

"DID protocol, sugar," Eve said with a nod.

I frowned and glared at them. "What is DID protocol?"

"Damsel in distress," Adam snarled.

"No fighting back, no sassing. Just let yourself be kidnapped and wait for us to come and kill them," Eve said matter-of-factly.

Bear snarled, and Ghost joined him in the arms-crossed pose. "Is that really the best idea?" Ghost asked, brow furrowing. "Like, isn't the idea that they *don't* get kidnapped?"

"The idea is that they don't get hurt," Garrett answered. "Adam will have a tracker on him—"

Adam grumbled again, and Eve gave him a sultry smile in response.

"—and complying within reason will buy them and us time to reach them without them being harmed. And this is in the *least* likely scenario," Garrett said.

"The 'least likely scenario' that has happened twice since we came up with the plan," Adam muttered. He sighed and turned to me. "I'm not complaining because it's frightening. I'm complaining because it's *boring*, and I didn't spend weeks learning hand-to-hand combat and marksmanship just so I could let some bozo tie my hands behind my back and stick me in an uncomfortable folding chair."

"No one's ever hurt you?" I asked Adam.

"Not since we implemented DID protocol," Eve said.

Adam's lips flattened in annoyance, and he shook his head. "No. They're never allowed to mess with me. It's always transport and waiting for some bigwig to show up. By the time they do, so does the cavalry."

I turned to my pack. None of them looked or felt happy about the idea, but King tried to offer me a smile, even if it was grim.

"Least likely outcome," he said.

Eve cleared her throat and caught my eye. "Do you think you could handle it?"

I gaped at her, wanted to shout *no*, that I would prefer she and the others take out the Wasted while leaving me in my nest with my pack, before I realized what she meant. Would I go feral if someone tried to kidnap me and Adam?

"I don't know," I admitted.

And for some reason, Eve smiled. She was a little crazy, or she knew something she wasn't telling the rest of us, or both.

I turned back to the betas and alphas waiting and recalling their names in my head—Grim, Mikey, Wave, and Frost.

"Are you going to let me get kidnapped?" I asked them.

"Not a fucking chance," Wave answered immediately. "Bear would take my nuts."

Bear grunted in agreement.

Least likely scenario, I told myself. It would've felt even less likely if we hadn't needed a plan for it in the first place.

A plan to deal with any stray dogs who might be watching me or Adam or both of us. To wipe the slate clean before my pack and I moved on, together, and started a life. I wanted that life, and I wanted it without the looming threats of alpha gangs who wanted to buy me, or Omikron wanting to sell me.

"Okay," I said, nodding.

Adam sighed again, heavy and defeated. "Fine," he groaned.

"Fuck," Bear muttered.

———

"Stay inside, keep the guys close," King said, his hands cupping my shoulders, pale blue gaze fierce.

"Be careful. Don't get hurt and don't get caught," I answered.

King's hand caught my chin, lifting it a fraction, stare sparking as his mouth lowered to mine. "Be good, princess. Or you'll get a spanking when I get home."

That's a confusing set of directions and he knows it, I thought, already considering how I might go about earning that spanking.

He grinned at my expression, reading me too easily now, then kissed my forehead and crossed the parking lot to his bike. Ghost and Chance took his place in front of me, folding me in between the two of them.

"You're sure you're okay with this plan?" Chance asked. "I can stay here with you too."

I relaxed a little, recalling Chance fighting off the two Wasted who'd come sniffing. In the bond, Ghost's nerves wormed through my chest. If Chance stayed, Ghost would want to stay to keep an eye on the both of us.

"You trust the guys staying here?" I asked Chance.

"Definitely," Ghost said easily.

Chance shot him an annoyed glance and spent more time on

his answer. "I trust their motives. They'd protect you and your brother for the sake of it, and not just for the club or as a favor to King. So...yes," he said slowly, reluctantly.

I nodded. "Then I'm okay. Make sure Ghost doesn't get punched in the face again."

Ghost laughed and leaned in, tickling his beard against my tender throat, over Chance's marks.

"Maybe he can get hit from the other side. Straighten his face out a bit," Chance suggested, smiling at me.

I rose on my toes, catching that smile with my teeth, Ghost smushed between Chance and me, nibbling on my throat. We parted slowly, cheeks rubbing together until their scents mingled on my skin.

"Love you," I whispered to Chance, and I squeezed Ghost's hand in mine, sending the feeling along to him, even without being quite ready to give voice to the words.

Bear's arms circled my shoulders as they stepped away, and he pulled me back into his broad chest, both of us taking slow, deep breaths.

"You've kept me safe all this time," I said, and Bear grunted. He was still surly and reluctant, annoyed with the plan. But I knew Bear, and if he didn't think it was best, he would've told Eve and King and all the others to go fuck themselves. "You won't stop now," I said, twisting to smile up at him.

Bear sighed, crouching over me, creating a deep shelter with his arms. "Feel better knowing your brother has a tracker up his ass."

"Ew!" I squawked, elbowing Bear. "Is that true? Why do you know that?! Don't tell me."

He laughed and shook his head, smacking noisy kisses against my cheek. "Teasing you, Butterfly."

"Don't talk about my brother's ass," I muttered, trying to shake thoughts out of my head.

Bear turned me to face him, clasped my face in his hands, and waited for me to meet his eyes. I hadn't even been able to see this man when we'd met, to see those rich, dark eyes or the strong brow, his full mouth, and I'd still known to grab onto him with hands and teeth and not lose him.

"I love you," we said at once. Bear beamed down at me, leaning in and resting his forehead against mine.

"Time to roll out," King called from his position at the head of the ride.

Bear grumbled and I caught his mouth briefly, pressing a tender kiss there before we stepped away from one another. Adam was delivering a similar goodbye to his pack, the four alphas stepping into a Jeep they used on missions. At the door to the motel, our chaperones waited, steel-eyed and cautious.

Grim opened the door for me, nodding inside, but I waited until Bear was on his bike, engine revving, before I walked slowly backwards into the shelter of the clubhouse.

"My only regret is not joining them in wiping the desert floor with those Wasted fucks," Grim said at my side. He glanced down at me, a careful smile on his lips. He was tall and lanky, with tight copper curls and freckled brown skin. "But I'm proud to be here to keep an eye on you and your brother. Pack is important."

I nearly looked away as King and the crew pulled out of the parking lot. "Do you want a pack someday?" I asked.

"I always felt like I had one here," Grim said. "But now I think I'd like something closer to what you five have."

"Well, I hope you find it," I said. Adam joined us in the doorway, pressing into my side. "And I'm grateful for your help."

Grim nodded. "Let's get inside. We've got a long wait ahead of us."

I watched the dust cloud from the retreating bikes until it was only the small and shabby view of Dead End.

———

I KNEW the moment action hit with my pack, the spike of adrenaline sending both Adam and me up out of our booth seats at the bar, our chaperones watching us from the pool table.

"Hate this part," Adam muttered, pacing the floor, arms wrapped tight around his chest.

I found myself behind the bar, cleaning bottles and glasses, reorganizing as I fell inward, searching for the slightest flinch or spark of injury.

"It seems to be going smoothly?" I asked.

Adam nodded. "Pretty hands-off plan. And even if it goes sideways, we outnumber the Wasted easily."

I sighed, staring at the bottle of good vodka in my hand before reaching for a short glass.

"Whatever you're making, make two," Adam said, crossing to sit on a barstool.

I found the cranberry juice the beta girls hid and made us a pair of strong drinks, complete with lemon wedges.

"You love your pack, right?"

I looked up from the counter and found Adam staring at me, his eyes wide, lips folded in, waiting for my answer. He shook slightly, and I knew from our years together that his heel was jiggling against the stool.

"I do," I said, scooting the drink across the counter.

"So everything...it all worked out," Adam said, still too earnest, still shaking.

I opened my mouth to say yes, but I remembered the camera in the corner of my cell with Omikron, the stomach cramps from the drugs they'd used, being grabbed at and hauled around like an uncooperative doll.

"Are you angry with me?" Adam whispered, eyes watering, leaning across the bar. "For losing you that night?"

"No." I sighed, relieved by the truth, and by the second half of Adam's question.

It wasn't his fault Omikron had caught me in the shipping yard, drugged me unconscious, and dragged me away. Was I angry with Adam? Sometimes, in tiny ways. For making my life a battle. But I would've been angry if he'd left me behind too. There was no right answer, no solution to the life we'd found ourselves in.

"I love you," I said, reaching across the bar. "I love my pack." I recalled King talking about the future, about finding a home. I'd found mine in strong arms and bite marks and hungry kisses. But maybe there would be another, with warm lights in the windows and a porch swing.

"I love you," Adam echoed, squeezing my fingers roughly. "And I'm sorry. I won't ever let Omikron hurt you again. I'm so glad we're back together. And now we've got packs, and it's going to be so much easier to deal with them, and—"

"Adam!"

My brother and I stared at one another, our mouths both parted, and Grim glanced over briefly from the pool table, checking on us. My heart was in my throat, stealing my breath, and my cheeks burned.

"I can't," I whispered.

Adam remained frozen as I shook my head.

"I'm not going on the run again. I'm not chasing Omikron, or...or whoever. I can't," I said.

Adam's brow folded. "Oh. But...there are omegas out there still who need help."

I swallowed hard and resisted the urge to place my hand over my heart where I felt the feral clawing come alive. "I know. I know, I was one of them, but I...I can't, Adam. I'm sorry."

He sat back slightly, blinking and staring silently. The room was quiet, just the click of balls colliding, bumping into the edges of the pool table, falling with a snick into pockets.

"It's okay," Adam said at last, his shoulders sagging. He forced a smile to his lips, and slowly it relaxed into something real. "It's okay, of course. I want you to be happy. I always have. I just...got excited about being together again."

I rounded the bar and Adam turned on the stool to face me, arms opening and ready. He smelled like warm cookies, but also like cinnamon, gunsmoke, nectarine, and fresh herbs, like his pack. A pack who would fight the world, with him and for him.

"I know," I said, notching my chin over his shoulder as we hugged. "And we're not losing touch now. I'm not being stolen away or hidden."

Adam nodded and squeezed his arms around me. "Eve will love surprising your pack with unannounced visits."

I snorted. "Just don't bring fucking tear gas next time."

"No promises. We love dramatic flair," Adam said, leaning back and grinning at me. "I love you, kiddo."

"I love you, biggo," I answered, helping myself to the stool at his side, settling in to watch the game of pool.

Adam and I both caught our breath at the same time, reaching for our drinks.

"Fight's amping up. Everything okay on your end?" Adam asked me.

I nodded. "My team's good."

Our glasses clinked together at the same moment a rumble sounded from outside.

"Thunder?" Adam asked me.

But our guards all paused in their game of pool, and I shook my head. "They're not done yet," I called out, the eager animal in me pacing nervously. "It's not the Devils."

"Probably Wasted," Frost said, nodding to Grim and Mikey. "Go to them. Wave and I will check it out."

"Get down behind the bar," Grim said.

I grabbed Adam's arm, dragging him along with me. We had a plan. We had four men here to protect us. I needed to breathe.

"Hold up," Wave said, jogging to the edge of the room, sporting a grin. "It's just Skid. What are you doing back so soon, ass—"

I jumped at the echo of the sudden sharp cracks of sound in the room before my brain could translate their meaning. My eyes were fixed to Wave's body as it jerked back, a thin red cloud bursting from his chest. And then Frost's too.

Gunshots. Skid. Wave hit the floor, and Frost fell down behind a table, taking cover.

"Fuck, Mikey, take them into the kitchen," Grim shouted, shoving me and Adam after the beta before jumping up onto the bar.

Skid. Skid was one of the Devils. Those were his brothers reaching to their holsters, preparing to fire back. I gaped as Mikey and Adam dragged me through the swinging kitchen door, violent cracking bangs echoing behind us. Glass shattered on the bar, and I only managed to glance back once to see Grim firing into the room before I was pulled into the dark kitchen.

"Fuck, fuck, fuck," Mikey muttered, eyes swinging wildly around the room.

Adam snapped his fingers in front of Mikey's face. "We need to get out of here."

Mikey gasped and nodded, the panic solidifying into determination. "Back door. Run to the garage. The truck's still there."

"But Grim—"

"Grim knows what he's doing," Mikey said, grabbing my arm again, nodding at Adam. "He's gonna make sure I get you and your brother out safely. Fucking *Skid*," he spat.

Fucking Skid. "Call King," I breathed as we ran for the backdoor, the gunshots growing louder at our back.

"I will," Mikey answered.

"Call now!" I cried as Adam threw the door open. If Skid was here, had he led King and the others into a trap with the Wasted, selling out his own gang to their rivals?

The door banged open, and I winced at the sudden brightness crashing into my eyes, not sunlight but electric blue-white.

"Fuck." Adam stumbled to a stop at the glare of harsh headlights pointed in our direction.

I was blinded, panicked, my throat vibrating with a nervous snarl.

"Hand over the omega," a strong voice ordered from within the glare of the headlights.

"DID protocol," Adam whispered to me.

Mikey pushed me and Adam behind him, marching forward, gun raised in both hands. "Turn off the fucking highbeams, and—"

Bang!

Adam pulled me into his chest as I screamed, my body rattling.

Threat. Fight. Claw. Protect.

"Hand over the omega," the voice repeated, and this time Adam and I both shuddered. An alpha's bark.

"DID protocol," Adam reminded me. "It's okay, kiddo. Together. We can do it."

"Hand over—"

"We heard you!" Adam shouted back, raising his arms. "We're coming!" He nudged me and tapped his head against mine, adding in a whisper, "Together."

Together. I swallowed hard and nodded, stamping down my warning whine, my urge to run and bite and scream. Together. Adam had the tracker. We would go together. My pack was hammering into the bond, screaming for me in my chest. They would come.

I turned with Adam, keeping my head down, my eyes on my own feet shuffling, my fists raised even though I couldn't unclench my fingers.

Eighty-seven fucking percent my ass, Eve, I thought.

"Not *you*," the voice snarled. "Just the girl."

"What?" Adam asked, his steps stuttering.

"No!" I gasped as a pair of huge hands grabbed my shoulders. "No. No! No! *Adam!*"

I kicked and wailed as the figure in black lifted me from the ground, trapping my arms to my sides.

"Faith! No! Let her go! No!"

"Don't hurt him!" I screamed as another dark-clad figure stepped forward, shoving Adam to the ground. I kicked and the man holding me grunted but didn't release me.

The door banged open, and it was Grim and not Skid who came out, face bloodied and eyes wild.

"Faith!" Adam screamed, just in time for Grim to catch him by the chest, hold him back and pull him out of the way of a sharp gunshot firing.

"Adam! No! Noo!" I snarled and twisted, thrashing in the hold like iron around me. I was spun to face the headlights and blinded again, panic replacing clear thoughts, anger and terror uncaging the force inside of me.

Adam's voice was foggy in my head as my mind narrowed down to the arms around me. The thick, harsh scent of the alpha. The impact of my knee against some bone. The tear of cloth under my fingernails.

Not again. Not again, please.

Alphas! Come for me.

The glare of light broke away as I was shoved into darkness, into metal. Into another cage.

I breathed through my teeth, counted the pound of my own heartbeat in my ears, and listened to the drumbeat of the music from inside the Wasted's compound. My back was to the hard wall of the building, gaze bouncing between searching the open area around me and checking my phone.

Ghost was watching me from a safe distance, his nerves making mine worse, but he kept pushing Faith through to me, distant and fairly calm. The bond was a revelation, not just to be able to reach Faith—she'd always offered her feelings to me clearly—but to finally know the startling range of emotions Ghost possessed. It was overwhelming most of the time, picking through a simmering self-loathing buffeting against his pride and arousal for me, but it made sense of the man who'd been a facade to me for so long.

My phone brightened in my palm, a text from Bear.

Compound is clear.

Garrett had put together a dossier of the Wasted, a thick folder of their crimes within the club and prior to joining. We'd found more than enough evidence against the prez and his loyalists, and Jamie and Rory had organized a plan to get the rest out of the building. No prospects, no club ass, just the men who'd pooled together to buy my bondmate.

There would be an investigation, of course, but even if our club hadn't had the local officials in their pockets, no one would question the circumstances.

I placed the vent cover back on the wall, screwing it shut again, and crawled slowly along the base of the wall toward the back of the building where I'd be able to make a run for it. I paused at the corner, listening for boots on earth or voices speaking, and peeked carefully through the gap between the gutter and the wall.

Empty.

I frowned, searching the hazy, hot horizon for any sign of Skid. I knew that bastard couldn't run that fast, and he was supposed to place his accelerant at the same signal as me.

Fucker. I grit my teeth as I crawled forward. I would've heard Skid hollering if he'd gotten caught by the Wasted. None of our team could see us from this vantage. He'd either done his work early and decided to fuck off, or he hadn't gotten into position at all. There were no windows on this back wall, and I rose and jogged lightly to the small attached shed. Even from the outside, I could smell the chemicals, but I unjammed the door and opened it, arm over my nose and mouth.

The Wasted's little meth hut was cooking, burners boiling and gas thick in the air. A perfect set-up. And one that was probably going to blow early, since Skid hadn't waited for the signal. I shut the door, refastened the simple paper jam that would disintegrate in the explosion, and then ran across the short yard and down the scruffy hill, out of sight.

I answered Bear as I searched behind the hill. Skid's bike was gone too, asshole, which meant I needed to hoof it around to the others.

Western and southern posts cleared. Where the fuck is Skid?

I marched down the ditch, grimacing at the obvious waste left behind by the Wasted's parties.

Thought you just said south post was cleared, Bear texted back.

He did his shit and is MIA.

Bear responded to me with a dorky monocle emoji, and I rolled my eyes. He was as cutesy as Faith sometimes.

King's impatient. Better run our way, Bear added.

Nothing like running in motorcycle boots in the middle of the desert. But I also didn't want to get hit by a flying piece of Wasted ass in the explosion, so I picked up my heels and ran down the ditch to where it met the road.

Ghost pulled up on his bike, rare tension on his face.

"No sign of Skid," Ghost said as I jumped on behind him, ignoring the indignity of not having my own bike for the moment. "We're heading back to King."

"No, take me to Rider. I wanna know where that fucking asshole slunk off to," I said.

Ghost didn't argue with me, just revved his engine and turned back up the road.

The ground rumbled before we heard the boom, but neither Ghost nor I flinched at the early explosion. The smoke rose at my right, and I understood that the satisfaction in my chest was twisted and dark, but I had no regrets. Faith would be safe.

"I hope the others get down there to clean it up," Ghost shouted over his shoulder.

"Don't think Eve will miss the chance," I answered, leaning with Ghost as we turned a sudden corner and screeched to a stop.

Half the club was gathered there and my brother stood over his bike, ready to ride away. Our work was done. My own bike was there, not far, but I scanned the crowd.

No fucking Skid.

I swung my leg over the back of Ghost's bike as engines started to rev, ignoring my bike as I marched to Rider. The fire was roaring blocks away, a gray plume building in the sky. It would be called in soon.

"We need to go," Rider said to me, frowning.

"Where's Skid?" I barked back.

Rider's scowl dug deeper, but he glanced around him.

"He wasn't waiting for the signal, and he didn't wait for me down the hill," I said.

Rider shook his head. "News to me. Maybe he spooked and ran home. Maybe he's with King and the others."

"He's not, Rider! I fucking checked. Where is your goddamn cronie—" My voice choked off as my heart seized in a sudden flare of terror.

Behind me Ghost yelped. "Chance! Something's fucking—"

"Faith," I gasped, clutching my own chest. It wasn't pain; it was animal terror and jagged confusion.

Rider's eyes widened, looking between Ghost and me, the whole fucking club watching as I had a panic attack blooming from inside of me like an atom bomb.

Faith was terrified. My omega was in trouble.

"We have to go," Ghost roared.

I spun to my own bike, ready to follow, instinct imperative. I had to get back to Faith! The dread worsened, grew into anger, and my phone vibrated in my clenched palm.

"What the fuck is happening," I rasped.

"On our way," Bear snarled over the line. "Don't move. She and Adam are at the club. We have guys there."

But *we* weren't there, and we were her pack. She needed us, not Grim and Wave and the fucking others.

Except I was frozen, Faith's terror too strong and my own head too jumbled to do anything but process the racing demand of the bond.

"What's happening at the club?" Rider asked.

I shook my head. "Don't know, just...she's frightened."

She was going feral again, and it was getting worse by the second. Ghost growled at my back.

"Chance, I *need* to go—" Ghost growled.

The Jeep barreled around the corner, followed by the last of the club. Jamie was grim behind the driver's seat, Garrett and Rory braced in the back. And Eve...she was blood-splattered and vivid with anger, a live wire in the passenger seat.

"Sugar, you stay right there," she snapped, glaring at the face of her phone.

Adam's voice was tinny, and I ran forward to the side of the Jeep, searching for a glimpse of Faith in the background.

"I can't. I have the tracker and she doesn't."

"I don't care—"

"But I do!" Adam snapped. He was pale on the bouncing screen, running across the yard. "Grim and I are following her. You follow me. I am *not* losing her to Omikron again."

"You are such fucking trouble," Eve growled. "Do not get killed!"

"Yes, alpha," Adam said, and I caught a flash of Grim in the camera, the sound of an engine revving.

Omikron had Faith. I looked up, searching blindly around me for a moment, and found King at my side, pale and vibrating with a growl.

On the phone, a voice murmured and Adam glared off-camera before shaking. The view rattled, the garage briefly visible, and then Grim appeared, one side of his face wounded.

"Wave and Mikey are dead. By fucking Skid," Grim said, baring bloodied teeth. "I dealt with him myself. Frost is injured, can't ride, but he's stable. I won't lose your girl, King. Promise."

Skid. Skid. He'd set up the lab to blow—because whatever he wanted now, whatever he was doing, he was clearing the Wasted out of the way too—and then run back to the club.

For *Omikron*? It didn't make sense.

I twisted and found the club all staring at us, the two packs with their omegas in danger. Would they even give a shit? Rider wouldn't care what King lost, not now that he had the club for himself. And Skid was *Rider's* man. But if my brother had one good fucking quality, it was how ass-over-head in love with the club he was. Skid had killed Wave and Mikey. Wave was another legacy brother and he'd grown up with Rider.

I wove through the members of the club I'd lived in my entire life but never really felt like I belonged to, until I stood in front of the brother I'd never related to.

"Who was Skid helping?" I asked Rider. "Who would Skid have killed our brothers for?"

Rider gaped at me, but the club was turning to him now. "I knew fucking nothing about this," he said, but his eyes were growing wider as he stared at the faces around him.

He was supposed to lead them. He might be inclined to protect Skid, if the man were still alive, but he was dead, and the rest of the club would never trust Rider, even if he feigned ignorance.

"Chance, we need to follow Eve," King called, voice so close to a bark it took everything in me to keep from flinching.

"Who was Skid talking to, Rider?" I asked. I would go to my bike, let my brother deal with the fallout of his friend, but I'd seen those two together. Rider would know *something*.

Rider stared back at me, mouth shutting and the shock settling into a shield. *You are my brother. You should fucking* help *me*, I thought.

"Preston Bowers," Rider said, looking to King. "He went with me to meet up with Bowers, to get evidence for the trial. I noticed the number on Skid's phone, but I thought he was pulling petty shit, drugs and shit like that for him."

"Bowers," I repeated, turning to King.

King's eyes were narrowed. "We'll fucking eat him alive. Now let's go."

"We'll come with you, Prez," Buck announced, seated on his bike.

"No," King said. "Go to the club, check on Frost. Clean things up. This is pack business."

I hurried to my own bike, started it, and pulled out after King and Bear and Ghost. My brother was watching us from the cluster of the club.

Preston Bowers or Omikron, it didn't matter. We were getting our omega back, and then we were destroying whoever tried to take her away from us.

S cents, cloying and clawing at my lungs.

"Prest, I thought you said she was recovered."

Growls too close, my own answering.

"I saw pictures. She was crawling all over those alphas."

"We should've tried a subtler approach. Seduced her to join us. Now we're as bad as the bikers."

I snarled, my head down, the figures distorted through the curtain of my hair. Three alphas stood at the end of a fussy canopied bed, staring at where I cowered against the wall at the corner of the room.

The drive had been a dark and horrifying blur, but I'd kicked and clawed and screeched as they'd dragged me into the fancy house, forcing these alphas to send their beta staff scurrying out. We were alone. I was kidnapped. I would *kill* them.

"She has a bite mark. This is getting very messy, Preston," one of the men said.

"We just bite over the marks," another hissed back. Preston. Familiar and awful. "No one is going to contest our claim when the alternative is a fucking character like King or anyone from his gang. He offered her up to me in the first place, and we're the obvious better choice."

"Hmph. Do you hear that, you rabid little creature?" the third man called to me. "Once you calm down, you'll see. Someone call down to the kitchen, get some cake for her or something."

"We sent everyone away, remember?"

"Damnit."

"We should bite her first. The sooner we have the bonds, the better."

"You said this would be easy."

"We have her, don't we?"

The more I listened, the more I hated these men. These weren't alphas. They were lazy cowards.

There was a beleaguered sigh. "We have a snarling bundle that tries to scratch us every time we come close. We *don't* have a lovely omega to knot and breed and take to functions."

"It's been less than an hour," Preston drolled. "Watch. *Omega. Stand up and come here.*"

A bark. My muscles seized, legs trembling, the urge to bounce up from my corner running on urgent repeat.

This was not Omikron. These were just men, alphas who had stolen me because they thought they could get away with it. Thought they could bite me and take me away from my pack. Like King or Bear or even Ghost would give me up if their bite was cut. Like these men hadn't signed their death warrant by grabbing me.

So I stood, keeping my eyes just high enough to be sure they didn't come any closer.

"She's in better shape than the first time I saw her," Preston noted as I took one step forward and then another.

The demand of the bark softened with every step until I could breathe fully again.

"Something can be done with her, I suppose," one alpha said, crossing his arms over his chest. "For now, she looks like a bar rat."

I glanced up to glare at him. The three men in front of me were dressed tidily, even Preston, who'd made some beta lackey grab me from the bar's backyard as he'd barked commands. They were handsome in a plain way, and the room around me was rich in a boring way, furniture large and simple and the space far too open. It smelled sterile, aside from the bland scents in front of me.

I stiffened as the one in the middle stepped forward, moving around the edge of the bed. But he remained out of reach. One of his pack, the one on the right, had a bandage over his forearm from where I'd scratched when he'd reached for me. Good. They were wary.

"They don't see the potential in you," the man closest said. He was Preston. He was the alpha King had tried to pawn me off to, the one who liked to bark at me. His voice was smooth now, too sweet and patronizing. "I do. I saw it the day we met. You were wasted on that crew of half-hearted criminals, omega. You can be so much more here with us, have so much more. Any present you want, just say so."

"Let's not get carried away, Prest," the one on the right droned. "She ought to prove she's worth the trouble first."

I bared my teeth and snarled at the alpha, and Preston rocked back on his heels before straightening again. Coward.

I had to get out of here. I knew my pack would come for me, but I didn't want my bonds broken, even if they could be remade. I didn't want to wait to be rescued. I wanted to prove to these men why they should never have dared to grab me in the first place.

"*Behave*," Preston barked.

I flinched, but my snarl only grew louder. "Fuck *off*," I answered, lunging forward.

He didn't jump away this time but grabbed my arm, shaking me. "If you don't listen to your alphas, you're going to get—"

"My *alphas* are going to eviscerate you," I growled at Preston. "They're going to come here and tear this house and all of you apart, one piece at a time."

Over Preston's shoulder, one of the other alpha's frowned, and I knew that whatever Preston had told them, it hadn't prepared them for the reality.

"There's nothing they can do once we bond you," the alpha on the right said.

"There's no bond if you're fucking dead," I answered.

"I said, *behave!*" Preston roared.

And while I whined and shuddered at the order, it wasn't enough. I didn't know if it was because I was feral or because my bonds with my alphas were strong, but the bark only hurt. My arm swung, fist tight and ready, and the punch crashed into Preston's nose, the impact cracking into my knuckles and reverberating up my arm.

Preston howled, throwing me onto the bed, but he didn't make it more than one step before I was kicking.

"Preston!"

Preston Bowers, blond and tall and blandly good-looking, turned into an animal to match me. His nose and upper lip were bloody, eyes wild as he lunged for the bed. I was smaller, weaker, but wilder too, and more desperate. He wanted to tame me, and I wanted to *kill* him.

Another alpha joined in the fray, grabbing at my wrists, but the third backed away for the door. I snarled and screamed, kicked and hissed. I kept my teeth clenched, because these men were not Bear and I wasn't biting anyone but my pack, but eventually the two alphas' strength won out. My arms and wrists were pinned back, and Preston had caught my ankles, holding them apart in a bruising grip as he lunged over me, one knee on the bed.

Preston's face was red and savage above mine, spitting down at me as he fumed out poison.

"I've never liked all that nonsense the Omega Center spews about omegas finding their perfect matches by scent. My father's pack tamed and trained my mother, taught her how to behave, how to make the pack proud of her. Call me old-fashioned, but I think it will be fun to carry on the tradition." Preston bared a mean and bloody grin down at me before glancing up at the other alpha who'd wrestled me down. "Push her head to the side. I'm covering the bite now. Then we'll strip her and find the rest."

"There's some kind of commotion downstairs," the alpha by the door said in a small voice.

"Go and deal with it then," the one above me snapped.

He had to release one of my hands as he reached and pulled at my hair, but it was a miscalculation. I was still ready, thrilled, desperate to fight, and my nails dug into his cheek and over his jaw, down his throat.

The commotion was outside of the room now, and it was easy to hear with the door open. The alpha above me screamed, his hand connecting roughly with my cheek in a noisy slap, but he reared back, grabbing at the scratches on his face.

"Damnit, Ed, grab—"

I scratched Preston, punched him hard everywhere I could reach until he was wrestling at my hands, my ankles free to kick and shove him back.

A gunshot cracked, and Preston fell back against the wall in shock. Ed, the alpha who'd held my wrists, dropped down to the floor at the sound of the second shot.

"Let go of my fucking sister."

I caught my breath in a ragged gasp, gaping at Adam where he stood in the doorway, gun aimed at Preston. There were no nerves on his face, no shock, just a hard determination.

"My pack is on its way," Adam said. "Hers too. My friend has your packmate in the hall. If either of you move, I will shoot you for real this time. I have been trained by three former black ops agents and one still-active assassin, so I *will not miss*."

I scrambled for the edge of the bed, not waiting to see if Preston or his packmate were stupid enough to challenge Adam.

"My pack and I will destroy you," Preston hissed. "We have connections. I know the governor."

Adam blinked at the man on the floor, now sullied and scratched and bleeding. "I know the FBI," Adam said, shrugging. "I'm working with them to take down alphas who buy and kidnap unwilling omegas. So, uh...eat my dick?"

"Eloquent as always, sugar," an exquisitely sinister voice called from the hall.

Adam's shoulders sagged slightly, the livid energy seeping out of him. "Took you long enough," he said, but he kept his gaze and the muzzle of his gun pointed at Preston.

Out of the corner of my eye, movement darted forward, and I screamed Adam's name.

But Eve was stepping into the room, her own gun raised, and she didn't so much as blink before firing it, a dull and quiet pop exhaling from the muzzle. Preston's packmate dropped to the floor and Eve shifted, standing in front of me, blocking my view of the man she'd shot.

"Go into the hall," Eve said to Adam and me, turning to face Preston. "I will finish here."

"No," Adam snapped back.

I had no complaints. I gasped and ran for the door, colliding with King in the hall. His arms fastened around me, lifting me off my feet, and I got another brief glimpse of worthless grandeur, a spiral staircase and a chandelier and gleaming tile, before my face was buried in his throat, inhaling his rough scent like it was my only source of oxygen.

"I've got you, princess. Go to Bear. I'm dealing with Bowers."

I lifted my face just enough to see Bear reach the top of the staircase, gaze bright on my face, and I whined at the sight of him, of Chance and Ghost at his back, their expressions equally anxious and eager.

"I knew you'd come," I whispered, kissing King's throat.

He squeezed me tighter, holding on for a deep breath in spite of his order, and then finally released me. I dashed toward Bear.

"Take her outside," King said.

"Eve, you can't bite me *now*," Adam said, laughter growing distant as I ran.

"Then you'd better follow them," Eve purred to him.

Bear caught me and hauled me up into his chest, my legs hooked under his arm, cradling me close as he turned and started immediately down the stairs.

"There's a third alpha," I murmured.

"Gone," Chance said. It could've meant the alpha had managed to run, but I suspected the truth was simpler and more final. And I didn't care.

"You okay, slick?" Ghost murmured. "They bite you?"

"Didn't get the chance. I fought too hard," I answered.

"Good girl," Bear said, his voice balanced between a growl and a purr.

The walk to the door was short, and I thought I heard a second snap or bang as it shut behind us, but if that was the last I heard of Preston, it was plenty.

Grim was outside, speaking to Garrett as Jamie dressed the wound on his forehead. Rory was missing, but so was the third alpha, and I wasn't curious enough to ask questions. Adam ran from our group into Garrett's arms, the pair kissing roughly, but my brother pulled away a moment later, hurrying back to our side.

Bear set me on my feet and Adam grabbed me. "I'm sorry. I let them take you again. I couldn't not follow," he gasped into my ear. "I'm sorry, Faith."

I wrapped my arms around Adam, pressing my cheek to his. Burnt caramel and almonds, our stressed scents tangled.

"I'm okay. I knew I would be okay," I said, arms clasped fiercely around him, tears clawing up my throat. "You came right on time."

Gravel crunched behind me and I jumped in Adam's arms, but he didn't release me.

"It's done," King announced.

"We'll finish up here," Garrett said. "Give us a shout when you're home. We'll work the timing out, clean up the loose ends."

"Glad you found a weird super spy pack," I whispered in Adam's ear.

He huffed out a laugh and loosened his hold on me at last. He leaned back, searching my face.

"I'm okay, Adam," I said once more, and he swallowed hard and nodded.

"Love you, kiddo," Adam whispered.

"Love you too, biggo."

"We'll swing by within a week. Once we know everything is tidy," Garrett said.

"You feel confident this won't come back on us?" Grim asked, frowning.

"Not our first rodeo," Jamie said. "We'll be all right. You should get back."

"Come on, Butterfly," Bear murmured.

"I need her to ride with me," King growled.

"Actually, I think I need—" Ghost started, all three of my alphas reaching for me at once.

"She rides with me, Ghost ahead, King and Bear behind," Chance snapped, holding his hand out in my direction.

I glanced at my alphas, at King and Bear glaring at Chance and Ghost ducking his head.

"The three of you are half-feral with her right now. I'm the one with the clearest head. She rides with me," Chance repeated firmly.

"Smart," Bear grumbled.

"Fine," King growled.

Ghost just flicked me a grin as I slipped my hand into Chance's. He tugged me close, pulling my mouth to his for a rough kiss.

"Come on, birdy. They can fight over you in the nest," he whispered.

I turned back to Adam, but he was surrounded by his own pack. We were safe. We were with our people. I climbed on behind Chance and wrapped myself tightly around him until he grunted with the force of my grip. His hand rested over my arms briefly, and then his bike roared to life and we rode home on long, quiet stretches of road, just the harmony of engines surrounding me, as warm and rich as my alphas' purrs.

"Little longer," I said, my head leaned against King's shoulder.

"These eggs are burnt," he grumbled.

"I like them burnt. Wet eggs are weird," I answered, shrugging against him.

He sighed and stirred the scrambled eggs with his spatula once more. "Now?" he asked, a hint of pleading in his tone.

"You wanted to know how I like my eggs and I'm showing you," I said, grinning. "Ten more seconds."

He remained stiff at my side, and I could almost hear his thoughts counting grumpily down from ten. When his hand twitched to pull the skillet off the burner, I interrupted him.

"Now turn the heat off and let them cool in the pan."

"You like burnt *cold* eggs?" King asked.

"With ketchup," I added, turning to beam a smile at his scowl.

He shuddered. "Ughhh."

Chance tapped on my shoulder and I turned to face him, a mug of coffee held out between us. I glanced at its surface and then offered him a smile. "Paler."

Chance's eyes narrowed. "They don't make a shade of coffee paler than this. Do you just want milk?"

But he turned and marched back to the creamer.

"How are the trainees?" Bear asked me, entering the kitchen. He smirked as he found King sullenly keeping an eye over my eggs and Chance grumbling over my coffee.

"Improving," I said with a nod. "How's Ghost?"

"A natural, actually," Bear answered cheerfully.

I crossed to him, wrapping my arms around his middle. "You're a good teacher."

"A good pack knows how to please their omega," Bear said.

"Our omega may need to have her tastebuds refined," King muttered.

"Says the man who likes to eat a hot dog on a *dry* bun," I answered, not bothering to lower my voice. "The whole point is what toppings you like."

"Come on, go have a seat and I'll get these two in line," Bear said, patting my ass and nudging me toward the kitchen door.

It was early morning, and Rider's coronation party had taken place the night before, so most of the club was still sleeping it off. My pack had been more subdued, for obvious reasons. We would be leaving the club soon, but King had stayed to help with last-minute adjustments. So far, Rider was being what King called "tolerable" about the help.

I grinned as I found my brother and his pack sitting at a long banquet table put together by a bunch of the square tables around the bar. Ghost's task for the morning was ambience, and truth be told, I hadn't known what to expect.

Beer bottles ran down the tables as vases, each one holding three brightly-dyed daisies. He'd picked out paper plates with a blue floral trim and black handkerchief napkins. There was glitter confetti scattered over the table, and Ghost was holding out a chair for me, a small wrapped box waiting on the paper plate.

It was silly and sweet, and it was for *me*.

"We said no presents," I said, walking to Ghost.

He raised his eyebrows. "*You* said no presents. And we'd been working on this one before we found out today was your birthday."

I blushed, resting my hands on Ghost's chest and rising to my toes. He bent his head for me, smiling into the kiss. I'd been vaguely aware of my approaching birthday, but we'd had bigger things on our plate and it had snuck up on me in these past couple weeks since shit had blown up. Adam had been the one to spill the beans at last, cornering my pack to quiz them on their plans.

King was still peeved I hadn't said anything myself.

Whatever clean-up Adam's pack had done at Preston Bower's home, it had worked. It helped that there'd be a wealth of evidence linking the Wasted's meth dealings with the Bowers pack. I wasn't sure how much was true and how much was elegantly crafted by Eve and Adam. It seemed like even the officials knew the world was better off washed clean of those men.

"Sit," Adam urged. "We have presents for you too."

I laughed, pulling away from Ghost's greedy kisses, sliding into the chair he'd offered me. "I think you've all done enough," I said to the group.

"We're omegas, we like to be spoiled," Adam said with a wave of his hand.

Coming from my brother, who had steadfastly rejected his biology for as long as I'd known him, the words were a surprise. He'd reconciled himself to his designation—accepted it, even. Largely because he'd found a pack that allowed him to be himself as an omega.

I'd found a pack that allowed me to keep searching for myself, willing to follow me to whatever destination that search might discover.

"Okay. One plate of cold, ruined eggs and limp bacon for the birthday girl," King announced, marching through the door with Bear and Chance helping him carry steaming pans of food. "And a perfectly respectable spread for the rest of us."

"Thank you," I cooed, pulling my present aside so he could load my plate. A bristly kiss ruffled the top of my head before he pulled away.

"Happy birthday, princess," he whispered.

Chance placed my creamy coffee down and then took his seat on my left, waggling his eyebrows. "Open your present."

"Shouldn't I wait?" I asked.

"Your eggs are cold anyways," Bear pointed out, lips twitching.

And the present *was* sitting there, winking at me with metallic gold paper and a pretty blue ribbon tie. I snatched it up from the table as everyone passed our breakfast around. The box jingled as I diligently untied the ribbon and worked at the messily taped corners.

"Just rip it," Ghost said, taking a bite of a runny egg stacked on top of bacon and toast.

I ignored him, taking my time with the paper, smoothing it out and setting it aside.

"Would've gotten you a property patch, but we're leaving the club, so..." King shrugged.

"Disgusting," Eve muttered.

The box was white and a shiny blue droplet stone glittered as I lifted the lid. It was a charm bracelet, a gold chain with four bright charms. I lifted it up from the fluff inside, touching each one delicately. A silver bird, a gold Butterfly, a crown embedded with stones, and the blue droplet gem.

"It's beautiful," I said, blinking away a surprising sting in my eyes. Birdy, Butterfly, princess. Simple, sweet, and *mine*. "Thank you," I said, catching each of my pack's eyes.

"Our turn," Adam said.

I leaned toward Chance, and he took the bracelet from me, unlatching it to fasten around my wrist.

"My birthstone isn't aquamarine," I whispered to him, glancing at the blue stone.

Chance grinned and answered softly, "Ghost couldn't think of what else would work for 'slick.'"

I choked on a laugh. The droplet. What a dorky asshole.

Adam passed a thick manila envelope down the table, Bear and King giving it a curious glance and then offering it to me. It had a bright red bow attached to the outside and felt heavy in my hand. I pinched the metal closures open and shook the contents out onto the table.

Plastic ID cards, passports, birth certificates. I picked up one of the IDs and found my picture there, my name, and the tailed B for a beta designation. Another had my face with a new name and an omega symbol. There was even a card identifying me as an alpha.

"They'll all work. You get to be whoever you want," Adam said, watching me with bright eyes.

"We'll keep taking Omikron out one official at a time," Eve added. "You just worry about living your life. As you see fit."

I sorted through the identities, clipped together in little stacks of paper and plastic, until I found my own. Faith Robins, brown hair, brown eyes, omega. I set it on the top, and then gathered all of it up and slid it back into the envelope.

"Thank you, all of you. Thank you so much," I murmured, eyes welling, chest clenching sweetly.

Bear leaned in and kissed my forehead, and I wiped my tears away against his jaw.

"Our pleasure," Jamie said.

"Love you, kiddo," Adam said.

King cleared his throat and feigned a scowl at me. "You want your eggs any colder, I'll put 'em in the freezer."

I laughed and grabbed my fork at last.

———

"COME UP HERE," I whined, clutching the back of King's head.

"Pretty sure if I try to stand, I'm gonna slip and crack my head open," he muttered. "'Sides, I've got good access right here."

I glared down at him on his knees in Bear's fancy tub, my leg propped up on the ledge to reveal my sex to him. And to his wonderful mouth. He leaned in, kissing my pussy with all the tender affection he reserved just for me. I shivered and swayed into the hot water beating at my back, and then the sway grew wobbly.

King growled and his fingers tightened on my waist. "Damnit, we're both gonna crack our heads."

The shower curtain twitched, and Bear appeared, shirtless and grinning.

"Can I help?"

"Yes," I said, at the same time King frowned and muttered, "No."

"The tub won't fit you too," King added.

"Sure it will," Bear said, shucking off his pants. "Besides, I've got a plan."

He stepped behind me, a warm shield against the hot water, and then his hands were scooping under my thighs. I screeched, reaching back to clutch his shoulders, and King's eyes widened as I was spread and lifted before his face.

"That's a good plan," King rasped, grabbing onto the ledge to lift himself up. "Hold her still. She gets squirmy."

Bear snorted. "I know. I was here first."

"Excuse you both," I said, although they were right; I was already starting to squirm as King stroked his cock against my folds, hands stroking up and down over my chest, plucking my nipples.

"You're cute when you're offended, princess," King said, catching my chin to pull me into his kiss.

"You'll still be wiggling and wanting even after you've had your way with all of us, birthday girl," Bear whispered in my ear, nuzzling his cheek there. "We know you best."

I gasped as King thrust in and Bear worked me on the other man's length. They did know me best.

And later, damp with sweat and crowded with bodies, after I'd gotten my real presents from my men, I was still squirming and whining as Chance teased my ass.

"You and Ghost are too horny for your own good," Chance laughed down at me. "I've got you begging for me to fuck your ass and Ghost's cock trying to get in mine."

"Seems like an obvious solution is available," I panted out.

King and Bear were snoozing on the other side of the nest, but I had a feeling they'd wake up again if Ghost and Chance and I went another round. Or I could wake them up with my mouth. I was the birthday girl, after all. I deserved to be spoiled.

"Obvious is boring," Chance said, pale eyes sparkling. Ghost's hand wrapped around him, reaching for Chance's cock before Chance slapped it away. "I like to get creative. And Ghost likes when you suck him dry, don't you, Ghost?"

Ghost and I both groaned and I scrambled across Chance, who laughed at my eagerness.

"Happy birthday to me," I whispered, nuzzling against Ghost's cock, catching a hint of me already on his length.

"She's crazy," King muttered, rolling over.

"She's our crazy," Bear sighed out.

"She's fucking amazing," Ghost groaned as I hollowed my cheeks and slurped him down.

"She's ours," Chance murmured, kissing my spine.

And you're all mine, I thought, closing my eyes and letting their love beat harder and faster in my chest than my own heartbeat.

THE DAY we left Dead End was so hot the air wavered in front of us. We'd packed up every inch of the nest that morning, and there was sweat running down my spine as I shoved the last pillows and secretly stolen T-shirts into the backseat of the truck. The truck bed was full of boxes, my pack's belongings tucked away.

I paused, catching my breath and leaning against the backdoor, pulling my sunglasses down from my forehead.

"You ready?"

I blinked open my eyes, winced at the sweat on my eyelids, and found Eve in front of me. The Charger and Jeep were packed too, Adam's pack making their goodbyes to the Devils.

"I am," I said, a rare confidence steadying my heartbeat. "Nervous too. King hasn't told me much."

"He takes that fake name of his too seriously," Eve said, rolling her eyes, sweeping that sheet of black hair up to the top of her head. Even she was feeling the heat.

"It's his real name. Well, his real last name," I said, shrugging.

Her eyes narrowed. "What is his first name?"

Ulysses, I thought, my giggle fighting to escape. "Secret," I said, waggling my eyebrows.

She snorted. "I'll find it in five minutes flat."

A sudden impulse overtook me, a temporary insanity, and I stepped forward, wrapping my arms around my brother's feral assassin alpha. She was stiff in my arms, maybe disgusted, but she softened after a moment, patting my back in an awkward but adorable gesture.

"I like you too," she said.

The swinging door to the motel creaked and I smiled at Adam, who was holding up a phone. "I got a picture of that," he said.

Eve grunted and pulled away, but I caught the hint of a smile at the corner of her lips. "Let's get in the car. You know I hate the mushy bits."

"She loves them," Adam mouthed to me.

"See you on the road," I called as they walked to the Charger. They were traveling with us part of the way, buying me and Adam as much time together as we could before they went off to kill...whoever was next on their list, I supposed.

A large group of the Devils walked out of the building with the rest of Adam's pack, including Rider and Grim—or Graham, as he'd introduced himself to me later. As if on cue, my own pack rode around the corner of the building on their motorcycles. My breath caught at the sight of them, four ferocious figures on snarling machinery.

Bear, Chance, and Ghost had all turned in their cuts, and it was the first time I'd seen them around the others without the leather vests on that marked them as Devils. But King? King had the black leather on, darker marks over his chest and across his back, where he'd trimmed away the patches that marked him as prez and club member. It was almost shocking to see him stripped of the title, and I'd asked him this morning why he was keeping the vest at all.

He'd smirked.

"'Cause you creamed all over it, princess. No one else gets to fucking touch it."

Gross and romantic all at once.

He grinned at me now, and he wasn't stripped of anything. He was freer. We all were. No more cages.

"Good luck, wherever you're going," Grim called to me, as other Devils went to shake my bondmates' hands.

"Good luck to you here," I answered.

His eyes drifted over my head and his smile was tight. "Won't be the same without your pack. Might be time for me to move on too. We'll see."

He shrugged and slipped away before I could ask more, and I climbed into the truck, watching Chance receive an awkward handshake and manly back-pat combination from his brother. The crowd backed away as King revved his engine, the rest of my pack answering with their own mechanical roars. I turned the key in the ignition of the truck, revved the engine on neutral, and laughed at King's glare, his twitching lips.

It was time to go. The Charger bolted forward onto the road, zooming away in a cloud of dust, followed by the Jeep. We would catch up with them soon.

King and Bear pulled out in front and I followed them, Ghost and Chance at the rear, a protective procession with me ensconced comfortably in the middle, as usual. My foot was heavy on the gas, keeping up with my pack easily.

We had a long road ahead of us, and I was eager for every mile.

I traced my fingers over the words of the text that had arrived in the middle of the night.

All done. They're gone, and there's no record of us.

Omikron was gone for good. I hadn't seen Adam in months, hadn't heard from him in weeks, but apparently he and his pack had been busy.

Chance stirred at my side, the last of my pack left in bed with me this morning, and then joined me in squinting up at the screen.

"That mean what I think it means?" Chance asked, wrapping his arms around me and drawing me closer. Morning light was faint in my new nest, and without the rest of the pack, the room felt cozy but a little too large.

"Yeah."

"How do you feel?" Chance asked.

I licked my lips and he turned his head to stare at me. "I thought I'd be more...relieved?" His brow furrowed, and I cleared my throat. "I'm not afraid of Omikron now, but I...I haven't been for a while. I've *known* how safe I am here, with all of you. Taking down the last of Omikron is... I guess I'm just happy for Adam."

Chance's face relaxed, and he pressed a kiss to my shoulder. "You're right. You've been safe. It's nice to hear you've felt it too." He kissed my skin once more, passing King's bondmark and trailing down to my collarbone. His hair was getting long again, sliding through my fingers, and I sighed as he sat up, beautiful and otherworldly in the soft morning glow of the nest.

"Come on, let's catch Ghost and Bear before they leave for the morning."

I debated drawing him back under the covers with me for a slow morning sex session, but I could always drag him and King back to bed with me later. I dressed and followed Chance out of the nest, down the narrow spiral staircase.

Coffee was brewing and a skillet was sizzling. The morning light filtered softly into the large open living space, with a huge stove fireplace at the center that kept our home cozy in the drizzly northwest winters.

Bear leaned over the kitchen counter, watching me descend from the nest. "Morning, Butterfly," he greeted, catching King and Ghost's stares.

"You're up early," King said, flipping an egg in the skillet.

"To see me," Ghost said, hurrying to reach Chance and me at the bottom of the stairs.

I still used their old road names, although Bear mostly went by Courtney to the rest of the world now. They were still the men I'd met in Dead End, but we were less tense in our new life.

Ghost and Chance kissed slowly at the bottom of the stairs, and Ghost caught my arm, drawing me between them before I could pass by. Their lips landed over every available inch of me until I was laughing and twisting away. Chance smacked a final kiss over a faded bruise on my throat. He bit me less often now, just when I begged, but there was usually a mark from him somewhere on me.

"Breakfast inside or outside?" King asked.

He already knew the answer, and Bear was pulling open the sliding door that led to our balcony deck.

"Outside," I said, grabbing one of Bear's hoodies from the couch and sliding it over my head. Mornings were chilly up the mountains, even deep in summer.

I paused in the center of our cabin. King had found it before we'd left Dead End and kept it as a surprise. He knew me better than I'd even realized. The large main room was surrounded by windows, pine trees and maples and oaks rising high on every side of us. Opening the door to the balcony let in morning music, birdsong and the occasional chitter of squirrels who knew I left crumbs behind for them to steal.

It was private here, serene. We were the last stop on the narrow mountain road, and there was a cute pack of betas who had an organic farm down near the base, and traded their grown veggies and fresh eggs for the mushrooms and berries and roots I foraged on the mountain.

"I've got to get to the shop early today to finish up an engine, but I should be done not long after lunch," Ghost said, heading for the door that led down to our ground floor garage.

"I'm out early too. We should go down to the lake," Bear said. "Give our Butterfly an excuse to wear that bikini she just got."

"She wears it on the deck while I try to study," Chance said, winking at me.

"You're getting As, don't throw me under the bus," I answered.

"C'mere, princess, try these," King called.

Bear stopped me on the way, bending his head and kissing me with coffee-flavored lips. "Be a good girl today," he said.

"Train the alphas well," I said, nodding.

Bear had started a small community program in the nearby town, training alphas on designation, on caring for an omega emotionally as well as sexually. The local omegas would be lucky, but not as lucky as I was.

I joined King at the kitchen counter, a poached egg resting on top of what looked like smoked salmon and an English muffin. It was drizzled with a yellow sauce, and in King's defense, it looked and smelled *delicious*. But we both knew how this was going to go.

I accepted the fork he passed me and dug into the beautiful breakfast, wincing slightly at the sudden bleed of rich, yellow yolk over the plate. I took my dutiful bite, chewing slowly, swallowing hard.

King raised an eyebrow, waiting for the verdict.

"Too runny," I whispered, blinking up at him.

His eyes narrowed. "Brat. Go outside and wait for your breakfast."

"I liked the sauce!" I said.

"It was from a bottle," he groused, bumping me away with his hip. "*Out*."

I hid my grin behind Bear's massive sleeves and hurried out to the deck, closing my eyes against the flicker of sunlight through thick layers of leaves, listening to the larks that had nested above the house.

King joined me a few minutes later, passing me a plate of toasted English muffin, barely-cooked bacon, and nearly scorched eggs with a drizzle of hollandaise.

"Chance told me about Omikron," King said.

I hummed and took a large bite of my breakfast, batting my eyelashes at him as he scowled at the food. "This is perfect."

"Don't rub it in," he said, wrapping an arm around me and pressing a long kiss to my forehead.

He sighed out, and I read his relief in the bond, my gratitude answering. He'd been worried for me, even when I wasn't. I had good alphas.

"So what do you wanna do today, princess?" King asked.

"Do you have to work?"

"Nothing that can't wait till tomorrow," he said. King had gotten back into investing, but he always asked my thoughts on where the money was going. Down to our beta neighbor's farm. Ghost's bike shop, and Bear's alpha training. Helping clear the debt of a great winery about an hour away.

"Can we go for a ride?" I asked.

King grinned and chuckled. "You never have to ask me that twice. You ridin' with me or on your own bike?"

I took another bite of my breakfast, glancing down to the ground in time to watch a red fox scurry down the rocks and out of sight. This woods, this mountain, this cabin, and these men felt more like home than anything I'd known growing up. I felt more myself too, at ease in my own skin, sure of my tastes and interests, my decisions.

And somehow King—and Bear, Chance, and Ghost—always knew. It might've been the bond, or it might've been there before any one of them took a bite. They knew me.

King was smiling at me as I looked up.

"On my own," I said. I leaned in and rested my head on King's shoulder. "With my pack at my side."

THE END

ACKNOWLEDGMENTS

Thank you so much to all the readers who dove in head first to the Sweetverse and fell in love with this interpretation of the rich and wonderfully wide land of omegaverse. You've changed my life and I'm so grateful to you.

And for this book, thank you to:

Moonstruck Cover Design and Photography, who hit every mark for Faith right off the bat!

My best babe Whoop for listening to me whine, brainstorm, celebrate and who helped all along the way. Meghan Leigh Daigle, my loving and incredibly patient editor. Jess Whetsel for her keen perfectionist eye.

The Beta Babes: Jami, Amanda, Ash, and Megan.

My amazing Moongazers who cheer me on each and every step!

All my writing babes, near and far, who inspire and motivate me. Every month this group of authors and future authors grows larger and I can't tell you how incredibly lucky I feel to know you all.

My entire family, related and chosen for celebrating with me, feeding me when I'm exhausted, and cuddling my brain when it's all out of fuel.

www.ingramcontent.com/pod-product-compliance
Lightning Source LLC
Chambersburg PA
CBHW032106310726
48972CB00001B/122